British
Bachelors
Gorgeous & Impossible

Nina
HARRINGTON

Elizabeth
POWER

Jessica
HART

MILLS &
BOON

Published in Great Britain 2017
By Mills & Boon, an imprint of HarperCollins*Publishers*
1 London Bridge Street, London, SE1 9GF

BRITISH BACHELORS: GORGEOUS & IMPOSSIBLE © 2017
Harlequin Books S.A.

My Greek Island Fling © 2012 Nina Harrington
Back in the Lion's Den © 2012 Elizabeth Power
We'll Always Have Paris © 2012 Jessica Hart

ISBN: 978-0-263-93064-1

09-0417

When she found the strength to speak her words came out in a horrified shudder. 'Oh, no. No, Dad. Please, no.'

And he heard her. In an instant he whirled around from where he was crouching and glared at her in disbelief. Just for a moment she saw a flash of shock, regret and contrition drift across his face, before his mouth twisted into a silent grin.

And her blood ran cold.

Mario Collazo had made a name for himself as a celebrity photographer. It wasn't hard to work out what he was doing with a camera inside the hospital room of some celebrity that he had stalked here.

If that was true... If that was true then her dad hadn't come to see *her* at all. He had lied to her warm-hearted mother and tricked his way into the hospital. None of the security officers would have stopped him if he was the relative of a patient.

Ice formed in the pit of her stomach as the hard reality of what she had just seen hit home. Her dad never had any intention of visiting her. The only reason he was here was to invade this poor sick woman's privacy. Lexi had no idea who she was, or why she was in this hospital, but that was irrelevant. She deserved to be left alone, no matter who she was.

Lexi felt bitter tears burning in the corners of her eyes. She had to get away. Escape. Collect her mother and get out of this place as fast as her legs could take her.

But in an instant that option was wiped away.

She had waited too long.

Because striding towards her was a tall, dark-haired man in a superbly tailored dark grey business suit. Not a doctor. This man was power and authority all wrapped up inside the handsome package of a broad-shouldered, slim-hipped man of about thirty. His head was low, his steps powerful and strident to match the dark, twisted brow. And he was heading straight for the room where her father was hiding.

He didn't even notice she was there, and she could only watch in horror as he flung open the door to the woman's room.

Then everything seemed to happen at once.

'What the hell are you doing in here?' he demanded, his voice furious with disbelief as he stormed into the room, pushed aside the visitor's chair and grabbed her father by the shoulder of his jacket.

Her breath froze inside her lungs, and Lexi pressed her back farther against the wall.

'Who are you, and what do you want?' His voice was shrill and full of menace, but loud enough to alert the receptionist at the desk to look up and lift the telephone. 'And how did you get a camera in here? I'll take that, you parasite.'

The camera came flying out of the door and crashed against the wall next to Lexi with such force that it smashed the lens. To Lexi's horror she saw the young man at reception reach into his pocket and pull out a digital camera and start to take photographs of what was happening inside the room from the safety of the corridor. Suddenly the stillness of the hushed hospital was filled with shouting, yelling, crashing furniture and medical equipment, flower vases smashing to the floor, nurses running and other patients coming out of their rooms to see what the noise was all about.

Shock and fear overwhelmed her. Her legs simply refused to move.

She was frozen. Immobile. Because, as if it was a horrible train wreck, she simply could not take her eyes away from that hospital room.

The door had swung half closed, but she could see her father struggling with the man in the suit. They were fighting, pushing and shoving each other against the glass window of the room. And her heart broke for the poor woman who was lying so still on the bed, oblivious to the fight that had erupted around her.

The door swung open and her father staggered backwards into the corridor, his left arm raised to protect himself. Lexi covered her mouth with both hands as the handsome stranger stretched back his right arm and punched her father in the face, knocking him sprawling onto the floor just in front of her feet.

The stranger lunged again, pulling her father off the ground by his jacket and starting to shake him so vigorously that Lexi felt sick. She screamed out loud. 'Stop it—please! That's my dad!'

Her father was hurled back to the ground with a thud. She dropped to the floor on her knees and put her hand on her father's heaving chest as he pushed himself up on one elbow and rubbed his jaw. Only then did she look up into the face of the attacker. And what she saw there made Lexi recoil in horror and shock.

The handsome face was twisted into a mask of rage and anger so distorted that it was barely recognisable.

'Your *dad*? So that's how it is. He used his own daughter as an accomplice. Nice.'

He stepped back, shaking his head and trying to straighten his jacket as security guards swarmed around him and nurses ran into the patient's room.

'Congratulations,' he added, 'you got what you came for.'

The penetrating gaze emanating from eyes of the darkest blue like a stormy sea bored deep into her own, as though they were trying to penetrate her skull. 'I hope you're satisfied,' he added, twisting his lips into a snarl of disgust and contempt before looking away, as if he couldn't bear the sight of her and her father for a second longer.

'I didn't know!' she called. 'I didn't know anything about this. Please believe me.'

He almost turned, but instead shrugged his shoulders and returned to the bedroom, shutting the door behind him and leaving her kneeling on the cold hospital floor, nauseous with shock, fear and wretched humiliation.

CHAPTER ONE

Five Months Later

GOATS!

Lexi Sloane pushed her designer sandal hard onto the brake pedal as a pair of long-eared brown and white nanny goats tottered out in front of the car as she drove around a bend, and bleated at her in disgust.

'Hey, give me a chance, girls. I'm new around here,' Lexi sang out into the silent countryside, snorting inelegantly as the goats totally ignored her and sauntered off into the long grass under the olive trees on the other side of the road.

'Which girls? Lexi? I thought you were working.' Her mother laughed into her earpiece in such a clear voice that it was hard to imagine that she was calling from the basement of an historic London theatre hundreds of miles away. 'Don't tell me. You've changed your mind and taken off with your pals on holiday to Spain after all.'

'Oh, please—don't remind me! Nope. The agency made me an offer I couldn't refuse and I am definitely on Paxos,' Lexi replied into the headset, stretching her head forward like a turtle to scan the sunlit road for more stray wildlife. 'You know how it goes. I am the official go-to girl when it comes to ghostwriting biographies. And it's always at the last minute. I will say one thing—' she grinned '—I stepped off the hydrofoil from Corfu an hour ago and those goats are the first local inhabitants I've met since I left the main road. Oh—and did I mention it is *seriously* hot?'

'A Greek Island in June... I am *so* jealous.' Her mother sighed. 'It's such a pity you have to work, but we'll make up for it when you get back. That reminds me. I was talking to a charming young actor just this morning who would love to meet you, and I sort of invited him to my engagement party. I'm sure you'd like him.'

'Oh, no. Mum, I adore you, and I know you mean well, but no more actors. Not after the disaster with Adam. In fact, please don't set me up with any more boyfriends at all. I'll be fine,' Lexi insisted, trying desperately to keep the anxiety out of her voice and change the subject. 'You have far more important things to sort out without worrying about finding me a boyfriend. Have you found a venue for this famous party yet? I'm expecting something remarkable.'

'Oh, don't talk to me about that. Patrick seems to acquire more relatives by the day. I thought that four daughters and three grandchildren were more than enough, but he wants the whole tribe there. He's so terribly old-fashioned about these things. Do you know, he won't even sleep with me until his grandmother's ring is on my finger?'

'Mum!'

'I know, but what's a girl to do? He's gorgeous, and I'm crazy about him. Anyhow, must go—I'm being dragged out to look at gothic chapels. Don't worry—I'll tell you all about it when you get back.'

'Gothic? You wouldn't dare. Anyway, I look terrible in black,' Lexi replied, peering through the windscreen and slowing the car at the entrance to the first driveway she'd seen so far. 'Ah—wait. I think I've just arrived at my client's house. Finally! Wish me luck?'

'I will if you need it, but you don't. Now, call me the minute you get back to London. I want to know everything about this mystery client you're working with. And I mean *everything*. Don't worry about me. You just try and enjoy yourself. *Ciao,* gorgeous.'

And with that her mother hung up, leaving Lexi alone on the silent country lane.

She glanced up at the letters carved into a stone nameplate, then double-checked the address she'd noted down over the phone while waiting for her luggage to come off the carousel at Corfu airport, some five hours earlier.

Yup. This was it. Villa Ares. Wasn't Ares the Greek god of war? Curious name for a house, but she was here and in one piece—which was quite a miracle.

Checking quickly for more goats or other animal residents, Lexi shifted the hire car into gear and drove slowly up a rough gravel driveway which curved around a long, white two-storey house before coming to a shuddering halt.

She lifted off her telephone headset and sat still for a few minutes to take in the stunning villa. She inhaled a long breath of hot, dry air through the open window, fragrant with the scent of orange blossom from the trees at the end of the drive. The only sound was birdsong from the olive groves and the gentle ripple of water from the swimming pool.

No sign of life. And certainly no sign of the mystery celebrity who was supposed to have sent a minion to meet her at the hydrofoil terminal.

'Welcome to Paxos,' she whispered with a chuckle, and stepped out of the car into the heat and the crunch of rough stone beneath her feet.

The words had no sooner slipped from Lexi's lips than

the slim stiletto heel of her favourite Italian sandal scraped down a large smooth cobblestone, her ankle twisted over, and she stumbled against the hot metal of her tiny hire car.

Which left a neat trail of several weeks' worth of grime and bright green tree pollen all down the side of the Italian silk and linen jacket.

Oh, no! Grinding her teeth, she inspected the damage to her clothing and the scrape down her shoe and swore to herself with all of the fluency and extensive vocabulary of a girl raised in show business. The dark red leather had been completely scraped into a tight, crumpled ball down the heel of her shoe.

This project had better be a real emergency!

Even if it was so *totally* intriguing.

In the five years that she'd worked as a contract ghost writer this was the first time that she had been sent out on a top-secret assignment on her own—so secret that the publisher who'd signed the contract had insisted that all details about the identity of the mystery author must remain under wraps until the ghost writer arrived at the celebrity's private home. The talent agency was well-known for being extremely discreet, but this was taking it to the next level.

She didn't even know the name of her client! Or anything about the book she would be working on.

A tingle of excitement and anticipation whispered across Lexi's shoulders as she peered up at the imposing stone villa. She loved a mystery almost as much as she loved meeting new people and travelling to new places around the world.

And her mind had been racing ever since she'd taken the call in Hong Kong.

Who *was* this mysterious celebrity, and why the great secrecy?

Several pop stars just out of rehab came to mind, and

there was always the movie star who had just set up his own charity organisation to fight child trafficking—any publisher would be keen to have that story.

Only one thing was certain: this was going to be someone special.

Lexi brushed most of the pollen from the rough silk-tweed fabric of her jacket, then straightened her back and walked as tall as she could across the loose stone drive, the excitement of walking into the unknown making her buzz with anticipation.

A warm breeze caressed her neck and she dipped her sunglasses lower onto her nose, waggling her shoulders in delight.

This had to be the second-best job in the world. She was actually getting paid to meet interesting people in lovely parts of the world and learn about their lives. And the best thing of all? Not one of those celebrities knew that she used every second of the time she spent travelling and waiting around in cold studios to work on the stories she *really* wanted to write.

Her children's books.

A few more paying jobs like this one and she would finally be able to take some time out and write properly. Just the thought of that gave her the shivers. To make that dream happen she was prepared to put up with anyone.

Magic.

Swinging her red-leather tote—which had been colour-matched to her now-ruined sandals—she shrugged, lifted her chin and strode out lopsided and wincing as the sharp stones of the drive pressed into the thin soles of her shoes.

Hey-ho. They were only sandals. She had seen too much of the flip side of life to let a little thing like a damaged sandal annoy her. Meeting a client when she didn't even know their name was a drop in the ocean compared to the train wreck of her personal history.

It was time to find out whose life she was going to share for the next week, and why they wanted to keep their project such a secret. She could hardly wait.

Mark Belmont rolled over onto his back on the padded sun lounger and blinked several times, before yawning widely and stretching his arms high above his head. He hadn't intended to fall asleep, but the hot, sunny weather, combined with the latest bout of insomnia, had taken its toll.

He swung his legs over the lounger, sat upright, and ground the palms of his hands into his eyes for a few seconds to try and relieve the nagging headache—without success. The bright sunlight and the calm, beautiful garden seemed to be laughing at the turmoil roiling inside his head.

Coming to Paxos had seemed like a good idea. In the past the family villa had always been a serene, welcoming refuge for the family, away from the prying eyes of the media; a place where he could relax and be himself. But even this tranquil location didn't hold enough magic to conjure up the amount of calm he needed to see his work through.

After four days of working through his mother's biography his emotions were a riot of awe at her beauty and talent combined with sadness and regret for all the opportunities he had missed when she was alive. All the things he could have said or done which might have made a difference to how she'd felt and the decision she'd made. Perhaps even convinced her not to have surgery at all.

But it was a futile quest. Way too late and way too little.

Worse, he had always relished the solitude of the villa, but now it seemed to echo with the ghosts of happier days and he felt so very alone. Isolated. His sister Cassie had been right.

Five months wasn't long enough to put aside his grief. Nowhere near.

He sniffed, and was about to stand when a thin black cat appeared at his side and meowed loudly for lunch as she rubbed herself along the lounger.

'Okay, Emmy. Sorry I'm late.'

He shuffled across the patio towards the stone barbecue in his bare feet, watching out for sharp pebbles. Reaching into a tall metal bin, he pulled out a box of cat biscuits and quickly loaded up a plastic plate, narrowly avoiding the claws and teeth of the feral cat as it attacked the food. Within seconds her two white kittens appeared and cautiously approached the plate, their pink ears and tongue a total contrast to their mum. Dad Oscar must be out in the olive groves.

'It's okay, guys. It's all yours.' Mark chuckled as he filled the water bowl from the tap and set it down. *'Bon appétit.'*

He ran his hands through his hair and sighed out loud as he strolled back towards the villa. This was *not* getting the work done.

He had stolen ten days away from Belmont Investments to try and make some sense of the suitcase full of manuscript pages, press clippings, personal notes, appointment diaries and letters he had scooped up from his late mother's desk. So far he had failed miserably.

It certainly hadn't been *his* idea to finish his mother's biography. Far from it. He knew it would only bring more publicity knocking on his door. But his father was adamant. He was prepared to do press interviews and make his life public property if it helped put the ghosts to rest and celebrate her life in the way he wanted.

But of course that had been before the relapse.

And since when could Mark refuse his father anything? He'd put his own dreams and personal aspirations to one side for the family before, and would willingly do it again in a heartbeat.

But where to start? How to write the biography of the woman known worldwide as Crystal Leighton, beautiful international movie star, but known to him as the mother who'd taken him shopping for shoes and turned up at every school sports day?

The woman who had been willing to give up her movie career rather than allow her family to be subjected to the constant and repeated invasion of privacy that came with being a celebrity?

Mark paused under the shade of the awning outside the dining-room window and looked out over the gardens and swimming pool as a light breeze brought some relief from the unrelenting late-June heat.

He needed to find some new way of working through the mass of information that any celebrity, wife and mother accumulated in a lifetime and make some sense of it all.

And one thing was clear. He had to do it fast.

The publisher had wanted the manuscript on his desk in time for a major celebration of Crystal Leighton at a London film festival scheduled for the week before Easter. The deadline had been pushed back to April, and now he would be lucky to have anything before the end of August.

And every time the date slipped another unofficial biography appeared. Packed with the usual lies, speculation and innuendo about her private life and, of course, the horrific way it had been brought to an early end.

He had to do something—anything—to protect the reputation of his mother. He'd failed to protect her privacy when it mattered most, and he refused to fail her again. If anyone was going to create a biography it would be someone who cared about keeping her reputation and memory alive and revered.

No going back. No compromises. He would keep his promise and he was happy to do it—for her and for his family. And just maybe there was a slim chance that he would come to terms with his own crushing guilt at how much he had failed her. Maybe.

Mark turned back towards the house and frowned as he saw movement on the other side of the French doors separating the house from the patio.

Strange. His housekeeper was away and he wasn't expecting visitors. *Any* visitors. He had made sure of that. His office had strict instructions not to reveal the location of the villa or give out his private contact details to anyone.

Mark blinked several times and found his glasses on the side table.

A woman he had never seen before was strolling around inside his living room, picking things up and putting them down again as if she owned the place.

His things! Things he had not intended anyone else to see. Documents that were personal and very private.

He inhaled slowly and forced himself to stay calm. Anger and resentment boiled up from deep inside his body. He had to fight the urge to rush inside and throw this woman out onto the lane, sending her back whence she came.

The last thing he wanted was yet another journalist or so-called filmmaker looking for some dirt amongst his parents' personal letters.

This was the very reason he'd come to Paxos in the first place. To escape constant pressure from the world of journalists and the media. And now it seemed that the world had decided to invade his privacy. Without even having the decency to ring the doorbell and ask to be admitted.

This was unacceptable.

Mark rolled back his shoulders, his head thumping, his hands clenched and his attention totally focused on the back of the head of this woman who thought she had the right to inspect the contents of his living room.

The patio door was half-open, and Mark padded across the stone patio in his bare feet quietly, so that she wouldn't hear him against the jazz piano music tinkling out from his favourite CD which he had left playing on Repeat.

He unfurled one fist so that his hand rested lightly on the doorframe. But as he moved the glass backwards his body froze, his hand flat against the doorjamb.

There was something vaguely familiar about this chestnut-haired woman who was so oblivious to his presence, her head tilted slightly to one side as she browsed the family collection of popular novels and business books that had accumulated here over the years.

She reminded him of someone he had met before, but her name and the circumstamces of that meeting drew an annoying blank. Perhaps it was due to the very odd combination of clothing she was wearing. Nobody on this island deliberately chose to wear floral grey and pink patterned leggings beneath a fuchsia dress and an expensive jacket. And she had to be wearing four or five long, trailing scarves in contrasting patterns and colours, which in this heat was not only madness but clearly designed to impress rather than be functional.

She must have been quite entertaining for the other passengers on the ferry or the hydrofoil to the island from Corfu that morning.

One thing was certain.

This girl was not a tourist. She was a city girl, wearing

city clothes. And that meant she was here for one reason—
and that reason was him. Probably some journalist who had
asked him for an interview at some function or other and
was under pressure from her editor to deliver. She might
have come a long way to track him down, but that was her
problem. Whoever she was, it was time to find out what
she wanted and send her back to the city.

Then she picked up a silver-framed photograph, and
his blood ran cold.

It was the only precious picture he had from the last
Christmas they had celebrated together as a family. His
mother's happy face smiled out from the photograph, complete with the snowman earrings and reindeer headset she
was wearing in honour of Cassie's little boy. A snapshot
of life at Belmont Manor as it used to be and never could
be again.

And now it was in the hands of a stranger.

Max gave a short, low cough, both hands on his hips.

'Looking for anything in particular?' he asked.

The girl swung round, a look of absolute horror on
her face. As she did so the photograph she was holding
dropped from her fingers, and she only just caught it in
time as it slid down the sofa towards the hard tiled floor.

As she looked at him through her oversized dark sunglasses, catching her breath unsteadily, a fluttering frag-
ment of memory flashed through his mind and then wafted
out again before he could grasp hold of it. Which annoyed
him even more.

'I don't know who you are, or what you're doing here,
but I'll give you one chance to explain before asking you
to leave the same way you came in. Am I making myself
clear?'

CHAPTER TWO

LEXI thought her heart was going to explode.

It couldn't be. It just could *not* be him.

Exhaustion. That was the only explanation. Three weeks on the road, following a film director through a series of red-carpet events across Asia, had finally taken their toll.

She simply had to be hallucinating. But as he looked at her through narrowed eyes behind rimless designer spectacles Lexi's stomach began to turn over and over as the true horror of the situation hit home.

She was standing in front of Mark Belmont—son of Baron Charles Belmont and his stunningly beautiful wife, the late movie actress Crystal Leighton.

The same Mark Belmont who had punched her father in that hospital on the day his mother had died. And accused *her* of being his accomplice in the process. Completely unfairly.

When she was a little girl she'd had a recurring nightmare about being a pilgrim sent to fight the lions in some gladiatorial arena in Rome.

This was worse.

Her legs were shaking like jelly, and if her hand held on to her bag any tighter the strap would snap.

'What—what are you doing here?' she asked, begging and pleading with him in her mind to tell her that he was a temporary guest of the celebrity she had been paid to work with and that he would soon be leaving. Very soon. Because the other alternative was too horrible to imagine.

She'd thought that she had escaped her shameful connection to this man and his family.

Fate apparently had other ideas.

Fate in the form of Mark Belmont, who was looking at her with such disdain and contempt that she had to fight back the temptation to defend herself.

With a single shake of the head, he dismissed her question.

'I have every right to be here. Unlike yourself. So let's start again and I'll ask you the same question. Who are you and what are you doing in my house?'

His house? A deep well of understanding hit her hard and the bottom dropped out of Lexi's stomach.

If this was his house—was it possible that Mark Belmont was her celebrity?

It would make sense. Crystal Leighton's name had never left the gossip columns since her tragic death, and Lexi had heard a rumour that the Belmont family were writing a biography that would be front-page news. But surely that was *Baron* Belmont, not his business-guru son?

Lexi sighed out loud. She was jumping to conclusions— her imagination was running ahead of itself. This was a big house, with room for plenty of guests. It could easily be one of his colleagues or aristocratic friends who needed her help.

And then the impact of what he was asking got through to her muddled brain.

Mark had not recognised her. He had no clue that she was the girl he had met in the hospital corridor only a few months earlier.

They had only met for a few fleeting moments, and she

had certainly changed since then. They both had. And her sunglasses were a genius idea.

She inhaled a couple of breaths, but the air was too warm and thick to clear her head very much. It was as though his tall, powerful body had absorbed all the oxygen from the room.

A flicker of annoyance flashed across his full, sensuous mouth before he said, 'I don't take kindly to uninvited guests, so I suggest you answer my question before I ask you to leave.'

Uninvited guests? Oh, God, the situation was worse than she'd realised. He didn't seem to be expecting a visitor—any visitor. He had no idea that his publisher had sent a ghost writer out to the island! No wonder he thought that she was some pathetic burglar or a photojournalist.

Okay, so he had treated her unfairly in the worst of circumstances, but she was here to do a job. She glanced down, desperate to escape his laser-beam focus, and her eyes found the image of a happy family smiling back at her from behind the glass in the picture she had almost dropped.

It could have been a movie set, with a perfect cast of actors brought in for the day. Gorgeous film-star mother, handsome and tall aristocratic father, and two pretty children—with the cutest toddler on the planet waving at the camera. All grouped in front of a tall Christmas tree decorated in red and gold and a real fire burning bright in a huge marble fireplace.

What did Mark Belmont know about broken families and wrecked dreams?

Guilt about the pain her father had caused the Belmont family pinched her skin hard enough to make her flinch. But she ignored it. What her father had done had never been her fault, and she wasn't going to allow the past to ruin her work. She needed this job, and she'd be a fool to let her father snatch away the chance to make her dream come true.

Lexi opened her mouth as if to speak, closed it again, and then pinched her thumb and forefinger tightly against the bridge of her nose.

'Oh, no.' She shook her head slowly from side to side, eyes closed. 'The agency would *not* do this to me.'

'The agency?' Mark asked, his head tilted slightly to one side. 'Have you got the right villa? Island? Country?'

She chuckled, and when she spoke her voice was calmer, steadier.

'Let me guess. Something tells me that you may not have spoken, emailed or in some other way communicated with your publisher in the past forty-eight hours. Am I right?'

For the first time since she had arrived a concerned look flashed across his tanned and handsome face, but was instantly replaced by a confident glare.

'What do you mean? My publisher?'

Lexi dived into her huge bag, pulled out a flat black tablet computer, and swiped across the screen with her forefinger—being careful not to damage her new fingernails, which still carried the silver and purple glitter that had been the hit of the last show party in Hong Kong.

'Brightmore Press. Sound familiar?'

'Maybe,' he drawled. 'And why should that matter to me?'

Lexi's poor overworked brain spun at top speed.

He was alone in the villa. This was the correct address. And Mark *was* familiar with Brightmore Press. Lexi put those three factoids together and came up with the inevitable conclusion.

Mark Belmont was the mystery celebrity she had been assigned to work with.

And the bubble of excitement and enthusiastic energy that had been steadily inflating on the long journey from Hong Kong popped like an overstretched balloon.

Of all the rotten luck.

She needed the job so badly. Running a home in central London wasn't cheap, and this bonus would have made a big difference to how quickly she could start the renovations. All her plans for the future relied on having her own home office where she could write her children's books full-time. Walking away from this job would set her back months.

She stared at him wide-eyed for a few seconds, before sighing out loud.

'Oh, dear. I hate it when this happens. But it does explain why you didn't meet me at the harbour.'

Mark shifted his legs shoulder-width apart and crossed his arms. 'Meet you? No, I don't think so. Now, let me make myself quite clear. You have two minutes to explain before I escort you from my private home. And please don't think I won't. I've spent more time than I care to think about giving press conferences. My office has a catalogue of past interviews and press statements, covering every possible topic of conversation. I suggest that you try there—because I have absolutely no intention of giving you an interview, especially when you seem intent on damaging my property. Am I getting through to you?'

'Your property? Oh, I'm so sorry,' she murmured, scrabbling to pick up the picture and brushing off any dust from the silver frame. 'I did knock, but there was no answer, and the door was open. This is a lovely family photo and I couldn't resist peeking at it, so...' She gave a quick shrug of the shoulders and lifted her chin slightly. 'You should be more careful about security.'

'Really?' He nodded, his voice calculating and cool enough to add a chill to the air. 'Thank you so much for the advice, but you aren't in the city any more. We don't lock our doors around here. Of course if I'd *known* I was to have visitors I might have taken additional precautions. Which brings us to my earlier question. Who are you, and why are you here? I'm sure the two charming police officers who take care of this island would be delighted to meet you in a more formal setting. And, as you have probably realised, Gaios is only about three miles from here. And they are the proud owners of both a police car and a motorcycle. So I would suggest that you come up with a very convincing excuse very quickly.'

Police? Was he serious?

She looked warily into those startling blue eyes. Oh, yes, he was serious.

Her chest lifted a good few inches and she stared straight at him in alarm. Then she sucked in a breath and her words came tumbling out faster than she would have thought possible.

'Okay. Here goes. Sorry, but your peeps have *not* been keeping you up to date on a few rather crucial matters. Your Mr Brightmore called my talent agency, who called me with instructions to get myself to Paxos because one of their clients has a book to finish and they—' she gestured towards his chest with her flat hand '—are apparently a month past the final deadline for the book, and the publishers are becoming a little desperate. They need this manuscript by the end of August.'

She exhaled dramatically, her shoulders slumped, and

she slid the tablet back into her bag with a dramatic flour-ish before looking up at him, eyebrows high, with a broad grin.

'Right. Now that's out of the way I suppose I should in-troduce myself. Alexis Sloane. Otherwise known as Lexi. Ghost writer *extraordinaire*. And I'm here to meet a client who needs help with a book. I take it that would be you?'

'Well, of *course* I didn't tell you what the publisher had organised, darling brother, because I knew exactly what your reaction would be.'

Mark Belmont sat down hard on the end of the sun lounger, then immediately stood up again and started pac-ing up and down the patio, the sun-warmed stone hot under his bare feet. The temperature was a perfect match for his mood: incendiary. His emotions boiled in a turmoil of resistance, resolution and defiance touched with fury. Cassandra Belmont had a lot to answer for.

'Cassie,' he hissed, 'I could strangle you. Seriously. How could you do this to me? You *know* that this biogra-phy is too personal, too close to home, to ask anyone to help. Why do you think I've come all the way to Paxos to work on the book on my own? The last thing I need is some random stranger asking questions and digging into places I don't know I want to go myself. Communication is a wonderful thing, you know. Perhaps you've heard of it?'

'Relax.'

His sister's voice echoed down the phone, and he imag-ined her curled up on the sofa in Belmont Manor while her two small sons played havoc around her.

'Lucas Brightmore recommended the most discreet agency in London. Their staff sign cast-iron confidenti-ality agreements and would never divulge anything you tell them. I think it could work.'

'Cassie, you are a menace. I don't care how discreet this...*secretary* is. If I wanted a personal assistant I would have brought one. I have excellent staff working for me. Remember? And I would never, *ever* invite them here to the villa. I need privacy and space to get the work done. You know me.' His voice slowed and dropped lower in pitch. 'I have to get my head into the detail on my own before I can go public with anything. And I need peace and quiet to do that.'

'You're right. But this is not a business project you are evaluating. This is our mother's life story. It has to do her justice, and you're the only person in the family with the faintest bit of creativity. I know I couldn't do it in a million years. I don't have nearly enough patience. Especially when it comes to the difficult bits.'

Cassie took a breath and her voice softened.

'Look, Mark, this is hard for all of us. And it's incredibly brave of you to take over the project. But that makes it even more important to get the job done as quickly as you can. Then we can all get on with our lives and Dad will be happy.'

'Happy?' Mark repeated with a dismissive cough. 'You mean like he's happy about my plans to renovate those derelict cottages on the estate into holiday lets? Or the restructuring plans for the business that he's been blocking since Christmas?'

'Probably not,' Cassie answered. 'But you know as well as I do that it isn't about you or me. It has a lot more to do with the fact that he's ill for the first time in his life and he's just lost his wife in a surgical procedure she never even told him about. He doesn't know how to deal with that any more than the rest of us.'

Mark ran his tongue over his parched lips. 'How is he today?'

The delay before Cassie answered said more than the sadness inherent in her reply. 'About the same. This round of chemotherapy has really knocked him back.' Then her steely determination kicked back in, tinged with concern. 'You don't need to put yourself through this. Hand back the advance from the publisher and let some journo write Mum's biography. Come home and run your business and get on with your life. The past can take care of itself.'

'Some journo? No, Cassie. The press destroyed Mum's last chance of dignity, and I don't even want to *think* about what they'd do with a true-life *exposé* based on lies, innuendo and stupid gossip.' He shook his head and felt a shiver run down his spine despite the heat. 'We know that her friends have already been approached by two writers for hire looking for dirt. Can you see the headlines? Read All About It: The True Sordid Past of the Real Crystal Leighton Belmont.' He swallowed hard on a dry throat. 'It would kill him. And I *refuse* to let her down like that again.'

'Then finish the book our mother started. But do it fast. The agency said they were sending their best ghost writer, so be nice. I'm your sister, and I love you, but sometimes you can be a little intense. Oh. Have to go. Your nephews are awake and need feeding. Again. Take care.'

'You, too,' Mark replied, but she had already put the phone down.

He exhaled slowly and willed his heart rate to slow.

He had never been able to stay angry with Cassie. His sister had been the one constant in his father's life ever since their mother had died. She had her own husband, a toddler and a new baby to take care of, but she adored the manor house where they had grown up and was happy to make a home there. Her husband was a doctor at the local hospital whom Cassie had met when she'd taken their father for a check-up. Mark knew that he could totally rely on her to take care of their father for a few weeks while he took time out of the office.

She had even taken over the role of peacemaker on the rare occasion when he went back to Belmont Manor.

But she shouldn't have talked to the publisher without telling him about it.

Suddenly the decision to come to Paxos to finish the biography seemed ridiculous. He'd thought that being on his own would help, but instead he'd become more agitated and irritable by the day. He needed to do things. Make things happen. Take responsibility just like he'd always done. It infuriated him that he'd found it impossible to focus on the task he had set himself for more than a few minutes without having to get up and pace around, desperate for an opportunity to procrastinate.

Cassie was right. This biography was too close. Too personal.

His mother had always been a hopeless housekeeper, and organisation had never been one of her strong points. She'd liked the creative world, and enjoyed making sense of the jumble of random photographs, letters, newspaper clippings and memorabilia.

And he was just the same. An artist in many ways. His natural inclination was to push through the boundaries of possibility to see what lay beyond and shake things up. Little wonder that he was increasingly at loggerheads with his father's almost obsessive need to keep things in order. Compliant. Unchanging. Private and quiet.

Or at least that had been the case until six months ago. But now?

Now his father was on his second round of chemotherapy, his beloved mother had effectively died on a plastic surgeon's operating table, and his on-off girlfriend had finally given up on him and met someone she actually seemed to love and who loved her in return.

Mark felt as though the foundations on which he had based his entire life had been ripped out from under him.

His fingers wrapped tightly around the back of the chair until the knuckles turned white with the pressure.

No. He could handle this trauma. Just as he had abandoned his own life so that he could take his brother's place in the family.

There was no point in getting angry about the past.

He had given his word. And he would see it happen on his own, with the privacy and the space to work things through. The last thing he needed right now was a stranger entering his private space, and the sooner he persuaded her that the publisher was wrong and she could head off back to the city the better.

Think. He needed to think.

To stop herself shaking Lexi gripped her shoulder bag with one hand and pressed the other against the back of the leather sofa. She couldn't risk ruining her carefully contrived show of being completely unfazed as she looked at Mark Belmont, pacing up and down the patio next to the swimming pool, her cell phone pressed to his ear.

Only this was not the business-guru version of The Honourable Mark Belmont that usually graced the covers of international business magazines around the world. Oh, no. She could have dealt with that stiff, formally dressed office clone quite easily. *This* version was an entirely different sort of man: much more of a challenge for any woman.

The business suit was gone. Mark was wearing a pair of loose white linen trousers and a short-sleeved pale blue striped polo shirt that perfectly matched the colour of his eyes. His toned muscular arms and bare feet were tanned as dark as the scowl he had greeted her with, and the top two buttons of his shirt were undone, revealing a bronzed, muscular chest.

His dark brown hair might have been expertly cut into tight curls, but he hadn't shaved, and his square jaw was covered in a light stubble much more holiday laid-back than designer businessman. But, Lord, it suited him perfectly.

She knew several fashion stylists who would have swooned just at the sight of him.

This was a completely different type of beast from the man who'd defended his mother so valiantly in the hospital. This was Mark Belmont in his natural setting. His territory. His home.

Oh, my.

She could lie and pretend that her burning red neck was simply due to the heat of a Greek island in late June and the fact that she was overdressed, but she knew better.

Her curse had struck yet again.

She was always like this around Adonis-handsome men. They were like gorgeous baubles on display in a shop window. She could ogle them all day but never dared to touch. Because they were always so far out of reach that she knew she would never be able to afford one. And even if she could afford one it would never match the disorganised chaos of her life.

This particular bauble had dark eyebrows which were heavy and full of concern. He looked tense. Annoyed and anxious.

It had seemed only right to ring the publisher for him. Just to clarify things.

Only judging by the expression on his face the news

that her assignment was not a practical joke after all had not gone down well.

Normally her clients were delighted that a fairy god-mother had dropped into their world to help them out of a tricky situation.

Apparently Mark Belmont was not seeing his situation in quite the same way.

She had to persuade him to allow her to stay and help him with…with *what?* She still had no idea what type of book Mark Belmont was writing. Business management? A family history? Or…she swallowed…the obvious. A memoir of his mother.

Lexi looked up as Mark turned towards her from the door, lowering the phone, and searched his face for something—anything—that would help her make the de-cision.

And she found it. In his eyes of frosty blue.

The same eyes that had looked at her with such pain mixed with contempt on that terrible day in the hospital. When his heart had been breaking.

Decision made. If he could survive writing about his late mother then she would do her best to make the book the best it could be. Even without his help.

She could make this work. It would take a lot of effort, and she would have to be as stubborn as a stubborn thing in Stubbornland, but she could do it. She had stood her ground before, and she'd do it again.

Mark stood still for a moment, eyes closed, tapping the cell phone against the side of his head.

'If you're quite finished with my phone, Mr Belmont?' A sweet, charming voice echoed out from behind his back. 'It tends not to function very well after being used as a percussion instrument.'

Mark opened his eyes and stared at the offending cell phone as though he had never seen it before. He'd never used a purple phone in his life and he was extremely tempted to throw the offending article into the pool and leave it there. *With its owner. The hack writer.*

Fortunately for the phone, good manners kicked in and, holding it between his thumb and forefinger, he turned and extended his arm towards Lexi.

To her credit, she was not wearing a self-satisfied smirk but the same look of professional non-confrontational in-difference he was used to seeing from city suits around the boardroom table where some of his riskier ideas were discussed.

Except for him this was not a job. It was very personal. And even the idea of sharing his deepest concerns and emotions about his parents made him bristle with resent-ment and refusal to comply.

He hadn't built a venture-capital company from the ruins of his father's business without taking risks, but they had been calculated risks, based on information he had per-sonally checked and worked on until he'd known that the family's money would not be wasted on the investment.

This girl—this woman—in this ridiculous outfit had arrived at his home without his approval.

His sister might have confidence in the talent agency, but he knew nothing about the plan, and if there was one thing guaranteed to annoy him it was things being planned behind the scenes without his knowledge.

Cassie was perfectly aware of that fact, but she'd done it anyway. Her intentions might be excellent, but the real-ity was a little difficult to stomach.

A light tapping broke Mark out of his reverie, and he flashed a glance at the girl just in time to see her keying fu-riously into the cell phone, her sparkly purple-painted fingernails flashing in the sunlight. Although how she could see through those huge sunglasses was a mystery to him.

In the living room she had been more stunned than stunning, but in the bright white light reflected back from the patio her skin appeared pale and almost translucent, as though she hadn't seen sunlight for quite some time. The contrast between her English-rose complexion and the startlingly bright scarves wrapped around her neck was so great that it distracted him for a moment from the fact that she was talking.

'I'll be with you in a moment, Mr Belmont,' she said away from the phone. 'I'm just trying to find out the location of the nearest hotel on the island. Unless, of course, you can recommend one to me?'

She looked up and gave him a half smile—a pink-cheeked, polite kind of smile that still managed to brighten her whole face, drawing his full attention.

'I apologise for not booking accommodation before I arrived, but this assignment was rather last-minute. I'll need to stay somewhere close by, so I don't waste too much time travelling back and forth. Don't worry,' she added, 'I'll be out of your hair within the hour.'

'A hotel? That is quite out of the question,' he answered.

'Oh?' She raised her eyebrows and her fingers stilled. 'And why is that?'

Mark pushed his hands into his pockets to keep them from fastening around that pretty pale neck and squeezing hard.

'Well, for one thing there is indeed a small hotel in Gaios. But it is currently closed for over-running refurbishments. And secondly...' He paused before saying the words. 'Paxos is a very small island. People talk and ask questions. I hardly think it would be appropriate for you to stay in rented accommodation while you're working on a confidential project for the Belmont family. And I'm afraid that you certainly don't *look* like a package holiday tourist.'

To her credit, she didn't look down at her outfit to check if something was amiss. 'I don't? Excellent. Because I have no intention of looking like a tourist. I want to look like me. As for confidentiality…? I can assure you that I'm totally discreet. Anything you tell me will be in strict confidence. I've worked on many confidential projects, and none of my previous clients ever had any problems with my work. Now, is there anything else you'd like to know before I head to town?'

He lifted his chin and dropped his shoulders back, chest out, legs braced, creating the sort of profile his media consultants had recommended would be perfect to grace the covers of business magazines. Judging by the slight widening of her eyes, it was equally effective on the patio.

'Only this. You seem to be under the illusion that I've agreed to this arrangement. That is not the case. Any contract you might have is between my publisher and your agency. I certainly haven't signed anything. And I have a big problem with being railroaded. Which is exactly how I'm feeling right now. I dislike surprises, Miss Sloane.'

She lifted her chin, and instantly the firmness of the jawline on her heart-shaped face screamed out to him that this was a girl who rarely took no for an answer.

'It's unfortunate that you weren't expecting me,' she replied with a tight smile, 'but I can assure you that I have no plans to return home before this assignment is completed.'

She reached into the tiny pocket of her jacket, pulled out a small business card and presented it to him. 'I've just survived two long international flights, one hour on the hydrofoil from Corfu, and twenty minutes negotiating car hire with the charming Greek gentleman at the port to get here. I don't intend to leave until my boss instructs me to. So. May I suggest a compromise trial period? Let's say twenty-four hours? And if you don't find my services valuable, then I promise to jump into my hire car and get out of your life. One day. That's all I'm asking.'

'One day?' Mark echoed through gritted teeth.

'Absolutely.'

A smile warmed her lips, and for the first time since they'd met it was a real smile. The kind of smile that made the Cupid's-bow curve of her full lips crinkle girlishly at the edges and the pink in her cheeks flush with enjoyment. She was enjoying this. And she was clearly determined to make him do all the work.

'Very well. Twenty-four hours it is. In which case there is only one possible option,' he continued. 'You will be staying here at the villa with me until I decide whether I need your help or not, Miss Sloane.'

CHAPTER THREE

'You want me to stay here at the villa?' Lexi looked around the patio, then back towards the house. 'You did say you lived here alone, Mr Belmont? Is that correct? I'll take your silence as a yes. In that case, aren't you worried about what your wife or girlfriend will think about the arrangement? A single man living here alone suddenly has a young lady houseguest? There are bound to be questions.' Lexi glanced at him. 'Perhaps you have nieces?'

'I'm afraid not. Two nephews. Both under five. Go by the names of Charles and Freddie.'

'Shame.' She nodded and screwed up her face. 'How about cousins? Old schoolfriends? Casual acquaintances that just happen to pass by?'

'No subterfuge will be necessary, Miss Sloane. You can call yourself a business colleague or personal assistant for as long as you stay here. Take your pick.'

'Business colleague it is. Personal assistant smacks too much of a girl who organises your dry-cleaning, runs your office and buys presents for your lucky lady-friends—of which I'm sure there are many.'

Lexi leaned forward slightly towards Mark.

'I don't actually perform those particular duties, by the way. In case you're wondering. Ghostwriting. That's it. Okay? Splendid. Now, seeing as I'll be staying here, would you mind helping me with my suitcases? I do have quite a few.'

'What do you mean a few?'

Mark strolled over to the edge of the patio and stared at the tiny hire car. Lexi tottered past him and descended the two low steps that curved down to the driveway.

'You men have it easy.' She laughed, opening up the boot and heaving the two massive matching cases out onto the pebble driveway. 'A couple of suits and that's it. But I've just spent three weeks on the road with different events every evening.'

A cabin bag and a leather Gladstone bag followed.

'Clients expect a girl to wear different outfits for each film launch to keep the photographers happy,' she added, walking around to the passenger door and flinging it open. The top garment bag had slipped a little down the back of the driver's seat, so she tugged it free and folded it over one arm before grabbing hold of her travel bag with one hand and slinging the shoulder strap of her overnight case across the front of her jacket.

Lexi pushed the car door closed with one foot and looked around for Mark. He was standing open-mouthed, still watching her from the terrace as though he could hardly believe what he was looking at.

Lexi rolled her eyes, took a firmer hold of her bag and tottered across the pebbles of the car park onto the patio steps. 'Don't worry about me,' she said, 'I've left the heavy bags down by the car. Any time today will be good.'

'No problem,' Mark murmured under his breath. 'The porter will be right with you.'

He reached for his shoes, which he had stashed under the lounger. Unfortunately, as he bent over, Lexi tottered past his very fine rear end in her high-heeled sandals, and as he stood up his elbow jogged the overnight bag she was carrying.

At exactly the same moment the slippery silk fabric of her garment bag slipped down her arm. She snatched at it with the hand holding the travel bag, twisting her body round to stop it from falling to the ground.

And she took one step backwards.

The stiletto heel of her right sandal hit the smooth marble edge of the swimming pool, her right leg shot forward, she completely lost her balance and instinctively flung both arms out to compensate.

For one millisecond she was airborne. Arms twirling around in wide circles, both legs in the air, luggage thrown out to each side and the thin silk fabric of her overdress inflated up to her waist as a parachute.

She squeezed her eyes tight shut and prepared herself for a dunking in the swimming pool. But instead her feet lifted even higher off the ground as a long, strong arm grabbed her around the waist and another arm swept under her legs, taking her weight effortlessly.

Lexi flashed open her eyes, gave a high squeak of terror, and flung both her arms around Mark's neck by sheer instinct, pressing herself tight onto his shirt. Unfortunately she forgot that she was still clutching her travel bag for dear life, and succeeded in hitting Mark on the back of the head with it.

To his credit, he gave only a low, deep sigh instead of yelling like a schoolboy.

She opened her mouth to apologise, then closed it again. Her lungs seemed to have forgotten how to work and her breathing had become a series of short panting noises—which would have been perfect for a spaniel but which, from her lips, managed to sound both pathetic and wheezy at the same time.

She had *never* been picked up before.

And the last time she'd been this close to a handsome man had been on Valentine's night, when her ex-boyfriend had confessed he'd been sleeping with a girl she'd thought was her friend. So it would be fair to say that it hadn't ended well.

This, on the other hand, was turning out to be a much more positive experience.

Below his loose blue shirt Mark was muscular, warm and solid against her body, and in the position he was holding her their faces were only inches apart. His eyes locked onto hers, and suddenly it made perfect sense just to lie there in his arms while he took her weight.

Up close, she could see that his eyes were not a perfectly clear blue, as his mother's had been, but were flecked with slivers of darker blue and grey, so that under the shade of the terrace they looked like a cloudy summer sky.

His wiry dark brown hair was curled at the base of his neck with the heat of the afternoon, and she inhaled an intoxicating aroma of some fragrant shampoo or shower gel, freshly laundered linen shirt and something much deeper and muskier.

She had no clue what it was, but that extra something had the power to make her heart beat faster than was probably safe. So fast that it was all too easy to recall that she was here to work. Not to cuddle the client or to partially strangle him with her arms after trying to knock him out.

'I should have warned you about the pool. Are you okay now?' he asked, his voice low with concern.

She swallowed, and gave a smile and a short nod. Instantly the arm around her waist slackened and her brief adventure came to a halt as he slowly lowered her back down and her sandals made contact with solid ceramic tile.

Strange how her arms seemed reluctant to lose contact

with Mark's shirt and practically slid the full length of his chest—before the sensible part of her brain took over and reminded her that her agency contract included some rather strict rules about fraternising with the clients.

Lexi tugged down on the hem of her dress and pretended to be straightening her clothing before daring to form actual words.

'No problem. I prefer not to go swimming fully clothed, so thanks for saving me from a dunking. And sorry about the bag.' Her fingers waved in the direction of his head.

'Well, at least we're even,' Mark replied, gesturing with his head towards the swimming pool, where her garment bag was floating on the surface and making small glugging noises.

'Oh, drat,' Lexi replied and her shoulders slumped. 'There go two cocktail dresses, a business suit and a cape. The dresses I can replace, but I liked that cape.'

'A cape?' Mark repeated, strolling down the patio and picking up a long pole with a mesh net on the end.

'One of my previous clients started life as a professional magician, entertaining passengers on a cruise ship,' Lexi replied, preoccupied by watching Mark try to guide the wayward luggage to the side of the pool. Every time he got close the filter pump blew it back towards the deep end.

She winced the second time he almost had it close enough to reach.

'Fascinating man. He told me he'd kept the cape just in case he ever needed to earn a few dollars. I pointed out that after forty years in Las Vegas the chances of that happening were slim.' Lexi sniffed and gave a low chuckle. 'The rascal gave me that cape the day of the launch party for his autobiography. He'd decided that his pension didn't need boosting after all, and that at ninety-two he might be a little rusty. So we had one final performance. I was his glamorous assistant, of course. He supplied the top hat, plastic flowers and scarves. The full works. Then he patted my bottom and I threatened to cut him in half.'

She grinned. 'Happy days. It was a great party. What a shame that a vintage cape like that is going to be ruined after all of those years in showbiz…' Her eyes tracked slowly from the bag across to Mark, then back to the bag again, and she gave a dramatic sigh just to make sure that he'd got the message.

'Are you always so much trouble?' Mark asked, rolling up his trousers to reveal a surprisingly hairy pair of muscular legs before descending the steps into the shallow end of the pool and dragging the soggy garment bag onto the side.

'Oh, no,' Lexi replied in a totally casual, matter-of-fact voice as she grasped the handle and sloshed the bag farther onto the terrace, to join the other pieces of luggage she had abandoned there. 'I'm usually a lot more trouble than this. You should be grateful it was the shallow end. But these are early days.'

His reply was a snort and a brief smile illuminated his face. It was the first time she had seen Mark smile, and even in the hot afternoon sunshine she felt the warmth of it on her face. And was instantly filled with remorse.

She paused and focused on her bags before breathing out slowly, eyes down.

It was time. If she was going to do this then she had better do it now and get it over with.

Mark frowned and strolled over towards her. 'I'm sure you have enough dry clothing to last a few days. Is there something else I can help you with?'

Lexi looked up at him reluctantly and licked her lips, which were suddenly bone dry.

'Actually, there is one more thing I need to clear up

before we start working together. You see, we have met before. Just the once. In London. And not in the best of circumstances.'

She whipped off her sunglasses and hung them over the breast pocket of her jacket, looked up into his startled face.

'We weren't formally introduced at the time, but you'd just met my father in your mother's hospital room and you were rather preoccupied with escorting him out. Does that jog your memory?'

Mark paused, hands on hips, and looked at her. So they *had* met before, but...?

The hospital. Her father. Those violet-grey eyes set in a heart-shaped face.

The same eyes that had stared up at him in horror and shock after he'd punched that slimy photographer.

'Get out,' he said, cold ice reeling in his stomach, fighting the fire in his blood. 'I want you out of my house.'

'Just give me a minute,' she whispered in a hoarse, trembling voice. 'What happened that day had nothing to do with me. My father is completely out of my life. Believe me, I am only here for one reason. To do my job. As a writer.'

'Believe you? Why should I believe a single word you say? How do I know you're not here spying for your paparazzi father? No.' He shook his head, turning his back on her. 'Whoever is paying you to come here to my home has made a very grave mistake. And if you ever come near me or my family again my lawyers will be called in. Not to mention the police. So you need to leave. Right now.'

'Oh, I'll go.' She nodded. 'But I have no intention of leaving until we've cleared up some of these facts you're so fond of. Just for the record. Because I want to make something very, very clear,' she hissed through clenched teeth as she crammed every piece of clothing she could find from the soaked luggage into her handbag and vanity case.

'My parents were divorced when I was ten years old. I hadn't seen my father, the famous Mario Collazo—' she thumped the cape several times as she stuffed it farther down into the bag '—for eighteen years, until he turned up out of the blue at the clinic that morning. He'd begged my mother to give him a chance to make amends for his past mistakes and to rebuild some sort of relationship with me. And like a naive fool—' her voice softened '—no, make that a lovely, caring and heartbroken naive fool, she took the time to talk to him and actually believed him.'

Lexi shook her head and sniffed.

'She spent years sending me birthday and Christmas presents pretending that my dad still loved me. She mailed him photos and school reports every single year. And this year she'd also let him know that I was waiting for hospital treatment and asked him to come and see us when he was in London. And what did he do?'

Lexi threw her bag onto the patio floor in disgust and pressed a balled fist to each hip, well aware that she was being a drama queen but not caring a bit.

'He abused her confidence. He took advantage of a caring woman who wanted her daughter to have a relationship with her father. And she never even suspected for one moment that he'd set me up in that particular clinic on that particular day because he already knew that Crystal Leighton was going to be there.'

She lifted her chin.

'And I fell for his story just the same as she did. So if you want someone to blame for being gullible I'm right here, but I am *not* taking responsibility for what happened.'

Mark glared at her. Lexi glared back.

'Finished yet?' His voice was ice, clashing with the intense fire in his eyes. The same fire she had seen once before. It had terrified her then, but she *wasn't* finished yet.

'Nowhere close. My mum is a wonderful dress designer and wardrobe mistress. It took her years to rebuild her career after my dad left us with nothing. Her only crime—her fault—was being too trusting, too eager to believe he'd changed. There was no way she could have predicted he was using her. Oh, and for the record, neither of us got one penny of the money he got from selling those photos. So don't you *dare* judge her. Because that is the truth—if you're ready to accept it.'

'And what about you?' he asked, in a voice as cold as ice. 'What's your excuse for lying to me from the moment you arrived at the villa? You could have told me who you were right from the start. Why didn't you? Or are *you* the one who's unable to accept the truth?'

'Why didn't I? But I *did* tell you the truth. I stopped being Alexis Collazo when I was sixteen years old. Oh, yes. I changed my name on the first day that I legally could. I *hated* the fact that my father had left my mother and me for another woman and her daughter. I despised him then and I think even less of him now. As far as I'm concerned that man and his new family have nothing to do with my life, and even less to do with my future.'

'That's ridiculous,' Mark sniped back at her, quick as a flash. 'You can't escape the fact that your family was involved.'

'You're right.' She nodded. 'I've had to live under the shadow of what my father did for the last five months. Even though I had nothing to do with it. That makes me *so* angry. And most of all I hate the fact that he abused my mother's generous, trusting spirit and used me as an excuse to get into that hospital. If you want to go after someone, go after him.'

'So you didn't benefit at all?'

'We got nothing—apart from the media circus when your lawyers turned up and hit us with a gagging order. Are you starting to get the picture? Good. So don't presume to judge me or my family without getting your facts straight. Because we deserve better than that.'

Mark pushed both hands deep into his trouser pockets. 'That's for me to judge,' he replied.

Lexi hoisted the suitcases upright, flung on her shoulder bag and glanced quickly around the patio before shuffling into her sandals.

'I'm finished here. If you find anything I've left behind feel free to throw it into the pool if it makes you feel better. Don't worry about the cases—I'll see myself out. Standard social politeness not required.'

'Anything to get you out of my house,' Mark replied, grabbing a suitcase in each hand as if they weighed nothing. 'Rest assured that if we should ever run into each other again, unlikely though that may be, I shall not try my best to be polite.'

'Then we understand each other perfectly,' replied Lexi. 'As far as I'm concerned, the sooner I can be back in London, the better. Best of luck writing the biography— but here's a tip.'

She hoisted her bag higher onto her shoulder and nudged her sunglasses farther up her nose.

'Perfectly happy people with perfect families living perfect lives in perfect homes don't make interesting reading. I had no idea you were my client when I came here today, but I was actually foolish enough to hope you'd be fair and listen to the truth. I even thought we might work together on this project. But it seems I was wrong about that. You won't listen to the truth if it doesn't suit you. Apparently you're just as cold, unreasonable, stubborn and controlling as the tabloids claim. I feel sorry for you.'

And with that she grabbed the vanity bag and tottered across the patio. She was already down the steps before Mark could reply.

Mark stood frozen on the patio and watched the infuriating girl teeter her way across the crazy paving, the flimsy silk dress barely covering her bottom. How dared she accuse him of being cold and stubborn? That was his father's speciality, not his. It just showed how wrong she was. How could she expect him to believe her story and put aside what he had seen with his own eyes? Mario Collazo being comforted by his daughter on the floor after Mark had knocked him down. Those were the facts.

He had recognised who she was the second she'd taken off her sunglasses. How could he forget the girl with the palest of grey eyes, filled with tears, looking up at him with such terror?

He had frightened her that morning, and in a way he regretted that. He wanted no part of his father's arrogant, bullying tactics. But at that moment he had allowed anger and rage to overwhelm him. Justifiably. It had still shocked him that he was capable of uncontrolled physical violence. He'd worked long and hard to make himself a different man from his father and his brother.

Edmund wouldn't have wasted a moment's thought before knocking any photographer to the floor and boasting about it later.

But he was *not* his older brother, the golden boy, his parents' pride and joy, who had died falling from a polo pony when he was twenty-five.

And he didn't want to be. Never had.

Mark wrapped his fingers around the handles of the

wet luggage, his chest heaving, and watched the small figure in the ridiculous outfit struggle with the door handle on the car before lowering herself onto the seat with an audible wince as her bottom connected with the hot plastic. Seconds later her legs swung inside and the door closed.

So what if she was telling the truth? What if she *had* been used by her father that day, and was just as innocent a victim as his mother had been? What if her turning up at the villa really was a total coincidence?

Then fate had just kicked them both in the teeth. And he had handed that monster an extra set of boots.

But what alternative did he have? He knew what the response would be if his father or even his sister found out that he'd been sharing precious family memories and private records with the daughter of the stalker who'd destroyed his mother's last day alive. It would be far better to forget about this fearless girl with the grey eyes and creamy skin who'd challenged him from the moment she arrived. A girl whose only crime was having the misfortune to be the daughter of a slimeball like Mario Collazo. And she had defended her mother from an attack on her reputation. In anybody else that loyalty was something he would admire.

Oh, hell!

He'd spent the last seven years of his life trying to prove that he could take his brother's place, and then his father's as head of Belmont Investments. He took risks for a living and he liked it. And now this girl turned up out of the blue and accused him of being cold and unreasonable and unwilling to listen to the truth because it didn't agree with his pre-established version of the facts.

Mark dropped both suitcases on the patio. Perfect families living perfect lives. Was that what she really thought the Belmont family was like? Perfect?

Hardly.

He looked up. The hire car hadn't moved an inch. How did she do it? How did she make him feel so angry and unsettled?

And about to make a potentially very dangerous decision.

Lexi collapsed back against the driver's seat and was about to throw her luggage onto the passenger seat when something moved inside the car. She froze, and for one fraction of a millisecond considered screaming and running back to Mark as fast as her legs could carry her.

But that would make her wimp of the week.

Hardly daring to investigate further, Lexi slowly looked sideways and blinked through her blurred vision in disbelief at the two white faces with pink ears staring back at her.

One of the kittens yawned widely, displaying the cutest little pink tongue, stretching his body out into a long curve before closing his eyes and settling down to more sleep on the sun-warmed passenger seat. The other ball of white fluff washed his face with his paw, then curled back into a matching position.

A low chuckle started deep inside her chest and rambled around for a few seconds before emerging as slightly manic strangled laughter, which soon evolved into full-blown sobbing.

Lexi closed her eyes, slumped back against the headrest and gave in to the moment. She could feel the tears running down her cheeks as the deep sobs ripped through her body, making her gasp for air. *This was not fair. This was totally not fair.*

Swallowing down her tears through a painful throat, Lexi slowly cracked open her eyes and took a firm hold of the steering wheel with both hands, curling her fingers tightly around the hot plastic as if it was a lifeline to reality.

It took a moment to realise that with all the sniffing she had not heard the gentle crunch of Mark's footsteps on the gravel driveway.

She stared straight ahead at the olive and lemon trees as he slowly strolled over to the side of the car, then leant his long tanned forearms on the open driver's window and peered inside without saying a word.

They stayed like that for a few seconds, until the silence got too much for Lexi.

'There are cats. In my car. I wasn't expecting cats in my car.' She sniffed, and then flicked down the sun visor and peered at herself in the vanity mirror.

'And look at this.' She released the steering wheel and pointed at her eyes. 'It took me an hour to put this make-up on at the airport. And now it's totally wrecked. Just like the rest of me.'

She slapped her hands down twice on the dashboard, startling the cats, who sat up and yawned at her in complaint. 'Now do you understand why I never mention my dad when I'm working? Just the mention of his name makes me all…' She waved her arms towards the windscreen and waggled her fingers about for a few seconds before dropping them into her lap.

'I noticed,' he murmured, in a calm voice tinged with just enough attention to imply that he was trying to be nice but struggling. 'And, by the way, allow me to introduce Snowy One and Snowy Two. They live here. And they tend to snuggle on warm car cushions, towels, bedding, anywhere soft and comfy. You might want to think about that when you're working outside.'

Her head slowly turned towards him so that their faces were only inches apart. And his eyes really were sky blue.

'Working?' she squeaked. 'Here?'

He nodded.

'I don't understand. A minute ago you couldn't wait to see the back of me.'

'I changed my mind.'

'Just like that?'

He nodded again.

'Have you considered the possibility that I might not want to work with you? Our last conversation was a little fraught. And I don't like being called a liar.'

'I thought about what you said.' His upper lip twitched to one side. 'And I came to the conclusion that you might have a point.'

'Oh. In that case I'm surprised it took you so long.'

Mark stared back at her with those wonderful blue eyes, and for the first time she noticed that he had the kind of positively indecent long dark eyelashes of which any mascara model would be envious.

They were so close that she could see the way the small muscles in his cheeks and jaw flexed with the suppressed tension that held his shoulders so tight, like a coiled spring.

Mark Belmont was a powder keg ready to blow, and like a fool her gentle heart actually dared to feel sorry for him. Until she remembered that he had been doing all the judging and, until now, she had been doing all the explaining.

'I'm never going to apologise, you know,' she whispered. 'Can you get past that?'

'Strange,' he replied, and the crease in his brow deepened. 'I was just about to say just the same thing. Can *you* get past that?'

'I don't know,' she replied, and took a breath before chewing on her lower lip.

Time to make her mind up. Stay and do the work or cut her losses and go. Right now.

She felt Mark's eyes scan her face, as though he were looking for some secret passage into her thoughts.

Her fingers tapped on the dashboard, but his gaze never left her face, and she could hear his breathing grow faster and faster. He was nervous, but did not want to show it. And she needed this job so badly.

'Okay,' she whispered, her eyes locked on his. 'I am going to give you another chance.'

He exhaled low and slow, and Lexi could feel his breath on her neck as the creases at the corners of his eyes warmed, distracting her for a second with the sweet heat of it. Time to get control, girl!

'Here's what's going to happen,' she continued, before Mark had a chance to answer. 'First I'm going to drag what's left of my luggage back inside your lovely villa and find a nice bedroom to sleep in. With a sea view. And then we're going to write your mother's biography to celebrate her life. And when we're finished, and it's totally and absolutely awesome and amazing, and you're standing at the book launch with your family all around you, *then* you're going to say that you couldn't possibly have created this best-seller without the help of Lexi Sloane. And that will be the end of it. No more recriminations and no more blame. Just a simple thank-you. And then we get on with our respective lives. Do you think you can do that, Mr Belmont?'

'Miss Sloane...'

'Yes?' she muttered, wondering what conditions and arguments he was going to wrap around her proposal.

'My cat has just peed on your shoe.'

She looked down just as Snowy One shook his left leg

and then clawed his way back onto the car seat without the slightest whiff of contrition.

'Can I take that as a yes?' she huffed.

'Absolutely.'

CHAPTER FOUR

MARK woke just as the morning sunlight hit that one perfect angle where it was able to slant around the edge of the blackout blind and shine a laser beam straight onto his pillow.

He groaned and blinked several times, turning to glance at the wristwatch he wore 24/7. It was set to tell the time in each of the main financial markets as well as local time on Paxos. And at that moment they were all screaming the same thing. He had slept for a grand total of four hours since forcing himself into bed at dawn.

By 9:00 a.m. on a normal weekday Mark would already have showered, dressed, had breakfast and coffee and been at his desk for three hours. Insomnia had been his faithful companion for years—he'd hoped that being back on Paxos would help him to catch up on his sleep.

Wrong again.

Pushing himself up on the bed, which was a total wreck, Mark reached across to his bedside table for his glasses and tablet computer and quickly checked through the emails his PA had filtered for him. London was an hour behind Paxos, but the financial markets waited for no man and his team started early and worked late. They earned the huge salaries he paid them to make Belmont Investments one of the most respected London financial houses.

Ten minutes later he'd sent replies to emails that needed his personal attention and forwarded others to the heads of department to action.

Then he turned to the real nightmare. The restructuring plans which would secure the long-term stability and profitability of the company. It was going to be tough convincing his father that these difficult measures needed to be taken, and they had already been delayed for months following his mother's death and his father's illness.

But the real problem was his father. He had built up Belmont Investments by taking a low-key, low-risk approach that had worked well years ago. Not any longer. Not in today's financial market.

Mark flicked over to his own plan—the plan he'd been working on in the early hours of the morning when sleep had been impossible. It was dynamic, modern and exciting, and until now this plan had been a dirty secret that he hadn't shared with anyone else.

His father would hate it. But he had to do something to save the business. Even if it meant breaking through the unwritten rules his father had laid down—rules which came with all the obligations attached to being the next Baron Belmont.

Mark quickly scanned through one of the key implementation plans, and had just started to work on the projected time schedule, looking for ways to bring it forward, when he heard strange, cooing baby-love sounds below his bedroom window.

And they were definitely human.

Mark closed his eyes, dropping the tablet onto his knees with a low sigh.

Of course. Just for a second he'd forgotten about his uninvited and very unexpected houseguest. Miss Alexis Sloane.

No doubt fresh as a daisy, bursting with energy, and ready to get started on ripping his family history apart so she could collect her fee and head back to civilisation as fast as her cute, shapely and very lovely little legs could carry her.

A whisper of doubt crept into his mind.

What if he had made a mistake when he'd asked her to stay?

What if this was all some elaborate ruse and Lexi truly was intending to leave with all the Belmont family secrets tucked under her arm, neatly packed up to pass on to her paparazzi father?

For all Mark knew he could be handing Mario Collazo all the ammunition he needed to twist Crystal Leighton's life story into some sordid tabloid hatchet-job.

He slipped out of bed and padded over to the window to peek out onto the patio.

Lexi was bending down and was rubbing her fingers together in front of Emmy and Oscar, the feral cats who called this villa home and whose kittens had invaded her car. The cats clearly couldn't decide whether this replacement for Mark's soft-hearted housekeeper was friend or foe, and were taking the 'feed me and I'll think about it' approach. But at least she was making an effort to be friendly.

Mark almost snorted out loud. He'd made the mistake of bringing his one-time fiancée here for a weekend break. She'd been horrified that he allowed 'vermin' so close to the house, and actively shooed the cats away at every opportunity in case they contaminated her clothing—which had confused Emmy and Oscar so much that they'd kept coming back to find out what was going on.

She'd lasted three days before stage-managing an emergency at the bank.

Pity he hadn't picked up on the clue that the beautiful girl had enjoyed the kudos of being the future Baroness Belmont a lot more than she'd liked him and his ordinary life.

He pulled back the blind just an inch and watched Lexi dangle a piece of ribbon up and down, inviting the cats to play with this strange new toy. Her childlike laughter rang out in the sunshine and was so infectious that he couldn't help but smile in return.

It struck him all at once that his life revolved around people who were very different from the girl he was looking at now. Lexi was pretty, dynamic and confident enough to challenge him and defend herself against what she saw as unfair treatment.

If this was an act, then she was playing her part very well indeed.

The girl he was looking at—okay, ogling—seemed to have no off button. No dial he could turn to slow her down and make her start conforming a little to other people's expectations.

She had surprised him by telling him who her father was before they'd started work.

A shrewder person might have kept quiet about that little bombshell until the cheque had cleared.

Honesty and integrity. He admired that. Even if she *was* the daughter of a man he despised. And, unless he had lost his knack of judging people, she was telling the truth about not knowing she'd be working with Mark.

Overall, a fascinating, intriguing and very unsettling package. Who probably didn't realise that as she bent over the back of her hipster slim-fit trousers, which were probably extremely fashionable in the city, had slid way down past her hips, exposing the top of what passed for her underwear. And providing him with a splendid and tantalising view of a smooth expanse of skin divided by a tiny band of what appeared to be red lace.

Considering the hot weather, and the tightness of her trousers, it was just about as uncomfortable and unsuitable a combination as he could imagine.

But if her intention was to make a man's heart pound rather too fast, she had succeeded brilliantly.

She was skipping across the patio now, perilously close to the swimming pool where he had held her so close against his body—and had enjoyed every second of it. Enjoyed it rather too much for comfort.

That was it. She made him feel...uncomfortable.

Of course that had been until he'd looked into those remarkable violet-grey eyes and instantly been transported back to the horror of that morning in a London clinic when his world had collapsed around him. And that was not uncomfortable. It was damning.

Mark released the blind and took off his glasses.

Perhaps it was just as well that he knew who her family were. She was way too attractive to ignore, but that was as far as it went—as far as it could ever go.

There was no way around it. Lexi Sloane was part of his past. The question was, would she be able to help him get through this project so he could move on to his future?

Because if he had made the wrong choice, then bringing Lexi into his life could be the worst decision he'd ever made.

Lexi sang along under her breath to the lively trance track blasting her eardrums while she flicked through her cellphone messages, sending off fast replies to the most urgent and deleting what she could.

She was just about to switch to emails when Adam sent her yet another text. That had to be the fourth in the last twenty-four hours.

Please. Call me. We need to talk.

'Oh, I don't think so, loser. You don't tell me what to do. Not any more,' Lexi hissed, moving on to the next message. But the damage was done: her eyes and brain refused to connect and she put down the phone in disgust.

The last time they had spoken face to face had been in the hall of Adam's apartment. Both of them had said things which could not be unsaid. And then she had embarrassed herself by slapping him harder than she'd ever hit anything in her life.

Girls did that when they found out their boyfriends had been cheating on them.

What a fool she'd been to pin all her hopes of happiness on the one man she'd thought was a friend. She should have learned from her mother's experience not to let personal feelings interfere with her judgement. And that was exactly what she'd done. Stupid girl.

She wasn't going to live in Gullible Girl City again. Oh, no. At least not until her home office was ready and her children's books were in the shops.

Then she might think about dating again. If…

She held the thought as she caught a blur of movement in the corner of her eye and turned her head just as Mark strolled into the room. He was wearing loose navy trousers and a very expensive-looking navy polo shirt. His hair was dark and slick, as though he had just stepped out of the shower.

Mark Belmont looked like heaven on legs.

And with one single glance she was instantly hit with a sudden attack of the killer tingles.

The kind of tingles that left a girl feeling hot, bothered, brainless and desperate enough to do something really stupid. Like forgetting that Mark was her client. Like wanting to find out what it felt like to run her fingers through his hair and feel his breath on her neck.

Bad tingles. *Very* bad tingles.

Not ideal qualities for a professional writer.

This was the man who'd accused her of being her father's accomplice and almost thrown her out yesterday. As far as Mark Belmont was concerned she was here to work. And that was all. She had to keep her head together!

It was time to turn on a cheery nonsense gossipy voice and the fixed smile that had become her standard mask to the world. Busy, busy, busy. Chatter, chatter, chatter. That was the role she played. He wouldn't be able to get a word in edgeways, and she could keep her distance.

Deep breath. Cue, Lexi. Action!

'Good morning, Mr Belmont.' She smiled, nervously rearranging the cutlery to hide her complete mental disarray. 'I hope you're ready for breakfast, since I've been on a mission of mercy and made the village baker and shopkeeper very happy. But please don't be worried about your reputation as a ladies' man. I told them I was only here for a few days to help with a business project and I'd be heading back to the office ASAP.'

Oh, and now she was babbling about his love life. Great. Could she be more pathetic?

'My reputation?' Mark repeated, staring at her through those incredibly cute spectacles as he leant against the worktop, his hands in his trouser pockets. Casual, handsome, devastating. 'How very thoughtful of you. But why did you think it necessary to go on a mission of mercy?'

'I was brave enough to rummage around inside your freezer looking for breakfast. Behind the bags of ice cubes were a few ancient, dry bread rolls, which crumbled to pieces in my hands and were only fit for the birds, and an assortment of unlabelled mystery items which, judging by their greyish-green colour, were originally of biological origin. But they did have one thing in common. They were all inedible.'

She stopped cutting bread and looked up into Mark's face. 'It's amazing what they have in small village shops on this island.'

'Food shopping,' he replied, running the fingers of one hand through his damp hair. 'Ah. Yes. My housekeeper stocked up the refrigerator last week, but of course I wasn't expecting visitors.'

'No need to apologise,' she said as brightly as she could. 'But it has been my experience that we can get a lot more work done if we have food available in the house and don't have to run out and stock up at the last minute. And, since the room service around here seems to be a little deficient, some creative thinking was required.'

He peered over her shoulder and the smell of citrus shower gel and coconut shampoo wafted past. She inhaled the delicious combination, which was far more enticing than the food and did absolutely nothing to cure her attack of the tingles.

But as he stepped forward Lexi heard his stomach growl noisily and raised her eyebrows at him.

'It seems that I *could* use some breakfast. Um… What did you manage to scavenge?'

'Since I don't know if you prefer a sweet chocolatey cereal breakfast or a savoury eggs, bacon and tomatoes type breakfast, I bought both. I've already had scrambled eggs and toast, washed down with a gallon of tea.'

'Tea is disgusting. But eggs and toast sound perfect if I can persuade you to go back to the frying pan. I'll take care of my coffee. It's one of my few weaknesses. I'm very particular about what coffee I drink, where it came from and how it was made.'

'Of course, Mr Belmont,' Lexi replied, with no hint of sarcasm in her voice, and turned back towards the cooker.

'It's Mark.'

'Oh,' she replied, whizzing round towards him and making a point of taking out her earphones. 'Did you say something?'

Mark crossed his arms and narrowed his eyes, well aware that she had heard what he said but was making a play of it since she had just scored a point. 'I said, since we will be working together, I would prefer it if you called me Mark.'

'If that is your instruction, Mr Belmont.' She smiled and relaxed a little. 'I'd be very happy to call you Mark. But only if you call me Lexi in return. Not Alexis, or Ali, or Lex, but Lexi.'

Then she turned back to the hob and added a knob of butter to the hot pan before breaking more eggs into a bowl.

'Breakfast will be with you in about five minutes, Mark. I do hope you like orange juice. That was the only—'

The sound of a rock band belted out from her cell phone, and Lexi quickly wiped her hands on a kitchen towel before pressing a few buttons.

'Anything interesting?' Mark asked casually as he reached for the coffee.

'I always receive interesting messages.' Lexi twisted to one side and peered at the display. 'But in this case they were two new messages from my ex-boyfriend, which are now deleted. Unread, of course. Which I find deeply satisfying.'

'I see. I thought you might be a heartbreaking sort of girl.'

'It cannot be denied. But in this particular situation it transpired he was cheating on me with a girl who took great satisfaction in enticing him away from me.'

Mark's eyebrows went skywards and his lips did a strange quivery dance as his hands stilled on the cafetière. 'He cheated on you?' he repeated in an incredulous voice, then shook his head once before going back to his coffee. 'Do you always share details of your fascinating-but-tragic love life with people you've only just met?' he asked with a quick glance in her direction.

Lexi shrugged, and was about to make some dismissive quip when it struck her that he was actually trying to have a conversation this morning.

That was different.

He'd barely said a word over their light dinner of crackers, cheese and sweet tomatoes apart from commenting on the local red wine. The meal had been so awkward that she'd felt she was walking on eggshells every time she tried to break the silence.

She wasn't complaining, and it helped that she now wasn't the only one talking, but she wasn't used to having one-to-one, intelligent, hangover-free conversations with her clients at this time in the morning. Perhaps Mark Belmont had a few more surprises for her?

'Oh, yes,' Lexi replied with a shrug as she added lightly beaten eggs to the sizzling butter in the pan and immediately started working the mix. 'But, if you think about it, my job is to help *you* share details of *your* fascinating-but-tragic love life with strangers whom *you* are never going to meet. This way we are both in the same business. I think it works.'

'Ah.' Mark pressed his lips together and gave Lexi a small nod as he carried the coffee over to the table. 'Good point. I should probably tell you that I am not totally thrilled by that prospect.'

'I understand that. Not everyone is a natural extrovert.' She shrugged just as the bread popped up from the toaster. 'But that's why you called me in.'

'I prefer keeping my private life just that. Private. I would much rather stick to the facts.'

'Are you speaking from past experience?' Lexi asked quietly, flashing him a lightning-quick glance as she quickly tipped hot scrambled egg onto a thick slice of golden toast.

'Perhaps it is,' Mark replied between sips of juice. 'And perhaps it isn't.'

'I see.' Lexi slid the plate onto the table. 'Well, I can tell you one thing. If you want this biography to work you're going to have to trust me and get that private life out for the world to see, Mark.'

His response was a close-mouthed frown which spoke volumes.

Oh, this was turning out so well.

Lexi nodded towards the food. 'Enjoy your breakfast. Then I really do need to find out how much work you've done so far on the manuscript. Perhaps you could show me your mother's study? That'd be a good place to start. In the meantime I'm off to feed the cats. Bye.'

And Lexi waltzed out of the kitchen diner on her wedge sandals, safe in the knowledge that Mark's stunned blue eyes were burning holes in her spectacular back.

CHAPTER FIVE

Lexi followed Mark through a door to a large room on the first floor, looking around in delight and awe.

Crystal Leighton had not had a study. Crystal Leighton had created a private library.

'How did you know my mother even had a study? I don't recall mentioning it.'

Lexi touched two fingers to her forehead in reply to Mark's question. 'Intuition. Combined with the number of rooms in this huge house and the fact that Crystal Leighton was an undisputed artist. Any creative person coming to this island would bring a fine collection of writing materials and reading matter with them. And when it's your own house… She would have a study. Elementary, my dear Watson.' She tapped her nose and winked in his direction. 'But this…' she continued, whistling softly and waving her arm around the room, turning from side to side in delight. 'This is…wonderful.'

'You like it?'

'*Like* it?' She blinked at him several times. 'This is heaven. I could stay here all day and night and never come up for air. Total bliss! I love books. Always have. In fact I cannot remember a time when I haven't had a book to hand.'

She almost jogged across the room and started poring

through the contents of the bookcases. 'Poetry, classics, philosophy, history, languages. Blockbuster fiction?' She flashed him a glance and he shrugged.

'I have a sister.'

'Ah, fair enough. We all need some relaxing holiday reading. But look at this collection of screenplays and books on the theatre. My mother would be so envious. Did I mention that she works as a wardrobe mistress? She loves reading about the theatre.'

'Every school holiday my mother used to stuff a spare suitcase with plays, books, scripts her agent had sent— anything that caught her eye.' Mark gave a faint smile and plunged his hands into his trouser pockets, nodding towards the shelves. 'I spent many wet and windy afternoons in this room.'

'I envy you that. And it's just what I need.' Lexi turned to face Mark, resting her fingertips lightly on the paper-strewn table in the centre of the room. 'Have you ever heard the expression that you can tell a lot about someone from the books they have in their home? It's true. You can.'

'I'm not so sure about that,' Mark replied with a dismissive grunt. 'What about the car magazines, polo-pony manuals and the school textbooks on biochemistry?'

She shook her head and waved with one hand at three particular shelves. 'Theatre history and set design. Fashion photography. Biographies of the Hollywood greats. Don't you see? That combination screams out the same message. Crystal Leighton was an intelligent professional actress who understood the importance of image and design. And that's the message we should be aiming for. Professional excellence. What do you think?'

'Think? I haven't had time to think,' Mark replied, and inhaled deeply, straightening his back so that Lexi felt as though he was towering over her. 'My publisher may have arranged your contract, but I'm still struggling with the idea of sharing personal family papers and records with someone I don't know. This is very personal to me.'

'You're a private person who doesn't like being railroaded. I get that. And I can understand that you're still not sure about my reason for being here in the first place.' She glanced up at his startled face and gave a small snort. 'It's okay, Mark. I'm not a spy for the paps. Never have been. No plans to be one any time soon. And if I was stalking you I would have told you.'

Lexi turned sideways away from the table and ran her fingers across the spines of the wonderful books on the shelves. 'Here's an idea. You're worried about sharing your family secrets with a stranger. Let's change that. What do you want to know about me? Ask me anything. Anything at all. And I'll tell you the truth.'

'Anything? Okay, let's start with the obvious. Why biographies? Why not write fiction or business books?'

She paused and licked her lips, but kept her eyes focused on the books in front of her. To explain properly she would have to reveal a great deal of herself and her history. That could be difficult. But she'd made a pact with herself. No lies, no deception. Just go with it. Even if her life seemed like a sad joke compared to Mark's perfect little family.

'Just after my tenth birthday I was diagnosed with a serious illness and spent several months in hospital.'

'I'm so sorry,' he whispered after a few seconds of total silence.

She sensed him move gently forward and lean against the doorframe so that he was looking at her.

'That must have been awful for you and your parents.'

She nodded. 'Pretty bad. My parents were going through

a rough time as it was, and I knew my father had a path-
ological hatred of hospitals. Ironic, huh?' She smiled at
him briefly, still half-lost in the recollection. 'Plus, he was
working in America at the time. The problem was, he
didn't come home for a couple of months, and when he
did he brought his new girlfriend with him.'

'Oh, no.' Mark's eyebrows went north but his tense
shoulders went south.

'Oh, *yes*. I spent the first year recovering at my grandmother's house on the outskirts of London, with a very
miserable mother and even more miserable grandmother.
It was not the happiest of times, but there was one consolation that kept me going. My grandmother was a wonderful storyteller, and she made sure that I was supplied
with books of every shape and form. I loved the children's
stories, of course, but the books I looked for in the public
library told of how other people had survived the most horrific of early lives and still came through smiling.'

'Biographies. You liked reading other people's life stories.'

'Could not get enough.' She nodded once. 'Biographies
were my favourite. It didn't take long for me to realise that
autobiographies are tricky things. How can you be objective about your own life and what you achieved at each
stage? The biography, on the other hand, is something
completely different: it's someone else telling you about
a mysterious and fabulous person. They can be incredibly
personal, or indifferent and cold. Guess what kind I like?'

'So you decided to become a writer?' Mark asked. 'That
was a brave decision.'

'Perhaps. I had the chance to go to university but I
couldn't afford it. So I went to work for a huge publishing
house in London who released more personal life stories
every year than all of the other publishers put together.'

She grinned up at Mark. 'It was *amazing*. Two years later I was an assistant editor, and the rest, as they say, is history.'

She reached her right hand high into the air and gave him a proper, over-the-top, twirling bow. 'Ta-da. And that's it. That's how I got into this crazy, outrageous business.' Lexi looked up at him coquettishly through her eyelashes as she stood up. 'Now. Anything else you'd like to know before we get started?'

'Only one thing. Why are you wearing so much make-up at nine o'clock in the morning? On a small Greek island? In fact, make that *any* island?

Lexi chuckled, straightening up to her full height, her head tilted slightly to one side.

'I take it as a compliment that you even noticed, Mark. This is my job, and this is my work uniform. Office, movie studio, pressroom or small Greek island. It doesn't make any difference. Putting on the uniform takes me straight into my working head—which is what you're paying me for. So, with that in mind, let's make a start.'

Lexi pulled down several books from the shelves and stacked them in front of Mark.

'There are as many different types of biography as there are authors. By their nature each one is unique and special, and should be matched to the personality of the person they are celebrating. Light or serious, respectful or challenging. It depends on what you want to say and how you want to say it. Which one of these do you like best?'

Mark exhaled loudly. 'I had no idea this would be so difficult. Or so complex.'

Lexi picked up a large hardback book with a photograph of a distinguished theatre actor on the cover and passed it to Mark.

She sighed as Mark flicked through the pages of small,

tightly written type with very little white space. 'They can also be terribly dry, because the person writing is trying their hardest to be respectful while being as comprehensive as possible. There are only so many times an actor can play Hamlet and make each performance different. Lists of who did what, when and where are brilliant for an appendix to the book—but they don't tell you about the *person,* about their *soul*.'

'Do you know I actually met this actor a couple of times at my mother's New Year parties?' Mark waved the book at Lexi before dropping it back to the table with a loud thump. 'For a man who had spent fifty years in the theatre he was actually very shy. He much preferred one-to-one conversations to holding centre stage like some of his fellow actors did.'

'Exactly!' Lexi leant forward, animated. 'That's what a biographer *should* be telling us about. How did this shy man become an international award-winning actor who got stage fright every single night in his dressing room but still went out there and gave the performance of his life for the audience? That's what we want to know. That's how you do justice to the memory of the remarkable person you are writing about. By sharing real and very personal memories that might have nothing to do with the public persona at all but can tell the reader everything about who that person truly was and what it meant to have them in your life. That's the gold dust.'

Mark frowned. 'So it all has to be private revelations?'

'Not all *revelations*. But there has to be an intimacy, a connection between reader and subject—not just lists of dry facts and dates.' Lexi shrugged. 'It's the only way to be true to the person you're writing about. And that's why you should be excited that you have this opportunity to make your mother come alive to a reader through your book. Plus, your publisher will love you for it.'

'Excited? That's not quite the word I was thinking of.'

She rubbed her hands together and narrowed her eyes. 'I think it's time for you to show me what you've done so far. Then we can talk about your memories and personal stories which will make this book better than you ever thought possible.'

Lexi sat down at the table, her eyes totally focused on the photographs and yellowing newspaper clippings spilling out of an old leather suitcase.

Mark strolled towards her, cradling his coffee cup, but as she looked up towards him her top slipped down a fraction and he was so entranced by the tiny tattoo of a blue butterfly on her shoulder that he forgot what he was about to say.

'Now, I'm going to take a leap here, but would it be fair to say that you haven't actually made much progress on the biography itself? Actual words on paper? Am I right?'

'Not quite,' Mark replied, stepping away to escape the tantalisingly smooth creaminess of Lexi's bare shoulder and elegant neck. 'My mother started working on a book last summer when she was staying here, and she wrote several chapters about her earlier life as well as pulling together those bundles of papers over there. But that's about it. And her handwriting was always pretty difficult to decipher.'

'Oh, that's fine.'

'Fine?' he replied, lifting his chin. 'How can it possibly be *fine?* I have two weeks to get this biography into shape, or I miss the deadline and leave it to some hack to spill the usual tired old lies and make more money out of my mother's death.' Mark picked up a photograph of Crystal Leighton, the movie star, at the height of her career. 'Have you any idea how angry that makes me? They think they know her because of the movies she worked on. They haven't got a clue.'

He shook his head and shuffled the photograph back into the same position, straightening the edges so that each of the clippings and photographs were exactly aligned in a neat column down one side. 'I don't expect you to understand how important this biography is to me, but she is not here to defend herself any more. Now that's my job.'

Lexi stared at Mark in silence for a moment, the air between them bristling with tension and anxiety.

How could she make him understand that she knew exactly what it was like to live two lives? People envied her her celebrity lifestyle, the constant travel, the vibrancy and excitement of her work. They had no clue whatsoever that under the happy, chatty exterior was a girl doing everything she could to fight off the despair of her life. Her desperate need to have children and a family of her own, and the sure knowledge that it was looking less and less likely ever to happen. Adam had been her best chance. And now he was gone… Oh, yes, she knew about acting a part.

'You think I don't understand? Oh, Mark, how very wrong you are. I know only too well how hard it is to learn to live with that kind of pain.'

She watched as he inhaled deeply before replying. 'How stupid and selfish of me,' he said eventually in a low voice. 'I sometimes forget that other people have lost family members and survived. It was especially insensitive after what you've just been telling me about your father.'

'Oh, it happens in the very best of families,' she said with a sad smile. 'Your mother died a few months ago, while I've had almost twenty years to work through the fact that my father abandoned us. And that pain does not go away.'

'You sound very resigned—almost forgiving. I'm not sure I could be.'

'Then I'm a very good actress. I've never forgiven him and I don't know if I ever can. A girl has to know her limitations, and this is one of mine. Not going to happen. Can we move on?'

Lexi looked up into Mark's eyes as she asked the question, just as he looked into hers. And in the few seconds of complete silence that followed something clicked across the electrically charged space between them.

'And just when I thought you were perfection,' he whispered, in a voice which was so rich and low and seductive that the tingles went into overdrive.

Lexi casually formed the fingers of both her hands into a tent shape, raised an eyebrow and stared at him through the triangular gap between her fingers.

'There you have it. I have flaws, after all. You must be incredibly disappointed that a respectable agency sent you a defective ghost writer. You should ask for a discount immediately. And I shall officially hand back my halo and declare myself human and fallible.'

Mark smiled. 'I rather like the idea. Perhaps there *is* hope for the rest of us?'

'Really? In that case,' she breathed in a low, hoarse voice, 'let's talk about your baby photos.'

And Mark immediately swallowed the wrong way and sprayed coffee all over his school reports.

They had hardly stopped for over three hours. He had made coffee. Lexi had made suggestions, dodging back and forth to the kitchen to bring snacks.

And, together, somehow they had sorted out the huge

suitcase bursting with various pieces of paper and photographs that he had brought with him from London into two stacks, roughly labelled as either 'career' or 'home life.' A cardboard box was placed in the middle for anything which had to be sorted out later.

And his head was bursting with frustration, unease and unbridled admiration.

Lexi was not only dedicated and enthusiastic, but she possessed such a natural delight and genuine passion for discovering each new aspect of his mother's life and experience that it was infectious. It was as though every single scrap of trivia was a precious item of buried treasure—an ancient artefact that deserved to be handled with the ultimate care and pored over in meticulous detail.

It had been Lexi's idea to start sorting the career stack first, so she knew the scope and complexity of the project right from the start.

Just standing next to her, trying to organise newspaper clippings and press releases into date order, made him feel that they might *just* be able to create some order out of the magpie's nest of thirty years' worth of memorabilia.

He couldn't remember most of the movie events that his mother had attended when he was a boy, so photographs from the red carpet were excellent markers—and yet, for him, they felt totally repetitive. Another pretty dress. Another handsome male lead. Yet another interview with the same newspaper. Saying the same things over and over again.

But Lexi saw each image in a completely different way. Every time she picked a photograph up she seemed to give a tiny gasp of delight. Every snippet of gossip about the actors and their lives, or the background to each story, was new and fresh and exciting in her eyes. Each line provided a new insight into the character of the woman who'd been a leading lady in the USA and in the British movie and TV world for so many years that she had practically become an institution.

Dates, names, public appearances, TV interviews—everything was recorded and checked against the film-company records through the power of the internet, then tabulated in date order, creating a miraculous list which they both agreed might not be totally complete, but gave the documented highlights.

And from this tiny table, in this small villa on Paxos, in only three hours, they had managed to create a potted history of his mother's movie career. All backed up by photographs and paper records. Ready to use, primed to create a timeline for the acting life of Crystal Leighton.

Which was something very close to amazing.

He wondered if Lexi realised that when she was reading intently she tapped her pen against her chin and pushed her bottom lip out in a sensuous pout, and sometimes she started humming a pop tune under her breath—before realising what she was doing and turning it into a chuckle because it had surprised her.

Every time she walked past him her floral fragrance seemed to reach out towards him and draw him closer to her, like a moth to a flame. It was totally intoxicating, totally overwhelming. And yet he hadn't asked her to wash it off. That would have been rude.

The problem was, working so closely together around such a small table meant that their bodies frequently touched. Sleeve on sleeve, leg on leg—or, in his case, long leg against thigh.

And at that moment, almost as though she'd heard his

innermost thoughts, Lexi lifted up the first folder of the second stack and brushed his arm with her wrist. That small contact was somehow enough to set his senses on fire.

Worse, a single colour photograph slipped out from between the pages and fell onto the desk. Two boys grinned back at Mark from the matte surface—the older boy proud and strong, chin raised, his arm loosely draped across the back and shoulder of his younger brother, who was laughing adoringly at the person taking the photograph.

Mark remembered the football match at boarding school as though it were yesterday. Edmund had scored two goals and been made man of the match. Nothing new there. Except that for once in his life nerdy Mark Belmont had come out from the wings and sailed the ball past the head of the goalkeeper from a rival school.

And, best of all, his mother had seen him score the winning goal and taken the photograph. She had always made time in her schedule if she could to attend school sports days.

Edmund had called him a show-off, of course. And maybe he'd been right. Mark had wanted to prove to at least one of his parents that he could be sporty when he wanted.

He inhaled slowly through his nose, but just as Lexi stretched her hand out towards the photograph he picked it up and pushed it back on the pile.

Not now. He was not ready to do that. Not yet.

But there was no escaping his companion's attention to detail. Lexi instantly dived into the stack and retrieved the photograph.

'Is this your brother?' she asked.

He took a moment and gave a quick nod. 'Yes. Edmund was eighteen months older than me. This was taken at our boarding school. The Belmont boys had just scored all three of the goals. We were the heroes of the hour…' His voice trailed away.

Out of the corner of his eye he realised that she was standing quite silent and still. Until then it hadn't dawned on him that her body was usually in constant motion. Her hands, shoulders and hips had been jiggling around every second of the day, which was probably why she was so slender. This girl lived on adrenaline.

But not now. Now she was just waiting—waiting for him to tell her about Edmund.

He picked up the photograph and gently laid it to the far right of the table. Recent history. Too recent as far as he was concerned.

'He died seven years ago in a polo accident in Argentina.'

If he was expecting revulsion, or some snide comment, he was wrong. Instead Lexi gently laid her fingertips on the back of his hand in a fleeting moment of total compassion. And he felt every cell of his skin open up and welcome her in.

'Your poor mother,' Lexi whispered, only inches away from him.

He turned his head slightly. Her eyes were scanning his face as if she was looking for something and not finding it.

'That must have been so heartbreaking. I can't imagine what it's like to raise a child to manhood and then lose him.'

Her gaze slid down his face and focused on a family snap of his mother. Not a studio press release or a publicity shot. This was a photo he had taken with his pocket camera when his mother had been manning the cake stall at a local garden fête. She was wearing a simple floral tea dress with a white daisy from the garden stuck behind one ear. But what made her really beautiful was the totally natural expression of happiness she wore.

It was just as hard as he'd thought it might be, looking at the photograph and remembering her laughing and chatting and waving at him to put down the camera and enjoy himself.

Lexi ran a fingertip ever so gently across the surface of the print. He steeled himself, ready to answer her question about how the famous actress Crystal Leighton had come to be working behind the counter of a country village fête.

That was why, when she did ask a question, it knocked him slightly off-balance.

'How old is your sister?

'Cassie? Twenty-seven,' he replied, puzzled. 'Why do you ask?'

'Because I'm going to need to talk to her about Edmund. I know she's a lot younger, but I'm sure she can remember her eldest brother very clearly.'

'So can I,' he retorted. 'We were at school together—more like twins than brothers.'

'And that's the point. You're too close. You can't possibly be objective, and I wouldn't expect you to be. He was your best friend and then you lost him—and that's hard. I'm so sorry. You must miss him terribly,' she whispered, and her teeth started to gnaw on her full lower lip in distress.

The deep shudder came from within his chest, and it must have been so loud that Lexi heard it. Because she smiled a half smile of understanding and regret and looked away. As though she was giving him a moment to compose himself.

Just the thought of that generous gesture flicked a switch inside his head that went from the calm controlled setting straight to the righteous anger mode.

This woman, this *stranger* who had walked into his life

less than twenty-four hours earlier, was giving him a moment to bring his pain back under control.

Nothing she could have done would have made him more furious.

How *dared* she presume that he was unable to control himself?

That he was unable to do the job he had set himself because of the foolish, sensitive emotions in the gentle heart he had suppressed for all these years?

He'd learned the hard way that the Belmont men did not talk about Edmund and how his death had wrenched them apart. No. Instead they were expected to shoulder the extra responsibilities and obligations and carry on as though Edmund had never existed.

Lexi pressed both hands flat against the table, lifted her head and looked into his eyes.

And, to Mark's horror, he saw the glint of moisture at the corners of her own eyes—which were not violet after all, he realised, but more of a grey colour in the diffused warm light coming in through the cream-lace curtains from the sunny garden outside. Her eyelashes were not black, like his, but dark brown, with a tint of copper. The same colour as her hair—well, most of it. The places that weren't streaked with purple highlights.

But it was those amazing eyes that captivated him and dragged him helplessly into their depths. Multiple shades of grey and violet with blue speckles gazed back at him, with the black centres growing darker and wider as her eyes locked onto his and refused to let go. And he simply could not look away.

Those were the same eyes that had stared up at him in total horror that morning in the hospital. The same eyes that were now brimming with compassion and warmth and delight. And he had never seen anything like it before.

His mother had used to say that eyes were the windows to the heart.

And if that was true then Lexi Sloane had a remarkable heart.

But the fact remained—just looking into those eyes took him back to a place which shouted out, loud and clear, one single overpowering word.

Failure.

He had failed to protect his mother.

He had failed to replace Edmund.

He had let his parents down and was still letting them down.

And just the sight of his mother's pretty face looking back at him from all these photographs was like a knife to the heart.

'How do you do it?' he demanded through clenched teeth. 'How do you do this job for a living? Poring over the pain and suffering of other people's lives? Do you get some sick pleasure out of it? Or do you use other people's pain in order to make your own life feel better and safer in some way? Please tell me, because I don't understand. I just don't.'

He was trembling now, and so annoyed by his own lack of self-control that he brusquely slipped his hand out from under hers, turned away and strode downstairs to the patio doors, pulled them open sharply and stepped outside onto the cool shaded terrace.

Well, that was clever. Well done, Mark. Very slick. Taking your problems out on the nearest person, just like your dad would.

He closed his eyes and fought to control his breathing. Minutes seemed to stretch into hours until he heard the gentle tapping of Lexi's light footsteps on the tile floor behind him.

She came and stood next to him at the railing, so that they were both looking out across the pool towards the cypress trees and olive groves in total silence.

'I don't do this job out of some sick pleasure or self-gratification. Well…' she shrugged '…apart from the fact that I get paid, of course. No. I do it to help my clients record how they came through the traumas of their lives to become the person they are now. And that's what other people want to read about.' She half turned at the railing. 'I was serious when I told you how much I loved reading about other people's lives. I love meeting people. I love hearing their life stories.'

Her fingers tapped on the varnished wood. 'Just in case you haven't noticed, every family in this world suffers pain and loss, and every single person—every one—has to survive horrible trauma which changes their lives forever. That includes me, you and all our families and friends. There is no escape. It's how we deal with it that makes us who we are. That's all.'

'That's *all?*' He shook his head. 'When did *you* become an expert in sorting out other people's lives and their histories for them? You're hardly perfect yourself—not with *your* father.'

The temperature of the air dropped ten degrees, and the icy blast hit Mark hard on the forehead and woke him up.

He hadn't meant to sound bitter or cruel, but suppressed emotion and tiredness swept over him like a wave and he needed a few moments before he could very, very slowly relax his manic hold on the railing and start to breathe again. He was only too aware that Lexi was watching his every move in silence.

'I apologise for that outburst, Miss Sloane. It was uncalled for and unnecessary. I thought that we could get past what happened at the hospital but apparently I was mistaken. I can quite understand if you would prefer not to work with me after my rudeness. In fact, if you pack your bags now, you should be able to catch the ferry which leaves at four. I'll make sure your hire car is picked up at the harbour, and that the agency pays your full fee. Thank you for your help this morning.'

CHAPTER SIX

LEXI stared at him as the hot sun beat down on her shoulders.

Yesterday Mark had listened to the truth about her father and still given her a chance to work with him. Now he had thrown her heritage back in her face—and then apologised to her for it.

He was the most contrary, annoying and confusing man she had met in a long time. But under that bravado something told her that he was okay. Intensely private, ambushed into having her at his house, but okay.

And she was not giving up on him.

'Oh, I'm well aware that I am very far from perfect. Stubborn, too. Put those two things together and the result is that I'm not going anywhere,' she replied with a lilting voice, and raised both hands, palms forward. 'This happens all the time. Who in their right mind wants to talk about the pain of the past? It's human nature to push all this turmoil into a box and lock the lid down tight so we can get on with our daily lives.'

And I should know.

She glanced from side to side, but the only living creatures within sight were the four cats along the wall. 'I'm not allowed to talk about other clients, because those confidentiality agreements I sign are completely watertight, but believe me—I've worked with some people and I don't know how they get through the day with all the baggage they're carrying. I thought I had problems until I worked with *real* survivors.'

'Is that what we are? Survivors?'

'Every single one of us. Every day. And there's nothing we can do about it. Although I do know one thing.'

He slowly exhaled. 'I can hardly wait to hear it.'

'I'm famished!' she exclaimed with an overly dramatic sigh, in an attempt to break the tense atmosphere with a change of topic. 'Can I suggest we break for lunch before we start on your mum's personal life? Because I have a feeling…' she looked at him with a grimace '…that we may need some fortification to get through it. And my body armour is back in London.'

'Famished?' Mark replied, blinking for a few seconds as though his brain was trying to process the words. Then his shoulders seemed to drop several inches, his back straightened and his head lifted. 'Of course. In that case it's my turn to provide lunch. Prepare to have your taste buds tantalised by one of the excellent tavernas on the coast. How does a big bowl of crisp Greek salad followed by succulent freshly caught sea bass and chips sound? But there's one condition. We don't talk about our jobs or why you're here. Do we have a deal?'

Lexi's mouth watered at the thought of it. Her last proper meal had been in Hong Kong two days earlier. Although lunch for two in a beautiful restaurant by the ocean could be mighty distracting if it meant sitting across the table from Mark for several hours, sharing delicious food.

'Lunch in a restaurant?' She baulked. 'Do we have the time?' She thought in panic of the mountain of paperwork they'd just left behind. 'There's a lot of work to do here.'

'Which is why the fresh sea air will do both of us a

world of good. I've been cooped up inside for the last three days. I need a break and a change of scene.'

'Why don't you go on your own?' She smiled, nodding her head. 'It'll take me a few hours to read through these typed pages in detail. I'll be quite happy with bread and salad.'

'You can do that later,' he shot back and looked at her through narrowed eyes. 'Unless, of course, there's another reason why you'd prefer not to eat lunch in public with me. Jealous boyfriend? Secret fiancé? Or simply worried about my table manners?'

He tilted his head and the tingles hit her the second those blue eyes twinkled in her direction.

'Just say the word and I can provide excellent references for both my sobriety and my familiarity with cutlery.'

Lexi rolled her eyes. Mark was clearly determined to avoid what they had left behind in that suitcase of memories, so she relented enough to step back from the balustrade and shake her head.

'No jealous boyfriends—or girlfriends, for that matter— no secret fiancé, and I'm confident that your table manners will be excellent. Okay, we have a deal.' Her face softened. 'However, there is one tiny problem.'

His eyebrows lifted.

'Oh, yes, I know it's hard to believe. I hate to admit this, but I didn't have the heart to move the kittens out of the car last night. Can we walk there? Catch the bus?'

Mark pushed his right hand into his pocket and took a step closer, filling the air between them with a few inches of warm masculine scent. He pulled out a set of keys and swung them into his left hand. 'No problem. I'm ready to go. How about you?'

'You mean now? I need a few minutes to get changed and grab a bag,' Lexi replied and twirled her forefinger towards her head. 'And do my hair and put some make-up on.'

He looked at her open-mouthed for a few seconds, and then did a complete head-to-toe scan of every item of cloth-ing that she was wearing. And actually smiled as he was doing it.

Lexi crossed her arms and glared at him. She felt as though his X-ray vision actually bored right through her trousers and the off-the-shoulder tunic to the brand-new red-lace lingerie beneath. Her neck was burning with em-barrassment, her palms were sweating, and the longer he looked the more heated she became. This was not doing much good for her composure.

'Oh, I really wouldn't worry about that,' he murmured. 'Especially about your hair.'

'What's wrong with my hair?' Lexi asked, flicking her hair out from inside her collar and away from the back of her neck. 'Is there a dress code where we're going?'

A peal of pure exuberant laughter came out of Mark's mouth and echoed around the garden. The sound was so astonishing, so warm and natural, that Lexi blinked twice to make sure she was looking at the same person. *Where had that come from?*

And could she please hear it again? Because his whole face had been transformed into a smiling, almost *happy* version of the usual handsome-but-stern exterior. And her poor foolish heart jumped up and did a merry jig just from looking at him.

She'd thought Mark handsome before, but this was tak-ing it to a new level.

'You'll be fine,' Mark replied, looking rather sheepish at his outburst of jollity. And then he held out his hand to-wards her, as though he was daring her to come with him.

'I'm going to need five minutes,' she said, trying to

sound bright and enthusiastic as she slid past him and tried to ignore his hand. 'Just enough time for you to bring the car around.'

'You don't need five minutes,' he replied with a grin, grabbing her hand and half dragging her off the patio and onto the gravel drive. 'And who said anything about a car?'

'Your carriage awaits, madam.'

Lexi stared at the motorcycle, then at the boyish black crash helmet Mark was holding, then back to the motorcycle. She stepped out onto the gravel and walked slowly around the vehicle, examining it from a number of angles.

Mark waited patiently for a few seconds as Lexi stopped and nodded her head several times, before declaring, 'This is a scooter.'

'Your powers of observation are quite superlative,' he replied, fighting the urge to smile and thereby shatter even more of her expectations.

'It's a very nice scooter,' she continued, 'and very clean for a boy, but…it's still a scooter.'

She seemed to suck in a breath, then shook her head twice and looked up at him with total bewilderment on her face.

'But *you* can't ride a scooter! It must be against the rules for English aristocrats to ride scooters. At the very least I expected some swanky sports car worth more than my house. This is incredibly shocking.'

'I take delight in thwarting your expectations. For where we're going, two-wheeled transport is definitely the best option.'

And with that he calmly unfastened a second crash helmet from the back seat and presented her with it. The helmet was red, with a white lightning arrow down each side and the words *Paxos Pizza* in large black letters across the front. Not something you could easily miss.

'Ah. Yes. Cassie's helmet came at a bargain price. That was the only one my pal Spiro had left in a medium.'

She looked dubiously at the helmet that he was holding out to her.

'The only one? I see. And you're quite positive that we shouldn't take my hire car?'

'Quite,' he replied. 'I would hate to disturb the cats.'

'Ah,' she said, 'of course. The cats. A man clearly has to have priorities.'

Without saying another word she slid her shoulder bag over her head and across her chest, took the helmet out of his hands, swept back her hair and slipped the helmet on. All in one single sleek movement. She fastened the chin-strap as though she had been doing it all her life.

His silent admiration just clicked up two points.

'Don't say a word,' she murmured, glaring at him through slitted eyes.

'I wouldn't dare.' Mark patted the seat behind him. 'You might want to hold on to me when we set off.'

'Oh, I think I can manage. Thank you all the same.'

She was standing next to him now, one hand planted firmly on each hip, weighing up her options. Although she was only two feet away, he could hear her mind ticking. The air crackled with tension.

'You should be warm enough,' he said quite calmly. 'We're not going far.'

And with that he started the engine and clicked down into first gear.

Then he checked the chinstrap on his helmet, wriggled his bottom into the driver's position and faced directly ahead. Without looking back even once to check what she was doing.

Ten seconds later the bike lurched slightly to one side as she settled herself on the small pillion passenger seat.

That was his cue to enjoy a totally secret wide-mouthed smile, which he knew she wouldn't see.

'Hang on!' he called, and without waiting for a reply opened up the throttle and set off slowly down the drive. He checked the road was clear and they were on their way.

Warm summer air, thick with pollen from the olive trees and scented with pine resin, caressed Lexi's arms and bare legs as the scooter tootled down the main road heading for the coast.

She leaned back on her arms and gripped on to the grab-rail behind her seat, her muscles clenching and rattling with every bump in the road. Strange how she hadn't noticed the potholes in the comfort of her hire car. She was certainly feeling every one of them now.

She hated being a passenger. But she had to admit that the view in front of her was impressive enough. Mark's broad shoulders filled his shirt, and as he stretched forward on the scooter she could see the muscles in his arms move effortlessly through the controls. His top wasn't quite long enough, which meant she had occasional tantalising glimpses of the band of skin above his snug-fitting trousers.

Far too tantalising.

Dratted tingles.

Lexi turned her head slowly from side to side, looking for distraction in the stunning Greek countryside as they sped along at about twenty miles an hour. Lemon trees, bright purple and pink bougainvillaea, and pale oleander bushes filled the gardens of the houses they passed on the small country road. Dark green cypresses and pine trees created a perfect skyline of light and shade under the deep azure blue of the sky.

And all the time she could glimpse a narrow line of darker blue in between the trees, where the Ionian Sea met the horizon.

The sun shone warmly on her exposed skin and she felt free and wild and ready to explore. She felt so completely liberated that, without thinking about it, she closed her eyes and relaxed back to let the wind cool her throat and neck. Just as she did so the bike slowed, making a sharp turn to the left off the main road onto what felt like a farm track.

Lexi snapped her eyes open and instinctively grabbed Mark around the waist, her heart thumping. She could feel his muscles tighten under her hands, warm and solid and mightily reassuring.

He glanced back just once, to give her a reassuring smile, before reducing his speed and leaning the scooter through bend after bend of steadily narrowing and even more bumpy road until they came to a passing point outside a stunning tiny white church and he came to a slow, graceful stop.

They had arrived. At the end of the road.

'Did I mention that the rest of the way is on foot?' he asked in an innocent voice.

Lexi replied with a scathing look and glanced down at her gold wedge sandals. 'How far do I have to walk?'

'Five minutes. Tops. It's just at the end of the donkey trail and then through the olives.'

'Five minutes? I'll hold you to that. Of course you *do* realise that your terrible secret is now out in the open?' Lexi grinned, heading down the rocky path between the high drystone walls that separated the olive groves. Pine needles from the conifers softened her tread.

Mark swallowed hard. 'Any one in particular? I have so many.'

'This is undoubtedly true. I was, of course, referring to the secret life of The Honourable Mark Belmont, Company Director. The outside world knows him as the suave financial wizard of the London stock market. But when Mr Belmont comes to Paxos? Ah, then the other Mark emerges from his chrysalis. *This* version enjoys riding his scooter—in public—drinking the local wine and entertaining cats. So that only leaves one question. What other hidden talents are yet to emerge?'

His reply was a quick snort.

'Landscape painting, perhaps? No. Too sedate. How about speedboat-racing?' Lexi stretched up and ran her fingers through the low-hanging branch of an olive tree. 'Or perhaps you're the olive king of the island and have vats of the stuff back at Belmont Manor, ready to challenge the Greek olive-oil market? That'd suit your aristocratic swashbuckling style.'

He chuckled out loud now. A real laugh, displaying his perfect teeth. 'Swashbuckling? Not exactly my style. And, in answer to your question, I'm no water baby. But I can heartily recommend the local olive oil.'

'You don't swashbuckle *or* swim?'

'Never.'

'Seriously? When you have that lovely pool at the villa?'

He froze, half turned and then looked at her for a split second, still smiling. 'Swimming was for pupils who preferred sport to studying. Apart from my stellar football experience, which was definitely a one-off, sport was not on my timetable. And it strikes me that I've been answering a lot of questions. Your turn. What hidden talents does Lexi Sloane have up her sleeve? What's *her* guilty pleasure?'

Now it was Lexi's turn to smile, but she shot him a quick glance as they walked along before speaking again.

'Apart from good food and wine, you mean? Ah. Well, as a matter of fact I *do* have a guilty pleasure. I write children's stories.'

Mark made a strange strangled sound but carried on walking.

'Children's stories? You mean teen vampire love and schools for wizards?'

She sniggered. 'Mine are meant for a much younger audience. Think talking animals and fairies.' She stopped walking, dived into her shoulder bag, brought out her favourite notebook and flicked to a particular page. 'I worked on this one during the night when I couldn't sleep.'

Mark turned around on the narrow path and took a step towards her, peering at the notebook she held out.

To Lexi's delight his eyes widened and a broad grin warmed his face, as though she'd lit a fire inside him which drove away the darkness of the morning with its brightness.

'That's Snowy One and Snowy Two.' He laughed, flicking over the page. 'These are wonderful! You didn't mention that you did the illustrations, as well. When did you find the time to draw the kittens?'

'I cheated and took some photos before dinner yesterday. They were perfect models and quite happy to stay in position for at least a couple of seconds while I found a pose I liked. Then I worked the photos into the stories.'

She took the notebook back and just for a fraction of a second her fingertips made contact with Mark's hand. And, judging by his sharp intake of breath, he felt the connection just as powerfully as she did. He immediately started gabbling to cover it up.

'Well, I am impressed. Are you planning to have your

stories published or keep them for your own children to enjoy?'

And there it was. A direct hit. Bullseye. Right between the eyes!

My own children? Oh, Mark, if only you knew how much I long to have children of my own.

Tears pricked at the corners of her eyes. *Stupid.* She should be able to handle the question better than this. But he'd hit her with it out of the blue. That was all. She could cope.

'Published, I hope,' she replied through a burning throat. 'One day.'

'Excellent,' he replied, his warm voice brimming with feeling. 'In that case I look forward to reading your stories to my nephews at the earliest opportunity.'

Lexi picked up his lighter mood and went with it gladly. 'Ah. Do I have to add bedtime story-reader to your long list of accomplishments?'

He smiled. 'I try. Actually...' He paused long enough for Lexi to look at him, then shrugged. 'Sometimes reading those stories is the best part of my day. We have a great time.'

With startling suddenness he turned away from her and started down the track, but the sadness and need in his voice were so powerful that Lexi stayed frozen to the spot.

Two things were clear. He loved those boys. And Mark Belmont was going to be a wonderful father to the lucky children he so clearly wanted in his life.

And her poor heart cried at the thought that she would probably never experience that joy.

Just as the thought popped into her head Mark glanced back towards her, and Lexi slid the book back into her bag and pretended to rummage around as she casually replied, 'I don't have any food with me except breath mints.'

Then she looked around her and raised her eyebrows. 'And, while I appreciate that this is a lovely spot, and I'm enjoying the countryside, something tells me that there won't be a restaurant at the end of this very winding footpath. Am I right?'

'Perhaps.'

'Sorry?'

'It's a long story.'

He gestured with his hand down the path and set off slowly. 'You were talking earlier about collecting impressions about a person by where they liked to live and what they read. And it struck me that you might find it easier to understand who Crystal Leighton was when she wasn't being a famous actress if I showed you her favourite place on the island. I haven't been here in a long time, but this is very special. If we're lucky it won't have changed that much.'

'What kind of place are you talking about?' Lexi asked, astonished that Crystal had chosen somewhere other than her lovely villa. 'And what makes it so special?'

'Come and see for yourself,' Mark replied in a hushed voice that she had never heard him use before.

Lexi followed him through a cluster of pine trees, pushed through some fragrant flowering bushes next to a stone wall, and stepped into a private garden.

And what she saw there was so astonishing that she had to clutch on to Mark for support. His reaction was to instantly wrap one long muscular arm around her waist to hold her safe against his body.

They were standing about six feet from the edge of a cliff. A real cliff. As in the type of cliff where, if you stepped forward one inch, you'd find yourself flying through space for a long time before hitting the sea below.

Their only protection from the dizzyingly close edge

was a waist-high stone wall, which had been built in a wide curve in front of a low stone bench.

But it was the view that grabbed her and held her even tighter than Mark. All she could see in each direction was an unbroken band of sea and the azure sky above it. She felt like an explorer standing on the edge of a new world, looking out over an ocean no one had ever seen before, with nothing but air between her and the sea and the sky. And all she had to do was reach out and it would be hers.

To her right and left were high white cliffs of solid rock, studded with occasional stunted pine trees like the ones she was standing next to now. Far below, the sea crashed onto a collection of huge boulders at the foot of the cliffs.

'There are huge caves under the cliff here,' Mark said as though he was reading her thoughts. 'Big enough for the tourist boats to go into. But we're quite safe. There are hundreds of feet of solid rock below us.' As if to prove the point he grabbed her hand and practically dragged her to the stone wall, so that they could look out together over the tops of the hardy bushes and bright flowering plants clinging to the cliff face at the open sea.

'This is the nearest I've ever come to being on the prow of a ship,' Lexi breathed. 'Oh, Mark. This is…wonderful. I can see now why she chose this spot.'

'You should come back at dusk and watch the sun setting. It turns the whole sky a burning red. It's a wonderful sight. And, best of all, it's totally private. No cameras, no people, just you and the sea and the sky. That was why she loved it so much here. That's why she spent hour after hour on her own up here with just a picnic and a book. Alone with her thoughts. Away from the press and the movie business and everything that came with it.'

Lexi glanced up at Mark's face but his attention was totally fixed on the horizon, where the sky met the sea.

His eyes were the colour of the ocean. His fingers were still locked on to hers and she could feel his heart pound with each breath.

And her heart melted like cheese under a grill.

She had not intended it to. *Far from it.*

She couldn't help it. The fire in his voice and in his heart burned too hot to resist.

Which was why she did something very foolish. She squeezed his hand.

Instantly he glanced down at his fingers, and she caught a glimpse of awareness and recognition that he had revealed a little too much of himself before he recovered and released her with a brief twist of his mouth.

'Last Christmas she tried to persuade me to take some time off to celebrate Easter with her on the island. Just the two of us. But I said no. Too much work.' He sniffed, looking out towards the islands in the distance. 'Ironic, isn't it? I have the time now.'

'She knew you wanted to come back. I'm sure of it. How could you not? When you write about the last few months of her life you should put that in. It would be a lovely touch to end her story.'

She instantly sensed his solid-steel defences moving back into place.

'I'm not ready to write about how her life ended. I'm not sure I ever will be.'

'But you have to, Mark,' Lexi urged him softly, ignoring just how close the cliff edge was so she could step in front of him, forcing him to look down at her face. 'You're the only one who can tell the truth about what happened that day. Because if you don't someone else will make it up. I know that for a fact. Your mother is relying on you. Don't you want the truth to come out?'

'The truth? Oh, Lexi.'

She lifted her hands and pressed her fingertips to the front of his shirt.

He flinched at her touch, but she didn't move an inch and locked her eyes on to his.

'I was only there for a few seconds that day, but you saw what happened in its entirety, and you know why it happened. That makes you unique.'

'What happened?' he repeated, his eyes scanning her face as though he was looking for permission to say what needed to be said and finding it. 'What happened was that I was half a world away from London when my mother collapsed with a brain aneurysm. Dad had sent me over to Mumbai to negotiate with the owners of a start-up technology firm, so I was in India when Mum's friend called me out of the blue. It was the middle of the night, but there's nothing like hearing that your mother's been rushed to hospital to wake you up pretty fast.'

'How awful. No one should have to take a call like that when they're so far away.'

'The next twenty-four hours were probably the longest and most exhausting of my life. But if anything it got worse when I finally arrived. Cassie had met me at the airport. I'll never forget walking into that hospital room. I hardly recognised her. She had tubes coming out from everywhere, she was surrounded by medical staff, and I couldn't understand why she was still comatose. She looked so lifeless, so white and still.'

He shook his head and closed his eyes as Lexi moved closer towards him.

'I think I must have been too exhausted at that point to take things in, because I remember asking Cassie if she was sure there hadn't been some terrible mistake—this wasn't our mother after all. But then the doctors whisked us all out to one of those beige and green so-called relatives' rooms and the truth finally started to hit home.'

He half opened his eyes as Lexi looked into his face. 'Our lovely, beautiful mother hadn't come to London to stay with her old friend and talk charity fundraising. She'd come to have plastic surgery. She didn't tell us in advance because she knew we'd try and talk her out of it. According to her friend, she'd planned the surgery months earlier, as a Christmas present to herself. Because she needed the boost to her confidence.'

'Oh, Mark.'

'She had the operation Monday morning, collapsed on the Monday evening, and slipped away from us on Thursday morning. While I was standing in a police station in central London, being cautioned for attacking a member of the press. Your father.'

Mark snapped his fingers, and the sound ricocheted out into the serene calm air and seemed to penetrate Lexi's body. She jerked back in shock.

'*That's* how fast your life can switch.'

Lexi felt tears roll down her cheeks, but she couldn't speak. Not yet. Not until he was ready.

'The surgeon kept telling us that if she'd survived the aneurysm she could well have been brain-damaged or disabled, as if that would help in some way. It didn't.'

'How did your dad get through it?' Lexi asked.

'He didn't,' Mark whispered. 'He fought off cancer a few years ago, and was in remission until her death destroyed him. He's never been the same since. It's as though all the light went out of his world. He's fighting it, but he's determined to do it alone and there's not one thing Cassie or I can do except make his days as bright and positive as possible.'

'And do you think this book will help? Is that why you agreed to do it?'

'Cassie thinks it's the one thing keeping his spirits up. He wants it to be a celebration of her life instead of some nonsense tabloid journalists will put together from media press kits to make a profit from some scandalous headline.'

'But what about you, Mark? What would help *you* to grieve for her?'

'Me? I don't know where to start. Sometimes I can't believe that I won't ever see her again or hear her voice. I don't want to think about all the future events and special occasions in my life where there will be an empty chair with her name on it. And then there's the guilt. That's the toughest thing of all.'

'Guilt? Why do you feel guilty?'

He closed his eyes. 'Let me see. Never having time to spend with my own mother one-to-one because of the obligations I took on when Edmund died. Always cancelling lunch dates with my biggest fan at the very last minute or having to cut short telephone calls because of some business meeting. Oh, yes, and let's not forget the big one. The reason she had plastic surgery in the first place.'

Mark lifted his head and looked directly at Lexi. She could see moisture glistening at the corners of his eyes, but was powerless to speak in the intensity of his gaze.

'She told her friend that she was having the surgery because she didn't want to let me down at my engagement party. She didn't feel beautiful enough to stand next to me and my future bride's aristocratic family. So she went to London on her own and went through surgery on her own. *For me.* Have you ever heard anything so ridiculous in your life?'

CHAPTER SEVEN

'OH MARK,' Lexi whispered in amazement. 'Why do you think your mother felt that way? She was stunningly beautiful.'

Mark looked up as a flock of seabirds circled above their heads before flying over to the cliffs to nest. 'Pressure. Competition from other actresses for work in TV and movies. Every time we met she talked about the disappointment of being turned down for the roles she really wanted to play.' Mark sighed. 'She couldn't get work, and it was obvious she was finding it tougher and tougher to bounce back from each new rejection. Her agent gave up even trying to interest the movie studios. There was always another beautiful starlet just waiting to be discovered, and in the end it wore her down.'

'But Crystal Leighton was still a big star. People loved her.'

'Try telling that to the casting directors. The truth is she'd been desperately unhappy for a very long time and it showed. She'd lost her spark. Her vitality. Her joy. And it was there on her face for the world to see.'

'So it wasn't just about your engagement party, was it? That was just an excuse for having the work done. Please don't feel guilty about something you have no control over.

From what you tell me, it doesn't sound like you would've been able to change her mind.'

Mark exhaled slowly and Lexi felt his breath on her face. She lifted her right hand and stroked his cheek with her fingertips as his eyes fluttered half-closed. 'I didn't realise you were engaged,' she whispered, desperate to prolong the sensation of standing so close to him for as long as possible. Even if there *was* a fabulous fiancée waiting for him back in London.

'There's no reason why you should. It never happened. It's over now,' Mark replied, his brow furrowed and hard. 'We'd known each other for years, we mixed in the same circles, and I think it just became something other people expected us to do. I never proposed and she didn't expect me to. It was simply a convenient arrangement for both of us. We were friends, but I wasn't in love with her. Two months ago she found someone she truly cares about, which is how it should be.'

'Did your mother know you felt that way?'

'I don't know. We never talked about it. We don't talk about things in our family. We skate over the surface for fear of falling into the deep icy water below. And all my father cared about was making sure there'd be another Belmont son to inherit the title.'

Mark shook his head, his mouth a firm narrow line. 'I thought for a while that I wanted the same thing. That perhaps having a wife and a family might bring the Belmont family back together again. But it would only have made two more people miserable and led to an embarrassing divorce down the line. I can see that now.'

Lexi's brain caught up with what Mark was saying and a cold hand gripped her heart in spite of the warm breeze. 'You were prepared to do that?' she asked, trying to keep the horror of his situation out of her voice and failing. 'To marry a girl whom you didn't love? Then have a baby with her to provide a son to inherit the estate?'

'Oh, yes. The old rules are still in force. Even Cassie's boys don't stand a chance. Unless I persuade some poor girl to give me a son, the next Baron Belmont will be my least favourite cousin. And both of *his* boys are adopted, so they can't inherit, either. So that's it. Nine hundred years, father to son, and it all comes down to me.'

Lexi sucked in a breath and exhaled slowly. 'How can you stand it? How can you live like that?' she asked in a trembling voice. 'Bringing a child into this world should be something for two people to celebrate—not an obligation you can tick off the list.'

And at least you're able to have a son. Have you no idea how lucky you are?

Then she looked into Mark's sad eyes and all of her fight drifted away. 'Sorry. That was unfair. You have a duty to your family and they need you.'

His response was to rest his forehead against Lexi's and take her hand in his, stretching out each of her fingers in turn, as though they were the most fascinating objects he'd ever seen.

'Now do you understand why I'm struggling to finish her biography?' he asked, his voice low and trembling. 'People will expect my mother to have enjoyed a fabulous life full of fun and happiness and excitement. Movie stars like Crystal Leighton aren't supposed to end up living a bitter, cold existence, racked with disappointment and low self-worth. With a son who was never there for her.'

He clasped both her hands between his and held them prisoner before asking the question Lexi had been dreading but had somehow known would come.

'How will you write *that* story, Lexi? How do you tell

that kind of truth without destroying my father and my family at the same time?'

'That has to be your decision, Mark,' she replied, in as low and calm a voice as she could manage. 'I can tell you how to make this book a true celebration of her life. And I know that the dark and the shade only make the happy times seem brighter. That was a part of her life and you can't avoid the truth.'

'The truth? That's a strange concept from someone who writes stories for a living. Let me tell *you* the truth,' he murmured, his voice trembling with emotion. 'The truth is that I need to get back to London. Away from the manor. I have to focus on the future and learn to live my own life, not a second-hand one—that's precisely what she would want me to do.'

And then Mark released her fingers, pressed one hand to her cheek, tilted his head and, with the most feather-light touch, kissed her.

Lexi was so startled that she was rendered speechless. The pressure of his lips was so warm and soft that her eyelids fluttered closed and she almost leant forward for more—only to find him gone. And she immediately cursed herself for being so weak and foolish.

'Thank you for listening. I can't finish this book, Lexi. I can't put my family through the pain.' He took a step back and looked out over the cliffs to the wide blue ocean in front of them. 'Sorry, Lexi. The biography is cancelled. I'm going to return the advance to my publisher. I can deal with the fallout with my family, and it's better to do it now rather than later, in the full face of the media. Thank you for helping me to decide to move forward in my life, not backwards, but I don't need your help any more. You can go back to London. Your work here is finished.'

* * *

Lexi fought to bring her heartbeat back to normal before stomping up to Mark, who was standing at the stone wall looking out towards the islands on the horizon.

'Finished? Oh, no, you don't, Mark Belmont.'

Mark turned back to face her, startled. 'I beg your pardon?'

'And so you should. Because right now it seems to me that you are running away from a challenge just at the point when it starts to get interesting.'

He smiled and shook his head. 'I've already told you that you will get your fee. Don't worry about it.'

She stepped forward, grabbed his arms and turned him sideways, so that he was not quite so scarily close to the edge of the precipice.

'I'm really not getting through to you, am I?' She rolled her eyes. 'I refuse to let you walk away from the only chance you'll ever have to put the record straight about Crystal Leighton. Yes, that's right. I am not going anywhere. And neither are you. I've been hearing a lot about family obligations, but nothing about how the real Mark would choose to celebrate his mother's life and work if left to himself.'

'That option is not available. I don't have a choice.'

Lexi clamped her hands over her ears. 'Not listening. Of course you have choices. You're the one who decides what to do with the life you've been given. So you're going to be the next Baron Belmont? That's amazing!'

She lowered her hands and smiled at him. 'Think of all the good you can do in your position. Starting with celebrating the life of your wonderful mother.'

One more step pressed her against his chest. 'Take the risk, Mark. Take this week out of your life and do the best you can. Because together I know we can create something stunning and true and authentic. But I need you on my team. Come on. Take the risk. You know you'll always regret it if you don't. And I never took you for a quitter.' Her voice softened. 'Do it out of love, not out of obligation. Who knows? You might actually enjoy it.'

His finger traced a line from her cheek to her neck and the tingles made her want to squirm.

'One week?' he whispered, his breath hot on her face.

'One week.' She play-thumped him on the chest. 'Now. Where's that lunch you promised me? I've been desperate for Greek salad for the last hour.'

It was a very silly hour of the morning when Lexi finally gave up tossing and turning, pulled her pillow from under her head and attempted to throw back the covers from her comfortable double bed.

Only she'd twisted so much that the fine cotton sheets had wrapped around her like an Egyptian mummy, and after a few minutes of kicking and elbowing her way free she knew what silkworms must feel like. She felt so hot that even the single sheet was a weight on her skin. The simple air-conditioning unit was trying its best, but with the double glazed windows closed the bedroom felt airless and stuffy. And so desperately, desperately quiet.

Somewhere in the house a clock was striking every quarter-hour with a musical chime, but apart from that comforting sound the house was completely silent—as though it was a sleeping giant waiting for some magical spell to be broken to bring him back to life.

It was such a total contrast to the background hubbub of the large international hotels she usually stayed in and the city noises that surrounded them.

Lexi tiptoed over to the balcony door and peeked out through the hand-worked lace curtain. Slowly and quietly sneaking open the door, she stepped outside, closing it behind her.

She could see light coming from the living rooms of the house on the other side of the olive grove. Moths fluttered against the light above her head, but no mosquitoes, thank goodness. Down below in the garden, solar-powered lights illuminated the pathway to the pool and a barbecue area. A white cat pattered across the patio tiles towards the swimming pool—probably the Snowys' dad Oscar, going for a drink. But apart from that all was still, calm and serene.

Lexi looked out over the treetops and soaked in the silence as though she was drinking the contents of a deep well of cool, refreshing water. True silence like this was so rare in her life that when it happened she took the time to appreciate the tranquillity, no matter how temporary it might be.

Especially after today's scooter ride to the viewpoint.

It was going to take a while to process everything that Mark had told her. And what about that fleeting kiss? Oh, boy. Had he really no clue as to how totally tantalising it was to have had a taste of his mouth, so tender, even for such a fleeting second?

He'd made an effort to keep their conversation on neutral ground during their brief lunch at the lovely harbour at Lakka before going straight back to work. And this time they had both been enthusiastic and motivated. The tide had turned. Now Mark wanted this book as much as she did.

Perhaps it was this villa that had made the difference.

Everything seemed so still. So full of possibility. A white clean space just begging to be filled with activity and life and—

A loud clattering, quickly followed by a low mumble, banged out on the wooden floorboards and she practically jumped over the railing. The sound ricocheted like a bullet around the terrace, shattering the deep silence.

Holding her breath, she clung on to the railing and listened for any further indication of movement. Or for the sound of his voice.

He did have a remarkable voice—deep and intense, yet quiet. With that faint touch of an American accent. It truly was quite delicious.

She wondered for a moment what it would be like to hear that voice speaking her name with intimate, loving tenderness. To fall into those strong arms and not let go for any reason.

No! Wipe that image from your brain!

If she wanted a fantasy she would stick to thinking about her mother's engagement party and all the work they needed to do to make it as magical as possible.

So what if she was attracted to him? It was only natural. But there could never be anything between them. And she had better remember that.

Lexi took another step along the small balcony, gazing out over the olive groves towards the sea.

A ship was sailing on the horizon, the rows of coloured lights on its decks bright and sharp against the darkness of the night. Perhaps it was a cruise ship, or a large ferry from Italy. And above the ship the sky was a breathtaking blanket of stars. She leant on the balustrade and stood on the tips of her toes, but the overhanging wooden eaves were blocking her view.

There was only one thing for it: she would have to go outside to get the full benefit of the night sky.

Lexi skipped lightly down the staircase, carefully turned the creaking handle of the heavy door that opened onto the patio, anxious not to disturb Mark, and stepped out onto the stone floor.

She stood silently with her head back for a second, lost in the bliss of cool air against her skin. A gentle breeze was blowing in from the sea between the pine trees, and Lexi could smell flowers and pine resin mixed in with the slight whiff of chlorine from the swimming pool.

A tiny sliver of new moon peeked out from behind one of the cypresses across the lane, and the only light was from the solar-powered lamps around the car park and stone steps leading to the house. But as she made her way gingerly towards the side garden in her bare feet even that background light was blocked by the house.

Perfect! Lexi stopped, pressed her back against the wall, and looked up towards the night sky.

Without streetlights or a city glow, the sky was wonderfully dark and clear of cloud. Spread out above the trees was a magnificent display of stars which seemed dazzlingly bright in the unpolluted air. She even recognised a few of the constellations, although they were aligned in slightly different shapes from the ones she knew in England.

It was stunning. Without realising it Lexi exhaled a long, slow sigh of deep satisfaction and relaxation. Her shoulders slumped with pleasure.

'Stargazing? Can't blame you. It is rather spectacular.'

She practically jumped out of her skin.

There was a creak from the sun lounger at the far end of the patio, and as Lexi's eyes became more accustomed to the low light she saw Mark stretched out flat, hands behind his head. He seemed to be fully dressed, and she could only hope that her thin pyjamas were not too transparent.

'Well!' She tried to keep her voice light, jovial and her heart from exploding. 'This is a surprise. The famous businessman Mark Belmont is actually a closet astronomer. One more attribute to add to your résumé.'

He chuckled, and his voice was low, deep and resonant in the absolute stillness of the night.

'Guilty as charged,' he replied. 'Always have been. Even had a telescope at one time—much to my family's amusement. My sister could probably find it somewhere in the attic if needed. How about you? Long history of solar exploration in your family?'

'Oh, just one of my many talents,' Lexi replied and was just about to make some dismissive quip when it struck her that from the tone of his voice he sounded relaxed and comfortable. At home. Unencumbered with responsibility.

So she fought back the urge to be sarcastic and strolled over towards his lounger in the dark. Except that her bare toes connected with something solid on the way.

'Ouch!' She winced. 'What have I just banged into?'

'That would be the other lounger,' he replied, sounding concerned. 'Any damage done?'

'To my toe or your furniture?' she asked and flexed her toes. 'No, I don't think so. I still have some movement. I can't speak for the other party.'

'Excellent,' he replied. 'Then please feel free to sprawl and enjoy the free floorshow. No charge.'

'Well, in that case, I think I might just do that.' Lexi smiled as she sank her bottom into the sumptuous cushion and stretched her legs out. 'Oh, that's better.'

They lay there without speaking for a few minutes, disturbed only by the sound of the cicadas in the olive groves and the occasional car horn from miles away. It was so bizarrely quiet that when a weird whooping, screeching noise broke the silence Lexi sat bolt upright and clutched the sun lounger in alarm.

'What was that?' she whispered.

'An owl. They nest in the trees,' Mark replied. 'So, tell me more about your star-watching.'

Lexi knew from the warmth of his voice that he was smiling as he said it. 'I can't say it was a popular hobby in my family, but I've always been fascinated by the stars.' She snuggled deeper into the lounger and tried to find a comfier position. 'I can still remember the first time one of the teachers at school told us that each star was actually a sun and probably had a moon and planets going around it.'

Lexi chuckled. 'He had no idea what he'd started. I dragged my poor mother out on cold winter nights, huddled up outside the back door of our little London house, just to stare up at the sky. I remember asking her if there were people like us living on those planets around those stars, looking back at us at that very minute.'

'What was her reply?' Mark murmured in the dark.

'She said there probably were creatures and possibly even intelligent beings living on those planets, orbiting around suns we can't even see because they're so far away that the light hasn't reached us yet from those distant worlds.' She paused for a second. 'Which totally made my head spin. Clever woman, my mother.'

Except when it came to choosing husbands. Then she was a disaster.

'Do you still live with her? In your little house in London?'

'Mum? No. I moved out earlier this year—although we still live in the same part of London. I spend a lot of time overseas, but we make the time to catch up with each other every few months. Our telephone bills are pretty enormous. It works well. She recently got engaged, so the next few months are going to be a bit wedding-crazy.'

Lexi pursed her lips for a second. The conversation was starting to get a little personal, and way too close to home for this audience. Especially when it came to her parents.

'How about you, Mark? Tell me about your place in London.'

'I have the penthouse apartment in my office building.'

'You live in your office building?' she replied, realising even as she spoke that her voice was stinging with criticism.

A low snort came from the other lounger, but when he spoke Mark's voice was clear and honest, rather than embarrassed or apologetic for living above the shop. 'It suits me very well. I'm single and busy. And the views across the city are pretty spectacular from my balcony. But the stars? Ah. Not so spectacular.'

Lexi exhaled slowly. 'It must be wonderful to have this house to come back to any time you want and look at the night sky. You do know that this is every writer's dream? A quiet rural retreat where they can focus on simply being creative. It's magical.'

The silence seemed even more intense and Lexi squeezed her eyes closed. Why had she said that? *Stupid girl.* He might think she was angling for an invitation. Or more.

'That's the problem,' he replied in a very quiet voice. 'It is magical, but most of the year the place stays empty and the only people who benefit are the cats and my housekeeper. We're always so very, very busy. Always so much to do just to stand still.'

The sadness in his voice pierced Lexi's gentle heart.

She hadn't expected to like him or care about him, but she did. More than was good for her. She knew now that his family life wasn't perfect and happy after all, and she was sorry for that. So much loss and pain changed people, and not always for the better. But Mark? Mark still had that spark, even if it was hidden deep inside.

And the thought that he might lose that spark sent a shiver down her back. She quivered and rubbed her arms.

'Feeling cold?' he asked.

'A little,' she replied. 'Probably time for me to head back inside.'

She heard a low grunt and a shuffle as Mark swung himself off his lounger and took the two steps towards her. Before she had a chance to speak he had taken both her hands in his and was lifting her to her feet.

'We stargazers have to stick together,' he murmured, pressing his body against the length of her back with his arms around her waist. A delicious glow of warmth and strength filled Lexi's body and she instinctively leant back to enjoy the heat from his closeness.

Mark raised one arm and pointed to a bright star on the horizon below the new moon. 'I used to read all those exciting comics about mysterious invaders from Venus or Mars. Scared myself silly. I suspect that's why my dad bought me the telescope. So that hard science could replace dreams and fantasy stories about aliens and spaceships.'

'And what about your mum? What did she say?' Lexi struggled to keep her voice steady in the face of this sudden intimacy.

'Oh, she kept bringing me the comics. Keeping my mind open to every option. I loved her for that.'

'She must have been quite remarkable,' Lexi whispered into the night.

'Yes. Yes, she was.' He paused before going on. 'Thanks for talking me into carrying on with her biography. I think it's going to be a grand celebration.'

Lexi lowered her head and turned around so that she was facing Mark.

'You're most welcome. Good night. I hope you sleep well.'

She touched her cool fingers to either side of his face, and brushed her lips against his in a light kiss which was just a tiny bit longer than the one he had given her at the viewpoint. His lips were warm and full and inviting, and she hesitated for just a moment in the darkness before moving away.

Mark seemed to freeze. Then he took hold of her shoulders, pulled her tight into his body, stepped forward until her back was resting against the wall of the house, cushioned by his arm, so that when he kissed her, her pliant body had somewhere to go.

This was nothing like that first hesitant kiss in the sunshine. This was the kiss of a man determined to drive logical thought from her mind as he pressed harder, exploring her tongue and lips while taking the weight of her body in his muscular arms.

Her hands moved up from his shoulders and into his hair, which was as wonderful and sensual as she had imagined.

But she had broken the spell by moving. And he eased back, drawing her on wobbly legs away from the wall.

She hung on to him, her head against his chest until her breathing calmed, then looked up into his smiling face. His thumb brushed against her lower lip, sending tingles to places she really did not want to be tingling.

'You are really quite irresistible. Do you know that?' he whispered.

She managed a nod. 'You, too.'

He stifled a grin. 'But probably not a good idea. All things considered.'

Then he tapped her on the nose. 'It won't happen again. Good night, Lexi. Sleep well.'

She watched him stroll into the house. Sleep? After that kiss? Was he *kidding*?

CHAPTER EIGHT

'You bought me shoes?' Lexi stared at Mark open-mouthed, dangling the plain tan-leather flat sandals from one finger so that she could ogle them from every angle.

He winced, and nodded his head towards the local shop only a few feet away from the waterside restaurant where they were sitting.

'If you really hate them I won't be in the least offended. Take them back for an exchange. But the range is rather limited compared to what you're used to.'

Her eyes widened in disbelief. 'Hate them? What are you talking about?' She leaned forward over the remains of their lunch of kebab, Greek salad and hot grilled herb pitta. 'You're the first man ever to buy me shoes. This is an historic occasion. They're even the right size. I am amazingly, stunningly speechless. And I have no intention of taking them back. I may even wear them. How about that?'

He raised his water glass to her in tribute. 'The cats and I thank you for your understanding. I had a stern word with both kittens and they promise never to pee on your shoes again.' He played with a piece of bread before asking, in the most seductive voice Lexi had ever heard in her life, 'Do you really like them?'

'They are totally awesome sauce,' she murmured across the table in an equally low voice. 'Yes. I like them.'

She sat back under the sun umbrella and sipped her wine as she looked around at the harbour and the line of yachts moored in the marina in the warm bright sunshine.

'I must say, Mr Belmont, that you treat your lady guests remarkably well. A waterfront location only feet from the Mediterranean, a delicious meal, splendid local white wine—and shoes. I am impressed.'

'Thanks. I thought it was only appropriate since I have a pre-published children's author with me—that, and the small fact that we've been slaving away in that stuffy study for two days and hardly coming up for air.'

She looked at Mark over her glass.

Slaving was one way of putting it.

The constant struggle to avoid touching his body as they negotiated around each other in the small space had driven her mad with frustration.

Sometimes she could almost feel the tension between them.

But he had kept his word and not made any moves on her. And she was grateful…wasn't she? She couldn't give in to the feelings. That would mean trouble for both of them and would only end in heartbreak. She had to hold it together and fight temptation for a few more days. Just. A. Few. More. Days.

In the meantime she could enjoy his company. Memories of meals like this were going to have to sustain her on many a lonely night in a foreign hotel for a long time to come.

'It's been worth it, Mark. The book is shaping up really well, and the work we were doing this morning on your village school was lovely.' Lexi clinked her wine glass against his water beaker in a toast. 'To team work.'

'I'll drink to that. Speaking of which, I have a mission to accomplish—and you are the ideal person to advise me.'

'Ah,' Lexi replied, rubbing her hands together. 'Business or personal?'

'Personal. I have to buy a present for my nephew Freddie before I head back. Two years old and already interested in everything animal-related. I was thinking of a soft toy, but he has a room full of those already. Any ideas?'

Lexi rested her arms on the table and chuckled. 'I am no expert on toddlers. But tell me what sort of things he likes to do. What kind of games does he enjoy?'

Mark's face instantly relaxed into an expression of pure delight. 'Here. This might help. They are both total scamps, but you have to admit they're adorable.'

He dived into his trouser pocket and pulled out a state-of-the-art smartphone which made Lexi drool with envy. His fingers moved swiftly over the keyboard and a few seconds later he scooted his chair closer to hers so that she could watch the surprisingly clear images come alive on the small screen.

His body was pressed tight against hers all along one side of her capri pants and sleeveless top, and at another time and another place she would have called it a cuddle. He was so close that she could feel the golden hairs on his tanned arms against her bare skin, the heat of his breath on her neck, and the smell of his expensive designer cologne filled her head.

The overall effect was so giddying that it took her a moment to realise that he was looking at the phone rather than her, and she forced her eyes to focus on the video playing on the screen.

It was Mark. Playing with two of the cutest little boys on a sandy beach. They were making sandcastles and Mark, dressed in shorts and a T-shirt, was helping the youngest to tap the sand into his bucket with great gusto while his brother danced around with a long piece of seaweed. All three of them were laughing their heads off, and seemed to be singing silly, glorious nursery rhymes. Pure childish joy and delight beamed out from the brightly coloured images in front of her. They looked so happy.

Mark with his nephews. Caught in the moment. Living. Showing his love in every single laugh and smile and hug.

She glanced up at this man whose face was only inches away from hers. He was the real deal. He had taken time out from his international business to go to the beach with his nephews and simply enjoy them.

Her heart broke all over again.

Only this time it was not for Mark. It was for herself.

When had she ever done that? When had she made the effort to spend time with her mother's soon-to-be step-grandchildren or her friends' children? Or her neighbours? She hadn't. She'd chosen a job where the only children she met belonged to her clients—that way she could share their family life second-hand.

The truth of the life she had created for herself jumped out from that simple holiday video that Mark kept on his phone because he loved those boys so very much and it slapped her across the face. Hard.

She'd told herself that she wasn't ready to adopt a child as a single mum, after seeing what her mother had gone through, but the truth was simpler than that.

She was a fraud. And a liar. And a coward.

She was too scared to do it alone. Too scared to take the risk.

And here she was, trying to tell Mark Belmont how to live his life, when he was already way ahead of her in every way. He had chosen to fill his life with real children who loved him right back. Damn right.

'I think the best thing is probably to trawl the shops and throw myself on the mercy of the lovely ladies who work there.' Mark smiled, totally unaware of the turmoil roiling inside her head and her heart.

And she looked into those eyes, brimming with contentment and love for those two little boys, and thought how easy it would be just to move a couple of inches closer and kiss him the way he had kissed her under the stars. And keep kissing him to block out the hard reality of her empty life.

Bad idea. *Seriously* bad idea.

She could never give him, or any man, the children he wanted. And nothing she could do was going to change that.

Suddenly it was all too much. She needed to have some space from Mark. And fast.

'Great idea,' she gushed. 'I think I'll take a walk and meet you back here.'

Throwing her new sandals into her bag, Lexi stood up and, with one quick wave, took off down the stone wall of the harbour towards the port before Mark had a chance to reply.

White-painted wooden fishing boats with women's names lined the harbour between the marina and the commercial port, and Lexi forced herself to try and relax as she sat down on a wooden bench under the shade of a plane tree and looked out across the inlet to the open water between Paxos and Corfu.

The hydrofoil was moored at the dock and had just started loading passengers. For one split-second Lexi thought about running back to Corfu so she wouldn't have to face Mark again. All she had to do was buy a ticket and she could be on her way before he even knew she was gone.

Leaving Mark and his life and Crystal Leighton's biography and everything that came with it behind her.

Stupid, self-deluded girl. Lexi sniffed and reached for a tissue.

Other passengers had started to mill about. A taxi pulled up and a gaggle of suntanned tourists emerged, loaded down with holiday luggage, laughing and happy and enjoying their last few minutes on Paxos. Local people, children, workers, a few businessmen in suits. Just normal people going about their normal business.

And she had never felt lonelier in her life.

A stunning sailing yacht with a broad white sail drifted across the inlet on the way into the long safe harbour at Gaios, and Lexi watched as it effortlessly glided through the water.

She was simply overtired, that was all. Too many sleepless nights and tiring days. She would be fine once this assignment was finished and she was back in London with her mother.

And what then?

Tears pricked the corners of her eyes. Her mother had found a lovely man who was almost good enough for her. And even better, he had given her the grandchildren—*his* grandchildren—that she longed for, whom she already worshipped and spoilt terribly.

So where did that leave Lexi?

Alone. Directionless. Existing rather than living. Filling her life with frenetic activity and people and places and travel. On the surface it looked exciting—a perfect job for any single girl.

How had she become the very thing that she despised?

A parasite, living her life through second-hand experiences, listening to lovely people like Mark talk about their families, sharing their experiences because she was too pathetic and cowardly to have her own love affairs, her own family.

The people on that boat were free to go where they wanted. Moor up anywhere, take off when they wanted. And she felt trapped. No matter how far she travelled, or whatever she had achieved in her life, she simply could not escape the fact that she was childless and would probably be so for the rest of her life.

So why had she not done something to change that fact instead of blocking it out? When had she turned her back on her dreams and thrown them into the 'too hard to deal with' box?

She had talked to her mother about giving up full-time work and writing her own stories, but it had always seemed like a dream.

Well, the time for dreaming was over. She had her own home and could work part-time in London to pay the bills. Surely there was some publisher who'd like to work on her children's books? It would probably take years to be a financial success, but she could do it. If she was brave enough.

Couldn't she?

Lexi was so distracted by the yacht as it sailed past that when her cell phone rang she picked it up immediately, without even bothering to check the caller identity.

'Lexi? Is that you? Thank goodness. I'm so pleased to have caught up with you.'

Great. Just when she thought things couldn't get any worse. It was the talent agency. Probably checking up on her to make sure that the project was on track.

'You're not going to believe who we have lined up for your next writing assignment, Lexi. Think America's favourite grandmother and cookery writer. It's the most *amazing* opportunity, but we do need to get you out to Texas on Sunday, so you can interview all of the darling children who are staying at the ranch. Of course it'll be first class all the way and... Lexi? Are you there? Hello?'

Mark flicked down the prop stand on his scooter, whipped off his crash helmet and looked out across the road towards the hydrofoil, then breathed a huge sigh of relief

Standing on the edge of the pier, on the harbour wall, was Lexi Sloane.

And as he watched Lexi drew back her arm and threw her purple telephone with all her might over her head and into the air.

She simply stood there, panting with exertion and the heat and horror as her precious link to the outside world, her business contacts, her lifeline to business that never left her side, made a graceful arc into the sea.

It hit the waves with a slight splosh and was gone.

Well, that was interesting.

Lexi hardly noticed that someone had come to sit next to her on the bench until he stretched out his legs and she saw the sharp crease on his smart navy trousers, and the black crash helmet cradled on his knee.

'Hi,' she said.

'Hello,' Mark replied. 'I didn't have much luck in the shops so I thought I'd join you, instead. Much more entertaining.'

They sat in silence, watching the hydrofoil crew help passengers onto the deck.

Lexi lifted her head and frowned, as though she had just woken up from a deep sleep.

'Did I just throw my phone into the sea?'

'Yes. I watched you do it from the car park. For a casual overarm technique it made a very nice curve for the few seconds it was airborne. Have you ever thought of playing cricket? Not much of a splash, though.'

'Oh. I was hoping I had imagined that bit. No chance I could get it back, I suppose?'

'Sorry. Your phone is probably covered by about thirty feet of salt water by now.'

'Right. Thirty feet.'

Mark sidled up to her on the bench. 'When I take an awkward call I often find it better to wait a few moments before replying. How about you?'

She shook her head. 'You see what people do to me? They make my head spin so fast that I throw my phone, that I need for my job and has all my numbers, into the sea.' She gesticulated towards the open water. 'There's probably a law against polluting the Mediterranean with small electrical items. Perhaps you could direct me to the local police station? Because I have to tell you, handing myself in and spending some time in solitary confinement sounds pretty good to me right now.'

She swallowed hard but no more words would form through the pain in her throat.

'Attractive though that option might sound, I have an alternative suggestion. I have a spare phone and a number of spare bedrooms which you are welcome to use any time you like. And I still owe you dessert. If you are available?'

'Available? Oh, yes, I am available. I'm always ready to step in at a moment's notice when they can't find anyone else. Why not? After all, I don't have a life.'

'Don't say that. You know it isn't true.'

'Do I? Then why is it that I choose to live through other people's experiences of a happy family life, and other women's children? No, Mark, I do it because I want to for-get for just those few days that I am never going to have children of my own. But it's crushing me. It is totally crushing me.'

And then lovely Lexi, totally in control as ever, burst into hysterical tears.

CHAPTER NINE

LEXI sat back on the sofa with her eyes closed. The patio doors were wide open and a gentle breeze cooled the hot air. It was evening now, and the only sounds were the soft hum of the air-conditioning unit on the wall, the cicadas in the olive grove and somewhere in the village some chickens being put away for the night.

The gentle glug of wine being poured into a crystal goblet filtered through Lexi's hazed senses, and she opened her eyes just in time to see Mark smiling at her.

'Feeling better now?'

She nodded. 'Almost human.'

And she meant it. She'd enjoyed a luxurious bath, with some amazingly expensive products Mark's sister had left behind from her last visit, and was now being cosseted and pampered by a handsome man.

The day was turning out a lot better than she had expected.

'I'm sorry about what happened at the harbour earlier, Mark. I don't usually burst into tears. But do you remember we'd been talking about how your mum had given up her career for a few years when you were small? So that she could take you to school in the morning and take you to see your friends and make cakes for your birthday parties?'

'Yes, of course. We loved it.'

'Well, sitting on that harbour this afternoon it hit me out of the blue that somewhere deep inside my head I know I'm never going to have that life—and like a fool I've been living through other people's stories.'

'What do you mean other people? You have a perfectly good life of your own.'

'Do I? All those celebrities I work with? I've been making a life for myself through their love affairs, their pregnancies, their children, their families—the good and bad and all the joy that comes with being a parent. That's what hurts. I've been using their lives as some sort of replacement for the family I'll never have—for the children I'll never meet. And that's not just sad, it's pathetic. Wake-up call. *Huge.* Cue tears.'

Her voice faded away and she tried to give Mark a smile as he kissed her on the forehead and pressed his chin into her hair.

'I think you would make a wonderful mother.'

Lexi squeezed her lips together and shrugged her shoulder. 'That's not going to happen Mark. That illness I was telling you about? I was diagnosed with leukaemia two months after my tenth birthday.'

Mark inhaled sharply, and his body seemed to freeze into position next to her on the sofa but he said nothing.

'I know. Not good. But I was lucky. I lived in central London and had a very quick diagnosis and treatment at one of the best children's hospitals in the world. I was in hospital for what seemed like forever. It was…painful and difficult to endure. My mum was there every day, and my dad phoned me now and then, but I knew he would never come.'

Her head dropped onto her chest and she twiddled the ring on her right hand. She paused and took a moment to compose herself before going on, and to his credit, Mark didn't interrupt her but gently stroked the back of her hand, as if reassuring her that he was there and ready to listen to anything she had to tell him.

'The day I was due to be discharged from hospital I remember being so excited. I can't tell you how wonderful it was to see my own home again, and my own room with all my things in it. Best of all, my dad was there. Waiting at the front door. With his suitcases. For a few precious moments I thought we were going on holiday somewhere warm, so I could get better. And then he closed the door, and he wouldn't let me hug him or kiss him because he said I was still getting better and he had a cold. Then he turned to my mother and told her that he had met someone on location in Mexico and had decided to make a fresh start with this girl and her daughter. He picked up his suitcases, opened the door, walked down the path to a huge black limousine and jumped inside.'

Her brows twisted and she had difficulty continuing. 'I couldn't walk very fast, and my mother... She was running after the limo, screaming his name over and over. Telling him to stop, begging him to come back. But the car didn't stop. It went faster and faster. When I caught up with her she was kneeling in the road, watching the car speed round the corner, taking my dad away from us.'

Bitter hot tears pricked the corners of her eyes and Lexi blinked them away.

Mark sat next to her on the sofa and wrapped his arm around her shoulders. 'You don't have to talk about it.'

'Yes, I do,' she answered. 'Because the past never goes away. There's always something there to remind you, and just when you think you're on a happy track and can forget about it and move on—*smack!* There it is again. Staring you in the face.'

'How did you ever get over that betrayal?'

'Oh, Mark. You never get over it. My mother taught me to focus on the best memories we had as a family. But she never really understood why I felt so guilty, and that guilt consumed me for years. Until I saw what he was really like.'

'You felt *guilty?* I don't understand why the ten-year-old Lexi would feel guilty about her father leaving.'

'Can't you see? I was the one who got the cancer. I was the one who forced my dad to have an affair with a beautiful actress on a movie set because it was too upsetting and painful for him to come back and deal with my illness and pain. I was the one who drove him to find another daughter who was prettier than me and healthier and cleverer and more talented and...'

Her voice gave way, unable to sustain the emotion any more.

'Parents aren't supposed to abandon their children,' Mark whispered. 'Sometimes I regret going to university in America. I loved being with my friends in a wonderful country where the world seemed open and full of opportunities to explore and to do business. I just forgot that my family needed me back in England. I could never have imagined that one day my mother wouldn't be there at the airport to take me home. We missed so many weekends and holidays together.'

'Young people leave home and follow their hearts and careers. Your mother knew that. Her little boy had grown up, with his own life to lead. She must have been so proud of you and what you've achieved.' Her voice faltered and she stroked his face with her fingertip as she went on. 'We're so very similar in many ways. We're both survivors. I came through cancer. I watched my mother going through torment as my father cheated on us both, then struggle to balance life as a single working mother with a sickly child.'

'Is she happy now?'

Lexi nodded. 'Very. She's taking a chance and getting married again. Brave woman!' She grinned at Mark. 'I think that's why finding out Adam cheated on me was so hard. In the past I could have laughed it off. Joked that it was his loss. But somehow this time it really did feel as though I was the one who'd lost out. He didn't have the courage to tell me what the real problem was. Apparently he wanted children after all.'

'Had you spoken to him about children?'

'Of course. That was why I was in the hospital. Having tests to find out if there was anything I could do to improve my chances. I do have more options than I ever thought possible, but they made it clear that the treatments are very gruelling and there's no guarantee of success.'

'So it didn't bother him that you couldn't have his children?'

Lexi turned and looked at Mark. There had been a touch of coldness in his voice.

'He said he would be happy to adopt at some point, but it was never going to happen. Adam was doing loads of location work, and I was travelling more and more. These past few months we hardly saw each other.'

'I'm sorry that it didn't work out. It's hard on you. So very hard.'

'Perhaps that's why I want to write children's stories— I can make up a happy ending and send a child to sleep knowing that all is well with the world and they are safe and happy, with loving parents who care for them. Maybe all of the love I have will filter through to those children

I'll never get to meet or hug through my words on the page.'

Lexi swallowed down her anguish and looked into his eyes.

Fatal mistake.

It meant she was powerless to resist when Mark shifted closer to her and reached up to hold her face in his hands, gently caressing her skin, his eyes locked on to hers.

And then he tilted his head to kiss her.

His full mouth moved in delicious slow curves against hers, and she closed her eyes to luxuriate in the tender kiss of this warm, gentle man she'd soon have to say good-bye to.

She put her arms around his neck and kissed him back, pressing hotter and deeper against his mouth, the pace of her breathing almost matching his. It was a physical wrench when his lips left hers and she gasped a breath of air to cool the heat that threatened to overwhelm her.

'I was hoping there was another very good reason why you might want to stay on Paxos instead of heading back to London so soon,' he whispered in her ear, before his lips started moving down towards her throat, nuzzling the little space under her ear.

At which point the sensible part of her brain admitted defeat and decided to have some fun, instead.

'You mean apart from the excellent accommodation and room service?' She batted her eyelashes.

'Absolutely,' he replied with a grin. 'I'm talking about the full package of optional extras here.' He tapped her twice on the end of her nose and lowered his voice. 'I don't have to go back for a few days. And there's nowhere else I would rather be than right here with you. Take a chance, Lexi. Stay. Let me get to know you better. Who knows? You might like me back.'

He shifted slightly and looked away. 'Besides, the cats would miss you terribly if you left now. They're waiting to—'

Lexi silenced him with one fingertip pressed against his lips.

'It's okay. You had me at the word *cats*.'

Lexi turned over and tried to find a comfy position. Only something solid and man-shaped was in the way. She cracked one eye open, then smiled with deep satisfaction.

Warm morning sunlight was flooding into the living room and reflecting back from the cream-coloured walls in a golden glow that made everything seem light and fresh.

It had not been a dream.

She really had just spent the night on the sofa with Mark Belmont.

At some point Mark had suggested going into the bedroom, but that would have destroyed this precious connection, which was so special and unique. She didn't need to take her clothes off and jump on him to show how much she cared.

Lexi snuggled into the warmth of his chest, and Mark's arm wrapped around her shoulders and drew her closer into his body.

Lexi's hand pressed against the long tantalising strip of bare chest she'd created by unbuttoning his shirt in the night. She closed her eyes and moved her forehead against the soft fabric of the shirt, inhaling its fragrance. It was musky, deep and sensuous, and totally, totally unique to this remarkable man.

'I have a question,' she murmured, her eyes closed.

A deep chuckle came from inside Mark's chest, and Lexi could feel the vibrations of his voice under her fingertips. It was weird that such a simple sensation made her heart sing with delight at the fact that she could be here, in this moment, enjoying this connection. No matter how fleeting or temporary it might be this was very special, and she knew that Mark felt the same.

'Out with it,' he growled, 'but it had better be important to disturb my beauty sleep at this hour of the morning.'

'Indeed,' she replied, trying not to give him the satisfaction of a grin. But it was too hard to resist, and she slid out of his arms and propped herself up on her elbow to look at Mark's face.

'Do you know that you have two grey hairs on your chest?' she asked in a semi-serious voice. 'And one just here.' Her forefinger stroked down the side of Mark's chin against the soft stubble, then tapped very gently at the offending hair.

'Are you offering a personal grooming service?' He smiled.

'Oh, if required a freelance writer should be ready to carry out any duties necessary to complete a task. No matter how odd or dangerous or *icky* the task.'

'I had no idea,' he said gravely, 'of the horror you must face on a daily basis.'

'Explorers going out into the unknown,' Lexi replied, her left hand making a sweep of the room. 'Armed only with a designer wardrobe and a make-up bag. Not for the faint-hearted. And that's just the boys.'

She lowered her head and rubbed her nose against his. 'It is, of course, essential that a writer should investigate local customs, which must be observed wherever possible,' she whispered in a low, sensual voice as her lips made circles around his mouth. 'So important. Don't you think?'

'Absolutely,' he replied, his mouth moving down the side of her neck.

Lexi closed her eyes and lifted her chin so that he could fit more closely into her throat.

'Were you thinking of any in particular?'

'Actually, I was… Oh, that's good.' Lexi sucked in a breath as Mark nuzzled aside the neck of her stretchy T-shirt and started kissing along the length of her collarbone. 'I was thinking about how people celebrate important dates in the year.' Her words came out in a rush as her breath suddenly seemed to be much in demand. 'Wedding anniversaries, Christmas, Easter and…' She slid down a gulp of anxiety and uncertainty before she said the word which would either be a horrible mistake or a wonderful way to connect them even more.

'And…?' a low husky voice breathed into her ear.

Lexi opened her eyes. She wanted to see how Mark responded to what she was about to say.

'Family birthdays,' she replied gently, hardly daring to say the words in case they brought back bad as well as wonderful memories. 'Like today, for example. Your mum's birthday.'

Mark was silent for a moment, and then he smiled and lay back on the sofa cushions. He looked at her—really looked at her—his eyes scanning her face, looking for something. For a few terrible moments Lexi felt that she had made a terrible mistake. But the words were out and couldn't be taken back.

'Clever girl. Mum would have been sixty today.'

He stretched out the full length of the sofa with a sigh, his head on her lap and one of his arms flailing onto the floor, his eyes staring at the ceiling. Mark seemed so totally natural and relaxed in her presence that it made her heart sing.

'Would she have hated turning sixty?' she asked quietly. 'Or would she have taken it in stride? Just another day?'

Mark was silent for a moment, before he looked up at her and gave a small shrug.

'Hated it. With a passion. I remember her fiftieth birthday party in London. She went to the gym every day for six months. Facials, Botox, hairdressers galore. Trips to Paris for flattering outfits. The works. Just so she'd look amazing in the photographs on that one night. And it worked. I remember those photos appearing across the world in every newspaper and gossip magazine. Crystal Leighton looking ten years younger. Or was it twenty? She made headlines at that party. She even announced a new contract with a make-up company at the same time. All part of the plan to revitalise her career and keep her name on the front page.'

He broke into a lopsided loving grin. 'She loved being the centre of attention at big events. The adulation, the crowds, flashguns, photographers. Mum could sign autographs for an hour and not get bored with it. There was no way she'd ever allow herself to be anything less than spectacular.' His grin faded. 'But that was in public.'

He reached up and pushed a lock of her hair back behind the ear with two fingertips, as though he'd been doing it all his life, and she revelled in the simple touch of his skin against hers.

'Crystal Leighton was totally professional in every way when she was at work. But her fans forgot that when she got home at night she took off her war paint and designer clothing and Crystal Leighton became Baroness Belmont. Wife and mother. And I don't think anyone truly saw her for the remarkable woman that she was.'

'Then tell them. Help them to understand.'

Mark started to sigh with exasperation, but Lexi pressed her hand hard against his chest and he stilled under her touch.

'You and your family are the only people who knew who she truly was. And now you have the power to celebrate that wonderful woman who was your mother.'

'I don't—'

'I know.' Lexi smiled. 'You don't want to hurt your family by revealing how very unhappy she was at the end. That's why I'm here. I'm helping you write a memoir. Not a dry list of dates and all the films she was in—anyone can get that from the internet. No. This is going to be a personal memoir.'

Lexi tapped a finger against his forehead. 'I want to release all those wonderful stories and precious memories you have inside your head and make this a *real* memoir which only you and your family could write. That's what is going to make this book so remarkable and real. And that's how you're going to give your mother the best birthday present she could ever have had. Because you know homemade presents are always the best.'

'A birthday present? I like that idea. Can we have birthday cake and bubbly?'

'I'm astonished that you have to ask. And a monster-sized birthday card. Just tell me what kind of cake takes your fancy and I'm your girl.'

'My girl? Is that right? Well, how could I possibly resist an offer like that?' His face relaxed and he blinked several times. 'Lemon drizzle. She liked lemon-drizzle sponge. With a dusting of icing sugar. No fancy cakestands or anything. Just an ordinary lemon-drizzle sponge. And a gallon of boiling hot tea to wash it down with. I'd completely forgotten about that until this minute.'

'Crystal Belmont's lemon cake,' Lexi replied in a far-away voice. 'Oh, my. That's lovely.'

Lexi sat up so quickly that she felt dizzy, and Mark's

head dropped onto the cushion. 'That's it! You are *so* clever.' She bent forward and touched her lips against his.

'It's been said before, but not frequently in this particular situation. Please explain before my head explodes.'

'The title for the memoir! I've been racking my brain all week to come up with an interesting title which will make your book stand out on the shelves.' She beamed down at Mark and shook her head slowly from side to side. 'I hate to say I was right, but sometimes I amaze myself. You have everything you need to write this story inside your head. My job is to make it into a book. And I can't wait to get started.'

Lexi flung back the light cover from her legs, swung her body off the sofa, and was on her feet and reaching for her sandals in an instant.

'Right. Time to make a list. So much to do and so little time.'

'Lexi?'

She looked back at Mark, still lying flat on the sofa with a certain smile on his face.

'Can't we do that later?' he implored. 'Much later?' And he waggled his eyebrows at her.

She sniffed at his cheeky grin. 'Work now, cuddle later, you scamp. You have a lot to do today. I'll get the coffee started while you're in the shower—then straight to the computer so we can start dictation. This is going to be *so* much fun!'

Lexi skipped out of the door before Mark could grab her and employ his best powers of persuasion to make her stay.

He could hear her humming happily as the plain leather sandals he'd bought her clapped along the tiled floor towards the ground-floor bathroom.

Telling Lexi about his mum's birthday parties? That

was new. But maybe she was right? Maybe there was a chance he *could* write this biography as a celebration of her life and make it a positive, happy thing, with only a tinge of sadness.

Mark linked his hands under his head and lay back as the sun filled the room with bright morning light. It was going to be another hot sunny day on Paxos, and from deep inside his body came a warm feeling of contentment that bubbled up and emerged as a smile that surprised his face.

He had slept for eight hours straight on a very uncomfortable sofa with a woman in his arms. For the first time in many years he hadn't snapped awake to reach for some electronic gadget and check his email, compulsively making sure he hadn't missed an important message about the business while he wasted time sleeping.

He could hear Lexi moving around in the kitchen. The hiss of water into a kettle. Cups rattling on the worktop and metal spoons hitting the olive wood tray. Was this the soundtrack to happiness he'd been looking for all his life? Or simply the joyful noise that came with sharing your home with this whirlwind of a girl?

He had found someone he wanted to be with in the last place on the planet he'd ever expected to. In this wonderful house that held so many memories of his mother and happy childhood holidays.

How could he have known that the path to happiness would lead right back to where he'd once been so happy? How ironic was that?

Belmont Investments and the manor were not important any longer.

This was where he wanted to be. *Needed* to be. With Lexi.

And now she was here. And he felt an overwhelming, all-powerful connection.

Finally. It had happened. He'd known lust and attraction. But this sensation was so new, so startling, that the great Mark Belmont floundered.

He was falling for Lexi Sloane.

'Mark?' Lexi popped her head around the door. 'Perhaps you should telephone your dad. He might need to hear your voice today of all days.'

And then she was gone, back to the kitchen before he had a chance to answer, singing along to a pop song, oblivious of the fact that she had thrown him a bomb and he'd caught it single-handed.

Telephone his dad? On his mother's birthday?

Oh, Lexi.

This lovely girl really had no idea whatsoever just how much it would take for him to lift the telephone and make that call. What would he say to his father? What *could* he say?

All his father cared about was the heritage of the estate and how his only remaining son was going to ensure their lineage was carried on. And Mark's failure to get married and produce an heir was starting to become a problem.

Mark swung his legs over the sofa and ran his hands down over the creases in his trousers.

His engagement had been a catastrophe—a disaster meant to placate his parents. He knew that his father blamed him for letting his fiancée go.

Failure. Yet again.

And here he was, falling for a girl who couldn't give him children. Couldn't give him the heir that he was supposed to provide.

More failure.

What was he doing with Lexi? What was he *thinking?*

The answer was only too clear. He wasn't thinking at

all. He was living and reacting and loving life, and he had Lexi to thank for that.

It didn't matter what happened in the future. It didn't matter one jot. He'd have to deal with the consequences when they happened. They both lived in London. They were both single. And, unless he had completely misread the signals, she felt the same way about him. And that was too special to give up.

Since Edmund had died Mark's life had been filled with obligation and duty. He loved his family too much to let them down. But Lexi was right. They were both living second-hand lives.

All that mattered was right here and right now.

Living in the moment. He quite liked the sound of that.

Without a second's further delay, Mark stretched up to his full height and headed off to the kitchen. Time to entertain the cats and drink coffee on the terrace with the woman he simply couldn't bear to be apart from.

CHAPTER TEN

'You have a whole hour to titivate yourself,' Mark joked, jumping into Lexi's hire car and cranking down the anti-cat-invasion window, 'while I'm on my perilous, swash-buckling mission to track down two bottles of champagne and the local version of lemon-drizzle cake. I'll be back with the swag before you know it.'

Lexi stuck her head through the window and kissed him swiftly but firmly on the lips. 'You'd better be.' She grinned. 'I have my favourite dress ready and waiting, and matching shoes that the cats haven't peed on yet.' She winked at him. 'It's going to be a lovely birthday party. And please bring back more doughnuts for breakfast.'

She kissed him again, and again and one more time for luck, before waggling her nose against his with a giggle, then standing back and waving as he sped off down the road towards the biggest town on the island.

Lexi stood and watched the car until it turned the cor-ner onto the main road, carrying inside it the man she was already longing to see again. She felt as though part of her was somehow missing without Mark by her side.

The cool and unhappy man she had met only a few days earlier was gone, replaced by a remarkable, talented, gentle-hearted man who loved to laugh and enjoy himself.

He knew her faults, her history and he certainly knew

about her dad. And yet he still wanted to be with her. Which was so very amazing that it made her head spin.

And now she had a lovely birthday-party dinner to look forward to, followed by drinks on the terrace watching the sun go down, and then maybe a little stargazing. If they weren't otherwise occupied.

Delicious!

Was it any wonder that she adored him? Perhaps a little too much, and way too fast… But she adored him all the same.

Well… Now it was her turn to dazzle and give him a treat in return.

Lexi skipped up the steps to the house, waving at the sun-kissed cats on the way, and took the stairs to the first floor two at a time.

Clothes first. Then hair and miracle make-up. Mark Belmont would not know what had hit him—because tonight he was going to get the full works.

Let the titivation ensue.

Twenty minutes later Lexi was still humming a pop song under her breath as she jogged from the shower to her bedroom and flung open the wardrobe door.

Her designer cream-lace lingerie would have to do. But she hadn't been kidding about her favourite dress.

No wild patterns, flowers or multi-coloured designs this time. Just a completely sweet confection of flowing gold lace over a plain cream-silk shift dress picked out by her mother with her expert eye.

Elegant. Understated. Knockout.

She had only worn the dress once before, at the Valentine's Day party when her mother had announced her engagement. Somehow it had never seemed lively or colourful enough for any of the movie functions in Hong Kong, but now—in this villa, on this tiny island, with only Mark and the cats to see it—yes. She was glad she had hauled it through so many airport departure lounges.

The cream silk felt cool and luxurious against her moisturised skin. Sensuous and smooth and just what she needed. She smoothed down the lace overskirt and admired herself in the full-length mirror, turning from side to side for a few seconds before smiling and giving herself a quick nod in admiration.

'Not too bad, girl,' she whispered to herself with a wink. 'You'll do nicely.'

But now for the killer touch. Lexi reached into a shoe bag with the name of a famous Asian shoe designer on the front and pulled out a pair of pale gold kitten-heeled satin mules.

They were limo shoes and always would be. No excuses. These shoes were designed for fine wool and silk carpets, not country stone patios, and had cost more than she'd ever paid for shoes in her life even if they had been on sale. But she didn't care.

So what if they'd only ever seen red carpets before now? She was wearing them for Mark, who was all that mattered.

A little giggle of happiness bubbled up from deep inside her chest and Lexi bit her lower lip in pleasure as she slipped on the mules and posed in front of the mirror.

It had been such a long time since she had felt so light. So joyous. So very happy.

Yes. That was it. *Happy*.

This was so strange. Before this week, if anyone had asked if she was happy she would have answered with some glib statement about her magical, awesome life.

Not now. Not any longer. In a few short days Mark had shown her what real happiness could be like.

Until now she'd been living her life through other people's experiences, and now it was her turn to love. Not simple contentment, not settling for the best she could but true happiness with someone she loved.

Lexi inhaled sharply and pressed her fingertips to her throat.

Loved?

Was that it? Was that why she felt that she had been waiting for Mark all her life?

Breathing out slowly, Lexi tottered the few steps across to Crystal's library and ran her fingers down the rows of photographs Mark had chosen to feature in the opening chapters of the book.

They'd spent three glorious days together, laughing and chatting, and all the while Mark had dictated wonderful anecdotes, happy memories of his mother's life and the people she'd met, the things she'd done.

If only he could come to terms with the sad moments. Then it would be a remarkable biography. And she was happy to help.

Happy to do anything that meant she spent as much time with him as she could.

Looking at the photographs now, she could see that each image captured a moment in time when the young Belmont family had been happy together. Before things had changed and they'd lost that easy familiarity.

Her fingers rested on the photo she'd picked up on her first morning at the villa. The schoolboy Mark and his brother Edmund, arms around each other, muddy, happy and proud on the football pitch.

There was so much love shining out from the flat matte surface.

Edmund the older brother. Heir to the estate. The next Baron Belmont.

A shiver of unease ran across Lexi's shoulders and she

scanned the photographs, looking for some sign of where things had changed.

And there it was. Mark must have been in his early twenties when this photograph had been taken at some movie award ceremony. He was standing next to Crystal, who looked stunning, but that spark, that easy, relaxed expression that Lexi had come to know on Mark, was missing. Snuffed out.

It was more than grief at losing his brother. It was as though the heavy weight of being the only son and heir to the Belmont estate was sitting on his shoulders, pressing him down.

It truly was a shame that Cassie's boys would never inherit the title.

An icy feeling quivered and roiled inside Lexi's stomach and she slumped down onto the nearest hard chair.

Bad choice. Because the chair faced a small round mirror on the wall opposite. And as she glanced at her reflection all the energy and fun and joy of the day drifted away, leaving behind the cold, hard reality she'd managed to stuff deep into the 'too difficult to handle today' box.

Shame that she'd chosen this minute to let it out.

Because suddenly her lovely dress and shoes felt like a sad joke.

She did not have any future with Mark. How could she when she was unable to give him the son he needed to carry on his family name and title?

Sniffing away the tears, she stared at photo after photo through blurred vision.

His family meant everything to him.

It was so unfair. So totally unfair. Just when she thought she'd found the love of her life. Staying with Mark, loving Mark, sharing her life with Mark would force him to decide between his family and her.

And she couldn't do that to him. She loved him too much to put him in that position.

What was she going to do?

The sun was already low in the apricot-tinged sky when Mark pushed through the cypress and olive trees onto the secluded circle of stones facing the cliffs and the open sea.

But at that moment not even the view from this special place his mother had used as her escape could compare with the lovely woman sitting so quietly with her eyes closed and her head leaning back on the sun-warmed bench.

It staggered him that one look at her beautiful face could send his senses into a stomach-clenching, mind-reeling, heart-thumping overdrive.

What was it about her that made him feel like a schoolboy on a first date?

His heart raced just at the sight of her, and it was as if he'd dreamt this marvellous creature up out of his imagination—because she was too special to be real.

Lexi's skin and dress were lit by golden and pink sunlight, creating the illusion that she was lit from within, that she was the source of the light. Shades of gold. Apricot and pink.

She looked stunning.

No amount of clever studio lighting would be able to recreate this unique combination of place and time, and Mark instinctively knew that this image would stay locked in the safe and secure place where he kept his most treasured possessions: wonderful memories of love and happiness forever.

Not in printed photographs which could be recreated inside the pages of a biography for others to read. But inside his head and heart, where the real Mark Belmont had been kept safe until now.

Waiting for someone to release him from the constraints he'd made for himself to get him through the obligations he'd accepted for his family.

That someone was Lexi Sloane.

And he loved her for it.

Time to step up and prove that he was good enough for her.

But as he moved the dry pine needles covering the stones on the gravel path crunched beneath his smart shoes, and her eyes flicked open and she looked at him.

And in that one single glance any doubt he might have had was wiped away.

He was in love. Not for the first time—but for the last.

She was the one he wanted. For good.

Lexi stretched her arms out so that they rested on the back of the bench and smiled. Waiting for him to speak. As he came closer he saw something more than relaxed confidence in that smile. Confusion, regret. And apprehension. She was nervous.

Oh, yes. He recognised *that* look only too well. His stomach was suddenly ice.

She was leaving him and she didn't know how to do it without hurting his feelings. He was grateful for that sensitivity, but it wouldn't make the next few minutes any easier.

Her fingers started to curl into tight knots of tension, but she instantly blocked the move, stretched out her fingers and turned it into the casual brush of a stray dry leaf from the stonework as he strolled closer.

'Hello,' she said with a small smile. 'I hope you don't mind, but I couldn't bear to miss my last sunset. Looking for me?'

Here it comes, he thought, *and she doesn't know how to handle it.*

'I'm not used to being stood up,' Mark replied. 'Came as quite a shock. Especially since my mission was completely successful, and our party food is ready and waiting back at the villa.'

She raised her eyebrows. 'Congratulations. I...er... waited for you.' Her fingers waved in the direction of the main road. 'But I got lonely.'

He winced. 'Ah. Thanks for the note. It was good to know that you hadn't been kidnapped by pirates or called back to write some other biography at the last minute. Sorry I was late. I was tied up on the phone to Cassie, trying to organise a surprise thank-you present for you.'

Her mind reeled with the impact of what he'd said, and she slid back down onto the hard stone bench and looked up at him in astonishment.

'A thank-you present? I don't expect a present, Mark. I'm just doing my job—your publisher is already paying me a great deal of money to be here.'

'Then think of it as a bonus. From the family.'

'The family? You mean the family who doesn't know who my father is? *That* family?'

Mark tapped his forefinger against his lower lip as he nodded, and then broke into a smile at her stunned face. 'Yup. I loved what you said about having your own writer's cottage, hidden away in the woodland. Well, I have woodland on the Belmont estate. Beech woods, oak, maple and hornbeam. And they are beautiful. Stunningly beautiful, in fact. Which got me thinking that clever people who write children's stories—' he tapped her on the end of the nose '—might care to test out one of the cottages to see if they work as country retreats for artists and writers. What do you say, Lexi? Are you willing to take the risk and give it a go?'

In the absolute stillness of the secret place the air was filled with the sound of nature: flying insects in the olive groves on the other side of the footpath, and birds calling on the clifftops where they nested. But Lexi did not hear the sea-birds. She was way too busy fighting to keep breathing in a controlled manner.

Because they both knew that he wasn't just talking about renting a cottage. Oh, no.

Mark lowered his body onto the bench next to her and stretched out his long legs towards the sea wall, his splayed fingers only inches from hers.

One side of his throat was lit rosy pink by the fading sun as he twisted his body to face her, apparently oblivious to the damage he was causing to the fine fabric of his trousers, which stretched to accommodate the muscled thighs below.

'What do you say?' he repeated, his blue eyes locked on her face, his voice low and intense, anxious. 'Would you be interested in moving into my world? Say yes. Say you'll run away from the city and come and write your children's stories in one of my cottages. Trust me, I will make sure that your new home has everything you could possibly want. It'll be so perfect that you'll never want to leave.'

Trust him? Trust him with her life? Her future? Her love?

'Why me?' she asked, her voice almost a whisper.

His response was to slide his long, strong fingers between hers and lock them there. Tight. A wide grin of delight and happiness cracked his face.

'For the last five months I've done everything I can to avoid going back to my home. You've helped me see that

Belmont Manor is where I belong. I can't run away from home forever. But it's missing one thing which would make it truly special.' He flashed a cheeky smile. 'The woman I'm looking at right now.'

Her dream of finishing her stories.

Her own home with someone who loved her.

This amazing man was offering her the chance she had been waiting for, working towards every second since she'd started writing down her grandmother's children stories all those years ago. This man she'd met only a few days ago, yet she felt she'd known him all her life.

He was holding her dream out to her, confident that she could do it. All she had to do was say yes and it would be hers.

Lexi leaned back and her sides pressed against the stone.

She inhaled a deep breath, trying to process words when his body was only inches away from her own, leaning towards her, begging her to hold him, kiss him, caress him.

She swallowed hard down a burning throat and tried to form a sensible answer.

'Belmont Manor? I don't understand. I thought you couldn't wait to leave your father and run your own life in the city?'

'It dawned on me that I have to *talk* to my family about the important things in my life now and then. Strange concept. But I'm getting used to the idea and it might just work. And of course there is one final reason why you are the only writer I would ask to test out my writers' retreat.'

Lexi let out a long slow breath as his fingertips moved over her forehead and curled around the layers of her hair before caressing her neck in slow, languorous circles.

'Why is that?' she whispered, almost frightened at what he might say next.

'It's not every day that I get the chance to make a girl's

dream come true. I want to read your stories to my nephews one day. Will you let me into your life to help you do that?'

Suddenly it was all too much for her to take in.

Let her into his life? Make her dream a reality because her cared for her?

She looked out towards the distant horizon, where the calm ocean formed a line with the apricot sky, and was instantly transported into her happy dream of what life could be like. Writing in her little wooden retreat in the forest all day. And then maybe the tantalising prospect of being with Mark every evening, sharing their lives, their dreams and their hopes for the future.

Future. The reality of what he was proposing hit her hard.

Idiot girl! Who was she kidding? They *had* no future.

By looking down and taking both of Mark's hands in hers she managed to regain some composure so words became possible.

'This is a wonderful offer, and I'm sure that I would love it there, but you know I have to work as a contract writer to pay the bills, and I can't accept your charity. Or your pity.'

His fingers meshed into hers and he raised one hand to his lips, gently kissed her knuckles before replying.

'Last I heard writers can work from home and be quite successful. You're so talented, Lexi—you can do this. I know you can.'

The pressure in her chest was almost too much to bear as she looked into his face and saw that he meant it. He believed in her!

'You'd do that? You'd put up with having me hanging around the place? Even with my horrible taste in music and annoying habits?'

'If it meant I could be with you? In a heartbeat.'

Mark's words seem to echo inside her head. Her chest and her whole body were filled with their overwhelming joy and deep love.

She forced herself to look up into his face, and what she saw there took her breath away. Any doubt that this man cared about her was wiped away in an instant.

No pity, no excuses, no apologies. Just a smouldering inner fire. Focused totally on her.

'And now you've gone quiet. I find this worrying,' he joked.

'I can't think, Mark. This is all too new and terrifying. I need to try and get my head around what's going on, make sense of it all. Can you understand that?'

'What's going on is that you have come to mean a great deal to me—more than I could ever have expected. Not for one minute did I believe that anyone could reach inside me and open up my heart, make me vulnerable again.' He grabbed hold of both her hands and held them tight against his chest. 'It's taken me years to build up so many layers of defences. This suit of armour I've created is even more impressive than the one standing in the hall at Belmont Manor. But I needed it so no one could hurt me and break my heart again. And then you walked into my life—my empty, busy and on-the-surface so-successful life—and you smiled at me. And ever since that moment my life hasn't been my own any more. It just took a while for the message to get through.'

He must have seen the terror in her eyes and felt her fast breath on his neck, because Mark took a second before smiling and lowering his voice.

'And now I'm doing it again. Rushing ahead of myself just to keep pace with you.'

He kissed her fingertips one by one.

'Don't you understand, Lexi? You've taken me hostage.

Heart and soul and mind. You've become part of me. And you feel the same. I hope—no, I *know* that I am part of you, so please don't try and deny it. Because I can see it in your eyes and feel it in your touch.'

And suddenly she couldn't stand to look into his eyes and say what she had to. It was just too painful.

His presence was so powerful, so dominating, that she slid her fingers away from his and pushed herself off the stone bench and across a few steps to the cliff wall.

Sucking in cool air, she looked down the steep bank towards the sea below, to the crashing waves on the boulders at the foot of the tall white cliff to her right.

She could jump into Mark's arms and leap into the deep, warm ocean of life with him, knowing that he would hold her up and not let her drown. But one day the waves of his obligations would crash over their heads and they would both drown in a sea of bitterness and despair from which there was no going back.

She couldn't bear it. Not when Mark had a chance to find someone else and have a happy married life with children to carry his name and his heritage to more generations.

She loved this man too much to allow him to sacrifice everything he held sacred. Just to be with her.

The very thought that he'd offered her that amazing gift filled her heart and soul with happiness and a sweet contentment that they'd at least shared these few precious days together. That was going to have to be enough.

Mark was standing behind her now, and she felt the light touch of his hands on each side of her waist.

Lexi immediately pulled his hands closer to her body, so that she could grasp them to her chest as it rose and fell. His knuckles rested on the exposed skin of her throat and neck, and the heat of the delicate touch and the gentle pressure of his chest against the back of her dress warmed her body as nothing ever had before.

He was the flame that had set her world on fire, and she knew beyond any measure of doubt that no man could ever touch her heart the way Mark had.

He was the love of her life.

Which was precisely why she was going to have to walk away from him.

All she had to do now was turn around and tell him to his face.

Slowly, inch by inch, she lowered his hands and slid her fingers out, one by one, until they were only in contact at the fingertips, before turning around within the circle of his arms.

But she couldn't do it. She surrendered to her desire for one last time and pressed her head onto his chest, her arms around his neck, hanging on for dear life, pulling his head lower.

His eyes flickered at her touch, and she had to blink away tears as his nose pressed against her cheek, his mouth nuzzling her upper lip as his fingers moved back to clasp the back of her head, drawing her closer to him.

His hard body was against her, rock-solid, safe and secure, and so loving that the overall effect was more than intoxicating.

And then his mouth was pressing hotter and hotter onto hers, his pulse racing below the fine cloth as he pushed her lips apart and explored her mouth. One of his hands made slow circles on the small of her back, then higher, while the other caressed the skin at the base of her skull so gently that she thought she would go mad with wanting Mark so much, needing him to know how much she cared.

She felt carried away on a sea of love and deep connection that she could happily drown in and not regret for a moment.

Maybe that was why she broke away first, leaning back just far enough so that he could brush away the glint of tears away from her cheeks.

'Hey. Don't cry, gorgeous. I'm going to be right there with you, every step of the way.'

And he was kissing her again, pressing his soft lips against her throat and tilting his head so he could reach the sensitive skin on her neck.

Her eyes closed and she leant back just a little farther, arching her spine, supported by his long fingers as they slid down to her hips. Lexi stopped breathing and inwardly screamed in frustration because her body was enjoying itself far too much for her to reply. And her heart and mind sang.

She closed her eyes tight shut and focused on the sound of her own breathing. Only it was rather difficult when the man she wanted to be with was holding her so lovingly, keeping her steady on her wobbly legs, her toes clenched with tension inside her shoes.

Tempting her. Tempting her so badly she could taste it. She wanted him just as much as he wanted her. This was going to be their last night together, and…

No. If she gave in now there would be no going back. She would never be able to walk away. And neither would he. No matter how much she wanted to stay in his arms, she had to be brave for Mark's sake.

She just had to find the strength to get through this.

Lexi inhaled slowly, then whispered into Mark's shoulder, 'I don't think that would be a very good idea.' She dropped back so he would have to stop kissing her. 'In fact,' she continued in a trembling voice, 'it might be better if I started packing. I have an early flight tomorrow.'

The air escaped from his lungs in a slow, shuddering hot breath against her forehead.

It took her a few seconds to form the words she had to say. She was almost too afraid.

Her voice stayed calm, despite the thumping storm of confusion and resignation building in her chest. 'You know why we don't have a future together, Mark. You need to have a son to inherit your title and I can't give you one. And nothing we say or feel is going to change that fact.'

As soon as the words left her mouth she regretted them. The man who had been holding her so lovingly, unwilling to let her move out of his touch, stepped back. Moved away. Not physically, but emotionally.

The precious moment was gone. Trampled to fragments.

His face contorted with pain and closed down before her eyes. The warmth was gone, and she cursed herself for being so clumsy.

She had lost him.

'I was never supposed to be Baron Belmont,' Mark replied, his voice low and rough. 'That was my brother's job. Ed was the heir apparent, my parents' pride and joy. As far as my parents were concerned Edmund was the golden boy, the eldest son, whom they'd groomed since junior school to take over the company business and the estate. So when he died…it destroyed the family plans completely. And broke my mother's heart forever. It was as simple as that. The entire family collapsed.'

He looked into Lexi's face and smoothed back her hair with his fingertips.

'I was the second son, Lexi. As different from Edmund and my father as it was possible to be. I had to leave my world behind and take over the obligations that came with being the next Baron Belmont. I had no choice. I *had* to take over as the next heir. And everything that comes with it. Including making sure that I married early and produced a son to carry on the name.'

He closed his eyes. 'Working on my mother's biography has shown me just how much I've sacrificed to take his place—and how much I need to claw back my right to personal happiness. And that means *you,* Lexi.'

'You know that I can't have children.' Her voice quivered as she formed the syllables, and she only just managed the words before her voice failed. 'But you can. And that is why I have to let you go.'

Mark shook his head slowly and his chin dropped so their foreheads were touching. His breath was hot against her skin as the words came stumbling out. 'I can see where this is going, but you are *so* wrong. I want you and only you. Can you understand that?'

Lexi took a slow breath and squeezed her eyes tight shut, willing away the tears. 'And I want you. So very much. I'd given up hope of ever finding someone to love. But you need to have a son of your own. Somewhere out there is a very lucky woman you can cherish and who will be able to give you that son. And it's not me.'

'Another woman? Oh, Lexi.'

He straightened and drew back, physically holding her away from him. Her hands slid down his arms, desperate to hold on to the intensity of their connection, and her words babbled out in confusion and fear.

'We had a wonderful few days together, Mark. And I am so grateful to you for that.'

He'd turned away from her now, and paced back towards the bench, one hand clenched onto the back of his neck

'Grateful? Is that it? You're *grateful?* How can you walk away from what we have? I know you care about me, Lexi—please don't try and deny it.'

The bitterness in his voice was such a contrast to the loving man she'd just been holding that Lexi took a breath before answering. 'I do care about you—more than I can say. Can't you see? That's why the last thing I want to do is trap you into a relationship which will end in bitterness and disappointment, no matter how hard we both try.' She stepped forward and gently laid her hand on his arm as she looked into his face. 'You know I'm right. You're going to be a wonderful father, Mark. I just know it.'

She gulped away the burning sensation in her throat and looked into those wonderful eyes, so full of concern, and told him the truth—because nothing else would do.

'This is breaking my heart, Mark. I can't be with you any more. It's time to escape this perfect fantasy and get back to our ordinary lives. And if you love me then you have to let me go, Mark. Let me go. While we still have our precious love intact.'

'Lexi!'

The only thing that stopped Mark from running after her down the gravel footpath that led back to the villa was the heartbreak in her words and the unavoidable truth that he *did* love her—enough to stand, frozen, and watch her walk away.

Lexi sat in the very front row of the hydrofoil, facing the bow window at the front, so that her head was right in front of the TV showing cartoons with the sound off.

Her once-white linen trousers were a total mess, her blouse worse, and the only shoes she had with her were the flat tan leather sandals that Mark had bought her after they'd shared lunch that day in Gaios.

The elegant Greek woman sitting to her left was totally absorbed with cuddling and kissing a black toy poodle with red bows in its curls, which was getting ready to doze off for the hour-long journey.

Lexi was vaguely aware of tourists with their suitcases being loaded on at the harbour, filling up the seats behind her, their voices a blend of English and Italian accents. Some were yawning with the happy contentment of a sunny early morning call, but most were chatting away, couples and families enjoying the last day of their holiday before flying home.

She envied them that serenity. Her mind was a maelstrom of confused emotions and regret and loss, and she hadn't even left the island yet.

She felt as though time had stood still since she'd last spoken to Mark at the viewpoint.

It had taken only minutes to strip off her dress when she got back to the villa alone, to throw on the same trousers and loose blouse she'd been wearing that morning and cram everything from the wardrobe and drawers into her bags. He had not returned by the time her luggage was loaded into the car.

The cats had been sitting on the wall of sun-warmed stone as she'd turned the car around and driven through the wide entrance and onto the main road. When Snowy One had sat up and called to her she'd almost lost the will to go ahead with it.

Coward! She should have waited for him to come back. But that would have meant staying the night in the villa. And she was just not up to it. She would have given in and spent the night in his arms. And not regretted a second of it. That was the hard part.

Instead she'd held herself together long enough to drive down a country sideroad near Loggos and park her car well off the road, under the trees and away from the traffic and houses, before finally surrendering to the tears and anguish and exhaustion of the day. At some point in the night she'd fallen into an uncomfortable sleep for an hour or two before light broke through the trees above her.

She'd dropped her luggage off at the travel agent in Gaios when she'd handed back the hire car just as soon as the office opened that morning. She didn't need her expensive gowns and shoes for where she was going. This time her suitcases would be travelling cargo by themselves, and at this precise moment she really couldn't care less if they made it back to London or not. Everything she needed, everything she could not replace, was either in her huge shoulder bag or carried safe inside her heart. Where it would be locked away forever.

The burning in her throat emerged as a whispered sob, muffled by the sound of the hydrofoil engines starting up.

The sea was as smooth as a mirror, with only a gentle ripple to reflect back the jewelled sparkling of the rising sun. It was stunningly beautiful. A new hot sunny morning had dawned and her heart was breaking. She looked out of the hydrofoil windows, streaked with droplets of salt water from the seaspray.

The dew on the windows reflected back the fractured image of a woman who'd thought she knew what she wanted and had been proved completely wrong by someone so remarkable, so talented and so very lovable, that it took her breath away just thinking about him.

He would be awake now—if he had managed to sleep at all.

She wiped at the glass as the hydrofoil moved out into open water and headed towards Corfu, leaving behind the narrow green strip of the island with its white limestone cliffs that formed her last sight of Paxos. And the man she loved.

CHAPTER ELEVEN

MARK stood under the shade of the huge oak tree at the bottom of the drive as Cassie's golden retriever went tearing off across the lawn in search of a squirrel.

He looked up into the flame-tinged dark green and russet oak leaves above his head, so familiar to him that he sometimes forgot that tall oak trees from Belmont had been used to build the great wooden sailing ships that had made up the navy for so many kings and queens over the centuries.

Belmont's heritage. *His* heritage. And now he was paying the price for that.

Mark turned and started walking down the driveway between the two rows of mighty oak trees, back towards the magnificent Elizabethan manor house that was his family home. Belmont Manor.

The September late-afternoon sunshine had turned the buff old limestone to a warm, welcoming glow that brought to mind old hearths and the long history of the generations who had lived there. Purple and red ivy tinged with green clambered up the right block of the E-shaped house, but ended well below the curved stone decoration on each turret.

It was a solid house, almost six hundred years old, and barely changed over the centuries because the men had either been in London at court or busy fighting for their country. The heavy stone walls were broken up by rows of narrow mullioned windows which filled the rooms with coloured light, but never quite enough.

Looking at it now through fresh eyes, he couldn't fail to be impressed by the grandeur of the huge house. And yet this was his home. The place where he'd spent the first ten years of his life until he was sent to boarding school. But even then he'd come home to Belmont most weekends and every holiday. And he'd totally taken it for granted—just as he had with so much else in his life. Such as parents who would always be there to welcome him home, and a brother who would inherit the title and the house and all the obligations that went with it. Leaving the second son free to live his own life.

That was then. This was now.

Time to make a few changes.

Mark walked slowly through the beautiful timbered hallway and chuckled to himself at what Lexi would make of the suit of armour standing in the corner, and the family shields over the huge stone fireplace. She would probably want to wear the armour and invent some entirely inappropriate alternative descriptions for the heraldic symbols on the shields.

But as he strolled down the narrow oak-panelled corridor towards his father's study his smile faded. Everywhere he looked there was something to remind him of his mother. A Chinese flower vase or a stunning Tudor portrait, perfectly matched to the oak panelling and the period of the house. Right down to the stunning needlepoint panels which decorated the heavy oak doors. She'd always had the knack of finding the perfect item to decorate each room with such loving care and detail. It had taken her thirty years to do it, but in the process she'd transformed the dark and gloomy house he'd seen in family photographs into a warm, light family home.

This house was a celebration of her life, and Lexi had helped him to see that. Helped him to see a lot of things about his life in a new light.

He didn't need to be here in person today. He could have simply telephoned. But that was the coward's way out and he was through with that way of life. He had left that behind on Paxos three months ago.

Lifting his chin and squaring his shoulders, Mark strolled up to the half-open door and pushed it wide. His father looked up from his usual leather chair and waved at him to come closer. The gaunt look following his cancer treatment had faded. Charles Belmont was still slight, but he'd put on weight and was looking much more like the towering captain of industry and natural leader he had always been.

'Mark, my boy. Great to see you. Come and take a look at this. The advance copies of your mother's book arrived this morning. The printers have done a half-decent job.'

His father lifted up the hardback book and passed it to Mark, who had chosen to stand, rather than sit in the chair on the opposite side of the desk from his father as though he had come for a job interview.

'Excellent choice of photographs. Natural. I could not have chosen better myself. You did a remarkable job, Mark. Remarkable.'

And to Mark's horror Charles touched his nose with his knuckle to cover up his emotion. Strange: Mark did exactly the same thing and had never noticed it before.

Mark looked away and made a show of examining the cover's dust jacket and flicking through the first pages of his mother's biography. The publishers had chosen the very first photograph that Lexi had picked up that day on

Paxos, of his mother at the village fete. She looked happy and natural and full of life.

The photo worked brilliantly.

'Thank you, Father. But I can't take the credit for going with this particular photograph. That was Lexi's Sloane's idea. She thought it might help if people saw the real Crystal Leighton instead of some shallow movie star.'

'Damn right.' His father nodded. 'The girl's got a good head on her shoulders. And it did you good to meet someone outside the business world.' He nodded towards the book. 'I didn't just mean the cover. The stories you tell and your memories of happy and not-so-happy times brought her back to me in a way I didn't think possible. I don't have the talent for it. You clearly do.'

His voice dropped and he sat back in his chair, legs outstretched, tapping his fingers on the desk.

'Your sister is worried about you, Mark. When your mother was alive you would talk about what was happening in your life. But now…? I don't know what's going on in your head. We talk about the business—yes, sure. You even convinced me to go ahead with converting the cottages, and so far we're right on track with that risky business plan of yours. But since you got back from Greece you haven't been the same man. What do you want? More control of the business? The manor? Shout it out, son.'

'What do I want?'

Mark put down the book, strolled over to the window and looked out across the sunlit lawns. This was the first time in many, many years that his father had even asked him how he spent his day, but it was true that he had changed. They both had.

'Actually, I've been asking myself the same question an awful lot since I got back from Paxos. And the answers are not always comfortable,' he replied.

'Tough questions demand tough answers,' his father muttered dismissively. 'Let's hear it.'

Mark half turned back towards him. 'I want to stop feeling guilty for the fact that my mother couldn't tell me she didn't feel pretty enough to stand by me at my engagement party. That would be a start. I know now that there was nothing I could have done differently at the time,' he added softly, 'but it still makes me angry that she didn't trust us enough to share her pain.'

'Of course it makes you angry,' his father replied with a sniff. 'She didn't tell me, either. I thought she was perfect in every way. I can't understand her decision any more than you can. But she was an adult, intelligent woman who knew what she was doing. And don't you *dare* think it was about your blasted engagement. Because it wasn't. It was about her own self-worth. And if you're angry—fine. We can be angry together.'

The tapping continued.

'What else is on that list of yours? What about this girl who helped write the book?'

Mark took a moment to stay calm before making his reply. 'Actually, she's the reason I'm here today. Lexi has it in her head that marrying a girl who can give me a son is more important to me than finding someone I want to spend the rest of my life with. Three months ago she might have been right. Not any more. Not now.' He looked over his shoulder and made eye contact. 'I'm sorry, Father, but chances are that Lexi and I will *not* be able to give you the grandson you were hoping for. The Belmont line will probably end with me.'

The air between Mark and his father almost crackled with the fierce electricity of the tension between them.

'Even if it means that the title passes to your cousin Rupert? The spoiled brat who threw you out of a boat on the lake when you wouldn't let him row? This girl must mean a great deal to you.'

'She does. More than I can say.'

Mark heard the creak of the leather chair behind him, but didn't turn around to his father because of the tears in his eyes. A strong, warm arm wrapped around his shoulders and hugged him just once, then dropped to the window frame so they were both looking out in the same direction.

The intimate contact was slight, but so incredibly new that it seemed to break down the final barrier Mark had been holding between himself and his father for so many years. They had made real progress over these past three months, but this was new. He turned his head towards him.

'I'm pleased to hear that you've met someone at long last. I had almost given up on you. From what Cassie tells me, Alexis is not responsible for what her father did. She loves you enough to do the right thing, and sacrificed her personal happiness for yours. In my book that makes her someone I would like to meet. You deserve to have some love in your life, Mark. Your mother was right. You should get out more.'

He nodded once, then gestured with his head towards the book on his desk.

'If there's one thing your mother's story tells us it's that we loved her and she loved us. More than we knew. And in the end that's the only thing that matters. I am jolly glad that Crystal Leighton came into my life and made me the happiest man alive for so many wonderful years. And gave me my three wonderful children. I blame myself for what happened after Edmund. Tough times. Hard to deal with. I was not up to the job.'

Then he looked up into the sky and his voice turned wistful. 'I should be the one apologising to you, not the other way round. You're right. Don't give your inheritance another thought. The future can take care of itself. You're the man I always knew you could be, and I'm proud to have you as my son.'

Mark took a deep breath and startled his father by giving him a slap on the back. 'I'm pleased to hear it—because I'm heading off to London tomorrow to try and persuade her to give me another chance. Thanks, Dad. I'm pleased you like the book. And thank you even more for bringing Lexi Sloane into my life.'

'What are you waiting here for? Go get your girl and bring her home so she can meet the family. And don't you frighten her off with all this pressure about having sons. It's about time we had some fun around here.'

Dratted device. Lexi shook the small battery-powered sander in the vain hope that playing maracas with it would actually squeeze out enough power to finish the living-room wall.

No such luck. The sander gave a low whine and then shuddered to a halt as the battery gave out.

'Oh, come on, you stupid thing,' she snapped. 'I charged you for three hours this morning. The least you could do is work.'

She sat down on the arm of the sofa in the middle of the room. It was covered with a dust sheet and had been for weeks, while she stripped off the old wallpaper and repaired the holes in the plaster. Now came the dusty part. Sanding away the bumpy walls until they were smooth.

For the last twelve weeks Lexi had filled her days and nights with work that should have provided the perfect distraction.

But it was no use.

Apparently no amount of physical hard work on the

house could replace her obsession for Mark Belmont. He filled her days and nights with dreams and fantasies of what could have been; what had been lost. Worse, every time she looked at her children's stories of kittens having great adventures she was transported back in her mind's eye to the original inspiration and the sunny garden of Mark's villa on Paxos. The wonderful house and the man who owned it.

She could only hope that he wasn't as miserable as she was. Even if the view was particularly delightful from the balcony of his no doubt sumptuous penthouse apartment.

With a low sigh, Lexi replaced the sander on its charger and turned off the trance music that was giving her a headache.

She needed air.

Lexi walked the few steps from the living room to her freshly decorated kitchen, grabbed some juice out of the refrigerator and stepped out onto the tiny patio where she had replaced the traditional redbrick paving with buff-coloured sandstone slabs. Bright red geraniums and herbs spilled out from terracotta pots close to the kitchen door, and a simple wooden trellis still carried the last of the climbing roses.

A precious ray of September sunshine warmed her face and the tiny olive bush in the brightly coloured pot she had painted next to her wooden chair. The colour on the paint tin had been described as 'Mediterranean Blue.' But it was not the same. How could it be? Nothing in her life could be the same again.

She was still standing in the sunshine watching the sparrows on the bird table ten minutes later, when the front doorbell rang. She jogged back to fling it open, a pencil still logged behind one ear, expecting to see the postman.

It was not the postman.

'Mark?' she gasped, staring at him, hardly able to believe her eyes. 'What are you doing here? I thought you'd
moved to—'

'No. I changed my mind about New York. I'm having
way too much fun right here in Blighty.'

She swallowed and then gave a low sigh, blinking away
tears.

He was here. On her doorstep. Tall, gorgeous and over-
whelmingly tinglicious.

'Is your dad okay? I saw the pictures from the film festival when he accepted that lifetime achievement award on
behalf of your mum. He looked a bit shaky.'

He reached out and touched her arm, his fingers light
on the sleeve of her boiler suit. 'Dad's fine. He's still recovering, but he'll stick around long enough to make my
life interesting for some time to come. Thanks for asking.
The emotion of the night got to all of us. I'm sorry you
weren't there to help us celebrate.'

There was an awkward pause, and just when her resolve gave way and she felt that she simply had to say
something, *anything,* to fill the silence, Mark suddenly
presented her with a gift-wrapped square package tied
with a silver ribbon.

'I know that you'd prefer me not to contact you, but I
thought you might want to have your personal copy of the
biography. Signed, of course,' he said, his voice dry and
hesitant. 'My dad is planning a private launch party in a
few weeks, so this is a sneak peek. And, by the way, the
Belmont family would love to have you there. It wouldn't
be the same if I couldn't thank you in person on the big
night. I haven't forgotten what you said. You deserve the
credit for making this book a reality.'

She looked at the package, then back to Mark in silence, and then her shoulders dropped about six inches and

she slid the yellow washing-up glove from one hand and wrapped her fingers around the book. She pulled it towards her for a second, then looked down at the paint splattered overalls and socks she was wearing and shrugged.

'Sanding. Plastering. Bit of a mess. Not sure I'm ready for smart book-launch parties.'

'You look lovely,' he replied in a totally serious voice, but his eyes and mouth were smiling as his gaze locked onto hers. 'You look like *you*.'

He tilted his head to one side and gave her a lopsided grin which made him look about twelve years old.

And her poor lonely heart melted all over again.

'What have you been doing with yourself these past few months?' he whispered. 'Travelling the world? Seeing the sights? Tell me about all the wonderful exotic locations your clients have whisked you away to. Africa? Asia?'

She smiled back, her defences weakened by the wonderful charm and warmth of this man who was standing so very close and yet seemed beyond reach.

'Actually, I've been working on my own projects right here.' She waved her right hand in the air and looked up at the ornate plasterwork ceiling of her hallway. 'I thought that I might stay in one place for a while.' Her voice quivered a little and the silver bow on the gift-wrapping suddenly became the focus of her attention. 'Try and get my bearings after…'

She swallowed, almost losing control at the thought of Paxos, and quickly changed the subject. 'But I can see what *you've* been doing,' she whispered, giving him a half smile. 'You finished the book. Does you dad love it as much as you hoped?'

'He does. He had to go back into hospital for another round of chemotherapy. It was tough. But when I brought the manuscript in to check on a few details… It was one of

the few times in my life that my father has held my hand
and cried. Going through the chapters together changed us.
Made us talk about things I had put off for way too long. It
was good. Actually, it was better than good. It was grand.
What was the phrase you used? Oh, yes. *Awesome sauce.*
The book is awesome sauce. And I have you to thank for
making that happen.'

'Not just me. He should be proud of you.' Lexi stroked
the wrapping and pressed her lips together, her mind reeling from the fact that Mark was so close. She longed to
touch and hold him and tell him how much she had desperately missed him… But she knew that would only make
things a lot worse.

'I'll read it later, if you don't mind. I need to get back
to my decorating.' She waved her yellow glove back inside the hallway. 'Lots to do.' She half turned to step back
inside, then glanced back at him over her shoulder. 'But
thank you for bringing me this in person. I hope it gets
stunning reviews and puts some ghosts to bed. For all of
us. Good luck, Mark. To you and your family.'

Time stood still for a few seconds as Lexi remained in
the doorway, hating to say goodbye.

'Lexi. Can I come in? Just for five minutes? I really
do need to talk to you.' Then he pulled back his arm and
shook his head. 'Forget that. That's what the old Mark
would have said.'

He stepped forward so quickly that Lexi was still taking in a sharp breath when he wrapped his arms around
her back and pulled her sharply towards him. Looking
into her startled eyes, Mark smiled and pulled her even
tighter, so that the only thing separating their bodies was
the book he had just given her.

'I would much rather have this conversation on your
doorstep, so that the whole of London can hear me tell

you that I've been totally miserable these past few months without my sparkly Lexi by my side. In fact I missed your irritating sparkliness so much that I stopped being grumpy and decided to be a better man, instead.'

Her heart turned a somersault. 'Oh, you were grumpy. But I wasn't always sparkly, so I think we're about even.'

'Sparkly enough for me. And please don't make me lose my place in my speech. I was just getting to the apology—where I grovel at your feet and beg your forgiveness for being such an idiot that I let you go without fighting harder to persuade you to stay.'

'In that case I shall try not to be sparkly. Because I quite like the sound of that part.'

'I rather thought you might. Only I'm a bit out of practice when it comes to grovelling. In fact, this is a first, so you'll have to forgive me if I get it wrong.'

Lexi tugged off her other glove and pressed her free hand onto Mark's chest. He inhaled deeply with pleasure at her touch.

'On the contrary.' She smiled. 'I think you grovel quite beautifully. But you can stop now. There's something I'd like to show you.'

She grabbed his hand and half dragged him down the narrow hall and into the kitchen of her tiny terraced house.

'Do you remember all the photographs I took of your kittens on the terrace at the villa? Well, here they are.'

She pointed to the row of printed pages which ran the full length of the kitchen wall. 'On the left side of the page is a photo of the kittens, and then on the right side are a few lines of the story.'

'Is that Snowy One peeping his head out from my stone wall?' Mark asked, laughing at the cutest white kitten with pink ears, pinker tongue and a cheeky grin. 'It is—and here's Snowy Two, halfway up the trunk of the olive tree next to the table-tennis table. I think it was the moment when it dawned on him that going down might be slightly trickier than climbing up. "Once upon a time in the land of sunshine there lived a family of positively pampered cats,"' Mark read slowly, then snorted and looked back at Lexi. 'Well, that certainly is true. My housekeeper feeds them chicken when I'm away!'

Lexi took a step to his side and read out the rest of the page. "'There was a mummy cat, a daddy cat and two kittens. Their real names were Snowy and Smudge, but most days they ended up being called other names—like rascal, scamp, trouble and mischief.'"

'Oh, that is perfect. These are wonderful, Lexi.' He sighed warmly and walked, with her hand still held in his, from photograph to photograph. 'I knew you were talented. But these are magical. Truly wonderful. Cassie's boys would adore these stories.'

Lexi paused and looked up into his face. 'But not *my* boys, Mark. I know there's a small chance that medically I could have your son, but lurching from month to month with hope and then disappointment is no way to live. It wouldn't be fair on either of us. And that hasn't gone away.'

'No, it hasn't,' he replied, lifting a strand of hair and pushing it back over her forehead as he slid away her bandanna. 'But I know now that a life without love in it is no life at all. *You* are the only woman I want in my life. Plus I'm going to need some help with childcare. Ah…yes.' He smiled at her stunned face. 'That reminds me. I should probably mention that I plan to adopt. Two girls and two boys would work well, but I'm flexible. There are an awful lot of children out there who need a loving home where they can be spoiled rotten, and I suspect that we would be very good at that.'

'Adopt? Four children? You would do that for me?' Lexi

asked, suddenly feeling faint, horrified, stunned, amazed and thrilled to the core.

'In a heartbeat.' Mark shrugged and drew her closer. 'You are the girl for me. And that's it. Those children will be blessed with the most wonderful mum. And I'm going to be right there every step of the way. In fact, I'm rather looking forward to being a dad.'

'Wait a minute,' Lexi replied and shook her head. 'You seem to be forgetting something very important here. I was the one who couldn't face the hard time ahead of us. Not you. I was the coward. You made me feel loved and treasured, and it was so intense and so beautiful I couldn't deal with it, Mark. I just couldn't believe it was possible that any man could love me so much. And I ran. And I shouldn't have. I should have stayed and fought harder to make it work. I am sorry for that. I just couldn't believe it was real. I couldn't believe you wanted me.'

Her head lolled forward so that her dirty, dusty forehead was resting on his beautiful dark suit.

'Believe it,' he murmured, his chin pressed on top of her hair. 'Because it's true.'

He tipped her chin up so that she could look into his eyes, and the intensity and depth of what she saw there choked her so much that her breath came out in deep sobs.

'I telephoned your mother yesterday and personally invited her to the book launch. She was a tad surprised to hear from me, but we got along splendidly after I mentioned that I am completely besotted with her daughter and my sole objective in life from this moment is her complete happiness.'

'You said that to my mum?' Lexi gasped. 'Wow. That must have been an interesting conversation. You do know that she'll hold you to it? Wait a minute... I spoke to her last night and she never said a word.'

'Um… We made a pact. She wouldn't tell you that I was coming round so long as I promised to kidnap you from your world of plastering and whisk you off to a luxury hotel for an afternoon of pampering in the spa, a fine meal and hopefully some debauchery.'

She slumped against him. 'Oh, that sounds so good.'

'There's more. Your delightful and charming parent happened to mention that your home-decorating project was sucking time away from your writing. This cannot be permitted to continue. Children everywhere need to see these stories as soon as possible.'

He grinned and winked. 'The Belmont estate has a wonderful team of builders and decorators who will be happy to help my girlfriend in her hour of need. They are currently on standby, ready to burst into action at a moment's notice and get busy on your charming London house while you spend the weekend with my family at the manor.'

'That's—that's very generous, but I couldn't possibly accept… And…girlfriend? What manor? And you winked at me. You *winked.* Things really have changed.'

'I thought it was about time I started to be spontaneous. And I was hoping that if I played my cards right you might let me share this bijou gem of a home with you. It's far better than any clinical, empty penthouse. And, best of all, you are in it.'

He cupped Lexi's head between his hands, his long fingers so gentle and tender and loving that her heart melted even more.

'I love you, Alexis Sloane. I love everything about you. I love that you are a survivor. I love that you have come through so much and still have so much love to give to the world. I am so proud of everything you have achieved, and I want to be there when you go on to even greater things. I believe in your talent and I want to share my life with you.'

'You love me?'

He nodded. 'Yep. I love you. All of you. Especially that part of you that doesn't believe that she deserves to be loved. Because that's the bit I fit into. Say yes, Lexi. Say *yes*. Take the risk and let me into your life. Because you are not a coward. Far from it. You are the bravest woman I have ever met.'

'I would have to be brave to be *your* girlfriend,' she sobbed, spreading tears and plaster dust all over his suit. 'But give me ten minutes to get packed and I'll show you how much I've missed you every second of every day we have been apart.'

'You don't need to pack. Where we're going clothing is entirely optional.'

'Oh, I *do* love you,' she replied, flinging her arms around his neck and kissing him with every ounce of devotion and passion and repressed longing that she could collect into one kiss—a kiss that had them both panting when she released him.

'Wow.' He grinned, blinking, gasping for breath, his eyes locked on hers. 'Really?'

'*Really,* really. I love you so very, very much. Enough to stand up to anyone who even tries to break us apart. No matter who it is. Oh, Mark, I've missed you so much.'

His hands stroked her face and he grinned, his eyes sparkling with energy and life. 'Excellent. Because I've already invited your mother and her fiancé to meet the Belmont clan at the manor tomorrow. I cannot wait a moment longer to show you off.'

She gasped. 'My mother? And Baron Belmont? Now, *that's* something I want to see. He won't know what's hit him.'

'I have no doubt. But they're all going to have to get used to the idea. This is the first day of the rest of our lives,

Lexi. Tell me what you want to do and where you want to go and I'll take you there.'

Lexi took in a long breath and looked into the face of the man she loved—the man who loved her in return and was offering her the world on a golden platter. 'Then take me back to Paxos and that secret garden on a clifftop. And this time we are going to watch the sunset together. Forever.'

EPILOGUE

LEXI strolled into the luxurious reception room of one of London's most exclusive gentlemen's clubs and paused to take in the sumptuous interior which had already sent her mother into raptures over the ornate plasterwork, stunning Art Nouveau statuary and hand-painted Chinese wallpaper.

Deep brocade-covered sofas and crystal chandeliers added to the opulence—but they were lost on Lexi. Her high-heeled sandals sank into the fine Oriental carpet as she stood on tiptoe to find the one person she needed and wanted so badly to be with on his special day.

And there he was. Elegant in his favourite charcoal cashmere suit and the pale pink shirt she had ironed for him that afternoon, chatting away to Cassie and his mother's showbiz friends in front of a huge white marble fireplace. His father had one arm around Mark's shoulder and was laughing out loud, his head back, relaxed and happy, as one of London's most famous theatre actors shared an anecdote about the old days when he worked with Crystal.

The love and the warmth of the scene added to the familiar heat that flashed through her body the moment she saw Mark's eyes focus on her from across the room, inviting her to join him.

Clusters of elegant people were gathered around the tables, flicking through the pages of *Mrs Belmont's Lemon Cake,* some smiling and some wiping away tears. All affected by the woman Mark had captured so brilliantly in the pages of a book that was surely going to soar up the best-seller lists.

Her reward for wending her way across the room was a warm hug from Cassie and a kiss on the cheek from Charles. But it was Mark who gathered her to him, his arm wrapped tightly around the waist of her simple pleated silk plum cocktail dress so that she was locked into his side.

'You look even more amazing than normal, Miss Sloane. And that is saying something!' he whispered into her hair.

'Well, thank you, Mr Belmont, but I think the jewellery might have something to do with that.' She grinned, pressing one hand to his mother's stunning diamond-and-sapphire necklace which Mark had placed around her neck only minutes before they'd been due to leave her house for the party.

'Oh, no. You are already sparkly enough for me. This is just a finishing touch for the rest of the world to see.'

The sides of his mouth lifted into an intimate smile that made her heart soar as he tapped the end of her nose.

'Ah. Lexi. There you are.' The smiling owner of Brightmore Press charged forward, waving the biography in his hand. 'Splendid job. Just splendid. Huge success. I need to say a few words to our guests, but I'll be right back.' He looked at her over the top of his black spectacles. 'And don't you *dare* leave before we have a chat about that series of children's books you've promised me. I've already booked a page in our Christmas catalogue. Catch you later!'

He sped off to grab Baron Belmont.

Mark squeezed Lexi's waist as she smiled up into his

face. 'Well, I suppose I shall have to get used to having my own name on the cover for a change.'

'This is only the start,' Mark replied, then laughed out loud. 'They already know that I couldn't have written this book without you. Get ready for the time of your life, Miss Awesome Sauce. There's no holding you back now—and I am going to be right there by your side, cheering you on. All the way.'

*****

BACK IN THE LION'S DEN

ELIZABETH POWER

To Alan, with love always.

Elizabeth Power wanted to be a writer from a very early age, but it wasn't until she was nearly thirty that she took to writing seriously. Writing is now her life. Travelling ranks very highly among her pleasures, and so many places she has visited have been recreated in her books. Living in England's West Country, Elizabeth likes nothing better than taking walks with her husband along the coast or in the adjoining woods, and enjoying all the wonders that nature has to offer.

CHAPTER ONE

HE could hear the music coming from the fitness class before he reached it. A strong pulsing rhythm reverberating down the corridor.

On either side of him, behind glass partitions, enthusiasts were treading rubber and pumping muscle. He knew he cut an incongruous figure in his dark business suit, white shirt and tie, and was aware that two young women playing squash on one of the courts he was passing had stopped their game to watch him.

At six feet three and powerfully built, with the sleek black hair and rugged features of a Celtic heritage, he was used to the attention his presence elicited from the opposite sex. But while he might usually have spared a glance towards an admiring female today Conan Ryder's mind wasn't distracted from its purpose.

Ignoring their blatant interest, he strode determinedly on, the green-gold of his eyes remaining focused on the partly open door to the room where the beat was coming from. His broad shoulders were pulled back in a deliberate attempt to stem the adrenalin that was coursing through his body.

No one made him feel like this! The fight for the composure he prized pulled his jaw into a grim cast. Especially not a woman—and particularly not a woman like Sienna Ryder! He had a request to make—that was all. A request she'd probably refuse so that would mean a verbal battle with her to get her to do what he wanted. But he would win in the end. After that it was a matter of making the necessary arrangements and getting out.

'That's good, Charlene! Let your hips do the work! That's lovely! You're a natural! Let it f-l-o-w…'

He heard her voice above the beat as he pushed open the door with the flat of his hand. Clear. Encouraging. In control.

The lively rhythm was still pounding as he met the class head on and twenty pairs of female eyes turned his way, but his interest lay only with the petite figure of the young woman in a sleeveless red leotard and black leggings who was still directing the class with her back to him.

Her short dark hair was expertly shaped into the nape of her neck, its boyish style only adding to her femininity. Skin lightly tanned, the perfect proportions of her small, slim body were clearly outlined by the clinging clothes, yet there was a remarkably lithe fitness about her that hadn't been so apparent when she had been married to his brother.

Coming up behind her, he let his gaze sweep over the graceful line of her neck and shoulders to the small butterfly tattoo he recognised just above her right shoulderblade, and felt a tug of unwelcome awareness at the very core of his masculinity. He found himself having to clear his throat before he stooped to make himself heard.

'I'm sorry to interrupt your workout, but you were proving far too elusive. How does anyone get in touch with you? By carrier pigeon?' Past hostilities gave a hard edge to the deep resonance of his voice. 'Or would I have had more luck trying telepathy?'

Shock had registered in her eyes as she'd swung round— big blue eyes that met the green-gold of his now with a spark of contention, acknowledging the coldness in his tones.

'Hello, Conan.' Her smile was bright and forced, her small oval face assuming that look of cool detachment he remembered so well. 'It's lovely to see you again too.'

Her sarcasm wasn't lost on him, but then he saw the blood

drain from her cheeks as she said starkly, 'Daisy? Is she all right?'

Her concern for her child was obvious, even if she hadn't shown the same regard for his brother.

'How would I know?' he lobbed back across the fading beat. 'I haven't seen her in nearly three years!' Censure stiffening every inch of his strong, lean body, he watched her dark lashes come down as that moment of panic gave way to undisguised relief as it dawned on her that he couldn't possibly know anything about the welfare of his niece. 'I've been trying to reach you for days, but your landline's ex-directory, and each time I've called at the house you've never been around.'

She looked almost startled. Perhaps she had never expected him to find out where she lived. 'We've been busy.' It was a flat refusal to enlarge upon anything concerning her private life. 'Why did you want to see me anyway?'

Tension pulled in his jaw at the rising level of female hormones in the hall. Now that the music had stopped he could feel those twenty pairs of eyes looking him up and down, as though they had never seen a man before in their entire lives.

Impatiently he demanded, 'Can we talk somewhere else?'

Gesturing for her class to continue as another track started to play, Sienna simply jerked her head towards the open door.

Reaching it first, Conan caught the scent of the freshness of her skin as she stepped past him into the corridor. He noticed the sway of her slim hips as he followed her out, and with another stab of something way down in his loins noticed the shape of her firm buttocks, tantalisingly separated by the deep lines of the leotard, the narrow span of her waist as she went ahead of him with her head high, her back as proud and straight as any ballerina's.

'What do you want?' she challenged, swinging to face him.

Her blood was racing just at the sight of seeing Conan Ryder on her turf. He was as hard and handsome as she remembered him. Business entrepreneur. Billionaire. And her late husband's half-brother.

He was right, though. It *had* been three years—or as good as—since she had fled from Surrey to her home town just outside London, escaping his cruel taunts and his accusations with an eighteen month old toddler in tow. Three years since that tragic accident of Niall's that had left her widowed and her child fatherless.

It was clear from Conan's disparaging manner that his opinion of her hadn't changed. Now, alone with him, she felt less like the confident, self-sufficient woman she had become, and more like the emotionally dependent girl who had taken the lash of his tongue with no means of defending herself. Nothing that would explain her actions, why she had lied, her obvious guilt. Not without baring her very soul to him, and there was no way she was ever going to do that.

Closing her mind against the bitter pain that threatened to well up inside of her, she murmured in a voice that was near to cracking, 'For what reason could you possibly want to see me?'

'Not you.' Those incisive words cut across her with the precision of a scythe. 'Daisy. I'm here to insist you let Daisy come back with me.'

'What?' Her stomach muscles tightened at painful echoes of the past. *'I'd do everything in my power to take Daisy away from you.'* Yet her hackles were rising too, at the sheer arrogance of his statement, making her respond with, 'Insist? You *insist,* Conan?'

'She's my brother's child,' he reminded her harshly. 'She also has a grandmother she hasn't seen.'

'She also has a mother who wasn't good enough for any of you—remember?' It was a pointed little cry. Poignant, bitter and accusing.

Conan's black lashes swept down over the glittering green of his eyes—thick long lashes, she'd always thought, that most women would give their eye teeth to achieve. His face was lean and hard, high cheekbones stark against the proud nostrils that flared momentarily above his angular, darkly shadowed jaw, and the taut line of his wide, uncompromising mouth was compressed.

'All right,' he breathed heavily at length. 'I know we've had our differences.'

'Our differences?' She almost laughed in his face. 'Is that what you call them, Conan? Being accused of being an unfit mother and an unfaithful wife?'

His penetrating eyes hardened like chips of green glass, but all he said was, 'Yes, well…' It was clear he didn't want to discuss the accusations he had made. 'That doesn't alter the fact that you had no right to deprive Daisy of her family.'

'I had every right!' The star-shaped studs in her ears glinted as she brought her head up sharply, colour touching her cheeks at his glaring audacity. A confrontation with him was bad enough, but being so scantily dressed made her feel at even more of a disadvantage—especially since he was so big and so potently male. 'Niall was all the family she had. Niall and me!' That wasn't strictly true, Sienna thought, because there were her parents, although she didn't see them that often since their move to Spain.

'Niall was my brother.'

'Yes, well…a pity you didn't remember that when he was alive!'

She had hit a raw nerve. She could see it in the way that sensuous mouth of his hardened, and in the way his irises seemed to darken like woodland pools at dusk. Perhaps being reminded of how he, a self-made billionaire, had refused his own brother help when he'd been in desperate financial straits didn't sit too comfortably on his conscience. With lethal softness, however, he said, 'You still want to goad me with that?'

Something warned her to be on her guard and not to antagonise him unnecessarily. Even so, the raw pain to which he had subjected her three years ago, with his implacable assumptions and his inexorably cruel accusations, had her uttering tautly, 'I don't want to do *anything* with you, Conan Ryder.'

His gaze grazed over her shoulders, touching briefly on the swell of her small firm breasts. He was unpitying and unscrupulous and she didn't like him, and yet she felt the sick stirrings of a ridiculous heat lick along her veins.

'Did I ever ask you to?' he enquired silkily, the cruel mockery that played around his mouth leaving her in no doubt as to what he meant.

No, he hadn't, she thought with an inexplicable little tingle along her spine, and she had never thought of him as anything other than her husband's elder brother. Of course she'd been aware of his countless attributes during those two and a half years she had been married to Niall. What woman wouldn't have been? she reasoned resentfully. He was good-looking, dynamic, and unbelievably wealthy. He was also a dark and silent entity she'd never quite been able to fathom out, although his ruthlessness and insensitivity had been all too apparent at the end. She would have had to be an android not to have *noticed* him, at least. But she'd loved Niall. Loved him with a passion that had nearly driven her insane...

'If I remember correctly,' he was saying icily now, 'you were too busy breaking your marriage vows without any help from me—though I doubt it would have taken much more than a snap of my fingers, even with your lover in the picture.'

'He wasn't my lover! And you're still as misguided as you ever were if you think I would ever have thought about setting my sights on a man like *you!*' Memories of the last time she had stood and faced him like this clawed at her consciousness, the ugly scene forever etched on her memory. 'For your information, Conan—'

I loved your brother, she had been about to say, but broke off as the door to her gym class opened, enveloping them in a pounding rhythm.

A young woman came out, her smile for Conan openly inviting before she crossed behind him to the women's cloakroom, forcing him to move closer to Sienna.

In her tight, revealing clothes she suddenly felt naked beside him, and the air left her lungs so that it felt difficult to breathe.

This close to him she could smell the lemony fragrance of his cologne. It didn't help either that he was so formally dressed, probably having just come from some high-flying meeting, she guessed grudgingly, where he'd made multi-million-pound decisions that would increase his global fortune tenfold! But his nearness was stifling, and Sienna took a step back—which was so obvious that he couldn't have failed to realise why.

Apart from the lift of an enquiring eyebrow, however, fortunately he made no comment.

'My mother needs to see Daisy,' he stated as the cloakroom door closed quietly behind him. 'So do I.' Sombre lines were etched around his mouth and jaw and a deep groove corrugated the healthily tanned skin of his forehead. 'My mother hasn't been herself lately...' He couldn't bring himself to tell her what was really wrong, how worried he was about Avril Ryder; he wasn't going to beg. 'And I feel she would benefit from a visit from her only grandchild. She hasn't seen her since she was eighteen months old. Neither of us has.'

'And you think you can just come here and take Daisy away? Just like that? That I'd even allow it?' Fear rose in her again but she forced it back. 'She doesn't know you, Conan.'

'And whose fault is that?'

'She doesn't know you,' she reiterated, ignoring his censuring demand. 'Neither of us does.' Or did, she amended bitterly, reminded of his heartlessness, his lack of compassion—not just towards her, but towards his own brother.

'I'm the child's uncle, for Pete's sake! Not that you've ever given her the chance to find out. There have been no photos. No contact. Do you know what that's been like for Avril? Her *grandmother*? Don't you think she's had enough to contend with in losing Niall—without losing his baby daughter as well when you took her away?'

'I was driven away,' she breathed fiercely. 'And you seem

to forget…I lost something too.' Her eyes were shielded, their lids heavy with the pain of remembering. 'I lost a husband. And I had to contend with a lot of accusations and blame. Don't you think I felt bad enough without being made to feel I was responsible for what had happened to him? That I was responsible for his drinking and getting into debt? I knew what you thought of me—both of you. You made it clear often enough that you thought Niall had married beneath him.'

'I've never said that.'

'You didn't have to! It was there in every last criticism of everything I said—everything I did. Your mother could scarcely contain her shock at him marrying a barmaid! Albeit a temporary one, until I could get my career on track! But that was the crux of the matter, wasn't it? You were determined not to like me from the start.'

'I'm not responsible for my mother. As for me, I only acted on what I observed with my own eyes.'

'And what was that? Besides my supposed infidelity, that is?'

Condemnation set his features in harsh lines, so that he looked like one of the warring Celts whose blood still pumped through his proud, pulsing veins. 'You know very well. Niall was weak where money was concerned. He was living above his means and you did nothing but encourage him.'

Because she hadn't known. Because she'd been too young to recognise the signs: his irritability, his drinking too much, his mood swings.

'"Bled him dry",' she reminded him. 'That was the phrase I believe you used.'

He didn't negate or deny it. How could he? Sienna thought grimly. He wasn't a man to pull his punches, or hide behind lies and subterfuge—as she had—whatever else he might have done.

'I can't talk about this now,' she uttered quickly, hearing the last track on the album she'd selected earlier come to an abrupt end. 'I've got to get back to my class.' This meeting with Niall's brother was more traumatic than she'd ever have imagined possible, and it was with aching relief that she pulled herself away.

'You'll do as I ask, Sienna.'

She stopped in her tracks, swinging round to face him again, her eyes wide with defiance and disbelief.

'Oh, will I? And what do you intend to do to try and bully me into it? Concoct some tale about my being an unsuitable mother and get an injunction to try and take Daisy away from me, as you threatened before?' Beneath her bravado was a sick anxiety that he might try to do just that—somehow use his power and influence to get even with her for how he believed she had treated Niall.

'I didn't come here for that.'

'No. You just want me to hand her over without all the hassle. Well, I'm sorry, Conan, but the answer's still no. Daisy's not going anywhere without me, and I'm certainly not putting myself back into the lion's den, thank you very much!'

'Oh, I think you will, Sienna.'

'And what makes you so sure?'

'Conscience, sweetheart. If you have one.'

Her small chin came up as she said bitterly, ignoring the patronising way in which he had addressed her, 'Like you, you mean?'

She didn't wait to catch any sniping response.

Making sure Daisy was asleep, Sienna kissed the little girl's soft cheek before extinguishing her bedside lamp, unable to resist stroking the silky chestnut hair that curled against the pillow.

Like Niall's, she thought poignantly, pulling the duvet up over the chubby arm wrapped around her pink hippopotamus. Daisy had inherited her father's colouring, not hers.

Going back downstairs, she opened the back door to let in a big bouncing bundle of white shaggy fur, filled a bowl with the dog's supper, and then started the ironing—normal things she did every day, except tonight things felt anything but normal.

Meeting Conan again had opened up all the unhappiness of the past, forcing her to dwell on wounds she'd thought had healed, forcing her to think, to remember.

She had been just twenty when she had met Niall.

With her parents having sold their UK home to live abroad, Sienna had chosen to stay in England on her own. Her parents had always done their own thing. They liked sun, sea and sand, and Sienna had been happy for them, while relishing the prospect of occasional holidays in Spain.

She had been working as a receptionist at her local gym when she had met Niall. He had been a regular member there, and had often come into the bar where she had sometimes helped when it was short-staffed. She had instantly warmed to his wicked sense of humour. He'd been witty and charming, and just a little bit crazy, and she'd been swept off her feet before she had known what hit her.

Her parents had flown over for the wedding, which had been a short civil ceremony after a whirlwind romance. Faith and Barry Swann and Niall's mother—a barrister's widow— were poles apart, and while they'd tried to befriend her new mother-in-law it was clear that Avril Ryder hadn't really warmed towards them. It had also been clear to Sienna from the start that the woman believed she had trapped her youngest son into marriage by getting pregnant, which was something over which Sienna had been silently smug, proving her wrong when Daisy had arrived exactly a year to the day that they had married.

Conan had been at the wedding, interrupting some important business conference he'd been attending in Europe, and the cool touch of his lips on her cheek as he'd wished her well after the ceremony had been as formal as it had been unsettling.

It had been clear, though, that Niall looked up to his brother, and Sienna had understood why. Already approaching his late twenties to his half-brother's twenty-three, and spearheading a global telecommunications company, Conan Ryder had been a mind-blowing success—dynamic, wealthy and sophisticated. It had been apparent to Sienna from the start who Niall was trying to emulate in the way he spoke, in his image, even in that air of glacial composure that Conan exuded.

Niall had been a top sales executive working at Conan's head office, though not before pulling himself out of university and destroying his mother's hopes of him following his late father into the legal profession. Nevertheless, he had been good at his job, and determined that she would reap the benefits—from the clothes he had bought her to every conceivable luxury she had wanted in their modern four bedroom home, a house he had mortgaged only a few miles from his half-brother's Surrey mansion.

But he'd played as hard as he worked. Often too hard, Sienna remembered painfully, as she ironed the back of one of Daisy's little blouses for at least the third time. Because it had been that reckless sense of fun and that daredevil attitude towards almost everything that had killed him during those five days in Copenhagen at that stag party that had gone terribly wrong...

Pain and remorse pressed like twin bars against her chest, and she forced herself to breathe deeply to ease the anguish.

While he'd been alive he'd been driven: always trying to compete—almost obsessively so, she reflected—with his elder brother. But Niall hadn't had Conan's focus—or his ruthlessness, she thought bitterly. Because when Niall had got into dire financial straits and had asked his brother for help, just a couple of weeks before he'd died, Conan had refused. Niall had been devastated. It was only then that he'd told her how far they had been living above their means and just how much money they owed. She'd been too young and far too naive to realise it!

Both Conan and her mother-in-law had blamed *her* for her

husband's overspending, and for the worry she had caused, which had led to his drinking and his ultimate accident.

'It wasn't my fault!' she'd shot back at Conan that last day, just a week after Niall's funeral, hurting, agonised, reproaching herself for going along with everything Niall had expected of her—given her—even when her instincts had told her that he was wrong, or that it seemed he was being far too extravagant. 'And if *you'd* helped him when he came to you for help perhaps he wouldn't have got so drunk as not to know what he was doing!' she had flung at him bitterly, too overcome by grief to care what she was saying.

She had wanted desperately to cry. To break down. To alleviate the pain pressing like a dead weight against her chest. But standing there in the sumptuous drawing room of Conan Ryder's Regency home, where she'd come to return the last of Niall's things, her tears wouldn't come. She had felt only a numbing emptiness that had given her an air of spurious indifference—which had only cemented her guilt in his brother's eyes, promoting what he'd decided he already knew: that she'd been cheating on his brother.

'My brother was in trouble and you weren't even aware of it—too wrapped up in your spending and your...*boyfriend* to notice.'

'Oh, I noticed all right!' It was a bitter little cry, torn from beneath the veneer of icy detachment she was feeling.

'And you did nothing to help him.'

'I was his wife—not his nursemaid!' She realised how cold and brutal that sounded. She was trying to defend herself and failing miserably, wanting to scream at Niall for leaving her to face his family like this—alone. Hurt, angry, reproaching herself...

'My mother has expressed concerns that you aren't mature or responsible enough to look after a child—and quite frankly I agree with her. I want my brother's offspring to grow up as a Ryder, under this family's roof. Not in some other man's home, bearing some other man's name.'

'She'll grow up as I consider fit,' she assured him, stung by the things her mother-in-law had said. But then Avril Ryder—whom, she noted, hadn't emerged from her own wing of her eldest son's exclusive residence—had never made any attempt to conceal her disapproval of her other son's match. There was no way, though, that Sienna ever intended changing her child's name—even if she did end up with another man in the far distant future. 'You're not her father, Conan,' she reminded him coolly. 'Even if you'd like to think you are.'

'No.' Derision curved his uncompromising mouth at that. 'Fortunately I can't claim to be among those to have had the pleasure.'

Her hand clenched with the almost uncontrollable urge to lash out at him, to feel the sting of her palm as it met the hardness of his cheek which might shake her out of this numbing misery. But she'd decided that enough damage had been done already.

'I don't have to stay here and take this from you,' she responded quietly, hating herself for the tingle of awareness that had run through her at his blatant innuendo a moment ago. 'But if you're trying to make me feel cheap, then go ahead. I was never good enough for you, was I? *Either* of you,' she'd added accusingly. 'Is that why Niall made such a mess of things? Because he was made to feel he wasn't good enough either? Because he felt so overshadowed by his much smarter, richer and generally more favoured elder brother?'

If he'd looked angry before, he'd looked livid then, his proud nostrils flaring, the skin above his upper lip white with rage. 'You don't know what you're talking about,' he'd rasped.

'Don't I?' She went on goading him, unable to help herself, needing something—anything—to ease the burden of confusing emotions that were ravaging her. 'I know you did next to nothing to support him—in *anything*—and that when he came to you for help you refused him any financial backing! Well, don't worry! We'll be leaving tomorrow. You won't have to put up with me soiling this family's precious pedigree any more!'

'You take Daisy away from here and you'll have me to answer to. Is that clear?'

'As crystal! What do you propose to do?' she taunted. 'Sue for custody?'

'If it comes to it.'

'On what grounds?' she challenged, suddenly wary. 'That I'm an unfit mother?' Painfully she remembered the instances that had helped tar her with that particular brush—the circumstances that she couldn't explain even if she wanted to.

'If I find you wanting in that regard, I won't hesitate in applying for Daisy to be made a ward of court, most certainly.'

From anyone else she would have considered it an idle threat. From Conan it merely struck the deepest fear into her heart.

He was rich and powerful enough to make any court take notice of charges he made against her. And though she doubted that the Ryders would ever be allowed full custody of her daughter, she still feared what he might try to do with his staggering influence and his money.

'Well, perhaps I should marry my *boyfriend!*' she threw back desperately, pandering to his previous accusation. 'And then you wouldn't be able to do a thing! Stay away from me, Conan!'

She'd stormed out of the house and their lives without another glance back, paying off her debts and setting up home in the little terraced house she'd managed to mortgage with the small amount of capital left over from the sale of the house she had shared with Niall.

But now Conan had turned up again, still as judgmental as ever, and with a lethal maturity only acquired by three more years of honing that indomitable strength of character alongside his superb masculine physique. Of increasing his wealth and power and making himself one of the most talked about entrepreneurs of his generation—both in the playgrounds of the rich and in his corporate life. It amounted to three more years of getting what he wanted. And he wanted Daisy...

When the doorbell rang, she almost dropped the iron.

CHAPTER TWO

SHADOW—so named because of the patch of black fur covering the whole of one side of his head and one floppy ear—was barking frantically at the front door by the time Sienna reached it.

'Conan!' She didn't know why she sounded surprised. She had known he would come.

The dog was leaping excitedly up at him, with no regard for his designer tailoring, while Conan, with a face like granite, stood rigidly impervious, his nostrils flaring and his olive skin infused with something almost akin to anger.

'I'm sorry. He isn't usually like this,' Sienna apologised, rushing forward to grab the dog's collar. In fact, after bringing the six month old Shadow home from an animal rescue centre two years ago, she had been pleased when her pet had flown through obedience classes with the equivalent of a doggy distinction. Rather grudgingly though she decided that just the mere sight of a man like Conan Ryder was enough to make even a mere animal forget its manners.

'May I come in?'

With every nerve on alert, still holding the dog's collar, Sienna backed away to admit him.

Immediately the walls of the narrow passageway seemed to close in on all sides, the space between them shrunk by his imposing physique.

With a tightness in her chest, Sienna took another step back for an entirely different reason, releasing the dog which, after one brave sniff at the man's black designer shoes, trotted off to the comfort of the living room.

Her mouth dry, Sienna demanded, 'What's this all about, Conan? Because if it's about Daisy you've had a wasted journey. I thought I made my position clear this afternoon.'

For a split second something flared in his eyes. Anger? Retaliation? She wasn't sure. But with that strong self-command she had always envied about him he brought it under control, only the muscle that pulled in his darkly shadowed jaw disclosing any other sign of emotion.

'We parted on a rather bad note today. I thought it only right to try and rectify that.'

Oh, did you?

His dark head tilted towards the door at the end of the passageway, his meaning obvious, while an arresting movement of his devastating mouth caused a peculiar flutter in the pit of her stomach.

Conan Ryder being hostile was something she could deal with. Conan being charming was far more dangerous to her equilibrium.

'You'd better come through.' She wondered if he had detected that nervous note in her voice, and as she went ahead of him along the passageway could almost feel his eyes boring through her tight black T-shirt and jeans.

Too aware of him as she led him into her tiny sitting room, she sensed his brooding gaze moving critically over its rather jaded décor. 'Sit down.' She looked around the cramped little room in dismay. 'If you can find a space.' She darted to remove the pile of ironing from her one easy chair, dragging toys and a jigsaw puzzle box off the worn, rather lumpy-looking settee beside it.

Ignoring her, he was looking around at the rather shabby and tired-looking furnishings, the few sparse pieces of furniture that made up a wooden table and chairs, a rather stressed bookcase, a modest hi-fi system and her television.

'Is this how you're living?' Censure marked the hard lines of his face.

Eyeing him resentfully, with a pile of freshly ironed garments supported on her hip, Sienna snapped, 'What's that supposed to mean?'

Conan's mouth pulled down hard on one side. 'A bit of a change, isn't it, from what you were used to?'

'At least it's all paid for!' It was an anguished throwback to the girl who had blindly accepted every luxury without question—only to find herself plunged into widowhood with nothing but loneliness, a precious little toddler and a whole heap of debt.

'With what?' Derision laced Conan's voice as he sliced another detrimental glance around the sad little living space, finishing up on Shadow who was gazing up at him from his shabbily cushioned basket with suspicious eyes. 'You can scarcely earn much from that menial job you do at that gym.'

'And what's it to you?' She hadn't meant to snap. He'd come to try and patch things up, after all. But his criticism of her home and his disparaging reference to what she did when she had trained so hard—worked so hard—to keep a roof over her and Daisy's head was proving more than she could take.

'Everything—if I think my niece is being deprived of the most essential necessities when she could be benefiting from the help that her mother is too proud—or to selfish—even to consider.'

Sienna's hackles rose—not least because she *was* sometimes worried that her daughter was missing out on some of the things her little friends obviously enjoyed. Like bouncy castles on her birthday and pretty clothes; like the reliability of a car that wasn't breaking down every five minutes. Like a father who hadn't died and left her...

Regret mingled with anger—the anger she often reproached herself for feeling towards Niall and the way he had died when it had all been so avoidable. So pointless...

'Proud and selfish you might think me,' she quoted, pulling herself up to her full five feet four inches to face Niall's brother with a display of composure she was far from feeling, 'and perhaps I am. But as far as what I said to you three years ago, when you very kindly condescended to offer us financial assistance goes...' Her voice dripped pure venom. 'I don't retract a single word.'

The animosity she felt towards him lay thickly on the air between them. Conan felt it like a live thing, along with the silent, anguished accusation that rose like a torturing spectre from the darkest recesses of his mind.

You didn't want to help us when Niall was alive! We can do without any help from you now!

Heavily, with some private emotion seeming to stretch the skin taut across his prominent cheekbones, he pointed out, 'Even if Daisy suffers because of it?'

'She won't,' Sienna returned, with more conviction than she was feeling, glancing down at Shadow, who was making rather indelicate grunting noises as he delved violently into his fur.

'Then at least allow her to see her grandmother.' His denigrating glance towards the basket told her he probably didn't approve of her dog either. 'You have a duty, Sienna. To Niall's family as well as your own.'

'Duty?' She almost laughed in his face. What right had he to talk about *duty* when he had never really cared about his half-brother? When he had turned his back on him when Niall had needed him most? 'He never asked you for anything,' she accused bitterly, wanting to drive away memories that were too painful to remember. 'When he did...' She had to swallow to continue. 'He looked up to you and he needed you. He was desperate,' she muttered, 'and you just weren't there for him.'

'And you think *I* killed him? Drove him to drink so much that he overbalanced on that bridge when he took up his friends' ridiculous challenge to walk along that wall? Isn't that what you said?'

There was raw emotion in his voice—in the perfect structure of his hard-hewn features. Had he loved his brother after all? Despite everything? Or was it just a pricking of his conscience that was responsible for the darkening of his amazing eyes.

'I didn't know what I was saying.' Vainly she strove to redress the situation, to justify what she had thoughtlessly flung at him because of his accusations. If he'd loved Niall half as much as she had they would have lain heavily—would still lie heavily—on his conscience. 'As I said earlier—I'd just lost my husband.'

'And I'd lost a brother.'

She was right. Her words had left an indelible mark on him. She could see it—hear it in the dark resonant depths of his voice.

For a moment they faced each other like warring combatants—Sienna with her cheeks flushed, eyes glittering defensively, Conan's olive features tinged with angry colour.

He was every bit the Celt, Sienna decided distractedly, from his thick black hair to his strong, proud Gaelic bone structure. In his pride and in his daunting self-sufficiency. In that unmistakable air of command that surrounded him, which made him lead where other men could merely follow. Both brothers had been handsome men. Niall had had the cheek and the charm of his mother's Celtic bloodline, but it was Conan who bore his Irish ancestry like a blazing flag.

'My mother's unwell,' he stated, quietly and succinctly. 'She's very unwell.' In fact the doctors had told him that Avril Ryder didn't seem to have the will to recover. The dark fringes of his lashes came down to veil his eyes. 'I've brought her to stay with me in France.' He owned a spectacular villa these days on the Côte d'Azur, Sienna remembered from an article she had read about him. 'She needs cheering up, and I know her greatest wish is to see her only grandchild. You will come with Daisy, of course—I wouldn't expect anything else—and with the holidays coming up, I'll expect you to stay for the summer.'

A strong refusal sprang to Sienna's lips—but she couldn't express it. If the Ryders—Conan especially—only wanted to salve their consciences by making up for lost time with Daisy, that was one thing. They could go whistle for all she cared. But from the look on his face as he'd told her about his mother things sounded pretty serious. What if this was the last chance Daisy might have of seeing her grandmother? Sienna found herself considering reluctantly. Wouldn't she be doing her daughter a grave injustice by refusing to let her go? And if Avril Ryder *was* that sick...

The holidays *were* coming up, as he had said and her regular classes were coming to an end. She found herself assessing the matter before she had fully realised it. She did have individual training sessions to honour. Also, she couldn't afford to take that much time off without it eating severely into her already frugal budget. But if she did give in and condescend to grant his wishes, she'd be darned if she'd let Daisy go anywhere—or *stay* anywhere—without her!

'I—I can't take that much time off,' she found herself eventually admitting hesitantly. Though her ethics might be forcing her to do what anyone with half a conscience would do, she didn't want to suffer the indignity of Niall's brother guessing just how little money she had, or just how hard she was struggling to make ends meet. 'I would if I could, but I can't.'

Conan's eyes moved reflectively over her pleasingly toned and agile figure.

Of course, he thought, with an introspective smile touching the firm line of his mouth. He'd guessed she could use her job as an excuse. But women like her could be bought—for a price. Hadn't he seen evidence of it in the luxuries she had demanded from her husband? In the clothes and the designer jewellery? In the fast car she'd been happy to buy out of his limited funds before she'd found herself more interesting fish to fry?

'Wives don't come cheap, bruv...as you've yet to find out.'
Across the years he heard his late brother's almost bragging
statement after he'd warned Niall about his spending, and
remembered, some time later, accusing Sienna of taking his
brother for every penny she could get.

'I will pay you what you earn—I'll triple it,' he assured
her coldly. The reminder of the type of woman she was had
turned his heart to stone.

Now, why didn't that offer surprise her? she thought grimly.

'That's very generous of you.' Sienna gave him a bright,
unfaltering smile. 'But can you safeguard my position until I
come back?'

'If I have to.'

Of course. The Conan Ryders of this world could get anything they wanted. They snapped their fingers and lesser mor-
tals jumped to do their bidding. How stupid of her even to ask!

'I take it, then, that that's a yes?' he pressed.

She didn't answer, deciding to wait to tell him that if she
did agree to what he wanted she had no intention of taking a
penny of his precious money. Why spoil his mean and miserable opinion of her? she thought, following his gaze to where
it was resting on Shadow, who was making violent sucking
noises now as he burrowed with increasing ferocity into his
fur.

'Does that dog of yours have a problem with ticks?'

'No, he doesn't!' What *was* the emotion that was turning
down the corners of his superbly masculine mouth? she wondered. Disapproval? Dislike? And why was she even *looking*
at his mouth? she thought, annoyed with herself. Let alone
considering it superb?

Refraining from telling him that Shadow's problem sprang
from rolling on a chocolate wrapper while on his walk this
evening, much to the surprise and angry retaliation of a few
disgruntled wasps, she enquired breezily, 'Don't you like
dogs?'

A broad shoulder lifted beneath the tailored jacket. 'I can

take them or leave them. Let's just say I wouldn't choose to share my home with one.'

Well, tough! Sienna thought, but said brightly, and with some relish, 'That's all right, then. Because if you want to take Daisy and me away with you for the summer I'm afraid you're going to have to take us all.'

'I thought you said Conan never had much time for his brother?' Faith Swann commented when Sienna rang her parents to tell them where she would be going and why. 'That he was positively heartless towards him, and that Avril Ryder was always making you feel inferior and criticising the way you were bringing up my granddaughter?' Faith was fiercely protective of those she loved, and was constantly trying to persuade Sienna to bring Daisy to join her and her husband in Spain.

'He was—and she was,' Sienna averred, and though she hated having to acknowledge it she said, sighing, 'But they're Daisy's family too. And no matter how they treated me, or Niall, as his mother's not well I have to go.'

'I expect he can be quite persuasive,' her mother was remarking distractedly about her late son-in-law's brother. 'I only saw him in the flesh that once…' She meant at the wedding. 'But I saw a picture of him recently in one of our English newspapers,' Faith continued. 'He's quite a looker, isn't he? Not so obviously handsome as Niall was, but the more moody and magnificent type that a lot of women go for. At least he *looked* moody in that photograph,' she added with a little chuckle. 'Probably because he was caught hurrying from the executive lounge of some airport with his latest adoring companion. You know that chat show hostess? Petra Somebody-or-other?'

'Petra Flax,' Sienna supplied, not unfamiliar with the raven-haired beauty whose twice-weekly programme was a little too gossipy for her own taste.

'Just wait until I tell the regulars and our friends at the golf club that my daughter's hobnobbing with the likes of Conan Ryder.'

'Mum!' Sienna burst out, cringing at her mother's penchant for dropping names—the more influential the better. 'I'd appreciate it if you didn't.'

'Don't be silly,' Faith remonstrated, having clearly lapped up the news that Sienna was going to be in the bosom of her late husband's family. 'I'm proud that my daughter had the good sense to marry a man with such illustrious connections. So should you be.'

'Yes, Mum.' Sienna sighed resignedly, reminded of how much her mother enjoyed basking in other people's reflected glory, and remembering that it was those very traits of Faith Swann's that had gone a long way to letting Sienna and her family down with Avril Ryder and her friends on that one inauspicious occasion when their families had met.

'Don't take any notice of your mother. She means well,' Barry Swann placated, when he came on the line to talk to his daughter. 'I know you've always liked to play things close to your chest, but just remember we're here, love, if you need us. For anything at all.'

Strangely, that simple token of kindness from her father produced a welling of emotion in Sienna.

She'd never worried her parents with the reason for her estrangement from Niall's family, or with the extent of Conan's accusations—that he'd not only as good as accused her of being a gold-digger, but also of cheating on his brother. If she had, her father would have come over here to sort him out, she thought sadly, yet with a wry grimace, because she didn't give much for the chances of anyone who tried locking horns with Conan Ryder.

And anyway, what could she tell them? That Conan was right? That the morning he'd come looking for her to tell her that her husband had died he'd discovered she'd spent the night in another man's flat.

She shuddered at the prospect of all the hurt and anger that would follow if she did disclose the truth to them. She couldn't. Wouldn't! she vowed grittily, aching under the weight of it.

'Thanks, Dad,' she murmured gratefully, and rang off.

'So who's this guy you're going to be spending the summer with?' Jodie Fisher asked as Sienna, returning from some last minute shopping before Conan arrived to pick them up, joined her on her porch after locking up her clapped out little red saloon.

'He's my brother-in-law—and I'm not spending the summer with *him,* as such,' she corrected, keen to dispel any hopes her neighbour—a wild-haired blonde, who was noticeably pregnant and the mother of a four-year old—might be harbouring about her having designs on any man…least of all Conan Ryder. 'Well I am, but not in the way you think. My mother-in-law's sick,' she outlined, feeling a nagging unease about how the woman would receive her. She didn't elaborate to Jodie. Although Jodie was a good friend, often looking after Daisy at a moment's notice—as she had done today—Sienna hadn't confided to her exactly what the situation was with her late husband's family. Such things were private. She had simply told Jodie that they lived miles away and she didn't see them very often.

'You wouldn't be lying to me now, would you?' Jodie's attention was caught by something over Sienna's shoulder. 'Great Jumping Jacks! Wowee! Is that a BMW? Or is *that* a BMW? Is that *him?* No, don't tell me! Let me guess! He's pulling in here. It's him! What I wouldn't give for a brother-in-law who looked like that!'

Jodie was clearly knocked sideways. But why the man made every woman who cast eyes on him want to swoon at his feet was beyond her, Sienna though grudgingly, with a careless glance over her shoulder. Yet the dark magnetism of the man behind the wheel of the graphite grey monster that had just pulled up in front of her own pathetic little excuse for a car caused a peculiar fluttering way down in her stomach.

'It isn't what you think, Jodie,' Sienna told her when her friend continued to stand there agog. 'You've got a one-track mind where anyone who isn't hitched and as happy as you are—i.e. single and content—is concerned.'

'Don't give me that!' Jodie pooh-poohed, sending her a sceptical glance. 'You're too young to settle for contentment, and you can't hang on to the past for ever.'

'Well, perhaps content's the wrong word, but I'm adjusting to my life,' she admitted, only just stopping short of telling Jodie that the last thing she wanted was another man in her life. 'So if you're thinking I'd consider making a match with Niall's brother, then I'm afraid you're going to have to think again. He's far too arrogant, overbearing and too darn cocksure of himself ever to qualify as a contender for my affections, and—' She broke off, enquiring of her friend, 'What's wrong with your mouth?

Jodie was pulling faces, Sienna decided, as Shadow would have done, if he'd been able to, the day he'd rolled on that wasp-infested chocolate wrapper. When Jodie didn't answer, however, she went on, 'He's too rich, he's got a freezer cabinet for a heart and is about as approachable as a turned on water cannon. I wouldn't sleep with Conan Ryder if he was the last man on— *What?*'

Jodie's eyes had come into the equation now. But even as it dawned on Sienna what her neighbour was trying to tell her, too late she felt that prickling awareness she always felt when Conan Ryder was close, and caught his deep voice, low in her ear, as he told her, 'Don't worry. You won't have to. We have enough rooms in Provence for the family not to have to share with the guests.'

Those cool words were at variance with the warmth of his breath against her hair—an unintentional caress that sent tingles along her very nerve-endings. Or was it so unintentional? she wondered, her pulse quickening ridiculously. Because she didn't think he'd miss a single trick to try and unsettle her.

Impelled by good manners to introduce him to Jodie, she

tried to shake off the devastating effects of Conan's nearness. But before she could find her voice Jodie was shooting out a hand for him to take.

'I'm Jodie Fisher,' she pre-empted, smiling broadly at the dynamic-looking man whose bronzed chest oozed virility through a fine and fitted short-sleeved cream shirt, and whose long legs were encased in dark tailored trousers. Her cheeks were unusually flushed. Even being happily married and pregnant didn't stop a woman trying to get herself noticed by him, Sienna thought despairingly.

'The pleasure's all mine, Jodie.' His manner was charm personified. Never once in all the time she had known him had he smiled at *her* like that—with such sincere warmth— Sienna realised, annoyed with herself for even thinking it, and telling herself she hardly cared.

'Well, I'll be getting back to my hovel...' Still beaming, Jodie gestured towards the immaculately painted house next door for Conan's benefit. It made Sienna's look rather tired and dull in comparison. 'Daisy's in the garden with Shadow,' she told Sienna. 'Have a lovely time, won't you?' From the look she angled towards Conan as she was going out of the gate it was obvious what she meant.

'You'd better come in.' Alone with him, Sienna was determined not to let it bother her. 'We're nearly ready.'

Daisy was standing mixing play dough on a low table as they came out through the little galley kitchen, chattering happily to her pink hippopotamus, seated on a tiny chair, and the dog, which was stretched out with its head raised, listening interestedly to every word of the childish patter.

'You've got no qualms about leaving a four-year-old with that animal?' Conan's disapproval was obvious.

'No. Why should I have?' Sienna shot back at him over her shoulder. 'Shadow would protect her rather than cause her any harm. "That animal"—as you call him—is as gentle as a lamb!'

Peeved by his attitude, which even now questioned her

suitability as a mother, she had to bite back the desire to tell him to mind his own business as she plastered on a smile and called out to Daisy, 'Come here, poppet! There's somebody I want you to meet.'

Grabbing her hippopotamus, the little girl ran up to them.

'Do you remember…Mr Ryder?' Sienna queried after some hesitation. For some reason *Uncle Conan* didn't spring easily to her lips—which was crazy, she realised, because that was who he was.

The little girl gazed coyly up at him, her hazel eyes studying him with a seriousness way beyond her years. Eventually she asked, 'Are you my daddy?' and something squeezed painfully around Sienna's heart.

Daisy had never known Niall—not properly anyway. And she certainly couldn't remember him. So wasn't it an obvious mistake for her to imagine that Conan might be her father?

Dropping to his haunches, Conan gazed—transfixed—at the little girl who was studying him so intently, and something ripped through him, taking his breath away.

It was Niall at four years old! Niall with his shock of bright hair and his sturdy little body and his frowning bewilderment at the world as he'd looked to him—his older brother—for answers…

The feeling in his chest was almost suffocating. Somehow, though, he recovered himself enough to respond to her question about being her father. 'No, Daisy, I'm not,' he murmured huskily.

Had she imagined that crack in his voice? Sienna wondered, noticing how long and tanned and utterly masculine his hands were as they clasped the tiny arms, although he stopped short of actually catching Daisy to him. But she *was* his late brother's child, and for the first time it struck Sienna just how much pain the separation between her and Niall's family might have caused them—all of them. It was something far too uncomfortable to dwell on.

'This is Daddy's brother. Your Uncle Conan. Do you remember me telling you about the little holiday we're going on today?' Daisy's shining curls caught the sunlight as she nodded zealously. 'He's come to take us back with him to see your grandmother.'

Daisy looked quickly across at the dog, which hadn't come running up to this disapproving stranger as he had the last time, but was keeping at a very safe distance today. 'And Shadow?'

'And Shadow,' Sienna echoed firmly, with a challenging lift of her chin towards Niall's brother. So he didn't like her dog? Well, too bad! Perhaps if she was lucky she could get Shadow to slobber all over him and shed hairs over the back seat of his stupendously expensive car!

'What about Hippo? Can I take him too?'

'Of course you can,' Sienna said warmly. Slicing a glance down at Conan's gleaming black hair, she wondered what he was thinking when his interest shifted from his niece to the rather worn and faded toy she was clutching.

Had he remembered *he* had bought it, for Daisy's first birthday? she wondered. And that with it he had brought a remarkably expensive bottle of champagne? A gift for her and Niall because it was their second wedding anniversary. Niall had telephoned only minutes before and apologised for not being able to get home early as promised for Daisy's birthday, without a word about their own celebration. She recalled feeling stupidly hurt, thinking how strange it was that Conan had remembered when his brother hadn't. But then Niall had had a lot on his mind, had been working hard for his little family. And he'd fallen over himself with remorse when he had come home just after midnight and seen the bottle of champagne that Conan had left. He'd made it up to her the next day with chocolates and flowers, promising never—*ever*—to forget again...

Battling with the turmoil of emotions going on inside her, she saw Conan's mouth compress in brief recognition of the gift he had given his niece. But then his hands dropped away from the little girl and, getting to his feet again, towering above them both, he said with a coldness that seemed to leave him untouched, 'Well? Are we ready to go?'

CHAPTER THREE

FROM luxury saloon to private jet, to the equally luxurious chauffeur-driven car that had been waiting for them at the airport, the journey to Provence had been as smooth and as hassle-free as only the journeys of men as mega-rich as Conan Ryder could be. A discreet cabin crew had catered for their every need while Conan worked on his laptop in a separate compartment of the plane, keeping Sienna topped up with refreshments and occupying Daisy with games and the odd edible treat. Even Shadow had slept most of the way, in the large, comfortable carrier provided for the purpose, oblivious to the fact that he was being whisked thousands of feet up over a glittering body of water, and down across vast swathes of unfenced and sunlit fields.

Now, with the concrete and the crowds of the bustling mainland coast behind them, they were travelling across wild and isolated land jutting out into a sparkling sea.

It was another world, Sienna thought, gazing at the tall pine trees that defined the landscape and concealed exclusive walled mansions from prying eyes. A world far removed from the one she knew. A billionaire's retreat.

As the car slowed to pass through electrically operated gates into the lush, meandering grounds of Conan's hideaway, Sienna gulped back a gasp. What she was looking at was no less than magnificent. A huge white modern terracotta-roofed villa built on various levels, with a profusion of flower draped balconies, balustrades and floor to ceiling windows enjoying dramatic views of the rocky coast above which they were perched, of looming mountains and a breath-catching expanse of azure water.

Conan was sitting in the front of the car, conversing with his driver in amazingly fluent French, and had said very little to her since leaving the airport.

Viewing his dark and striking profile with the same mixture of wonder and appreciation with which she would view a classical marble statue as he turned and laughed at something the chauffeur had said, she resolved never to let him see just how overwhelmed she was by his wealth and his dauntingly impressive house—or by him!

Sitting immediately behind him, however, little Daisy had no such qualms.

As the car drew to a standstill at the end of the long drive, she exclaimed excitedly, 'Is this where we're going to live?'

'Yes, Daisy.' Conan's voice was decisive, causing Sienna to look at him quickly with a little trickle of unease.

'For ever and ever?'

Ignoring her mother's questioning glare—deliberately, Sienna felt—Conan laughed rather menacingly, she thought. 'I think even you would tire of such delightful surroundings eventually.'

'No, I wouldn't,' the little girl lobbed back, certain of it. And if that conversation wasn't enough to unsettle Sienna, then her daughter's continuing enthusiasm made sure of it as Daisy asked her uncle, 'Are you going to live with us too?'

Trying to reject the unwelcome connotations inspired by that innocent enough question, as Conan's glance sliced across hers with something mocking in those green-gold eyes, she uttered quickly for his as well as her daughter's benefit, 'It's just a holiday, Daisy. Just for a few weeks. That's all.'

Something firmed the hard line of that sculpted masculine mouth, but the arrival of a couple of male members of staff to deal with their bags and let a grateful Shadow out of the back of the car precluded whatever he had been about to say.

Out of the car before Conan could come round to assist her, Sienna moved to catch Daisy's hand to stop her running on ahead. Or perhaps, subconsciously, she needed the little girl's support as much as her daughter usually needed hers, Sienna thought self-deprecatingly, nervous at suddenly finding herself on this unfamiliar, unfriendly, exclusively Ryder territory.

Surprisingly, though, Daisy made a small protest and tugged away from her, causing something not unlike resentment to rush up inside Sienna as the little girl ran over to grasp Conan's hand.

This unexpected action caught Conan totally unawares. With a sharp intake of breath that caused his chest to rise beneath the tailored shirt and his wide shoulders to stiffen, he glanced down at the little face beaming up at him, a blend of surprise and resistance coursing through his long, lean body.

'And to what do I owe this pleasure?' he asked the little girl.

Suddenly not sure of what to make of this tall, inflexible stranger, Daisy lost her courage, letting go of his hand. It still didn't deter her from skipping along beside him, or from shrugging off her mother's hand as it shot out to restrain her.

'Get used to it, Sienna,' Conan advised, quietly so that none of the others could hear. 'You've had her to yourself long enough, and now you're going to have to accept that she has other family she needs to get to know and spend time with. And if you can manage to curb your tongue with my mother while you're here you'll be doing us all a favour. As I've already explained, she's very unwell.'

Peeved by his smug and condescending attitude, itching to remind him that it was *she* who had been on the receiving end of Avril Ryder's disdain and disparaging remarks in the past, Sienna decided it wouldn't help to promote good relations between them and considered it best to remain silent.

Ignoring him, she called to Shadow, who was already sniffing his way round one of the marble pillars at the top of the steps, and was relieved when the dog bounded down to her at once.

There was solace to be found in ruffling his fur, Sienna decided, speaking soothingly to the animal as she attached a lead to his red tartan collar.

A member of staff took the dog as soon as they entered the house, and Sienna had the disconcerting feeling that she was relinquishing all her power to Conan Ryder.

'Don't worry. He'll be adequately catered for,' he assured her evenly, wise to her silent objection.

'But will he be *cared* for?' Sienna argued in protest. 'He was ill treated before he was rescued and needs special handling. He likes tea, and the odd bowl of tomato soup, and he always sleeps on my bed because he doesn't like being left in the dark.'

'Give me strength…' Those dark fringed eyes rolled skyward. 'He's a *dog,*' Conan reminded her, sounding exasperated.

So are you. She mouthed it at him with a scowl, across Daisy's bouncing curls, not wanting anyone else to witness what she knew was a very childish retaliation. But Conan Ryder was as hard and impervious to human frailty as his brother had always led her to believe he was—as she had witnessed herself in his treatment of his younger sibling. So what chance did a mere animal have against so much indifference and superiority?

A young maid called Claudette showed her and Daisy to their rooms on the first floor. Each had its own luxurious bathroom, and both bedrooms reflected more of what Sienna had seen so far of the villa's décor. Light, airy and spacious, with tasteful and predominantly white furniture, Daisy's room was smaller, and had touches of pink in its floral bedspread and at the windows. Sienna couldn't help thinking it had been chosen especially for her. The room was also just a step away from Sienna's across the wide landing.

Conan was waiting for them in the marble-floored hall

when they came back downstairs a short time later, and Daisy ran to him at once, just as she had outside.

For a moment, with that determined little hand clutching his, Conan felt the same surge of resistance as he had experienced before—like a barrier slamming down on his emotions. But the little girl was giggling up at him, as though defying him to try and frighten her off again, and, yielding a little, he allowed her merely a glimmer of a smile before casting an inscrutable glance towards Sienna.

Was that triumph in his eyes? she wondered. Because while he seemed not to overly welcome his niece's attention, she felt that after what he had said outside he was putting up with it simply to needle her.

His scrutiny, though, was causing her pulses to leap-frog.

Now, tingling from the way his gaze ran over her freshly brushed hair and the golden slope of her shoulders beneath her sundress, Sienna stepped out of the beautiful house onto a sun terrace above a garden that tumbled down to the rocky shoreline and the restless sea.

Avril Ryder was propped up on a recliner in the canopied shade of the terrace, a flower-draped pergola behind her filling the air with some exotic scent. A creamy throw over her legs, she looked thinner, Sienna decided, her hair greyer than she remembered beneath a wide-brimmed floppy hat.

'Oh, there you are!' Her smile for Conan faded as her gaze shifted to Sienna, her eyes keenly assessing behind tinted lenses. Without a word to her former daughter-in-law, however, she turned her attention to Daisy, still clutching the man's hand. 'At last!' The transformation in the woman's face was like the sun coming out after a long hard winter. Her smile was warm and genuine, lending a glimmer of life to the otherwise waxen face. 'Come here, child. Let me see you.'

Daisy ran to her without hesitation and let the painfully thin arms engulf her. Too thin, Sienna decided, silently shocked at Niall's mother's appearance. No wonder Conan was worried about her, she thought, aware now that he must be far more concerned than he was letting on.

Impassively, however, she murmured, 'This is your grandmother, Daisy.'

Looking up at the pale and weary-looking face, Daisy giggled and asked, 'Why are you wearing that funny hat?'

Sienna bit the inside of her lip, expecting the pale lips to tighten as she had seen them do so often in the past. But instead they were curving in a soft smile. 'To keep the sun off my head. It doesn't look all that pretty, does it? But it does its job.'

Sienna watched Daisy digest this for a moment. 'Are you really going to be my grandmother?' she enquired. 'I've always wanted two. My friend Zoe has two. Are you going to take me to the beach like my Aunty Nanny?'

Sienna could have sworn there were tears in the shaded eyes that had suddenly turned her way.

'It's what she calls Mum,' she explained simply with a little shrug. At forty-eight, Faith Swann considered herself far too young to be called a grandmother.

'And you, Sienna…?' A bony hand was stroking the soft tumble of Daisy's curls, those tired eyes continually returning to the child's face as though they couldn't get enough of what they were seeing. A shaft of pain sliced viciously through Sienna as she wondered if her mother-in-law had noticed Daisy's likeness to her lost son. 'How have you been?'

Sienna's response was tentative. 'I'm fine.' This was hardly the same woman who had made her constantly aware that she wasn't good enough for Niall—who had ultimately blamed her for what had happened to her younger son.

'I think we should leave them for a little while, don't you?' Sienna stiffened at the firm, masculine hand around her elbow, and caught Conan's reprimand, low and lethally soft against her ear.

'You can't possibly object?'

She couldn't tell him that her reluctance sprang from spending any more time than she had to alone with *him*.

'No,' she said tensely. 'I don't object.'

'Good.' The eyes that roamed speculatively across her face told her that the small inflexion in her voice hadn't escaped him. He gestured for her to precede him through the pergola along the pale stonework of a shrub-bordered, sun-baked path.

'I didn't realise your mother was so…unwell,' she said hesitantly, concerned. 'Unwell' seemed far too moderate a word to describe Avril Ryder's appearance. 'Is she going to be all right?'

'I sincerely hope so.' The skin was drawn tightly over Conan's hard-boned cheeks and Sienna realised he *was* far more worried than he was letting on.

'Perhaps having Daisy here will help?' she offered, feeling that same tug of remorse over having denied Niall's family the right to see his daughter.

'Yes.' The single syllable seemed dragged through Conan's clenched teeth. It was clear he was thinking along the same lines, she thought, feeling chastened. 'And you, Sienna. What have you been doing for the past three years?'

A slim shoulder lifted slightly beneath her floral print sundress—a cool blend of white and soft blues and greens, teamed that morning with a green lacy cropped bolero, which she had discarded as soon as they had stepped off the plane.

'This and that. Training for my diplomas and the rest of my gym qualifications. Visiting Mum and Dad.'

'In Spain.'

It wasn't a question, she was quick to realise. He had obviously been informed. It was just another black mark against her in the Ryder family's eyes, she'd always felt. That she was the daughter of a mere carpenter, who had sold up everything he had to go and run a wine bar for British ex-patriots with his wife on the Costa del Sol!

'And what about the man whose flat you were sharing the night your husband died?' His tone had turned as hard as the earth they were skirting on either side of the path, where an endless profusion of white roses made her almost heady with their fragrance. 'How long did *he* stay in the picture?'

'I'd rather not discuss it, if you don't mind,' she responded, turning away.

Her profile, he noticed, was proud and challenging, yet insufferably alluring. He felt that stirring in his blood, that primal desire he had always recognised for his late brother's wife, and always violently rejected with every bone in his body.

'I bet you wouldn't!'

Sienna's expression as she looked his way again was almost careless, her pink creamy lips set in a sexy pout. He had the almost unbearable urge to crush them beneath his, to feel her body stir as his was stirring—and the evidence would be apparent if he carried on thinking like this! he thought censoriously.

She gave a little shrug, nonchalant and dismissive, as though her actions in the past were of no consequence whatsoever. That action caused the strap of her dress suddenly to slip off her shoulder. Its bareness was provocative, like pale silk begging for his touch.

Sienna reached for the fallen strap, sucking in her breath as Conan did the same, getting to it before she could and slipping it back on her shoulder.

'Thank you,' she murmured, breathless from the shocking electrical impulses zinging through her at the merest touch of his hand.

'When did you have that done?' He meant her tattoo, and his voice was cool, composed, holding none of the turmoil that was going on inside her.

'On my eighteenth birthday.'

Something tugged at his mouth. 'Before you knew better.'

She ignored that statement, because that's what it was. Her tattoo was just another thing he didn't like about her, she realised, telling herself quite adamantly that she didn't care.

'Daisy has a lot of energy,' she expressed, wanting to get away from him and his flower-filled garden, finding both disturbing with her troubling awareness of his far too unsettling proximity. 'Do you think that leaving her with Avril for too long is a good idea?'

They had stopped on the path. 'For my mother's welfare?' From beneath his dark lashes he regarded her with a contemplative amusement. 'Or for yours, Sienna?'

Her throat going dry, she swallowed. Goodness! The man was perceptive!

'Why should I be concerned for *my* welfare?' she bluffed, her heart rate quickening, pretending not to understand as she sent a glance seawards to where a flotilla of sailboats sported their jaunty colours as they skirted the peninsula.

'Why are you always so jittery when you're alone with me?'

'I'm not jittery.' Who was she kidding? 'Why should it make me jittery being alone with you?'

'You tell me.'

The warmth of the sun on her skin was a sensuality she could well have done without, and the hum of Mediterranean insects only emphasised the pregnant silence between them.

'Is it because I'm the only one who knows your secret, Sienna?'

She looked at him quickly, her eyes hooded and wary. 'My secret?'

Her tone, Conan noted, was tinged with alarm. What else had she been hiding for those two and a half years she'd been married to his brother?

'The only one who knows the kind of girl you really are,' he elaborated.

'You *think* you know. *Knew,*' she corrected emphatically.

He laughed softly. 'Whose so-called "shopping trips" to London and all those wanderings around museums were just a smokescreen for an illicit affair.'

About to deny it strongly, she felt the significance of what he'd meant when he said he was the only one who knew suddenly dawn on her, so that unthinkingly she asked, 'You didn't tell your mother about your suspicions?' She found that amazing. 'You surprise me, Conan.' She would have thought he wouldn't miss a chance to tell Avril exactly what he believed he'd discovered.

'And break her heart more than it was broken already to find that her son's wife was cheating on him? Don't you think she was devastated enough?'

Emotionlessly, because she would never give Niall's brother the satisfaction of knowing how much she had been through herself, she uttered, 'Your discretion becomes you.'

'Which is more than could be said for your morals.'

'Yes, well...' Heated colour crept across her cheeks. 'That was what you wanted to believe. You wouldn't listen to anything I said when I tried to explain.'

'That you and this Timothy Leicester were just good friends?' He laughed again, more harshly this time. 'It's a worn-out cliché.'

'No, we were more—much more than that, Conan.' Her gaze glanced across his, hard and defiant. She recognised from the rigidity of his jaw the danger that lay in provoking him, and yet it was a danger unlike any she had known before...

It would be sheer folly to antagonise him, or to deliberately fuel his hostility towards her, and so she burst out truthfully, 'I was never unfaithful to Niall. I loved him!' It was wrung from the anguished depths of her heart.

'You'll forgive me if I don't wholly acknowledge the authenticity of that statement. After all, we both know your capacity for telling lies.' They were walking again, and with a courtesy that was incongruous with the harshness of his words he stopped to lift a low branch of oleander that was growing over the path, its stems heavy with pink blossoms, their sultry scent impinging on the air.

Sienna moved under it and felt her hair lightly brush his arm. The contact was unwelcome, unwanted and electrifying.

'Which brings me to the other reason.'

'Other reason?' She dragged her gaze from the blue water of a pool she had spotted on another level of the garden, glancing warily up at him as he let the branch go and fell into step beside her. 'For what?'

'For why you've always made every excuse under the sun to limit the time you spend alone with me.'

Had she? She hadn't been conscious of it.

Heart beating erratically, she responded, 'Simple. I just don't like your company.'

'That goes without saying. But it isn't just my company that disturbs you, is it, Sienna?'

What was it then? she wondered, glancing out at the last of the sailboats that were still within her vision on the sparkling water. Because she wasn't sure. Even when she'd been married to his brother Conan had disturbed her beyond belief. It was that raw animal energy that positively crackled from him that she found so unsettling, even without the dark enigma of his character, or the penetrating green-gold of eyes that seemed to strip her of her every secret—along with her floundering self-confidence—on those few occasions that she had come in contact with him. Eyes that assessed, judged and unhinged her so much that she was always glad to escape.

His ability to unsettle her, she realised despairingly, had only intensified with the years. But now, striving for equanimity, she murmured, 'I really don't know what you're talking about.'

'Don't you?' His smile was feral. 'Oh, I think you do.'

She wasn't sure when they had stopped walking, but now she felt the snare of those glacial green-gold eyes holding her as though in an invisible trap.

'I'm talking about sex, Sienna.'

With her heart suddenly hammering against her ribcage, she echoed, 'Sex?' She uttered a brittle little laugh. 'With you?' Her mouth contorted at the concept of such an idea, masking the furore of wild sensations going on inside her.

Conan's lips moved wryly, mocking, unperturbed. 'Well,

I wouldn't have put it quite so graphically as that,' he stated, watching the colour rise in her cheeks and seeming to relish every ounce of her discomfiture. 'I was talking chemistry—unlikely though I know that seems. But then since when did physical attraction ever have anything to do with *liking* the object of one's attraction, or even respecting them for that matter? And I know your respect for me is about as low on the scale of one to a thousand as mine is for you.'

'That makes it all right, then, doesn't it?' she snapped. 'I often get my kicks out of shacking up with men I can't stand the sight of!'

'Or with those who keep you in enough luxury to buy your affection until you find more interesting diversions elsewhere.'

'Like I did with Niall, I suppose?' she jibed.

'You might think it's something to hold up as a trophy, Sienna, but I don't. My brother was besotted with you.'

'Yes,' she acknowledged, closing her eyes, clenching her teeth against the well of emotion that threatened to engulf her, the unshed tears that were locked inside her and seemed doomed never to know the mercy of release.

Niall *had* been besotted. Adoring. Almost obsessive in his love for her, so that sometimes she'd felt stifled by the possessiveness that had sprung from his insecurities. She'd been someone to flaunt. To show off. To place on a pedestal so high that sometimes she'd been frightened of toppling off. And sometimes she'd felt—to use Conan's own words—like a trophy, a feather in Niall's cap to parade over the man he'd most wanted to impress: his richer, harder-headed and far more successful older brother.

As he watched the emotions that chased across her face, a groove deepened between Conan's thick eyebrows. Was she telling him the truth? Had she ever really loved his brother? Was that what was tormenting her? Plain and simple guilt? Or was it something else altogether?

'Remorse, Sienna?' He reached out and slid a hand around

the nape of her neck. He heard her breath catch, felt her body stiffen, the pulse beneath his fingers beating a frenzied rhythm.

'What are you hoping?' To her own ears she sounded afraid, and her breathlessness was betraying to him that it was herself she was afraid of, the sensations that were ripping through her just from the touch of those cool fingers on her heated skin. 'That I'll fall for you so you can dump me? Because that's about as likely as one of our spacecraft finding life on Mars tomorrow night!'

Way off in the distance the buzz of a speedboat encroached on the peaceful garden. Closer to hand, a gentle breeze played among the spiky leaves of the oleander tree.

'I've always lived by the premise that's anything's likely.' A complacent smile touched his lips. 'And we both know you weren't impervious to me even with two other lovers in the picture—don't we, Sienna?'

Fear clouded her eyes. 'You read it all wrong!'

'Did I?'

He was referring to the firm's dinner-dance that she had attended with Niall. Niall had been drinking with clients at the bar, trying to tie down a deal. Conan had come over to the table where she had been sitting alone and asked her to dance—just out of courtesy, she'd guessed.

In a dark evening suit, white winged collar shirt and bow tie, he'd looked particularly spectacular—hard and confident and sophisticated—and he'd had the air about him of a man you couldn't say no to—as he always had in his private life as well as in business.

She remembered the feel of that impeccably clad arm going around her as they'd taken to the floor. The way every nerve in her body had seemed to tense like a tuned up violin as his hand burned through the flimsy red fabric of her dress.

'The telltale flush on those beautiful cheeks...' Conan's words as he remembered shook Sienna back to the present. They seemed to have given him licence to trace the fine structure of her face. His fingers were long and skilful and she couldn't seem to stop him, held in thrall by a sensuality that was as dangerous as it was thrilling as he continued reminiscing. 'The dilated pupils. That nervous stammer that sprang from between those alluring and very provocative lips.'

I felt awkward with you! Embarrassed! But there was a reason for it! There was a reason for everything I did!

But she couldn't tell him that.

Don't tell anyone! For a fleeting moment the words echoed through her brain—anguished and imploring. *Promise me you'll never tell anyone! Especially Conan!*

She felt straitjacketed by her emotions—just as she had then. But she had made a promise and she would never renege on that promise, she thought bitterly. Not now. Not ever.

Facing the censuring clarity of that glittering gold gaze, she said with a forced air of resignation, 'Well, there you have me! It seems you were irresistible, doesn't it, Conan? But not any more.'

He laughed softly as he lifted her chin with a curved forefinger, noting the way her breath shivered through her nostrils before his gaze rested on the trembling lashes that half veiled the darkening blue of her eyes. 'No?' he murmured silkily.

'Aren't you worried I might try to *bleed you dry?*' she emphasised, taunting him with it, pulling back from him on legs that felt so much like jelly she was wondering how much longer they could hold her.

He merely laughed again, and said, 'You couldn't bleed me dry.'

Of course. He had far too many millions for that.

A deep bark followed by a childlike squeal of laughter filtered down from the terrace above them. To Sienna it was a welcome reprieve.

'Go and make yourself at home. Settle in,' Conan advised with a jerk of his chin towards where the sounds were coming from. 'But remember…you're playing a dangerous game,

Sienna. You won't find me half so much of a push-over as my brother.'

She almost ran from him, back along the path, eager only for the safe, simple demands of Daisy and Shadow.

CHAPTER FOUR

CONAN looked up from the laptop and out of his study window, relinquishing his interest in the spreadsheet he was updating in favour of the more interesting scene by the pool.

In a skimpy white crop-top and shorts, Sienna was engaged in a workout. Daisy was crayoning in a sketchbook on the marble tiles in the shade of the sun-umbrella above the table just behind her. The hairy mutt, he noted with a derogatory grimace, was lounging nearby.

His niece was stocky, like her father, he decided, some uninvited emotion softening the firm line of his mouth. She wouldn't ever inherit her mother's petite figure, but she was a well-behaved and pleasant child, he'd observed since their arrival two days ago, and if she lacked any sort of maternal control then it certainly wasn't evident.

Which was one point in her mother's favour if nothing else, he acknowledged rather reluctantly, surprised by the way just the thought of another sparring session with his brother's unscrupulous little widow could kick his libido into life, sending a burning ache down through the centre of his hardening anatomy.

Or was it just the way she was moving with those weights strapped to her ankles? Her slim, beautifully shaped legs lifting independently, her small breasts accentuated, as she lay with her hands behind her head, face turned upwards to the sun?

At that moment the little girl ran up to her. He watched

Sienna sit up, saw her smile as she pushed the hair out of the child's eyes. The tender action reminded him of those times on the periphery of his memory with his own mother, when there had been just the two of them—before everything had changed after Avril had married his stepfather and then given birth to Niall. He had learned to harden himself against moments like these—against those early memories—and he did it now, saving the data on his laptop and closing down the program he had been using.

Whether he was happy about it or not, he thought, Sienna was his guest, and relations between her and his mother had been strained to say the least since he had brought her back with him. That was probably why she had chosen to come out to the pool area now, while Avril was up in her room taking a nap. She had definitely been going out of her way to avoid too much contact with his mother, with the result that she was spending far too much time alone. Something he intended to rectify as of now!

Standing with legs apart, ankle-weights substituted with hand-weights, her body angled, with her raised arm forming a perfect arc above her head, Sienna lost track of the seconds she'd been maintaining the position as Conan appeared, coming across the terrace in a white linen shirt and pale chinos.

His masculinity was glaringly evident in the corded strength of his throat above the open 'V' of his collar and in the larger 'V' of dark body hair shading his chest beneath his shirt. His chinos were fitted enough to reveal the narrow-hipped strength of his lower body, and the taut musculature of his thighs. His feet were thrust into backless leather mules, as fit and tanned and virile as the rest of him.

Spotting him, Daisy scrambled to her feet, already running up to him with her colouring book.

His reluctant smile for the little girl made Sienna's stomach twinge with something indefinable before he squatted down on his haunches to look at the picture his niece was showing him. She caught his soft words of praise—not gushing, but understatedly genuine—before he said something else more quietly that had the little girl darting off in the direction of the house.

'Take the dog with you, Daisy,' his deep voice instructed, and an obedient click of her tongue had Shadow leaping up and bounding after her.

Sienna straightened from the exercise she'd been doing with her hand-weights, letting both her arms hang at her sides. Her heart rate was usually up a bit after she'd finished a workout, she realised, but the sight of Conan had her blood pounding as though she'd been running hard.

'Does everyone do what you tell them to?'

His smile was wry. 'Usually.'

She didn't doubt it—especially those who were on his sub-stantial payroll. He was the type of man for whom waiters and porters materialised like genies, while others, like Daisy and Shadow, vanished at will.

'I thought you were working? Avril said you were working at home today.'

Did he think she was gabbling? She certainly sounded as though she was.

'I was,' he said, coming closer. And when she could only stand and look at him, rooted to the spot by the breath-catching spell of his very aura, he added, 'I saw you from my study. I decided the time had come not to have you spending so much time on your own.'

She smiled a rather nervous smile. 'Did you bribe Daisy with some particular treat to get her out of the way?'

He made another wry movement with his mouth. 'Now, what on earth makes you think that?'

'I think you could bribe your way out of anything you wanted to.'

He laughed—a warm, deep sound that had her reminding herself of how ruthless he was when she realised she was in danger of forgetting it. 'I simply told her that Claudette has taken some pastries up to my mother, and that Avril has asked Daisy to join her.'

'That's nice,' Sienna expressed, glad at least that her daughter was forming a bond with her new grandmother, even if *she* wasn't.

Those slow strides brought him nearer, and Sienna's breath caught almost audibly in her lungs.

'May I?'

She handed him the moderate weights she was still clutching in her tense fingers, watching him assess their poundage, weighing them both together in one tanned and strikingly tapered hand.

Crazily, for a moment she considered those hands making a calculated assessment of her body, feeling, touching, moulding...

Shocked by the disturbing imagery, mentally she shook it away. 'I'm not hoping to be Mr Universe,' she elucidated, a little more sharply than she had intended when she saw his mouth twist almost mockingly. 'Just to keep myself toned up.' Perhaps he considered those weights light, but then in those strong brown hands four times as much probably would be! she thought, shaken by her wayward thoughts about him.

'I should hope not.' She could feel his gaze travelling down over her figure where a moment ago she had imagined his hands travelling the same path. 'You're perfectly acceptable as you are.'

Wishing she'd worn a bra, with a rush of colour to her cheeks she felt the betraying thrust of her breasts against the stretchy fabric of her top.

'The last time I saw you at a poolside you were wearing a swimsuit from Dior,' he reminded her, concluding his disconcerting survey of her body. 'And you were positively dripping with gold.'

Gold she had sold—along with all her other jewellery, her fast car, and the rest of the things he obviously believed she'd cared about! she thought bitterly. To pay off the debts she'd been left with after Niall had died.

'That wasn't me!'

'Wasn't it?' He laughed again, not so warmly this time, the sinews working in his strong throat. 'I'd recognise that figure anywhere—although I'd agree that nowadays you're certainly...fully toned.'

His scrutiny of her was electrifying, moving as it did with slow deliberation over the golden slopes of her shoulders, touching on the firm, yet willowy arms, and coming to rest with appreciative male satisfaction on the betraying fullness of her breasts.

'I mean it wasn't...' How could she explain to him how ostentatious she'd found that jewellery? How she'd worn it merely to please Niall, because he had bought it for her? And that the extortionately pricey swimsuit hadn't been something she would even have dreamt of buying for herself—let alone considered wearing! That she'd only been persuaded to after Niall had presented her with it as a substitute for the plainer, less tantalising one she'd chosen herself from her favourite high street store? 'I was a different person then, Conan,' she said tonelessly, with a dryness creeping up her throat. 'We all were.'

His sensuous mouth moved in contemplation before he laid the weights down with that casual grace of his on one of the glass poolside tables.

'Were we?' he remarked, turning his full attention back to her again. 'Does a leopard ever change its spots?'

'No, apparently not!' she flung back at him, hurting and angry, because there was no way that he would ever change his opinion of her. His prejudices were set in stone! 'I'm not staying here talking to you when you only came out here to try and antagonise me!'

She made to move past him, but the table was blocking her way on one side, and as she moved to go around the other he side-stepped, so that she couldn't pass without the risk of falling into the pool.

His hands were raised palm-outwards in defence against her verbal attack. 'Believe me—that wasn't my intention.'

'Wasn't it?' Hot colour stained her cheeks. Her eyes, in contrast, were dark and accusing. 'You wouldn't miss a trick in trying to have a go at me. You might think I'm guilty of sleeping around during my marriage, but at least I wasn't the one lusting after my brother's wife!'

Her words seemed to stun him rigid.

Feeling the waves of condemnation burning from him, and already regretting her rash remark, Sienna darted a glance around for the quickest means of escape.

'Would you mind repeating that statement?' he rasped, in a dangerously low voice.

Yes, I would! she thought hectically, wishing she could retract it. And, shamed into flight—desperate to get away from him—she turned and plunged headlong into the pool.

She had only swum a few metres when she heard the deep splash behind her, felt herself being rocked by the displacement of water, and realised with a small gasp of alarmed amazement that Conan was giving chase—fully clothed!

She did a blazing front-crawl to the other side of the pool, reaching it with a determined grab for the tiled edge. But with a small gasp of dismay she heard Conan coming up behind her, felt a strong, determined hand pulling her round.

For endless pulsing moments they glared angrily at each other, the sun beating down a relentless observer, striking bronze from the transparency of Conan's shirt where it now clung to his skin, burning across Sienna, though not as much as she was burning inside.

She had never seen him look so wild or so untameable, and she didn't know what galvanised her into what happened next. But as his curiously ravaged face dipped low she was lifting hers to meet it, their angry passion given rein in a mutually antagonised kiss.

Conan didn't know what he had been intending to do when he'd come after her, but this, he realised, plundering her soft eager mouth, was the only ultimate outcome. Maybe her words had struck a raw chord in him because of his long denial of his body's uncontrolled response to her. The wanting he had never allowed himself to entertain even when he had been shocked into realising how nervous she was in his arms during that dance that night, and how he obviously affected her. Even if she refused to acknowledge it, he thought grimly. But there was no need for denial or for any reservations now.

As he shifted his arm to pull her into the rock-hard length of his body Sienna made a guttural sound deep in her throat, clawing at the warm wetness of his rippling back with desperate and greedy hands.

She hated the man, and yet...

Driven by desire, and the intensity of a passion such as she had never known before, she gave in to its demands, letting her trembling hands slide up to tangle in the soaked black thickness of his hair, responding to that hungry, insistent masculine mouth with unrelenting demands of her own.

Oh! Dear heaven... She gave a tortured groan—a low, anguished sound from deep inside her. She wanted more than this! She wanted all the things she had been imagining with him, which were responsible for the self-degradation that had had her flinging that insult at him just now. She wanted him to—

Her thoughts were driven from her mind as his hands suddenly spanned her waist, lifting her up so her legs automatically moved around him.

Supporting her with his arm, he was tilting her head back, his mouth closing over her clinging top through which her nipples were protruding in unashamed arousal. Never had she known such wanting as his actions sent red-hot spears of desire piercing down through her body, igniting a flame at the very heart of her femininity.

She could feel his own arousal, pulsing and hard, and

moved against him like a wild thing as he pulled up her top so that his hands could claim the aching fullness of her eager breasts.

Sensations coursed through her, piling one on top of the other, feeding on each other. Sensations fuelled by a desire that had been driven by anger and yet which was now exploding in a furore of feelings such as she had never known.

She had been in love with his brother; she had thought she knew everything about sexual desire. But nothing in her life or in her short-lived marriage had compared with or prepared her for the driving urgency of this pure raw lust...

Cruelly she was reminded of their earlier confrontation, and of how much Conan despised her. It made her realise that was all that this...this madness was. Lust, she thought bitterly, and she wrenched herself away from him, her feet touching bottom, her face screwed up in disgust as she pulled at her top, turning her head away, unable to face the mocking derision she knew she would see in his eyes.

'What's the matter, Sienna? Can't you look at me?' His voice was surprisingly hoarse, and he sounded as breathless as she was.

Chancing a glance at him, she noticed that his eyes were fathomlessly dark, his eyelids heavy from the heat of his desire. His mouth wasn't derisive at all. The full lower lip pulled was taut, as if he was having some inner battle for control. Beneath that tantalisingly transparent shirt she could see the way his chest was rising and falling heavily.

'I didn't intend that to happen either,' he admitted.

'Didn't you?' Remaining hostile, she decided, was the only way of saving face. How else could she explain those moments of insanity that had gripped her? That had dictated her actions? 'I would have thought your greatest wish was to see me humiliated.'

His eyes narrowed as he searched her small, indignant features. Her eyes looked like smoky sapphires, and her mouth was pink and swollen from the mutually fierce hunger that even with all his sexual experience had still left him reeling, and so hard with wanting he felt a weakness spreading along his thighs. 'Is that how you feel?'

'What do you think?' she murmured indignantly.

'I think we were both in a state of high tension and both had to let off steam,' he stated pragmatically—almost laughably so in the circumstances.

Letting off steam! Was that all he thought it was?

Well, of course. What did you want it to be? a little voice inside Sienna jeered. He was Niall's brother—Daisy's uncle. Nothing more.

'Now, if you'll excuse me...' That familiar mockery was back on Conan's lips, yet it was incongruous with the huskiness of his voice and the inscrutable expression in his eyes. 'Much as I'd like to stay and bring this pleasurable little interlude to its natural conclusion, I have to get back to work.' And that was going to test his powers of self-discipline more than seemed humanly possible, he realised. Although the alternative was to stay and have her believe what she had accused him of earlier. When he'd always rejected *any* conscious attraction towards his brother's wife. 'Besides...I've never made love to a woman in anger—' such behaviour was unpardonable and beneath him, he thought, fighting the long-buried demons that were threatening to surface '—and I don't intend to start now.'

With one thrust of those muscular arms he propelled himself effortlessly out of the pool, water cascading from his magnificent body.

As he walked away, Sienna broodingly noticed how his shirt clung wetly to his broad back, accentuating every muscle, and how his chinos had moulded themselves to his firm, hard buttocks and his powerful thighs. A sharp ache of unsated desire pierced her small, excruciatingly aroused body.

What had possessed her? And what must he think of her? she demanded of herself shamefully, watching discreetly from under her lashes as he scooped up the mules he'd obviously kicked off to give chase to her. Her behaviour must only have cemented his opinion of the type of girl he thought she was, she decided hopelessly, for all his remarks about them both needing to 'let off steam.'

He was a man very much in command of himself—and of his actions, she accepted reluctantly, grudgingly admiring the economy and grace with which he moved for a man of his height and build as he grabbed a towel from one of the sun loungers he was passing and began rubbing it casually over his hair. And a man who would consider the consequences of everything he did and said, she realised, even while she was resenting him. A man of surprising strength of character. Of principle, even. A man completely and utterly in control. And recognising that—along with what he had said just now about not making love in anger—caused a ridiculous ache in her throat.

'How have you been today?' Sienna asked, striving to be friendly as she came across her mother-in-law the following evening, on her usual shady seat on the terrace. 'How are you feeling?' She sank down onto the elegantly wrought, deeply cushioned chair beside her. Daisy was already in bed and Conan had been out for most of the day. She should have been relieved, she realised, and yet his absence was too noticeable to be pleasant.

'As good as I'm ever going to feel, I imagine,' Avril responded. 'The doctors can't seem to make up their minds as to what's wrong with me.' Even her rather resigned little shrug seemed like an effort. 'Can you credit that? Conan pays them a fortune and they can't even come up with a simple diagnosis. One says it's simply post-viral syndrome. Another one even stuck his neck out and suggested I have ME.'

'And you can't get about?' Sienna queried, sympathising. 'Or take any form of gentle exercise?' From casual comments Conan had made, Sienna knew he wanted his mother to try and get about more.

'Exercise?'

From the way she said it, Sienna thought, anyone would think she'd suggested a trip to the moon.

'That's the answer to everything nowadays, isn't it?' Avril remarked rather derisively. 'Especially with you younger generation.'

It was a conscious slight, Sienna decided, against all her years of training, and for a moment she felt as though she'd travelled back in time and was again the tentative, insecure creature she'd been, who'd often had to bite her tongue and had been made to feel like an interloper in her husband's family. Now, undeterred, and with a wealth of experience of working with both the fit and healthy and the elderly, she said, 'It's the answer to a lot of things.'

'Not in this case, Sienna—though your concern for me, I must say, is rather surprising.'

Because old hostilities were still there, she realised. And barely concealed where Avril was concerned.

'I don't like seeing anyone sick or suffering,' Sienna explained, brushing a rose petal from the loose white skirt she had teamed with a pale blue camisole. 'Especially when they can be repaired.'

The woman uttered a feeble laugh. 'I'm past repairing.'

'No, you're not,' Sienna returned decisively.

She was well aware that Conan's mother was little more than sixty-five, and couldn't help wondering if the woman's depression and mysterious debilitating illness had swayed her towards such fatalism. She also couldn't help thinking either how alike Niall and her mother-in-law were—in that way at least. Because her younger son had shown the same kind of resignation about a lot of things. Unlike Conan, Sienna realised intuitively, who would bend the world to his will if he had to. But then he was only Niall's half-brother, and had been born with a different set of genes...

'You know, you're much more confident than you were,

Sienna.' She could feel his mother studying her from behind her smoky grey lenses. 'Confident. And much more…mature.'

'I've had to be,' Sienna remarked, cringing as she recalled the optimistic young bride Niall had first brought with him into this family circle—a circle she'd fitted into as badly as the proverbial square peg!

'You didn't have to do it alone.' She meant bringing up Daisy, and Sienna felt her stomach muscles tightening. 'Conan tells me your parents are still in Spain. And yet they get to see her?' she expressed, when Sienna nodded.

When *she* hadn't. That was clearly what the other woman was saying.

'I'm sorry.' Sienna stared at the bright blossoms draping the flower-decked pergola, not knowing, in the circumstances, how she could have done things any other way. 'I really am.'

'There were faults on both sides,' her mother-in-law was admitting surprisingly. 'I realise that now. You were far too determined. Too strong-willed for a man like Niall. And far too young to take on the responsibilities of a wife and mother. You weren't…' Her voice tailed off, as though she'd thought better of expressing her views aloud.

'I wasn't the sort of wife you would have chosen for him?' Sienna supplied crisply, remembering this family's rejection of her a little less painfully than she once had.

'I know I might have made you feel like that.' A sigh seemed to shiver through the woman's thin frame, but all she added—as though it excused everything—was, 'He was my *son.*'

Despite everything, Sienna's heart went out to her, her lungs locking tight with emotion.

She didn't want to be discussing this—raking up the past. Her memories of that time, and of the situations she had been put into, which had helped condemn her in this family's eyes, still made her smart with the injustice of it all. And there had been none more condemning or unjust than Conan's scorching censure. But then what would *anyone* have thought of a mother who'd left her sick baby to go out partying? Without even bothering to ring up and check?

No, it was worse than that. Who had deliberately switched off her phone!

She could still see the condemnation in those green-gold eyes as he'd marched her away from that party. Still remember her desperation and panic over what might be wrong with Daisy, her futile attempts to make Niall's brother believe that her little girl had been fine when she'd left the house. To try and explain.

He hadn't listened, of course. Who would have? There had been far too much evidence against her.

Sick with self-remorse, she hadn't even been able to convince herself that she hadn't been that negligent. Not until later. Not until after her name had been reduced to mud in the Ryder family's eyes and they had notched up yet another black mark against her...

'If you'd been Conan's wife he would never have indulged you in the same way my younger son seemed to want to. He might be a very wealthy man, but he's not weak-willed and easily swayed like his brother was. I'm afraid if it had been Conan you'd chosen he'd soon have pulled you into line.'

No, he wouldn't! Sienna fumed silently. Because there had been no 'pulling into line' that had needed to be done. She was surprised though to hear Avril describe her younger son as weak. 'Then I must thank my lucky stars that that's one union you're never going to see,' she said with a forced little laugh.

'Am I missing something?' Conan's deep warm voice caused goose bumps to break out over Sienna's skin.

She hadn't seen him since he'd left to attend some business meeting that morning. Now, as he crossed the terrace to where they were sitting, wearing an impeccably cut silver grey suit, white shirt and silver tie, he looked so vital and dynamic against the backdrop of his luxury residence that the very sight of him took Sienna's breath away.

'What have you two been talking about?' he enquired smoothly.

Her nostrils dilated at the elusive spice of his aftershave lotion as he moved into their sphere, her senses filling with him, her body tingling as his gaze ran over her camisole and her feminine skirt. In spite of her fluttering pulse, and motivated by her memories of his insensitivity and by this frighteningly lethal power he seemed to have over her, she looked up into those rugged features to say pointedly, 'You.'

He was aware of the contention in her voice. It was evident in the way his mouth twisted in mocking amusement.

'For heaven's sake, Conan, take her away and do something with her!' Avril suggested, with more strength than she'd seemed capable of. 'Or she'll be having me jogging round the cape and back before I know where I am.'

'Well, that wouldn't be a bad thing, would it?' he expressed surprisingly with a wry smile at his mother—a smile that changed to one of heart-stopping sensuality as it came to rest on Sienna. 'It seems my mother's given me licence to do whatever I want with you…' The innuendo was unmistakable, and the light that flickered in the Celtic gold of his eyes as he offered her his hand burned with sensual mockery. 'So we'd better not disappoint her, had we?'

CHAPTER FIVE

IMPELLED by something stronger than her own will, she took the hand he was holding out to her. It was warm and strong and incredibly stimulating, sending a sharp *frisson* through her racing blood.

'Where are we going?' she asked, her fingers still in his as he brought her out across the front portico with its marble columns to the bright red convertible Ferrari standing on the drive.

'You'll see.'

'What about Daisy?' she asked, concerned, as he opened the passenger door for her.

'Daisy's asleep,' he assured her, surprising her with the knowledge that he must have checked up on his niece before joining her and Avril on the terrace. 'She's all right, I promise you.'

It came as quite a shock to realise that he was the only person whom she would have accepted that from without needing to check it out for herself. But why? she wondered, puzzled. When she didn't even like him? When he was the last man she would choose to be with? If she'd had a choice!

'I have to pick up some documents in Cannes,' he enlightened her as the Ferrari growled away. 'We won't be gone long, but I thought you might appreciate getting away from the house for an hour or so.'

Had he really thought that? she wondered, with an insidious warmth stealing through her—until she became aware of just how she was behaving.

Careful, she warned herself, realising that she was in grave danger of weakening towards him. As most women would, she accepted without any reservation, drawn as they were to those darkly aloof features and that uncompromising air of command mixed with that smoky sexuality of his that put every other man in the shade. But then they didn't know how unpitying he was, did they? she decided bitterly.

The air was pure and sweet as they drove through the forested hills, passing swathes of olive and citrus groves, and villages perched high above the sun-streaked sea.

'Do you come here very often?' she enquired, needing to say something because he wasn't.

'As often as I can. Long weekends. Bank holidays. But almost always for the summer.'

Breathing in the aromatic scents of wild herbs and lavender, Sienna returned, 'I can see why.' With its craggy coast, its mountains, and its interminable cypress trees piercing the dramatic blue of the sky, this landscape fitted him as if he was part of it. Unyielding. Implacable. Untamed. 'My parents always liked Spain, so we went there virtually every year,' she told him. 'Self-catering—that sort of thing. Cheap and cheerful, as Mum called it, but we had some great family holidays together.'

'That sounds good,' he remarked distractedly, making her wonder if he was just saying that. After all, what was camping on the Costa Brava compared with a billionaire's security-guarded villa in the South of France?

'What about you?' she murmured a little hesitantly, eager to know more about her late husband's brother. After all, he hadn't always been rich.

She knew he'd left home while still remarkably young, and according to Niall had had a variety of mundane and often laborious jobs until some lucky break and the right contacts had tested his entrepreneurial skills and set him on the road to where he was today. He'd made his fortune in telecommunications, she remembered, although his enterprises these days ranged from anything from technology to high finance. As a man, however, he was an enigma—he always had been—and he and Niall had been as different as wind and fire.

'What *about* me?' He was changing into a lower gear to take a winding road up the steep hillside, the action drawing Sienna's attention to his lean dark hand.

'Did you have family holidays?' she enquired, slamming down the lid on her speculation over how those strong skilled hands would know their way around a woman's body.

'Well, not quite as adventurous as yours sound,' he admitted dryly.

'Niall said you never knew your own father?' she ventured, aware that he'd been born illegitimate and that he might not want to talk about it.

'No,' he said uncommunicatively, seeming, from his curious glance in her direction, to have picked up on that rather breathy note in her voice at the turn her thoughts had taken about him.

'What about your stepfather?' She knew he had adopted Conan as his own son when Conan was four or five, and that the man had also given him his name.

'What about him?' His tone was frosty to say the least.

'Did you get on with him?'

'No.'

It was obvious from the lack of any further information that he clearly didn't like this probing into what was, after all, his very private life. And if she knew anything about Conan Ryder it was that he guarded his privacy like Fort Knox. His involvements with women, if reported upon, were done so with absolute discretion—such was the respect he seemed to generate with the world's media. And if he gave interviews— as he sometimes did—it was only ever in connection with the commercial side of his life. That was unless the paparazzi got hold of something they thought would be worth reporting and managed to photograph him unofficially—as they had at that airport with Petra Flax.

A covert glance at him through her dark lenses revealed a profile as harsh and forbidding as the cliffs above which they were driving, and the knuckles of those long tanned hands appeared white as they gripped the wheel.

With a little mental shrug Sienna delved into her skirt pocket for the cell phone she'd brought with her. 'Just checking on Daisy.' She felt the need to explain when he sent her an enquiring look, and guessed from the quizzical arching of his eyebrow what he was probably thinking. She hadn't always appeared to care so much.

It came back to her now—sharper than ever—the night Niall had telephoned, insisting she meet him at that party. A party she'd had no inclination to attend. She'd gone along for the sake of his job, leaving Daisy with their babysitter, after Niall had requested her support with some clients he was trying to close a deal with.

When Conan, with a face like a marauding Norse god, had turned up at that party a few hours later, Niall had been nowhere to be seen. Later she was to discover that he'd slipped away with his clients to a casino, leaving her to bear the brunt of Conan's pulsing anger alone.

What the hell did she think she was doing? he'd demanded. Enjoying herself regardless while her child had been taken ill and his mother and the babysitter were going half out of their wits?

She'd responded to his unrepeatable accusations as to the sort of mother he thought she was with defensive anger. Hadn't she checked her mobile at least a dozen times that evening to make sure she hadn't missed any urgent messages? No one had been more paranoid than she about leaving Daisy, and everything had been fine when she had left.

But when she'd taken her phone out of her clutch bag she'd been shocked to find it was switched off, and Conan's low opinion of her had only increased tenfold.

Later, when they were alone, Niall had admitted to her that it was he who had switched off her phone. "I just wanted you to relax," she remembered him saying, feeling a bittersweet ache for how much she had loved him—trusted him then. "You're always so wound up and worrying about her unnecessarily. And I knew I had my phone on me." He just hadn't thought when he'd left the party with those clients.

He'd bought her a pendant the next day. A golden heart on a chain with a diamond piercing its centre, virtually getting down on his knees and begging her to forgive him for showing her up in such a bad light with Conan and his mother. He'd only been thinking of her after all, she'd accepted, when all the fuss had died down. And Daisy had been all right. So she'd forgiven him. As she always had, she thought poignantly. Until that last time...

Conan's stop in Cannes was a ten-minute affair while he picked up some business papers from one of the prestigious hotels there. While he was gone, Sienna marvelled at the number of equally prestigious cars, the chic shops and the chic people who were patronising them. But the crowds along the palm-fringed promenade made her appreciate why Conan had chosen to buy a house in the peace and isolation of the peninsula, and she told him so when they were on the road again.

'I'm glad you approve,' was all he said, although she couldn't help wondering if he sounded pleased.

Because it became clear as they were driving back that he really had brought her out for no other reason than to enjoy herself, she asked, 'Why are you doing this if you despise me so much?'

Behind the dark designer lenses, his eyes didn't leave the road. 'Does there have to be a reason?'

'With you?' She stole a discreet glance at his ruggedly sculpted profile and those broad shoulders—he'd removed his jacket—and her stomach did a little flip. 'Oh yes, I think so.'

'Perhaps that incident between us in the pool the other day aroused my curiosity.'

'About what?' she croaked, thinking that that wasn't all it had aroused.

'About why a couple who—to put it a little less dramatically than you put it—don't appear to like each other should find themselves in the sort of unlikely situation we found ourselves in yesterday. Because do you know what I'd really like to do with you, Sienna?'

She had a good idea, but she didn't want to acknowledge it. Her heart was hammering and her mouth felt as dry as the Sahara. 'Put me on the first plane home?' she hedged.

'That would be the most sensible course of action to take, I agree,' he admitted. 'For both our sakes.'

'Then why don't you?'

'Because there's more than just ourselves in this to consider.'

'And if there weren't?'

'Then I'd take you home to bed and not let you out of it until we'd burned this whole crazy thing out of our systems. And do you know what's making it so hard to stop myself from doing that?'

With her pulses fluttering in response to what he had just said, she quipped unsteadily, 'No doubt you're going to tell me.'

'Knowing that you want it too.'

'Now, wait a minute...!' Confusion and embarrassment reddened her cheeks beneath the healthy lustre of her windblown hair. 'Just because we shared one kiss it doesn't mean—'

'That wasn't just a kiss.'

No, it wasn't, she thought. It was a culmination of something fuelled by hostility and resentment and which had been building with unstoppable force from the moment they had set eyes on each other again.

But, taking her silence for denial, suddenly he was pulling into a lay-by.

'What are you doing?' she challenged, her heart leaping, her throat contracting painfully as he turned off the ignition.

'What do you think I'm doing?' he murmured suggestively.

She shot him a warning glance and he laughed very softly.

'I thought you might appreciate the view,' he surprised her by saying, removing his sunglasses.

They were parked on a hilltop, with the shimmering sea below them, and it felt as though there were only the two of them in the world. It was late enough for the cicadas and lizards to have begun their evening chorus, and a late finch was chirruping in the scrubland beside the car. Affected by the sounds and scents of nature, and all the beauty around them, she found the stillness of the evening brought a painful lump to her throat.

'Why did you treat Niall so badly?' It slipped out before she could stop it, subdued yet quietly direct.

'Why did *you?*' he retorted.

She didn't answer, looking away from those harshly probing eyes towards the west, where the sun was turning the sky from brilliant gold to fiery red. What would it matter what she told him now? His brother was dead, and there were some things that couldn't be changed no matter what was said.

'Do I take it from your silence that you're admitting to that affair at last?'

Her head pivoted to face him. 'No!'

That cynical curl to his mouth told her he didn't believe her. 'Did you realise Niall was aware of it, Sienna?'

Watching the shadows that flitted across her face, Conan couldn't help thinking that she seemed shaken by his disclosure. In fact she looked positively shattered by it, he thought, surprised. But then what wife who had just found out that her husband had known about her extra-marital relationship wouldn't? he thought scornfully.

'He couldn't have been. I mean…there was nothing to be aware of,' Sienna uttered, bemused. And, as it dawned on her just what Conan was saying, 'You mean…he was the one who told you…?'

She couldn't go on. She felt hurt, bewildered—devastated.

She'd known that Niall had been insecure. Possessive. Even unsure of her. But not to the degree that he'd have expressed his concerns to anyone else...

'Why would he have had reason to suspect you if it wasn't true?'

His brother's flaying demand shook her out of the numbing shock of what she had just learned.

'Because just like you he wouldn't accept that a man I cared about could be anything other than romantically involved with me,' she flung at him bitterly.

'A man you cared about?' he underscored derogatorily, a black winged eyebrow climbing his forehead.

'Make of it what you will!' she snapped, folding her arms and clutching her elbows tight in a totally defensive gesture against all he was saying.

'My brother obviously did.' Conan was giving her no quarter. 'Did you even realise how crazy he was about you?'

'Yes.'

'And what was wrong with that, Sienna? Does a man's loving you make him somehow less of a man in your eyes?'

'Of course not!'

'Just an inconvenience, then?'

'No!'

'Then what were you doing that morning in another man's flat—especially one you *cared* about—' his tone was censuring '—if you weren't having an affair?'

Relaxing her arms a little, she said pointedly, 'Would you believe just visiting him?'

Harsh scepticism touched his mouth. 'I might if it hadn't been so obvious that you'd been sleeping there. Or if you hadn't been so ready to lie to your husband about where you were going every time you went "shopping" for the day, dragging your toddler along with you to witness your illicit little affair. So why did you—*if* you're as innocent as you say you were? Answer me that.'

She couldn't. Even now, hurting as she was from his brother's suspicions, the reason why she had been with Timothy Leicester that night stayed locked inside her, incriminating her, giving her no leeway to explain herself—just as it had then, three years ago. But at least she could try to defend herself against something.

'I lied because I couldn't mention Tim's name without Niall getting unnecessarily upset,' she supplied, admitting that much at least.

'And you find that surprising?' Incredulity marked features bathed bronze in the evening sun. 'In the world I inhabit — and I think most conventional couples—the presence of an old boyfriend on the scene would spark off the same reaction in anyone who happened to be the slighted partner.'

'He wasn't slighted—and Tim wasn't my boyfriend!' she asserted in self-defence.

'That wasn't the general consensus of opinion amongst the people my investigative team spoke to.'

'You had me *investigated?*' she whispered, her nose wrinkling in disbelief. She couldn't believe that Niall had been so unsure of her as to let his brother do something so underhand.

'My own idea,' Conan stated coolly, uncannily aware of what she was thinking, if not of the turmoil going on inside of her. 'There were those who knew you and this Leicester character who swore the two of you were an item—made for each other. They were even surprised you hadn't got married. Neighbours. Friends. Old acquaintances. It paints a somewhat less innocuous picture of the two of you, don't you think?' he suggested derisively.

'Because they'd all wanted us to!' she exhaled, angry colour touching her cheeks. 'And you had absolutely no right to question my friends or anyone else I knew like that!'

'I had every right when I saw what you were doing to my brother,' he sliced back, offering no apology. 'But don't worry. Those in question wouldn't even have guessed that they were being interrogated, let alone that your whiter-than-white reputation was being put under scrutiny. So what do you have to say for yourself now, Sienna? Still think you can convince me he wasn't an old boyfriend?'

'Obviously not!' she snapped, realising it was hopeless even imagining she could. The evidence against her was far too damning. 'Think what you like,' she sighed wearily, turning away. 'If you don't believe me, then that's your problem. Not mine.'

Only it *was* her problem, she thought despairingly, because she was only just beginning to realise that for some reason beyond her comprehension what Conan Ryder thought of her mattered. It mattered a lot.

'All you've done is put two and two together and come up with nothing!' she tagged on, turning towards him again, and wishing she hadn't when she noticed how his eyes were glittering gold beneath the sinking sun, and how the wind was ruffling his sleek black hair. 'Which just goes to show how narrow-minded you are!' she accused, angry with herself for noticing. 'As well as bigoted, single-minded and mercenary!'

'Is that all?' Instead of the anger she'd expected her accusations to generate, a slow smile was curling his stupendous mouth. 'Perhaps we recognise these things in each other, Sienna? Which could account for why we're so attracted to each other.'

'You don't attract me.' As an attempt at a bare-faced lie, it was so crass as to be laughable.

'Don't I?' he queried silkily. 'I'd beg to dispute that.'

You stupid, stupid fool! Of *course* a man like Conan couldn't be held up to challenge, she thought. He thrived on challenges. Knew how to take them on and overcome them. And now because of her stupid big mouth she was going to have to face further humiliation. Because he was right. She was so attracted to him that if he so much as touched her...

She suddenly tensed as his arm snaked around the back of her seat, his long dark hand coming to rest on the contrasting paleness of the leather.

As he leaned across her she pressed herself back against

the upholstery, hardly daring to breathe, yet found that the action had brought her into contact with the stirring warmth of his sleeve. She could feel the sensuality of the silk against the nape of her neck.

'Are you going to subdue me? Is that it?' she challenged shakily, her breathing so laboured it was difficult to speak.

He laughed very softly, his breath warm at her temple, the action gently stirring her hair. 'You don't strike me as a woman who would take that sort of treatment from any man—least of all one whom you believe despises you. You're much too liberated—too self-assured—to play the subservient little sex-slave. I want you as an equal, Sienna,' he purred deeply, his face so close to hers that she closed her eyes to blot out those darkly alluring features, feeling his breath as a sensual caress against her lips. 'Which is how I want you to want me. Giving as much as you take.'

He had moved his arm slightly, so that he wasn't even touching her now, but his words and the tonal quality of his voice along with the tantalising scent of him was a turn-on such as she would never have believed.

For the first time in her life the thought of what she wanted to do to a man—and not just any man but to him—was an aphrodisiac greater than any she had ever known.

She wanted to hide how she felt, but her breasts were already betraying her. She felt their burgeoning sensitivity, gasping deeply as his warm hand brushed across one taut hard peak so fleetingly that she might have imagined it.

Tense, wanting, she tilted her face to his, crazy for the feel of his mouth on hers.

'Oh, I'm not going to kiss you, Sienna.'

Her eyes flew open—not only at his declaration but at the amazing degree of self-control with which he had spoken.

'That would give you the opportunity of accusing me of instigating it.'

She couldn't believe what he was saying, or how unaffected he seemed to be after the effortless way in which he had aroused her.

'Why not? You did,' she snapped, burning with humiliation.

Unperturbed, he moved back to his own side of the car, fully in command of himself—and of her—as he started the ignition.

'At least try being honest with yourself, Sienna,' he advised, glancing over his shoulder before pulling back onto the public highway. 'If not with me.'

'I didn't want this,' she murmured, realising that with that defeated little statement she had admitted what her body had already told him. That it was true. She did want him. And with a desperation that hurt.

'Don't worry,' he rasped, looking at her tight strained features, giving the car full throttle as he took the road into the craggy hills. 'It won't last for ever.'

She didn't see him the following day, or the day after that, since he'd flown back to London for a conference. She spent the leisurely hours enjoying some quality time with Daisy, playing frisbee with her and Shadow on the private shingle beach, and building a kind of fragile peace with Avril.

Trying to let bygones be bygones, she brought her up to date with her little granddaughter's life, showing her early snapshots that she had brought with her for the woman to keep, as well as more recent photos of Daisy that were still on her cell phone.

She even encouraged Niall's mother to take a short evening stroll with her through the villa's spectacular grounds. She felt that Avril's problems might be more than physical, intuitively sensing that the woman was suffering from some sort of depression. From her training and experience with the older and less able-bodied people who joined the specialised courses she ran at the gym, she knew the benefits that gentle exercise could have on a person's well-being.

Consequently, when she went to bed that second night she drifted off to sleep feeling as though her day had been worthwhile—but woke up the following morning with a pounding head and aching all over.

'Tell Madame Ryder I'd better not come anywhere near her today,' she instructed Claudette, having sought her out in the villa's large modern kitchen. 'I think I'm going down with something. And keep Daisy occupied, will you?' she implored the little maid, who looked more than happy to be asked. 'I wouldn't want her to catch anything if I'm contagious.'

By lunchtime she was feeling so groggy she decided to go back to bed, annoyed at having to give in to sickness when she was never ill.

Some time during the afternoon Claudette came up with a tall and vastly expensive-looking vase of equally tall assorted flowers.

'From *madame,*' she informed Sienna, setting the vase carefully down on the high circular table that stood against the far wall, leaving Sienna surprised, though touched by the gesture.

Her room was above the terrace, and through the open window she could hear Avril's muted tones overlaid by Daisy's more eager and breathless ones. Shadow, loyal as always, was curled up asleep at the bottom of her bed. Lulled by the animal's gentle breathing, she began to relax, willing her aching body to let her sleep.

A sudden sound opened her eyes.

The dog was awake and alert. But not as awake and alert as Conan appeared to be as he came in, dressed for business as always, though his dark jacket had been discarded and his tie was pulled loose, the top button of his shirt unfastened, allowing a glimpse of the deeply tanned skin beneath.

'I understand you're not feeling well?' he said, without any preamble.

From the pillows, her hair dishevelled, her cheeks unnaturally flushed, Sienna pulled a self-deprecating face. 'I'm sorry.' She hadn't heard him knock, although she imagined he would have, and realised that she must have dropped off after all. 'You've got enough on your hands without having two sick women to worry about. I'm sure I'll be up and about again tomorrow.'

He didn't say anything, but just came over to the bed and felt her forehead. His touch was light, though his palm was strong and cool, and even now, feeling as she did, Sienna felt her body respond to it in a way that made her blood surge— and made her ache even more.

'You're burning up,' he remarked, his thick winged brows drawing together.

'I think I've got some sort of bug,' she said painfully. Why, if she had to be ill in somebody else's house, did it have to be his?

'Is there anything I can get you?' He looked so disgustingly healthy that Sienna couldn't imagine any virus or anything else ever daring to attack *him*. 'Do you need anything?'

She certainly didn't want him running around after her. Nor did she want his sympathy, she thought, silently fending off any suggestion of it. Not that he seemed to be offering any!

'Just for this to go.'

Fortunately Daisy came running in, scampering over to the bed and easing the inevitable tension coursing through Sienna. 'Mummy!' The little girl launched herself at her, her little arms going fiercely around Sienna's neck.

'I'm all right, darling. Mummy will be fine in a day or two.' She patted the adoring arms. 'You go with Uncle Conan.' Gently she disentangled herself from the affectionate embrace. 'We don't want you catching anything nasty, do we?' On her feet again, Daisy shook her head. 'Take her with you, will you?' she asked the man, blue eyes meeting green-gold over the little girl's bright, bouncy curls.

From a few feet away, he gave a nod of silent assent, before Daisy darted over to him.

'Mummy isn't well,' she informed him, clutching one

strong lean hand and looking trustingly up at his darkly aloof features.

'Then we'll just have to leave Mummy to get better, won't we?' he suggested, smiling indulgently down at the little girl. And the surprising warmth in the deep voice together with the sight of that little hand in his made Sienna's throat clog with unexpected emotion.

'If there's anything you need…' guiding Daisy away, he turned in the doorway '…let Claudette know immediately,' he instructed.

Claudette. Not him, she thought wretchedly as he went out with Daisy skipping beside him. Then suddenly Shadow took it on himself to desert her too, and shot out through the gap in the closing door.

Surely she hadn't wanted Conan to stay? How *could* she have wanted him to stay? she railed at herself, realising that she had. She could only justify the feeling by putting it down to the virus, which was obviously making her think irrationally, had her taking it to heart because he hadn't.

But how could a man as cold and heartless as Conan Ryder—except with Daisy of course—possibly sympathise with anyone who was ill? Especially someone he believed was as money-grubbing and deceitful as he thought she was.

A fact confirmed when he didn't return for the rest of the day—or the evening.

Claudette came up with Daisy for the little girl to give Sienna a goodnight kiss before going to bed, Shadow following at her heels. Even Avril sent up some of her best cranberry juice and a get-well wish through another servant, but there was no further sign of Conan.

Telling herself she didn't care one way or the other, Sienna tried to settle down. But her aches were getting worse, and despite the warm night she couldn't stop shivering—which meant she couldn't sleep, which in turn meant that she couldn't get Conan's cold indifference to her out of her mind.

It wasn't helped by the knowledge that he wouldn't hesitate

to take her to bed if the opportunity arose, which just confirmed what a hard and unfeeling louse he was.

But she'd known that already. So why was she feeling so disappointed in him? she berated herself, screwing up her face with the aches that seemed to be gnawing at her body. She wasn't, she told herself belligerently, through her restless, groaning fever. Unable to bear feeling so grotty any longer, she broke her rule never to resort to medication and took two paracetamol—which someone had left on the bedside cabinet with Avril's cranberry juice—after which her bone-deep aches began to subside.

She awoke while it was still dark, drenched to the skin, her nightdress sticking to her like a wet sheet.

It *was* the sheet, she realised, dismayed, trying to kick it off her legs, where it clung, unpleasantly clammy and cold.

Obviously taking the painkillers had reduced her temperature, she thought, which meant having to suffer this side-effect instead.

Grateful, though, that she wasn't aching any more, she slipped out of bed and into the *en suite* bathroom without putting on the light—which had been all right when she'd had some light filtering up from the grounds through the bathroom's frosted window. But someone must have drawn the curtains in the bedroom while she'd slept, she realised, after she'd shut off that only source of light, and she found herself having to grope her way back across the luxurious Indian rug, so damp she was already starting to shiver. She couldn't see a thing, and she needed to find a dry nightdress—fast!

Her clothes had been unpacked for her on the day she had arrived, and her nightwear and underclothes were all neatly folded, drowning in the space provided by an endless array of drawers. But not altogether *au fait* with her surroundings, feeling her way in the dark, she stepped off the carpet onto the richness of wood—and misjudged exactly where she was, colliding with the table where Claudette had placed the heavy vase of flowers earlier in the day, sending it crashing to the floor.

'Oh, *no!*'

Her legs were splashed from the water, and desperately she groped for a light switch—only to find herself blinking by the illuminated landing as the door burst open a few seconds later, and her own room was flooded with light.

'What the…?'

It was Conan who stood there, holding the door wide, his face an orchestra of emotions from surprise and concern to outright disbelief.

'I'm sorry.' It was all Sienna could say, seeing his gaze slip from her dishevelled state to the shattered pieces of vase lying on the floor. 'Was it very expensive?'

'Never mind about that,' he told her. 'What are you doing wandering about in the dark? And what the…?'

She must look terrible, she thought wretchedly, seeing his gaze raking over her, with her hair a tangled mess and about as glamorous as a compost heap, while he…

Only now did it sink in that he must have been undressing when he had heard the crash, because he was standing in nothing but the shirt he had been wearing earlier that day, which was fully unbuttoned and hanging open over a pair of dark briefs.

In normal circumstances she wouldn't have been able to take her eyes off that bronze, muscular chest, with its shading of black hair that arrowed down over his tight flat abdomen. Any more than she could have ignored the powerful thighs which, planted firmly apart and covered in the same fine hair, shouted of everything that was utterly virile and masculine. But her strappy nightdress was clinging to her feverish skin like cold wet polythene and her teeth were starting to chatter.

'I wanted a dry nightdress,' she was trying to say, but couldn't get it out because she was shivering so much.

'For goodness' sake!' In a few short strides he was beside

her, and, having sussed the situation, was tugging at the offending garment. 'Take this thing off!'

She started to protest, but he was already ripping it over her head, so that she was left standing naked in front of him, covered by nothing except her goose pimples.

'This isn't the time for modesty—unless you want to catch your death,' he advised, his mouth firming grimly. 'Here.' Having tossed the nightdress aside, he was shrugging out of his shirt, revealing his beautiful torso in all its glory. 'Put this on.'

Obediently Sienna slipped her arms into the silky fabric he was holding up for her. It felt warm and incredibly soft as she clutched her own arms, hugging its warmth to her, shuddering. Grateful. It smelt nice too. Like him. Lemony, tinged with spice, and somewhere in the mix a hint of musk...

'Now.' He had her by the elbow and was urging her back to bed, his other hand pulling back the covers. 'Get back in and—' He stopped mid-sentence, feeling the damp crumpled sheet. 'You can't sleep in that!' he remonstrated.

Before she realised it he had scooped her up into his arms. 'We've got to get you warm,' he insisted, ignoring her protests.

It was a miracle, Sienna thought distractedly, that Daisy hadn't been disturbed by all the commotion. She tried to ignore the feel of that warm, solid wall of muscle that she was being held against as Conan bore her down the landing to another room.

His bedroom! she realised at once, with her heart racing, seeing the enormous bed with its dark satin sheets, only half aware of the exclusive wood and the dark rich array of soft furnishings that defined it as very much a man's domain.

This time when he ripped back the sheet for her to climb in, he slipped quickly in beside her. Then, turning her onto her side with her back to him, he pulled her shivering body into the warm hard length of his.

She knew she should object—put up some resistance to

his taking control like this. But she needed him right at this moment, and his body was so warm…

Even through her fogged senses she recognised a deep sensuality, but she blotted it out of her mind, letting the warmth of him ease and comfort her, penetrate her shuddering body.

Her breathing was rapid and shallow from the virus, but gradually it slowed and became steadier as her shivers began to subside.

She felt sleepy and so…protected.

It was a half-conscious thought, so transient she didn't even question the strangeness of it as she drifted off, secure in the strength of his arms and in the cushioning warmth of his body.

CHAPTER SIX

WHEN she awoke she was alone.

Only the depression in the pillow beside hers assured her that she hadn't dreamt the whole thing. Plus the fact that she was still in his room—and in his bed! she realised with a self-ridiculing little grimace.

Surprisingly, though, she felt considerably better.

But where was he? And, more importantly, where was Daisy?

As her maternal instincts kicked in she scrambled out of bed, and was halfway across the room before she realised that she was still wearing Conan's shirt. The shirt he had helped her into after stripping her naked! The shirt she had been too shivery and unwell last night even to fasten!

Hearing a sudden soft knock on the door, she raced back to bed, only just managing to cover herself with the dark maroon sheet before the door opened and Claudette came in.

'Monsieur Ryder's instructions,' she declared in her heavily accented voice as she set a breakfast tray down on a marble-topped coffee table.

There was a jug of orange juice, and coffee in a silver pot, its aroma drifting tantalisingly towards Sienna. There were croissants too, she noticed, still warm from the oven, their buttery, freshly baked smell making her mouth water.

She was hungry, she realised, after eating scarcely anything the previous day.

'Claudette? Where's Daisy?'

The little maid paused in pouring juice into a crystal tumbler. 'I am not sure, *madame*. She had breakfast with Madame Ryder an hour ago, but I think Monsieur Ryder's taken her out with him.'

Without consulting her, or bringing Daisy up here to see her mother first? Sienna thought, stunned, wondering what could possibly have prompted such an action on Conan's part when he seemed to have had very little time for his niece since she had been there. Nevertheless, she couldn't help feeling that her role as guardian was being undermined.

'Oh…' she uttered, and hoped she didn't sound as hurt or put out as she felt.

'Is there anything else I can get you, *madame?*' Claudette asked helpfully as she finished rearranging things on the tray.

'No. Thank you,' Sienna said, embarrassed by what the woman must be thinking about finding Monsieur Ryder's sick young guest in Monsieur Ryder's bed. 'Oh—yes. Claudette…!'

The little maid was already on her way out.

'Do you think you could bring me some clothes?' She felt sticky and sweaty and she was longing for a shower. But she had no intention of risking anyone else in the house seeing her emerge from Monsieur Ryder's bedroom wearing only Monsieur Ryder's shirt!

'Oui, madame.'

The woman was back in minutes with fresh underwear, a casual check shirt and jeans, which she placed tidily over the wooden arm of a richly upholstered gold brocade chair.

'Shoes, too,' she said, placing them beside the bed, where Sienna was sitting with the sheet still pulled up around her, in a rather futile bid to conceal her betraying appearance.

Claudette was looking pleased with herself, as if she did this sort of thing all the time.

Which perhaps she did, Sienna thought suddenly, biting into one of the warm, moist croissants, wondering why the thought of Conan entertaining other women like this should bother her in quite the way it did. Women like Petra Flax.

'Claudette…' Wiping crumbs from the corner of her mouth, Sienna tried to imagine what reason Conan might have given his employee for Sienna being in his bed. In case he hadn't said anything, she felt she needed to put the record straight.

Now, though, as the woman waited for her to continue, Sienna merely shrugged. It was too complicated to try and explain.

After the maid had gone, she ravenously ate two of the croissants, finished her juice and a cup of coffee, and then, as Conan was clearly not around, took advantage of the facilities of his bathroom.

It was of a similar design to hers, though the long luxurious bath and the rest of the gleaming white suite was enhanced by a colour scheme of sage and dark green marble.

The sensuously appointed double shower was something she tried not to think about too much as she luxuriated in the steaming water from its powerful jets, while soaping her hair and her body with his citrus-fragranced shower gel.

Claudette hadn't thought to bring her a robe, so she grabbed Conan's when she'd finished, finding it hanging behind the door—a thick, white towelling garment that seemed to swamp her in its folds, and carried the disturbing and far too evocative scent of his body.

She was aching to see Daisy, though, and made short work of towelling her hair, needing to get downstairs and quiz her mother-in-law over where Conan had gone—and where he had taken his niece without *her* permission.

Standing in front of the mirrored wardrobe, teasing her hair into some semblance of order, she was trying to decide what she was going to say to him about it, particularly after he had rescued her from what would have been a very uncomfortable night, when the bedroom door suddenly creaked open just a crack—and then enough to allow a little grinning figure to scamper in.

'Daisy!'

Sienna's heart lurched as she swept her daughter up into

her arms. 'Oh, goodness! I've missed you!' She was hugging and kissing her as though she hadn't seen her daughter for months, breathing in her infant scent, revelling in the feel of her warm, familiarly solid little body.

'I got Uncle Conan to take me out 'cause my green crayon's all gone.' She spilled the words out, punctuating the statement with little breaths. 'Because you were asleep and no one else wanted to take me.'

'I expect they were busy, darling,' Sienna told her gently, trying to control her surprise as she stroked the soft chestnut hair.

'Uncle Conan told me to give you these.' Giving her some space at last, Sienna realised that the little girl was clutching a small bouquet of gaily coloured flowers. A couple of the heads were crushed from the ferocity of her affection, she noticed, sending a glance down at the crimson smudge staining the pristine whiteness of Conan's robe. 'He said you dropped all the ones Granny gave you.'

'Oh, darling…' Restraining a sob, taking the flowers from the small hand, Sienna hugged Daisy to her again—and only then became aware of Conan in a light, stylishly tailored suit, leaning with his arms folded against the doorjamb.

'We looked in earlier but you were asleep,' he said, straightening up to his impressive height and moving towards them. 'I thought you might have wanted to take Daisy yourself, but decided it best to let you sleep on.'

'Thanks,' Sienna uttered, ashamed to realise she had misjudged him, yet amazed that he had involved himself in something so trivial as a child's crayons. 'You didn't mind taking her?'

He shrugged, as though it was of little consequence, but didn't say whether he had or not. In fact he hadn't wanted to get drawn in at all. But when he had told the little girl that her mother wasn't well enough to take her out, and to use a different colour, she'd declared quite adamantly that grass could only be green, stamped her foot, and started to cry.

'Like most members of her sex, she knows just how to manipulate,' he commented dryly, and only that touch of humour on his lips stopped Sienna from coming back with some suitable retort. Not to mention that her body was responding to his impeccably tailored elegance and those deeply stunning features in a way that was far, far too disturbing!

'I take it you're feeling better?'

'Yes. Thanks,' she murmured, just the memory of how he had stripped her of that wet nightdress and carried her in here causing wings of colour to deepen across her cheeks. 'You were very kind.'

He laughed—a rather dispassionate sound. 'That's the first time anyone's ever accused me of that.'

Because "kind" didn't really seem to fit a man like Conan Ryder, Sienna thought, and the polite smile she gave him— like his laugh just now—was a little bit strained.

Hard, tough and practical. Those were the adjectives she would use to describe the man standing in front of her, she decided, setting Daisy down on her feet as soon as she started to wriggle.

'Uncle Conan?' With her hippo under her arm, she ran over to the man she seemed hell-bent on winning over, whether he liked it or not, grabbing one of his impeccably clad legs. 'Are you going to marry Mummy?'

Sienna, horrified, heard her.

Conan's forehead pleated in a kind of amused perplexity.

'Why on earth,' he said, with a curious edge to his voice, 'do you ask that?'

'She's in *your* bedroom.' The child looked coyly at her mother, as though she knew it was a subject that only adults should talk about. 'And she's got your dressing gown on.'

Conan's mouth pulled wryly as he glanced across at Sienna. 'So she has!' he declared, as though he had only just noticed.

His eyes were lingering on the swamping garment, which on him would probably only cover his thighs, Sienna thought, and a flood of warmth heated her body at the memory of those

virile thighs and just how he had looked when he had carried
her in here last night.

But now he was fully clothed, and as devastating to her
equilibrium as when he had been nearly naked. Particularly
when those perceptive eyes were raking over her as they were
now, taking in the rolled-back sleeves and the gaping neckline of the robe, which she had only just realised was revealing far too much of the upper swell of one breast, and which
her agitated fingers struggled to rectify.

'Why don't you go down and show your grandmother the
new colouring book we chose this morning?' he suggested to
his niece. 'I'm sure she'd like to see you using your new crayons. I'll send your mother down to join you as soon as she's
ready.'

Phew!

Sienna's relief was palpable as the little girl did as he advised and scampered away.

'Thanks,' she said again, placing the flowers down on the
table, envying the way he appeared so unfazed by the child's
remarks.

'All in a day's work.' The line of his mouth curved sensuously, sending Sienna's already hopeless defences against him
skittering like a retreating army. 'Does she always carry that
hippo with her?' he asked, with a jerk of his chin towards the
door he had just closed.

'She won't be parted from it,' she murmured unthinkingly,
suddenly nervous at finding herself alone with him.

A line deepened between those thick masculine brows,
and his gaze was so intense it felt as though he was probing
right down into her soul and sussing out that she hadn't really wanted to tell him that. That the simple gift he'd bought
for his niece's first birthday had eclipsed any other toy she'd
ever been given.

She hadn't played with it at first, Sienna remembered. It
had been just one more of the large number of cuddly toys
that had filled Daisy's bedroom. In fact she'd scarcely no-

ticed it for six months—not until after Niall had died. Then she had plucked it up one day and ever afterwards clung to it like a lifeline, taking it to bed, to playschool, wherever else she went, as though it somehow represented all the love and support and comfort that her father's absence had robbed her of. But Sienna couldn't bring herself to tell Conan any of that.

Now, trying to diminish the significance of what she had said, in case he read far too much into it, she shrugged, adding nonchalantly, 'Well, you know children. They go through these phases, don't they?'

'I don't know,' he said, in a surprisingly cool tone. 'I've never had any.'

For one crazy moment she had the strongest urge to ask him if he ever wanted any, but decided that that was a subject she didn't want to pursue with him either—particularly as he sounded less than enamoured of the idea.

'I'll get dressed and leave you to it,' she murmured, moving over to the chair where Claudette had left her clothes.

'Don't rush on my account,' he said dispassionately, turning away.

The bathroom beckoned. Privacy. A place where she could get dressed and then get out of there as smartly as she could. Except that her gaze moved too willingly towards where he was standing, with his back to her now, rummaging through one of the drawers, and she couldn't for the life of her tear it away.

Greedily her eyes ran over the wide sweep of his shoulders, tapered to perfection by the exclusive cut of his jacket, to his narrow waist and long, long legs. Very masculine legs that had rasped against hers as he'd warmed her in his bed. Even through her fever she had been mind-blowingly aware of him, had known that in any other circumstances she couldn't have lain with him like that, feeling the power of his arms and the rousing warmth of his body, without turning towards him...

And he would have taken her.

Gathering up her clothes, she felt her blood surge at the

memory. He had shown care and concern and overall commitment for her welfare, but he hadn't been able to conceal the physical evidence of his wanting her...

But he *had* shown that care—and to a woman he didn't even like. She was his least favourite person and yet he had held her through the night...

Trying to puzzle him out, her clothes clutched tightly to her, she heard the question that had been burning through her brain ever since she'd woken up this morning slip out before she could stop it. 'Why didn't you help Niall when he asked you to?'

The drawer closing hard on its runners was the only sound to intrude on the pregnant silence that followed. 'I had my reasons,' he replied, moving back across the room.

'What reasons?' Sienna persisted, swivelling to look at him as he crossed over to the wardrobe. 'What reason could be good enough for not helping your own brother? For just standing by while he got into such unavoidable debt?'

'Unavoidable?' With an eyebrow raised censoriously, he shot a glance in her direction.

Tension spread through Sienna's body. He thought *she* had been responsible for most of it.

'All right, then,' he rasped, taking a coat hanger out of the wardrobe. 'If you want to know the truth. I did help him.'

'You did?'

'At least, I tried to.'

'What do you mean?' she asked, screwing her face up.

'Where do you think the money came from for your fancy house, Sienna? For a large part of his investments? The backup? The loans?'

'But I thought—'

'You thought what? What you've always thought?' He tossed the hanger down on a chair and started shrugging out of his jacket. 'That I left my own brother to stew?'

'But Niall said—'

'I'm well aware of what Niall must have said. And, yes, all

right. That's how it must have looked,' he accepted, retrieving the hanger. 'As though I was a heartless bastard.'

Which was exactly what Niall had called him, Sienna remembered.

'Then why did he say it if it wasn't true?' Niall might have had his shortcomings, but he certainly hadn't been a liar, she thought, watching him hanging up his jacket.

'Because I did refuse him.' He was closing the wardrobe door. 'Later.'

'Why?'

'You won't like it, Sienna.'

She watched him move over to the table and drop his keys down beside the bouquet Daisy had given her. 'Because of me?'

He didn't answer. He didn't have to. His silence made it all too plain.

'I was sick of funding your lifestyle because Niall didn't have the gumption to control it. Any more than he had the commitment or the dedication for directorship.'

'That isn't true! I never asked him for anything! The car. The clothes. Every expensive gift he bought me!' Nothing had been too good for her, she remembered, with a surge of painful emotion pressing heavily against her chest, although she'd tried to dissuade him from spending so much, concerned about the cost. 'Niall worked hard,' she reminded Conan, because his brother *had* always been working. Using that unique Ryder charm on clients to secure deals. Striving to make himself as rich and respected and as successful as Conan was. Sometimes, she thought now, it had been almost painful watching him. 'He worked *hard*,' she reiterated. 'You know he did!

'But he spent more than he earned, Sienna.'

'So you decided to pull the plug? Because you thought I was the one spending it all?'

From the anguish scoring her face, he was almost willing to believe that she was telling him the truth. That she really didn't have a clue what had been going on. But whether she had or not, it didn't alter the fact that she was still a cheat...

'When I did have a change of heart and decided to throw him a lifeline he wouldn't even speak to me,' he informed her, the memory eating at him. Because however different their lives had been, or how diverse their characters, there had been an unbreakable bond between them, forged out of Niall's eternal yet unconscious need for guidance, and out of his own responsibility as the elder brother to see that he got it. 'I tried again—several times—even ringing him when he wouldn't see me, but he cut me dead on every occasion. Told me he'd sorted it out for himself.'

Which he had, Sienna thought. By mortgaging a house which, she was staggered to realise now, Conan had paid for. By securing extortionately priced loans she'd suddenly found herself responsible for. And for what? she wondered bitterly.

'Why didn't you tell me before?' she murmured distantly, clinging to the bundle of clothes she was holding like a shield. 'Three years ago?'

'What would it have achieved, Sienna?' he enquired resignedly. 'Absolution for myself at the expense of my brother's reputation?' The brother he'd always felt duty-bound to protect—from himself, if nothing else, he thought grimly. He had recognised his brother's weakness even from an early age. 'Especially when his grieving widow had only just emerged from another man's bed?'

Wearily, she said, 'It wasn't like that.'

'No, of course not.' He laughed humourlessly, refusing to believe her. Just as he had three years ago. Although he was unburdening himself, she thought, without any problem! 'Apart from which,' he went on, 'I didn't think Niall would have considered I was doing him any favours by telling his wife just how much financial support his brother had given him.'

'Then why are you telling me now?'

He was moving towards her with a purposefully predatory

stride, stopping only when he was breath-catching inches away from her. 'I think you know why.'

Yes, I do! she thought, weakened by his nearness, by his unmistakable scent that did things to her like no other man's had ever done, and by the mesmerising gold of his eyes.

Directed only by his will, she allowed him to take the small bundle of clothes she was clutching and drop them onto the chair, his eyes never leaving hers. She wondered if he could hear the way her heart was banging against her ribcage.

Her breath shuddered through her at those galvanising fingers against the nape of her neck. His hand curled around her, drawing her closer, and with her breath coming shallowly, she closed her eyes, her head dropping back of its own volition, her mouth tilted upwards to his.

His kiss was light, gentle, considered, bearing none of the demanding hunger he had shown in the pool. But his tenderness was torment and, made brave by the way he had treated her last night, and by the unbelievable things she had just learned about him, she slid her arms around his neck with a little murmur of acquiescence, wanting this as she had never wanted anything in her life.

He responded with an iron-strong arm around her middle, pulling her against the whipcord strength of his body.

Her own actions had loosened the belt of the bulky robe. She wasn't aware of it until his hand slid inside the parting garment, and she gave a throaty gasp as, with both hands sliding down to her hips, he pulled her against the rock-hard thrust of his masculinity.

The friction of his clothes was an aphrodisiac against her bare flesh, bringing her wriggling against him in involuntary provocation as each movement opened up a sensual heaven.

Her breasts were begging for his attention, their swollen peaks tightening into hard buds. With a small whimper she thrust them out to him in mindless invitation, flaunting her femininity before him with all the shamelessness of an abandoned nymph.

With the proficiency of a master, he read her body's silent language, drawing his tongue teasingly down the silken valley between her aching breasts, and chuckling softly at her stifled little groan of need.

One hand sliding under each breast, he cupped them as if they were prize roses, making her wait as he studied them with those darkly penetrating eyes, making her ache for him, making her silently beg.

Very gently he dipped his head to suckle first on one and then the other, tasting each sensitive tip before exploring the pink halo around it with his tongue.

His breath was unbearably sensual as it fanned the burning tip of each pale mound, increasing her pleasure with the cooling dew of his saliva, his actions slow and studied, exquisitely arousing, excruciatingly erotic.

Only it wasn't enough…

Sensations shuddered through her, sending shock-waves of pure pleasure right down to the aching heart of her femininity, the sensual message they carried clear and unequivocal.

She wanted him! Wanted him as she had never wanted any man. Wanted to be in bed with him as she had been last night—only without restraint and without the barrier of any clothes between them.

He didn't like her. But she would *make* him like her, she vowed to her own shocked consciousness, although that didn't matter now. All that mattered was that he wanted her as much as she wanted him. Driven by her need, she ground her hips sensuously against the hard structure of his and heard him groan with the agony of his own need.

Her hands were running over the fine silk of his shirt, exploring the warm contours of his chest, his flanks, and the hard straining muscles of his back.

She wanted to be naked with him. To feel his body slick and hot against hers. But as she started pulling awkwardly at the front of the immaculate shirt he slammed his hand over hers, holding it flat against his chest.

She could hear the thunder of his heart beneath her fingers, and there were slashes of dark colour along the sculpted lines of his cheeks. His eyelids were heavy, his eyes darkened by desire, but with a soft chuckle that was at odds with the raggedness of his breathing, he murmured, 'You aren't well enough for this.'

He was lifting her up, carrying her over to the big bed just as he had done last night. Only now, as she reached out to him, lying with her body unashamedly exposed to him by the gaping robe, it was only his dark-fringed eyes that caressed her supple nakedness, before he straightened and moved away from the bed.

A small moan of disappointment escaped her.

She couldn't believe it! He was picking up the phone on the bedside unit.

How could he be making a phone call at a time like this? she wondered through a mire of frustration, even if he *did* think he was being considerate in calling a halt to their lovemaking? Had he only been teasing her? Setting her alight only to douse the fire he had ignited with his disciplined self-control? And if so, why? Because he didn't like her? she thought despairingly. Because of what she still couldn't convince him she hadn't done?

'Yes, it's me,' she heard him say into the mouthpiece of what she realised then was the internal phone. 'Keep Daisy with you for a while, will you?' The phone pinged as he dropped it back onto its rest.

Aching with frustration, an arm flung out across the bedspread, her aroused body given added voluptuousness by the gaping robe, Sienna still couldn't believe it as she watched him stride across the room without so much as a glance in her direction—until, with a wild leap of her pulse, she heard him locking the door.

'Now…' he murmured, his mouth taking on an excitingly sensual twist as he turned back to where she was lying. 'Are you going to convince me that you are?'

CHAPTER SEVEN

COMING back across the room, Conan could feel his arousal straining against his trousers.

If Sienna was trying to test his restraint, he observed grimly, she was doing a very good job!

She was lying on her back with her legs drawn up to one side, with his robe covering only her arms and part of one shoulder like a pale frame for the soft lines and curves of her delicious body.

He guessed she was well aware of how tempting she looked. And if she wasn't, then she was certainly going to find out, he resolved, with a hard excitement throbbing through the lower half of his anatomy.

He allowed himself to take in the visual spectacle of all she was offering him. Skin like silk, from her lovely face and that natural complexion—paler today than it usually was—right down to her tantalisingly pink-tipped toes.

Her breasts were rising and falling sharply as he came and stood over her, their equally tantalising pink crests still swollen from his ministrations.

He restrained the strongest urge to spread his hands across them. Going for the erogenous zones first never had been his style, and he had never been a man to rush things if he could help it. Besides, he enjoyed the art of titillation and reward. It heightened experience, and in the lifetime of his sexual maturity he had never had any complaints.

Her breathing seemed to quicken as his gaze slid down her body.

Surprisingly embarrassed, she made to draw her legs up further, and gave a little murmur—a token of protest—as he took a slender foot in each hand to swivel her round, pulling her gently towards him with her legs a little way off the bed so that he could position himself standing between them.

Her body was so enticing that the throbbing in his loins became almost unbearable. Her waist was remarkably slim beneath those proportionately full breasts, her hips an inviting cradle above the apex of her thighs and the dark downy hair covering the very centre of her.

The silky triangle drew his gaze to the slick, secret haven of her femininity, and he allowed his eyes to linger there for a few moments before lifting his eyes to hers again and enjoying the flush of colour he could see staining her cheeks.

When she moved to pull the robe together he laughed and, bending over her, caught her hands, holding them fast in one of his so that he could continue his inspection, aware from her soft groan and her slumberous blue eyes that she was as aroused as he was.

Had his brother wanted her like this? Been driven mad by that body and that treacherously seductive mouth? he wondered, sliding his forefinger across its lower lip, feeling its inner warmth as her mouth parted to admit him, cushioning him—mimicking that ultimate act. Just as anticipating her surrender was driving *him* insane with wanting now?

Had *he* wanted her this much then too? Three? Four? Five years ago? he asked himself almost savagely, his mood incongruous with his actions as he drew his moistened finger with considered gentleness down the silken valley between her breasts. Was that why he had kept his distance from her? Why he hadn't wanted to believe Niall when he'd told him he suspected her of having an affair?

The purposefulness with which he pulled off his tie, tossing it aside before unbuttoning his shirt, reflected the grim path his thoughts had taken. Because the discovery that she was, and that she'd just been using his brother, had at the time rocked him like a tidal wave—especially in view of what had happened to Niall.

But now, as she reached for him, he realised he was just as much in danger of succumbing to her charms as his younger brother had been. Except that he was harder than Niall and far, far more experienced. Experienced enough never to let that happen. Because she was his now by tacit assent, to do whatever he liked with.

Which was to take her and take her until she screamed with the pleasure of it, he realised, hating himself even as his body hardened in scorching response to the thought of having her pleading and begging for him to end the pleasurable torture as he drove them both beyond ecstasy—before he walked away from her without batting an eyelid, letting her know exactly how it felt to be used.

Dragging his shirt down over his shoulders, Sienna allowed him to help her. Her fingers were clumsy—too eager—and fleetingly she wondered how the more sophisticated women of his acquaintance—and especially the likes of Petra Flax— would behave.

But the velvet-sheathed steel of his body drove her negative thoughts from her mind. He was with her, wasn't he? And even if this summer was all there was ever going to be with him she could accept that, couldn't she? A casual affair? People did. Other women she knew did it all the time.

'Conan...' She breathed his name like a reverent prayer, exalted by the way it felt on her lips, by being able to use it in such a way, like a coveted possession, something only granted to the favoured few.

Although probably more than a few, she thought with a mental grimace as she considered how many women might have sobbed out their pleasure on this same big bed. But she didn't want to dwell on that.

She wanted to explore him, and she used her hands and her

lips to make her intentions known, luxuriating in the strength of him as her teeth lightly grazed over the hard, undulating contours of a sinewy arm, and her fingers revelled in the pelt of hair that shadowed his deep bronzed chest.

'Turn over,' she breathed, thrilled and a bit over-awed by his glorious masculinity.

He laughed softly, doing as she asked.

She looked at him as he lay on his back with his eyes closed, his lashes thick and dark against the wells of his eyes, his hard mouth curving slightly, sensually relaxed.

Delicately she touched the tip of her tongue to his chest, letting it burn a trail over the dark line of hair that went down and down and disappeared under the waistband of his trousers, her senses imbued with his musky scent, the sound of his quickened breathing, and the salty taste of his skin.

'Are you going to take them off?' she suggested. Her hands were dealing with the buttons at his waist, her eyes bright with devilish excitement.

'I was hoping you were,' he drawled, his smile equally wicked.

Was he?

A little skein of excitement began unravelling inside of her.

He was hers to do with as she wanted. This big, important man with hidden depths to his character such as she hadn't realised until last night—and then again with that startling revelation this morning. She felt like a kid who had just been given a pomegranate and wasn't really sure what to do with it. Which was crazy, she thought, when she had been married for two and a half years! But then Niall had never encouraged her to take any initiative in their lovemaking. He'd always wanted to be in control, setting the pace and the rhythm. He'd wanted her submissive as he'd lost himself in her body. Idolising. Adoring. Dominating her...

Shaking the memory away, she slipped the zip down over the bulging fabric with surprisingly trembling fingers, as nervous as a schoolgirl on her first date.

'Do you usually let your women undress you?' she enquired, not wanting to imagine anyone else doing what she was doing to him, although she couldn't help it. Somehow she couldn't see Petra Flax feeling as gauche and awkward as she felt.

'That's none of your business,' he remonstrated softly, smiling at her cheekiness.

No, it wasn't, she thought, approving of him not telling her. He would be as discreet about his bedroom adventures as he was about the rest of his personal life.

'You're going to have to help me,' she said shyly.

'Really?' He was lying indolently on his back, and his face was a study in desire, from his heavy-lidded eyes and the flush staining the dark olive of his skin, to his full lower lip that was curling almost mockingly now. 'You disappoint me,' he said, before making quick work of dispensing with the hampering garment—and although Sienna knew he was only joking she felt his wry amusement like a shaming reprimand.

'Lie back,' she ordered, her heart fluttering nervously in her chest.

He was wearing little more than a black pouch that scarcely contained his manhood.

Sienna ran her hand lovingly across it, letting her palm size the dark bulk that was the most intimate part of his body. She gave him a self-satisfied smile, getting her own back when she heard the pleasurable groan that came from deep in his throat.

'I'll teach you to laugh at me,' she breathed, enjoying this sensual game with him that was thrilling and unexplored and totally new to her.

'Please do,' he murmured, his sexy mouth curling with wry anticipation, although his eyes were closed and his forehead crumpled in almost pained compliance.

Conan compliant! She almost laughed at the incongruity of it. Like a sleeping lion more like! she thought, considering the strength and power that could spring into action in a second, and a small frisson sizzled through her at the realisation that it was only the power of what she was doing to him that was keeping him still.

When she pulled down the last barrier—the only thing separating her from him—she closed her eyes and let her nervous hands caress him. He felt so hot and hard.

Emboldened by his groans of pleasure, she bent her head to taste him.

At the first touch of her mouth he shuddered violently against her, the power of his body arousing her in such a way as she'd never known she could be aroused from doing this to a man. Gently she used her breath to fan him, as he had done so expertly to her earlier across her aching breasts.

But, untutored in such a highly intimate game, she let her nerves get the better of her, and suddenly unready, feeling grossly inept with a man of such sexual prowess, she was murmuring like a fool before she could stop herself, 'I've never done this before.' She couldn't even look at him as she said it. She had never wanted to, she admitted to herself, feeling the dark clouds of her inadequacy threatening her, just as they had in her marriage. Not once, she remembered. Not until now...

She heard his breath shiver through him.

'Look at me,' he ordered deeply.

The eyes that met his when she raised herself up seemed guarded and... What? Conan wondered. Embarrassed? he considered, surprised. There was no doubt in his mind that she was telling him the truth.

So her previous sexual exploits, even in her marriage, hadn't included such adventurous intimacies, he realised with increasing surprise. Even though adultery had.

His grim acceptance of that, despite her continual denial, still couldn't diminish the rather chauvinistic pleasure of knowing that there was at least something left that he could teach her. But not today...

Her slender hand was resting on the flat plane of his abdomen.

Reaching down and clasping it in the lean strength of his, he said tonelessly, 'Maybe now isn't the time.'

A thin line appeared between finely shaped eyebrows.

Maybe it never would be, Sienna thought, wondering if her failure to please him meant he wouldn't want such an unsophisticated female in his bed again.

Desperate to do something that would keep him there, she marked a trail of butterfly kisses over the firm bed of his abdomen, her tongue lightly following where her lips had caressed, drawing a map of his body from his waist, down over his hip, from the sleekness of his skin to a thin, rough protrusion of flesh...

She sat up, staring at the jagged maroon line that ran diagonally across the outer side of his right thigh.

'Where did you get that scar?' Scars, she amended silently, noticing now that there were some smaller ones further up along his hipbone.

She could feel the tension that was suddenly flexing his powerful body, as though he had taken a breath and forgotten to let it out.

'Let's just say I had a difference of opinion with one of our canine friends,' he said dispassionately, releasing air from his lungs again.

'A difference...? You mean these are dog bites? How? When?' Sienna asked, horrified, running cool fingers caressingly across his flesh as though she could erase whatever had caused them.

'I was somewhere I shouldn't have been—and I paid the price for it.' Twice over, he remembered grimly. He didn't know what had been worse. The violent attack by that savage Doberman, or his stepfather's... A curtain came down over his thoughts, swiftly blotting out the memory. 'It was a long time ago.'

A long time ago, and yet he still bore the scars both mentally and physically, he reflected, quietly seething. And the reminder of that time, along with a sudden conscience-pricking thought as to what he was doing with his brother's little tramp of a widow, acted like a dousing of icy water over his skin.

'Conan…?'

As he lay there for a moment, trying to regain his zeal, her soft, enquiring whisper was all it took to pull him back.

And why not? he asked himself ruthlessly, moving as swiftly as a cat, hauling her up against him, before rolling them both so that she was lying beneath him. If anyone could help him wipe out his past then she could, he thought. Surprising though it was, she had the power in her small slender body and her contesting little opinions to excite him like no other woman had ever done.

She gave a deep moan of pleasure at the weight of him above her, her mouth as insistent as his as it parted for him in a mutual blending of searching tongues.

Her skin was soft and damp as he blazed a trail of urgent kisses down over her throat to the invitingly soft mounds of her breasts. He wanted to pour out his pent-up emotions against them. Take solace in the warm haven of her femininity. But how could a girl like her sympathise with the torments of his childhood? Or understand the demons that were riding him now?

She gave a soft whimper as though she was hurting and he raised himself up on his elbows. She was lying against the pillow, her beautiful eyes dark with desire, but her tousled hair was damp where it kinked around her temples, and there was an unnaturally high flush to the fine translucency of her cheeks.

What was he *doing?* he demanded of himself—though for a different reason this time. She looked all in, he thought. Exhausted, fragile, racked by her physical urges—totally unaware that, for him, this whole thing was little more than an act of revenge. To make her pay for how she had treated his brother and to salve his own conscience, if he was honest with himself, for his own contribution to his brother's reckless behaviour. She was unscrupulous, it was true, but she still wasn't well—and he couldn't use her like that.

'I think you'd better get dressed,' he advised, pushing himself up, away from her.

On his feet, he was already reinstating his clothes. 'I was right,' he said as she sat up, looking hurt and bewildered. 'This isn't a good idea.'

Abandoned as he closed the bedroom door behind him, not really sure of what she had done wrong, Sienna could only deduce, with a stinging slap to her pride, that it was her lack of sophistication and her failure to please him that had put him off.

Which was no more than she deserved, she reproached herself, for imagining she could make him like her—never mind allowing him to take such liberties with her body! She could only put it down to slight mental derangement caused by her very vulnerable state. She knew what he thought about her and it wasn't very complimentary! And even if her opinion of him had changed considerably since yesterday, it didn't mean that his had softened in any way towards her. It clearly hadn't! she realised shamefully. She would just have to be careful never to let him catch her off-guard again.

Daisy was helping one of the gardeners with his planting, Sienna noticed when, still embarrassed by the intimacies she had allowed herself to share with Conan, she came down into the garden a little later.

Ascertaining that the man didn't mind, and that Daisy wasn't hindering his work, she looked gingerly about her to see if Conan was around. He wasn't, but surprisingly she found Avril in her usual floppy hat, pruning a bright yellow shrub that bordered the terrace.

Intending merely to enquire how she was, and to thank her for the flowers she'd sent up to her room the previous day, she was even more surprised when, after she'd done that, the woman gestured her towards a shady bower clothed with climbing burgundy roses which cleverly screened a smoky glass-topped wicker table and two matching chairs. There was a large jug of iced orange juice on the table.

'I understand you had a bit of an accident last night?' the woman remarked, filling two tall glasses from the jug and handing one to Sienna.

So Avril knew about that, Sienna realised, her colour rising, wondering who had told Conan's mother—Conan or Claudette?—and also whether Avril knew that her younger son's widow had spent the night and half the morning in her elder son's bed!

'Yes, I'm sorry about the vase,' she said contritely, deciding to bluff her way through it. 'Was it valuable?'

'Not particularly. It was a gift from my late husband when we became engaged.'

'Oh, gosh! I'm sorry,' Sienna repeated, feeling awful.

Avril, though, was waving her apologies aside. 'Don't be. It wasn't one of my favourites. Besides, I'm surprised it survived this long.'

The woman was being surprisingly blasé, Sienna thought, over losing something that must have meant a great deal to her. She wondered if the other woman was putting on a brave face to spare her discomfort.

'I know I can't replace its sentimental value, but would you at least let me buy you another?' Sienna offered, still feeling dreadful about it.

'Don't be silly,' Avril scolded lightly. 'As you said, it's irreplaceable. So don't try.'

Feeling a little chastened, Sienna was surprised when a sun-speckled hand covered hers where it was resting on the table. 'Besides, if I want another Conan will buy me one.' There was a strangely wistful note in the woman's voice as she added, with an almost rueful smile, 'He usually supplies me with everything I need.'

Sienna felt her cheeks burning again just at the mention of

Conan's name, as sensual images of what had transpired in his room earlier caused her blood to race.

'He's a good son.'

An eyebrow cocked curiously under the floppy hat. Had Avril picked up on the rather breathless way she'd said that? Sienna wondered, dismayed, and was sure of it when the woman responded by advising, 'Don't imagine that you can get close to him, Sienna. Many women have tried—women who, if you don't mind me saying so, were a lot more steel-edged and sophisticated than you are. They've all been disappointed.'

'Perhaps he just hasn't found the right woman yet,' she returned, without thinking, and then wondered why she'd said it. Just as Avril must be wondering, she thought, when she saw that eyebrow climb even higher under the floppy hat. 'Don't worry. You've got no reason to fear that I'm likely to be taking another of your sons away from you,' she appeased, forcibly reiterating what she had promised Avril that evening Conan had come in and surprised them. And though she hadn't intended to sound bitter, she knew she did.

'Oh, I lost Conan a long time ago,' the woman startled her by saying. 'I think that's why I couldn't accept you as easily as I should have, Sienna. I couldn't bear the realisation I was losing my other son as well.'

Which she had—in the end. So pointlessly and so finally, Sienna thought, feeling for Niall's mother and yet amazed by her admission. She decided against reminding her that it was only her unfriendly attitude towards her younger son's new wife that had stopped her from gaining a daughter.

'What do you mean you lost him?' she pressed, needing to know what Avril had meant by that remark about losing Conan. 'How? I thought that you and he were—'

'Were what? Close?' A strained little laugh infiltrated the still scented air, and the face across the table was suddenly ravaged by some private emotion. 'We put on a united front,' she informed Sienna almost bitterly. 'This family's always been very good at that.' She lifted the glass in her hand and took a long draught of her orange juice. There was a small round patch of condensation on the table where the glass had stood. When she put it down, her face was turned away, as though she was studying the deeply perfumed roses interlaced with the latticework of the bower. 'I let him down, Sienna. And it's something for which I shall reproach myself for the rest of my life.'

'Let him down?' she prompted, puzzled. 'How?'

The woman gave her head a couple of quick shakes, as though she was trying to clear it of a subject that was too personal or too painful for her to talk about.

'You must have done something right,' Sienna assured her with a smile. 'Or he wouldn't have turned out quite as confident and successful and level-headed and…dependable as he is today.'

Another knowing look was angled in her direction. 'Well… he certainly seems to have scored a hit with you.'

She hadn't realised how much she had been eulogising and, blushing furiously, keen to distract Avril from suspecting how Conan affected her, she uttered without thinking, 'Where did he get those scars?'

'Scars?' Beneath the floppy hat both eyebrows lifted in questioning surprise.

So Avril hadn't known how intimate they had been. But she did now!

Sienna realised. Because how else would her daughter-in-law have known about those old wounds, she guessed Avril must be thinking, if she hadn't seen Conan totally naked?

'Didn't he tell you?' the woman enquired, somewhat cagily.

'Only that they were caused by a dog,' Sienna informed her, deciding to brazen it out. 'And he said something about being somewhere he shouldn't have been.'

'Which was in the grounds of a private business premises which had been securely locked for the night.'

'Conan?' Sienna queried, bemused. What was Avril saying? That he had been a tearaway? Was that what the woman had meant by losing him?

'Not quite what you're thinking,' Avril said knowingly, aware of the path Sienna's thoughts had taken. 'He went in after Niall—and after he had already warned him what would happen if he went over that fence. But Niall was born with a need always to do what was reckless and dangerous and downright inadvisable...'

Which was how he had had that accident, Sienna thought, guessing from that crack in his mother's voice that she was thinking the same thing.

'He wouldn't listen,' Avril was continuing. 'He was only just twelve years old to Conan's sixteen at the time, but he *had* to test his brother's authority. Had—as it turned out—to put his brother's life on the line. Because of course when Conan heard the rumpus, with the dogs barking and Niall shrieking, he just went over that fence into those grounds without a thought for his own safety. Niall was pinned down by one of the dogs, but the other one...'

She couldn't go on. She didn't have to. Sienna could visualise it all too clearly, even without seeing the anguish scoring the pale, fragile lines of her mother-in-law's face.

No wonder he'd seemed so...tense, she thought, her heart aching for him, when Shadow had jumped up at him that night he'd first called at her house. It also explained why he'd been so angry on that other occasion when Jodie had said she'd left Daisy in the garden with Shadow.

'He was in hospital for a couple of days,' Avril went on, her voice strung with the same anguish as she continued. 'And both boys were let off with a warning as there were no previous offences and my husband was such an upstanding member of the community.'

'But Conan was all right,' Sienna stressed, realising the distress that reliving the incident was causing his mother. 'It could have been far, far worse.'

'Oh, yes. He was all right,' Avril supplied with an undertone of acidity. Or was it remorse? Sienna thought, wondering why. 'And things would have stayed all right if my husband hadn't been determined to get to the bottom of it. He wasn't exactly a man known for his restraint. Niall was too frightened to tell him the truth, and it was beyond Conan's ethics to drop his brother into the front line of his father's anger. You see, Sienna, my husband could be a very intimidating man. So he made Conan pay—or tried to. He'd always made him pay for everything—except Conan was big enough and strong enough by then not to take it any more. He left the following spring and I didn't see him again for years, until after my husband died. As I'm sure you already know, Conan wasn't his son. He was the result of a one-night affair I had with a young pilot while I was on holiday in the Channel Islands. I was carefree, irresponsible and crazy. Crazily in love for those few hours, or so I convinced myself. I didn't even know his last name.

'Conan and I were close for those first few years. But then after I married Niall's father and my younger son came along the favouritism started, with Conan never being able to do anything right in his stepfather's eyes. He was so bitterly jealous of Conan—always goading him. Belittling him. I suspect it was my fault for loving Conan so much. He hasn't said as much, but I know he blames me for allowing it to happen. After all, I could have done something about it. Got him away from his stepfather. Divorced him. But in spite of all that I suppose I still loved him. And anyway, I was afraid that if I did it would be my word against his and he'd get custody of Niall—and that was more than I could bear to contemplate. So you see, Sienna, I sacrificed Conan's welfare for the sake of his brother and I shan't blame him if he never forgives me. Because I shall never, ever forgive myself for that.'

Stunned, Sienna regarded Conan's mother, her own features almost as harrowed. Avril hadn't meant to spill it out, she decided, and yet when all the pent-up anguish of a lifetime had started pouring out of her she hadn't been able to stop.

'Perhaps it's time to forgive yourself,' she suggested, doing as Avril had done earlier and slipping a hand over hers. 'I'm sure he doesn't think badly of you,' she murmured, her heart nevertheless going out to him. 'Otherwise he wouldn't worry about you quite as much as I know he does.'

'You know...you really are quite a perceptive and sensitive little thing.'

A rare warmth broke through the anguish scoring Avril's strained features. Like a chink in a wall letting the sunlight in, Sienna thought, giving her an insight into how beautiful the woman must once had been.

'I didn't ever dream that the little girl I resented would have the ability to make me open my heart to her—let alone try to make me feel better. And I *am* feeling a little better—both mentally and, I'm pleased to say, physically, too, over the past couple of days,' she expressed. 'Which is why I really don't want to see you get hurt. I know you have some sort of crush on Conan—there's no use denying it,' she interjected with a wry smile as Sienna made to try. 'Good heavens! I'm not altogether surprised—I've seen the effect he's had on women over the years. But I don't want to see you winding up unhappy over losing another of my sons, and I think you'd be on a collision course with disaster if you set your compass on Conan. He's too hard-bitten for you, Sienna. Apart from which, I think it's only fair to tell you that if you're living in the hope of his returning any feeling you think you might have for him, there's already one young woman of his acquaintance who considers herself first in the queue.'

She meant Petra Flax. Sienna didn't even need to ask. Not that she wanted to seem as though she was that interested, because she wasn't—was she? she assured herself. She'd made a big enough mistake in tying herself down the first time. She didn't have any plans for making the same mistake again any time soon.

'Good luck to her,' she murmured casually, excusing herself to go and check on Daisy, and deciding as she wound her way back through the scented garden that it was only because she'd been unwell that she felt so low.

CHAPTER EIGHT

CONAN woke up in bed, trembling and sweating. At first he thought he had caught Sienna's virus, until he realised it was only the effects of his dream.

Bringing her here had revived too many memories, he thought angrily. Of how much he had wanted her and how much he had beaten himself up over it, which in turn had reminded him of Niall, and of the darker past.

Getting up, he shrugged into his robe. The scent of her still clung to the garment from her wearing it two days ago, and, chastising himself for the way his body responded to it, he fastened the belt and went quietly downstairs without bothering to turn on a light.

Her shyness had surprised him. So had his own scruples. She had been ready for him, and yet he'd denied her. Denied himself, he thought with an ironic twist to his mouth and that familiar ache whenever he thought about her stirring in his loins. But why?

A prickly feeling down his spine lifted the hairs at the nape of his neck.

Feeling that he wasn't alone, he glanced round, his brows drawing together as he realised why. The dog had obviously padded down after him, and was standing in the doorway watching him.

A vision flashed through his brain. A set of bared white teeth. A huge snarling snout. And a black silhouette springing up out of the darkness. He felt the clamp of angry jaws, and the warm, bruising power of its body, then the pain and the fear. Fear such as he had never known before or since.

Clammy-skinned, he shook off the unwanted emotion in the way he had shaken off his dreams. 'You show up everywhere you're not wanted, don't you?' he drawled over his shoulder, opening the fridge.

The hiss of the cap being twisted off the bottle of mineral water he'd taken out was a soothing normality before he sat down with it on the cushioned cane sofa that ran along one wall, welcoming the burn of the chilled water as it slid down his throat.

Bringing her here wasn't doing much for his peace of mind or his self-respect, he thought self-deprecatingly. Because heaven only knew the feelings she generated in him weren't feelings he would normally have been too proud of. But then what man *would* be proud of harbouring such animosity towards his brother's widow, while wanting to do the most intimate things to her that his mind could dream up?

The dog padded over to him, unaware of his rising tension.

Or perhaps it was, he thought. Every cell in his body was shooting onto instinctive alert as the dog came much too close—close enough to lay a big hairy head on his bare knee.

Hesitantly he reached out, and with long tentative fingers ruffled the fur on the surprisingly gentle head. It felt warm, offering him a comfort he'd never expected to find.

'We're two of a kind, aren't we?' he murmured thickly, relaxing, experiencing for the first time a strange affinity with the animal. Didn't he come from the same ball-park as this four-legged freak? A nobody from nowhere? At least that was what his stepfather had tried to convince him he was. Of uncertain pedigree. With half his lineage unknown. The only difference was that this poor creature had been rescued, while there had been no one and nothing to rescue him.

Memories rose like dark demons, clouding his eyes and slashing harsh lines across his face, but forcefully he shook them away.

It was the past that had made him what he was. Driven.
Motivated. A success in the eyes of the world. Sometimes it
took all that he was made of to remind himself of that.

Hearing a sound, he glanced up, his wits sharper even than
Shadow's.

Or perhaps the dog was just wallowing in stringing out this
unexpected affection from him, he thought wryly, as its head
swivelled round a second after he'd spotted Sienna standing
in the doorway.

'Am I interrupting something personal?' she whispered,
sounding surprised as well as amused. 'Do the two of you
want to be left alone?'

She was wearing a short cotton polka dot robe, fastened
loosely over a matching nightdress which showed off the soft
movement of her breasts as she came in.

'What is it with the pair of you?' The barest smile touched
his lips, and a toss of his chin indicated both her and Shadow,
who had left him for this new and more appreciated visitor,
his long tail waving gently. 'Can't you leave a man to his own
devices without needing to invade his privacy?'

'I heard a sound. I looked in to see if Daisy was all right
and noticed that Shadow was gone. I just came down to see
where he was, but if that's how you feel…'

'Stay where you are.'

The deep, low command brought her head up, pulling her
round as she was about to make her exit.

'But I thought you said…'

'Your sex doesn't have the monopoly on meaning the opposite of what you say,' he advised, with something tugging
at the corners of his stupendous mouth.

'On what men *believe* is the opposite of what we say?' she
was quick to amend firmly. 'There's a difference.'

'As I'm well aware.'

Which he would be, she thought. Intuition alone assured
her that, regardless of his opinion of her, Conan Ryder was
a man who would respect women just as surely as he knew

how to pleasure them. The thought of what had transpired in his bed made her blood pulse quickly through her veins, so that it was a little breathlessly that she said, 'Are you asking me to stay?'

'Be my guest.'

She didn't take up his invitation to join him on the cane sofa. Sharing that particular seat would heighten her already screaming responses and make her more vulnerable to his devastating masculinity, and she wasn't sure she could handle the outcome of that, no matter how much she wanted it.

Instead she propped herself against the huge wooden table that stood in the middle of the room, her hands splayed out behind her.

'Do you want something to drink?' He gestured towards the fridge with the bottle he was drinking from.

Sienna shook her head, her hair a dark cap in the subdued light from the under-cupboard wall fittings which were all Conan had switched on. Her mouth felt dry, she realised, but it wasn't water that her foolish body craved.

Conan's mouth tugged carelessly on one side before his own dark head dropped back against the chintzy cushions of the sofa, the thick sweep of his lashes pressing down over the inscrutable gold of his eyes.

He looked hot and unusually tired, Sienna thought, glimpsing—surprisingly—a rare vulnerability behind that self-contained façade he presented to the world.

He was everything a woman could want, she realised, secretly studying him, her hungry eyes taking in the strong, lean bone structure that assured he would always stand out in a crowd, even without that added air of authority he exuded, or the head-turning lines of a physique that was primed to peak condition.

His reflexes were quick as a cobra's which, with that daunting ruthlessness, must have long ago earmarked him as a leader. Yet sensing vulnerability, remembering what Avril had told her, Sienna felt her heart swell with an emotion she didn't want to question too closely, and murmured in a voice made husky from that emotion, 'What's wrong?'

Her trembling question parted his lashes, bringing his unsettling gaze with unwavering directness to hers.

'Does something have to be wrong?' His smile, as he sat upright, said there wasn't. But there was, she thought, sensing it in every taut muscle of his powerful body. 'Do you know me so well that you think you can detect every nuance in my mood and character?'

'I don't think any woman could ever know you that well, Conan.'

His mouth moved contemplatively. 'You think I'm that deep?'

'I know you are.'

'And do you consider yourself qualified to plumb the depths?'

'I wasn't aware qualifications were required even if I thought of myself as a contender,' she breathed, wondering where this conversation had come from. 'Which I'm not.'

'And now I've upset you.'

'No, you haven't,' she said quickly, catching the sound of Shadow's claws on the quarry tiles as he trotted out of the kitchen, almost certainly to the comfort of Daisy's bed.

'Haven't I?' With his dark head cocked, Conan's gaze was far too shrewd, much, much too probing.

'It takes a lot more than that to upset me, Conan.'

There was a crack in her voice, he noted, that he couldn't quite account for. Contention, maybe, but if it wasn't then something was certainly affecting her.

She was outspoken, which he liked. In fact he found it distinctly refreshing. Most women he had known who were contenders for his bed had usually started out by agreeing with everything he liked, did and said—not challenging him at every given opportunity like this little madam. And yet that husky quality to her voice was doing untold things to his libido.

She was leaning back, supporting herself against the table, the action causing her robe to part and pushing up her beautiful breasts so that their soft upper swell was clearly visible to him above the simple nightdress.

He wanted her, he realised at that moment, swallowing a mouthful of cold water to try and temper his urges, more than he had wanted any woman in his life. Wanted her even as she was looking at him as doe-eyed as an innocent, and with that sort of anguished groove between her velvety eyebrows.

'Why are you looking at me like that?' he found himself asking her.

Sienna's breath seemed to shiver through her lungs, lifting her far too tender breasts to that hot masculine gaze.

Her lips parted as she dragged in air, hesitating, unintentionally provocative as she sought the courage to tell him, say the things she wanted—needed—to say.

'I only—' She swallowed, put off by that invisible barrier she could feel as tangibly as a shield of iron between them—a barrier she had always sensed Conan had deliberately erected between himself and the rest of the world. Like a dark and vigilant observer, aloof and protected by his own impregnable wall of immunity. 'Avril told me what happened when you got attacked by that dog. And about your father. I mean...' her throat worked nervously again '...your stepfather. What went on.'

Anger, like a dart of green lightning, flashed momentarily in his eyes, before his lashes came down, sweeping it away, leaving only a grim emotion that stretched his tanned skin taut across his angular features.

'What did she tell you? That he brutalised me mentally and physically?' He unfolded his long length from the padded seat and came towards her, the plastic bottle still in his hand. 'That he gave me the shelter of his home and the respectability of his name and made me pay for both of them through and through?' His bitterness was so palpable it dragged across her skin like the serrated edge of a knife.

'I'm sorry.' It sounded trite and utterly ineffectual against the depth of emotion that welled up for him from some hidden place deep inside her—such a breath-catching emotion that it was a moment before she could continue. 'She feels she let you down in not leaving him. That she put up with the way he treated you out of fear of losing your brother. She's tortured by it, Conan.'

'Is she?' he exhaled through the grinding tension of his jaw. 'And what else did she tell you? That he brutalised her too? That he made her pay for every occasion when she took my side against his? A respected barrister. A man at the cutting edge of his profession. A so-called "pillar of society."' Derision coloured his tone, his mouth contorting in distaste. 'He made her pay and never stopped making her pay until I was old enough to take matters into my own hands and knocked him flat.'

Sienna could feel the colour draining out of her cheeks, unable to imagine a man like Conan ever being driven into losing his cool like that.

'I see that she didn't,' he said grimly, assessing the shock and disbelief on her small blanched face. 'She wouldn't leave him, so in the end I had to. If I hadn't, I think I might have killed him.' He was so close now that she could feel the anger emanating from him as he put the bottle down on the table beside her. 'Life was intolerable for us all until I did. My mother was suffering and being made to pay because of me, and Niall was just caught in the middle.' He remembered his brother's tears and his frightened trembling, his sobbed and heartfelt promises—always sincerely meant after he had been too weak to admit to some wrongdoing—that he would never get him into trouble again. 'After I'd left my stepfather got what he wanted. His wife and his own son to himself, and from what I gather peace reigned from then on in the household. It seemed I was the source of all my stepfather's problems. The font from which all his jealousy sprang.'

The horror of all he had said sent a chill through Sienna,

causing her to shudder physically. Straightening up, she automatically put her hand out to him, her slender, pink-tipped fingers shaping the taut outline of one hard masculine cheek.

'I'm sorry. I'm so, so sorry.' Her feeling for him almost choked her, her words erupting from her on the tide of emotion that was flooding every fibre of her being.

His mouth lifted at one corner: a half smile—superficial, ironic, self-mocking.

'Is that why you were looking at me the way you were looking at me just now? Out of pity?' he challenged thickly. It struck him then that this was the first and only time he had ever bared his soul to anyone. It left him feeling uncomfortably exposed and vulnerable.

'I think pity would be wasted on you, Conan,' she said with unerring frankness. 'As well as being an insult,' she added tremulously, as she brought both hands into play to caress the soft towelling sheathing his broad shoulders, marvelling at how all that strength and latent power beneath her fingers could contain such a well of hidden anguish.

His smile this time was warm and unmistakably sensual, and Sienna's heart leaped as he caught her hand, turning it over to press his lips to the sensitive area of her wrist, allowing his teeth to graze gently along the inside of her arm. 'Clever answer,' he murmured silkily.

Riveted by his action, by his scent and his warmth and the breath-catching reality of his closeness, with a sensuous little shudder, she uttered, 'I'm not trying to be clever, Conan.'

His head lifted, his eyes meeting and locking with hers.

'No,' he breathed deeply in acceptance, and with his arm snaking around her waist very gently he drew her towards him.

She couldn't drag her eyes from his—not until his face went out of focus. Then she slid her arms around him, gasping into his mouth at the coldness of his right hand on her bare skin just above the back of her nightdress, from where he had been holding the chilled bottle.

'I'm sorry,' he murmured, scarcely lifting his mouth from hers, and yet she could still detect the warm concern in his voice.

'It's all right.' She sighed against the day's growth of stubble beneath his lower lip, because nothing he did to her would ever be anything but all right. She didn't know how she knew that, but she did.

His lips—like his arms—for all their strength were infinitely tender. So much so that she felt a well of emotion pressing against her chest. Because what she needed most of all right now was tenderness. Just as *he* did, she realised, with both hands coming up to cup his face, her tongue probing and exploring, melding with his as, with one arm supporting her back, he tipped her gently backwards until he was lying over her on the table.

'Oh, Conan…' Above the quiet hum of the fridge her voice was like a woodland nymph's—no more than a sigh lost on a transient breeze.

She wanted this, she realised now. Had wanted it from the moment he had taken her in his arms on the dance floor at that company dinner—refusing to acknowledge it, despising herself for even imagining what it could be like…

'Hush, hush.' He pacified her between the whisper of kisses over her face and throat, his tenderness so arousing that when he took her lips again, deepening the kiss with intensifying eroticism, she groaned her need into his mouth.

'Not now. Not yet,' he murmured with a teasing warmth in his voice, although she could tell from the way his breath shuddered through him that he was having difficulty keeping control. 'You belong in my bed, Sienna. Not here, like some cheap grabbed thrill with the boot boy—even if it is tempting to throw caution to the winds and savour the added thrill of the risk of being found out.'

How did he know that she felt like that? That she didn't care any more about who saw them? That she almost welcomed the idea of being discovered so that the whole wide world would know that this man was her lover?

And if she felt like that, then surely it must mean…

That she loved him?

But how could she? she wondered, shocked, when she had promised herself faithfully that she would stay immune. And not just with him, but with any man?

With her mouth welded to his, she sighed her despair against their mingled breath before he lifted her up, and with such little effort that she might have been weightless, carried her almost soundlessly up the marble stairs.

Did he know? He could tell what she was feeling—thinking—couldn't he? So how could she hide whatever this feeling was when her body was betraying her with its desperate need to be closer to him, craving his loving and his attention? When it always would, she thought hopelessly, just at a smile from him or a simple word…

His room was dimly lit, from where a gap in the curtains allowed the beams of a nearly full moon to creep through. But its shapes were familiar to her like the familiar surroundings of someone visually impaired.

Which she was, wasn't she? she thought with an abandoned excitement. Because they said love was blind, and she had to be blind if she could ignore the warnings of the person who knew him better than anyone about getting so intimately involved with him, if she wanted to scream out to the world that he was her lover as she had wanted to do downstairs.

He moved as stealthily as a panther across the room with her to the enormous bed, and she detected a hint of sensual amusement as he set her down on the cool sheet and said in a voice thickened from the strength of his desire for her, 'This is getting to be a habit.'

'Yes…' Her breathing was as laboured as his, her murmur a simple acquiescence of all they were going to do and what they were about to become, of the changing of the balance of their relationship for good.

And how foolish was that? An inner little voice tried breaking through her sensual lethargy to goad her, but she was already too far beyond the bounds of reason to listen.

Blotting out everything but the stimulating impulses that
were driving her, she was reaching for him as he slid in beside
her, discovering with a spiralling excitement from the warmth
of his hair-roughened skin that he had already discarded his
robe.

'Love me,' she murmured, pulling him down to her, offering her eager body to him with an abandonment which she
knew now she had never offered his brother. Not with this
cauldron of mutual need and desire, she thought.

And then Conan's lips and hands and the whole electrifying weight of his body numbed her to everything else but the
galvanising sensations that were driving her mindless for him.
Although the way he slowed the pace in measured, leisurely
adoration of her body kept her on fire until she thought she
would implode if he didn't grant her the release and fulfilment she craved.

When it finally came it had her gasping above the shuddering groans that accompanied his own burning orgasm, an all-
consuming mutual inferno of pleasure that lasted and lasted
and lasted.

It was such a profoundly moving experience that as the final
contractions throbbed out of her Sienna's emotions welled up
in scalding tears, which gave way to uncontrolled sobs that
shook her slender body.

Held against his shoulder, she let it all out, a torrent of hot,
unleashed emotion that she couldn't have held back if her life
had depended upon it.

'I'm sorry. I'm so sorry.' Ashamed, she tried to get up, but
the gentle touch of his fingers pressed her back as he raised
himself up sufficiently so that he could look at her.

'What is it? What's wrong?' he enquired, sounding deeply
concerned.

Sienna shook her head, unable to answer. How could you

tell a man who didn't particularly like you—let alone respect you—that making love with him had been the best experience of her twenty-five years? Ever. How could you do that unless you also told him that you thought you were falling in love with him? And only a fool would do that after all she had been through.

Sniffing back emotion, she shook her head again, trying to regain control, some degree of dignity.

'Do you always cry like this after you make love?' He sounded gently amused, yet surprised too.

'Don't all women?' she parried, grasping the clean, folded white handkerchief he'd just reached over and taken out of the drawer of his bedside cabinet.

'No.'

She smiled weakly, blowing her nose. 'Then it must be the effect you have on me.'

'Clearly,' he agreed, with a cocked smile. His thick winged brows were drawing together in puzzled bewilderment. What was she saying? That she hadn't been like this with any of the other men she'd known? Before he knew it, he was asking, 'What happened between you and my brother?'

Of course. He still believed she'd had a lover.

She didn't answer at first. How could she, she thought, when there were some things that were far too personal?

Striving to sit up, she was relieved when he permitted it this time.

'We were having problems,' she admitted, looking down at the handkerchief she was twisting in her hands. 'We always seemed to be arguing in the end.'

'What about?' he pressed.

'I don't know.' She gave a little shrug. 'Everything. Money. Daisy. His drinking.'

I'm sorry. I'm so, so sorry...

The regrets of that other time echoed down the years, but mentally she shook them away.

'Sienna?'

Lying on his side now, supported by his elbow, he could see the tension in her slender back—the way she was holding herself rigid as though she was fighting an inner battle with herself. One that hurt—like hell.

He placed a hand on her shoulder, his touch gentle but firm, and compliantly she allowed him to draw her back into the warm circle of his arms.

'His job. Being a father. His debts. I think it was all too much for him,' she murmured, her voice sounding far away. 'And he was always working so hard. Driving himself…' *To try and compete with you,* she added mentally, but didn't say it. 'We even stopped making love. I thought it was all my fault. Because I was tired looking after Daisy. I thought maybe motherhood had made me unattractive…'

Conan laughed softly, his eyes incredulous. 'Are you kidding? Your pregnancy, Sienna, made you blossom—and, believe me, it lasted.' He didn't tell her that there had been times when he'd found himself thoroughly envying his brother. Aside from all those other occasions, he thought, when he'd been a child, desperate for his stepfather's approval. For one ounce of the praise and affection his brother had taken as his birthright. 'I wanted you, Sienna.'

His comments had made her blush, he noticed, stroking her damp cheek, watching colour infuse the delicate skin. 'And it was mutual, wasn't it?' he prompted, thinking how her unexpected disclosure might go some way to explaining why she had taken a lover, even if it didn't excuse it. And why he had picked up on those pheromones she'd given off whenever she was alone in his company, but particularly at that dinner-dance that night. But was it because of *him?* Or had her lack of sex with Niall made her that desperate for a man? Any man? he wondered, finding the thought less than flattering, though he knew he had no right even thinking that way about the woman who'd been married to his brother. 'Tell me the truth.' For all his ethics about what was right and wrong, it was suddenly imperative that he should know.

'You overwhelmed me, that's all,' she dissembled, sitting up again. Because there was being straight with him, and there was being downright stupid. There was no way she was going to tell him exactly how she had felt when he had taken her in his arms that night because she had only just realised it herself. And because... Well, because she just couldn't, that was all. 'I know you don't want to accept it,' she tagged on, her blue gaze coming level with his, 'but I never cheated on your brother.'

His eyelids came down, concealing what he was thinking, his chest lifting and falling heavily.

Did he believe her? she wondered, aching for him to tell her so and realising now that she *had* to make him understand.

'Tim's mother and my dad were some sort of distant cousins. They were like family, and we all used to go on holiday together. When Tim's parents moved to Spain he was only seventeen, and he wanted to stay in England, so Mum and Dad let him move in with us. We used to go clubbing together, or to the cinema if one of us was at a loose end. He was part of the gang I kicked around with.' Her childhood playmate. The son of the couple she'd always called Aunt and Uncle. And, after he'd moved in, the big brother she'd never had. 'When Mum and Dad decided to move to Spain too, and I got my flat, they asked him if he'd keep an eye on me. There was never anything romantic between us,' she stressed, needing to convince him.

Because for Timothy Leicester there had never been anyone but Angie Thompson. Angie who had given him the runaround at school and at college, until just before she went away to university when she'd realised he was the nicest thing walking on two legs.

'I looked on him as a brother, and his girlfriend was like a sister to me until she went off to Brazil to save the rainforest. When you turned up at Tim's place that morning to tell me what had happened to Niall—I know how it must have looked, but you wouldn't listen to the things I've just told you—then or afterwards—when I tried to explain.' Because all he had seen in that one bedroom flat was a rumpled double bed, and belongings lying around that were exclusively masculine. And he had already been persuaded of her guilt, she remembered, by the people who had had her investigated. 'Angie was already in Brazil, and I knew Tim was planning to join her, but I—' She broke off, her breath coming shallowly, suddenly finding it impossible to articulate the words that would vindicate her. 'I just wanted to see him before he went,' she said instead.

'When I turned up with Daisy and decided to stay the night he gave up the bedroom and slept on the sofa. I tidied it up after he'd left for work,' she went on. So there had been nothing but her futile attempt—already muddled by the shock of learning about Niall—to convince his brother that he hadn't just stepped into an illicit love-nest. 'I was too upset to string two sentences together.' So numbed by what had happened and by everything that had driven her to Tim's that weekend that she hadn't even been able to cry. So Conan had decided she didn't care. 'I was also scared stiff of you,' she admitted, with a rather sheepish smile. 'As I said, you overwhelmed me.'

He inclined his head ever so slightly, in the briefest of acknowledgements. But of what? she wondered piercingly. That she was telling the truth? Was that what had brought his incredible lashes down over his eyes and made his breath seem to shiver through him? Or was it just relief in deciding at last that he wasn't sleeping with the enemy?

'And what about now, Sienna?' he exhaled, disappointing her because he didn't actually say he believed her. Although she hadn't actually told him everything, had she? she admitted to herself, already starting to tingle from the sensuality with which he pressed, 'Do I overwhelm you *now?*'

That sexiness of his voice and the way he was looking at her with such a febrile glitter in his eyes made her pulses start to throb, sending a resurgence of hot desire licking along her veins.

'No, you've just made me realise that I've got you exactly where I want you,' she murmured provocatively, pushing him back so that she could admire the flawed perfection of his amazing body.

Sensuously then, and very slowly, she anointed him with kisses, her tongue marking a path along the line of dark hair that ran from his chest, down over his waist to his tight, lean abdomen, straying only to pay particular attention to those angry slashes that spoke so vividly of his character, and were testimony to the sort of man he was.

A brave and honourable one, she thought, otherwise he wouldn't have shown such a strong sense of responsibility towards his weaker and reckless younger brother. And not just with those dogs, but in everything, she decided, her feeling for him ballooning inside her until it almost hurt keeping it to herself.

But she had to, she resolved grittily, guessing that he probably wouldn't welcome what he might think was a love-struck, clingy female in his bed any more than she intended to allow herself to become one. She understood now though why he'd threatened to take Daisy from her in the past, and why he'd vetoed the thought of any other man stepping into her life, and subsequently into Daisy's, when he'd had a stepfather as cold and brutal as he'd had.

Wanting to heal him more than she could ever express in words, and touching him in the most intimate place, she watched with darkened eyes as his face was scored almost with pain and his jaw clamped tightly as he groaned his need of her.

Made bold by his response, and the realisation of her strong yet reluctant love for him, she pleasured him then in the way she had wanted to please him since that first morning she'd woken up in his bed, driving him wild for her until he finally lost control and surrendered to the power of her femininity.

CHAPTER NINE

THE days that followed were halcyon ones for Sienna. She was living in a fragile bubble of happiness, she realised, which, like all bubbles, was by its very nature designed not to last.

Foolishly, though—and she knew she was being foolish—she allowed herself to enjoy the ecstatic feeling that she was floating on a cloud, buoyed up by Conan's insatiable need of her and hers for him, and kept there by the all-consuming fire of their lovemaking.

He could be excitingly passionate, she was discovering, when they had been made to wait to satisfy their intensifying and increasing appetite for each other because of the presence of Daisy and Avril, or simply because of the pressing demands of Conan's work. Unable to wait another second to satisfy their screaming hunger for each other, content that Daisy was safely preoccupied with Claudette or his mother, they would slink away like guilty lovers to some quiet area of his private beach, or out to the yacht he kept in the bay. There he would make hard and urgent love to her—just as her body demanded it—without any waiting or prolonged foreplay, driving her crazy with the knowledge that he wanted her with every breath of the passion with which she wanted him, and with shattering orgasms that left them both slick with sweat and gasping at the driving urgency with which he had taken her.

And then there were those other times, in the still of the night, between the sensuous satin of his sheets, when the rest of the world evaporated, when he would drive her delirious for him with a slow, calculated expertise that had her shuddering and sobbing for release. Then he would show her the true meaning of the phrase "sexual prowess" by bringing her to orgasm after multi-orgasm, before he finally allowed his amazing control to snap and lost himself in the hot and exquisite fulfilment her body offered.

Sienna would emerge the following morning, unable to conceal the glow in her cheeks, or the way her eyes were glittering like brilliant sapphires after a night of unparalleled rapture, her spirits high, her mood buoyant, while she ached for his lips and his hands on her body again with a craving that only making love with him could temporarily slake.

Conan, on the other hand, managed to appear remarkably unaffected—especially when they were in the company of other people. While meeting the pressing demands of his high-flying day-to-day business, or joining her and Avril for a drink on the terrace, or even inviting Sienna to accompany him for a meal out with colleagues, he stayed appropriately and yet amazingly aloof. Until he glanced across at her from behind his mother's chair or across a crowded table, and then the message in his eyes ignited a flame that would make molten heat pool in her loins and keep her on fire for him—sometimes for hours—until it culminated, as it always did on those occasions, in one of the hottest and most basic of couplings that was all the more thrilling for having been denied.

How they managed to keep their drastically altered relationship from Daisy and Avril and everyone else in the house—with the exception perhaps of Claudette—Sienna wasn't sure, except that Conan had enough discretion for both of them. He made no attempt to touch her if any of the others were around, or only in the most casual of ways. Like when helping her in and out of the dinghy when they had a family day out on the yacht, or giving her a hand up from the shingle where they had been playing with Daisy. And if Claudette alone wondered why there were two damp towels slung down on the base of his power shower, or two depressions on the pillows

on his enormous bed, or even that the bronze leather surface
of the desk she was polishing smelled of a sultry feminine
perfume when the sun touched it, then she was obviously
paid too highly—or, more probably, respected her employer
too much—to disclose his very private affair.

Because it *was* an affair. Sienna wasn't so completely swept
away not to realise that. After all, if she had been setting her
sights on marriage—which she certainly wasn't, she assured
herself—what could a girl like her ever hope to offer a man
like him?

And when it ended, as it surely would, she accepted—when
her euphoria was dampened by the thought of what she had
got herself into, how awkward would it be remaining in touch
with him—as she would have to, she realised, now that she
had agreed to bring Daisy to see her father's family as regularly as her job would allow? It was something pointed out to
her rather surprisingly, and not in so many words, by Avril
one afternoon, when Sienna was helping her cut some blooms
from the villa's magnificent white roses bushes.

'I hope you've thought about what you're doing, Sienna.'
The caution was so sudden and yet so patently clear that
Sienna looked up quickly from what she was doing and felt
one of the vicious thorns prick her finger. 'I hope you have,'
Avril emphasised. 'For all our sakes.'

Sienna turned away so that her mother-in-law wouldn't see
the colour that washed up into her cheeks, sucking hard on
her wound. The blood was bitter in her mouth—as bitter as
the meaning behind Avril's warning.

'I won't do anything that will ever stop you seeing Daisy
again,' Sienna promised, though a little shakily. Because
wasn't she doing exactly that? she berated herself, noticing
how much better Avril was looking than when Sienna had
first come here, despite the anxiety that was still lining her
somewhat gaunt features. The woman had more colour in her
cheeks these days, and she was getting stronger by the day,
taking on more adventurous tasks without getting breathless,

which was thanks in part to the regime of gentle exercise that Sienna had set out for her, but mainly, she suspected, because Avril was enjoying a new sense of purpose in being able to focus on her little granddaughter. Did she want to jeopardise all that through her own selfishness?

She was being a fool. She knew she was—had been telling herself since that night when she'd gone down to the kitchen looking for Shadow and found him with Conan, before she'd gone willingly into his arms and let him take her to bed. Hadn't she been advising herself day after day—when she managed to find some rational moment after he'd gone out and she could think with a clearer head—that she must call a halt to what was happening between them before it got out of hand? But she couldn't, she thought, ashamed of having to admit how weak she was where he was concerned. It was already out of hand.

Part of her had been half in love with him for a long time, she accepted now, although she hadn't realised it until that night. The night she'd discovered how unhappy his childhood had been, and she had opened up to him with everything that was caring and feminine in her when she'd realised just how cruel his stepfather had been and how isolated and undervalued he must have felt.

But if he hadn't then he might not have been so determined to make a success of himself, she thought, aching for the little boy who had felt like such an outcast, so underrated and alone. It was his childhood, most certainly, that must have contributed to that determination and to the steel-edged strength of his character, although he probably owed some of it to the young pilot who had fathered him, rather than Avril, who tended to let life ride roughshod over her, Sienna decided, thinking of the father who had never known Conan existed. But it had flawed him too, as his mother had already pointed out.

He didn't allow anyone close to him. So what right did she have to assume that one day he might—and that it would be

her, she wondered dispiritedly, when she wasn't even ready
to make another commitment herself? None, she told herself
bluntly. Yet in spite of the talking to she kept giving herself,
and the things Avril had just said, she couldn't help nursing
the hope of a woman already lost to love, even while wondering how she could possibly have got herself into such a mess.

They spent the last afternoon of Sienna's time in the South
of France making love in Conan's enormous bed, because
Avril had taken Daisy to a children's fête in one of the neigh-
bouring villages. Sienna had wanted to go with her daughter, thinking that the energetic four-year-old might prove too
much of a handful for Conan's mother. But the little girl had
protested, telling her very importantly that she was taking
her grandmother all by herself—which Avril had been quick
to second—and with Conan's chauffeur driving them to the
fête, and Claudette going along to take the strain off the older
woman, Sienna had reluctantly given in.

  Now, tender in the aftermath of lovemaking, she was lounging naked on top of the duvet, supported by pillows and one
arm behind her head, smiling as the bedroom door opened
and Conan came in with a tray.

  Having made love across lunchtime, and for the past couple of hours since, they were both famished, and Sienna had
welcomed his suggestion of bringing something up from the
kitchen. She could already smell the fresh crusty bread, and
noticed, with her mouth watering, the white and gold wedges
of the various cheeses he'd selected under a glass dome as
he set the tray down on the table he'd already placed beside
the bed. With his casual long-sleeved white shirt—tucked
loosely into his pale chinos—gaping virtually to the waist, he
looked the stuff of every woman's fantasy, and Sienna couldn't
take her eyes off that tantalising swathe of bronzed, hair-
roughened flesh while he was lifting the dome off the cheeses,
any more than she could ignore the musky scent that ema-

nated from him, and the scent of loving which still hung heavily in the room.

'Now.' He was tapping one of the cheese wedges with the curved end of the knife. 'What will you have?'

'You,' she breathed, her eyelids heavy from the sensual bonds which held her captive, finding it extremely erotic being naked when he was already dressed.

'You're decadent,' he murmured, his eyes glinting as he handed her one of the glasses of red wine he had brought up, his heated gaze roaming approvingly over her body.

'No. I'm not,' she countered, her excitement building just at the way he was looking at her. 'If I am, then it's your fault. Every little wicked thing I do, you're responsible for.' Taking a sip of the dark, full-bodied wine, she let the base of the tall glass rest on the dip between her tender, betraying breasts. 'Aren't you ashamed of yourself, Conan Ryder?'

He thought about what she'd said about his brother's interest in her waning, and wondered how any man could not want her. He could feel his urges rising again, but there were things that needed to be said.

'Don't do that.'

With her chin resting just above her chest, the glass tilted forward towards her, she was drawing her tongue suggestively around the rim of the glass while sweeping him a look of pure provocation.

'Why not?' Her smile teased, but she was all wide-eyed innocence as she did it again.

'Because if you don't stop it then I'm going to do something I'll be very ashamed of.'

'Like sending me back to bed with no dinner?' She giggled and slid down the bed, fully aware of the way what she was saying and doing was turning him on. 'Isn't that what you do with naughty girls who misbehave?'

'Sienna…'

Ignoring him, she wriggled further down the bed, with the base of the glass still pressed against the valley between her breasts, moving her hips so wantonly that the wine came precariously close to slopping out of the glass. 'Oops!'

'If you spill that…' Conan's voice warned of some delicious repercussions.

'Oh, dear!' She bit her lower lip in mock contrition. 'And it would be all over your nice clean sheets too.'

She gasped as the glass was suddenly whisked out of her hand.

'Sienna…we have to talk.'

His voice held all the gravity of something extremely serious. Like a doctor telling you there was no more room to hope. She heard it, but didn't want to acknowledge it—any more than she wanted to acknowledge that same seriousness mirrored in his eyes.

'We *are* talking,' she breathed tremulously, dark lashes pressed against the wells of her eyes so that she couldn't see that look of finality that was oh, so obvious in his eyes.

Tomorrow they would be flying back. What else was he going to tell her except that the holiday romance was over? No, not quite that—because it hadn't been a romance, had it? It had been the uncontrolled and desperate need of one man and one woman to do the most fundamental thing nature demanded of them. And if nature had had its way she would have been pregnant by him dozens of times over, she thought shamefully, except he had always been careful to take precautions.

As he was doing now, she realised, her senses leaping in wild anticipation, because her provocation had ultimately proved too much for him. She didn't need to open her eyes to recognise the sliding of the drawer in the bedside cabinet, and the familiar urgency of him ripping off his clothes.

It was quick and hot and hard, as once again she obeyed nature's demands in her hopeless, insatiable craving for him, taking him into her with her legs clenched tightly around his taut hard waist, her fingers locking with his on either side of the pillow high above her head.

When it was over she collapsed beneath him, gasping from the shuddering contractions that had had her crying out with an emotion that had been almost too much to contain.

Now, as he came down on top of her, breathing as heavily as she was, he pressed his lips against the satin slope of her shoulder. After a few moments, in a voice roughened by passion, he advised thickly, 'Don't fall in love with me, Sienna.'

She had, she thought hectically, wondering if he had guessed—and wincing a little as he withdrew from her, as so much loving by him today had made her tender. He was after all experienced enough to recognise when a woman's responses were for real.

Why not? she wanted to demand, just for the sheer hell of it. As if she didn't know! Men like him didn't fall for girls like her. And if the beautiful and sophisticated women that he usually mixed with couldn't penetrate that hard veneer, what hope did a girl of her humble background have of succeeding?

Feigning nonchalance, she uttered, 'I wouldn't dream of it.' She even managed a painful little smile.

'I mean it,' Sienna.' He didn't even look at her as he got up from the bed. 'If you do, you'll only get hurt.'

He could feel her gaze following him as he paced away to the bathroom. He felt like a heel, he thought, but he couldn't lie to her. She had come to him that night when he had most needed her tender femininity and he had taken full advantage of it—over and over and over again.

As he dispensed with the condom and got himself back into some sort of order he thought back to four weeks ago, when he had first brought her here, and particularly to that antagonised scene with her in the pool.

It had been his intention to have a fling with her. Get his anger and his rampant desire for her out of his system. But it hadn't worked out as simply as that. The more he had of her, the more he wanted. And the more he took, surprisingly, the more it seemed she was prepared to give. It didn't help his conscience either to discover that, far from the lying little cheat he had always believed her to be, she appeared to be open and honest and entirely different from the girl he thought he had known.

There was nothing of the high-maintenance, possession-loving creature who had worn her designer clothes and jewellery like trophies three years ago. She dressed very simply, never seemed interested in any of the exclusive shops whenever she had the chance to browse around them. And whenever he had taken her and Daisy out for the day she'd always tried to insist on paying for her and his niece's share herself.

She was proud and dignified and unbelievably desirable. She was also making him question his own actions—and he didn't like that. Whatever she said, she was getting too involved with him—and *he,* he realised, like a fool, was in danger of allowing her to. He didn't want to hurt her, but neither did he want an emotional involvement with her. Even if he was being brutal, she had to know.

She was standing by the bed, pulling on her blue chequered shirt, when he came back into the bedroom wearing his robe. A glimpse of her bare breasts above the tight clinging jeans almost threw his determination to the winds.

'Why are you looking at me like that?' Her heavy-lidded eyes, he noticed, were dark and brooding.

'Like what?' she replied curtly, knotting the ends of her blouse just above her tiny waist.

'Like I'm the big bad wolf and you're Little Red Riding Hood.'

Perhaps I feel like Little Red Riding Hood, she thought silently. Chased. Caught. Pounced on. And ravenously devoured. It didn't help telling herself, no matter how bad she was feeling, that she had done her fair share of the devouring too.

'I'm sorry if I've disappointed you,' he was saying, 'because I'm not the soft-hearted sentimentalist you might have convinced yourself I was.'

The sun picked out snatches of red in her gleaming black hair as she brought her head up. 'You? Soft?' she said with a brittle little laugh. 'I think any woman—or man—would have to have their head read if they *ever* made the mistake of thinking you were soft.'

'Then what's eating you, Sienna?'

What's eating me, she thought, as she turned away and made a show of straightening the duvet, is that I love you. And even though I've never said it, you've as good as thrown it right back in my face.

'Nothing,' she murmured with a little shrug.

He couldn't see her face, only the taut movements of her back, and the way her jeans clung smoothly to the contours of her delightful little bottom as she tried to restore some order to the wreck of his love-scented bed.

'I've never lied to you, or given you any reason to expect the promise of a commitment,' he added tonelessly.

Thumping a pillow with unnecessary force, she said coolly, without glancing round, 'Have I ever asked you to?'

'No.' His eyes were darkly reflective as he stood there watching her. He'd messed this up good and proper, he thought, wanting to kick himself, knowing that he should have had this conversation with her weeks ago. 'And I'm not suggesting that we should end what we have.'

'Really?' She spun round, clutching another pillow tightly to her chest. 'What exactly *do* we have, Conan? Great sex?'

Something tugged at one corner of his mouth. 'You must admit it's pretty spectacular.'

Which was an understatement! she thought. They had been slightly more than obsessed with each other! At least in bed.

'So you're saying we go on as we are? With no strings attached?'

'If you're prepared to do that. I just want to be open with you, so you know from the start where you stand and you can make a decision. Just as long as you're aware that I'm not proposing to marry you.'

He couldn't have put it more plainly.

'So you want us to go on having great sex, so long as it's kept on a purely physical level?'

'You don't have to make it sound so cold-blooded,' he remarked, reaching for his glass of wine, which still remained untouched on the tray he'd brought up before they had been overtaken by the scorching inferno that continued to consume them with no sign of ever burning itself out.

'Don't I?' She tossed the plumped pillow back on the bed. 'So what did you expect? My loving gratitude? There aren't many women who wouldn't feel a little put out by such a high-handed, presumptuous statement. "Just as long as you're aware that I'm not proposing to marry you",' she mimicked, her hands clutching her elbows, punctuating each word with a little shake of her body. 'Well, for your information, Conan Ryder, who said I *wanted* to marry you? If you must know, I had enough of marriage and so-called connubial bliss with your wonderful brother. Why would I want to jump in feet first and tie myself down to *you?*'

Of course, he thought. She hadn't had a particularly good time of it with his brother. But she was saving face. He was sure of it. It made him want to take her in his arms and kiss away her painful indignation. But that was just sex driving him—he was sure of that too—and suddenly he felt angry with her for making him feel so guilty.

'Well, that told me, didn't it?' he said, putting down his glass and holding the feeling in check as he played along with what he strongly suspected was an all-out attempt to maintain her dignity. His annoyance though was being swiftly replaced by something fast approaching admiration. The reaction of most women he dismissed from his bed after an affair had run its course was usually one of tears or bitter recriminations. Sienna wasn't outwardly displaying either. But then neither was he dismissing her from his bed. 'Which will just teach me to presume.'

'Yes, it will!' she underlined, wondering how—even when

there was no future in it—when she hadn't even expected him to offer her one—she was going to find the strength to walk away from all that he was proposing. Which was little more than pure and simple ecstasy until such time as he called the shots by deciding he wanted to move on. 'But just for the record... If I were to agree to what you're suggesting—which I'm not,' she tagged on hastily, 'aren't you worried that I really might fall in love with you? Or worse.' With a feigned and shuddering little laugh she lifted her eyes to the ceiling. 'Heaven forbid! You might suddenly find yourself in love with *me!*'

'Stop it, Sienna.' Suddenly he couldn't bear what he could see clearly she was doing to herself. He didn't want pretence. He would have preferred tears, or at best a tirade of abuse from her. 'I don't intend allowing myself ever to fall in love with you. It won't happen. Do I make myself clear?'

'As crystal.' But her voice cracked as she said it. Why should it matter? she challenged herself. When another commitment with a man was something she had been determined to steer clear of? When falling for him didn't mean putting herself back into the kind of emotional tyranny she had known before? Still reeling from his statement, however, she uttered with all the dignity she could muster, 'Could you at least tell me what puts you in a position so enviously above the rest of us that you're able to set such store by your own immunity?'

She was too far removed from his social circle for him ever to fall in love with. He still didn't like her. She satisfied him in bed but was far too shallow to satisfy his intellectual needs. The possibilities rang through her brain and none of them were complimentary. Or perhaps it was simply that he was in love with Petra Flax.

He had been pulling on his clothes, and his shirt was now hanging loosely over his chinos as it had been before they had both been overcome by their escalating need for each other.

'I came from one fractured family,' he told her grimly, pulling up his zip. 'I don't ever intend putting myself back into the hell-hole of another.'

His voice was so hard-edged she could feel the bitterness emanating from him. 'What do you mean?' she queried, frowning. How could any relationship he might choose to form with a woman possibly compare with the family life that he had had?

'I've no intention of becoming a stepfather to another man's child,' he shocked her by saying. 'Even if that child *is* my niece.'

Because he didn't care about his niece's mother enough. That was what he was saying, surely?

'I don't expect you to understand. Just trust me. It would be much too complicated.'

How? she almost asked, but managed to stop herself in time. Because that would be like openly admitting that she *did* love him and *was* looking for more permanence when she wasn't, wouldn't it? she reasoned hectically. But she couldn't just leave it like that.

'Even if I was saying I wanted something more—which I'm not—but some other woman might,' she felt she ought to tag on, 'how could Daisy—or any other woman's child—complicate things?' she pressed, unable to comprehend exactly what he was saying.

He thought of his loneliness, of his mother's fear of showing any affection towards him, of the rows and the jealousies and the divided loyalties that had eventually ripped them apart.

'I mean that eventually I might want children of my own. And closer blood ties are bound to create favouritism—jealousies. How could I be sure someone else's child wouldn't take second place to my own? Or I might try too hard not to let that happen and wind up being unfair to my own offspring. I'll marry eventually, but I'll never risk becoming the kind of father my stepfather was to me.'

You aren't that kind of person, she wanted to say, but he'd think she was only hankering after marriage if she did.

Instead, wanting genuinely to know, she asked tentatively, 'Are you perhaps worrying that you might follow him in other ways? That because of your upbringing you might wind up…' she was having difficulty saying it but she pressed on anyway '…wind up treating your wife and children in the same way he treated you and your mother?'

'By being physically brutal?' he supplied, looking appalled, not seeming to notice the way she winced as he said it. 'No. I abhor violence,' he appended, and from the way his firm mouth contorted she could tell he meant it—with a vengeance. 'I don't think there's a situation on earth that can't be resolved with diplomacy and communication. But a child needs its own father, and if it hasn't got that then nothing in the world is worth supplying what could only be a poor substitute.'

He meant that too, she realised, only fully understanding now, from the intensity with which he spoke, just how deeply his childhood had scarred him. But a poor substitute for what? she wondered bitterly. For a man who shrieked at his child until she screamed from the terror of it? For a man who flew into rages until she was afraid to take her baby home?

'Not that it affects me in any way,' she murmured, her throat raw from the anguish of remembering, 'but from a man of your obvious intelligence isn't that a rather short-sighted view? Do you imagine that every stepfamily in the land is suffering agonies of torment just because yours did? That every child who loses a parent—for whatever reason—shouldn't have the right to expect a loving surrogate father or mother in their place?'

'No,' he said, breathing out heavily through his nostrils. 'What I'm saying is that it wouldn't work for *me*. And if you think that's a rather short-sighted view—well, I'm afraid it's the only one I've got.'

Which was just unfortunate for her, Sienna thought, if she had been pinning her hopes on a wedding ring. Nevertheless she was hurting—but for him too, because he sounded so bitter, his voice harsh from the unforgettable misery of his childhood.

'Supposing one day you meet someone you really fall in love with and she has a child—or children?'

'It won't happen.' His tone was inexorable.

'How can you be so sure?'

'Because I'd be careful not to get involved with her in the first place.'

'What about me?' she ventured, trying to sound casual in spite of everything. 'Weren't you just a little bit worried that you might find yourself getting involved with me?'

'Not in that way,' he stated, and every syllable he uttered seemed to lacerate her heart.

'And what way is that?' she quizzed, swallowing emotion, unable to help the feeling that she was bleeding inside. For her being *involved* with someone could only mean being in love.

'I mean not with wedding bells and confetti and happy ever afters, Sienna. And if you've been imagining that that's where we were headed, then I'm truly sorry if I misled you.'

'No, you didn't,' she replied, chiding herself for caring so much when he had done nothing to indicate that she was any more than just another pleasurable diversion in his life—the kind he no doubt indulged in all the time with the opposite sex. Except, unlike the more sophisticated, far more sensible women who would normally share his bed, she'd been stupid enough to fall in love with him. 'Anyway, I wasn't thinking of myself in all this,' she put in, pulling her thoughts up quickly. Even if she was the worst possible kind of romantic fool for getting herself into this situation, there was no way Conan was ever going to know about it. 'I was thinking of you.'

'Me?' A self-mocking note of laughter escaped him. 'Lose no sleep over that, my dear deluded innocent. I can assure you I'm perfectly happy.'

'No, you're not. OK, maybe you are—but with such a closed attitude to life you're going to miss out on a lot.'

'I already did,' he reminded her tersely. 'And it isn't an experience I intend repeating with any other child. If my view doesn't particularly correlate with yours, all I can say is that—like you—I'm not merely thinking of myself in all this. I'm thinking of the wider picture and the family I ultimately make myself responsible for. Daisy's my niece,' he continued pragmatically. 'Nothing will ever change that. And as my niece I'll encourage and support her and see that she never wants for anything—if you'll allow me to do that—but I won't take on the role of a father in her eyes, and I sincerely hope that you haven't given her any reason to suspect I would.'

Hurting, angry, Sienna shot back in protest. 'I've done no such thing! I told you—I've got no intention of settling down with anyone!'

'Good. Then let's keep it that way. I won't ever try to step into Niall's shoes, or presume to imagine that I could give Daisy—or any other man's child for that matter—the understanding and emotional stability that only her own father could have given her.'

Which was a joke in itself, Sienna thought bitterly, resisting the urge to tell him just how 'emotionally stable' his younger brother had been.

'And if you're still harbouring any ideas about pitying me, then you can dispense with them now. If you'd lived through the undesirable set-up I lived through, you'd realise that I'm being totally practical.'

'That's not being practical, Conan,' she advised, realising how strongly he believed it. 'That's being afraid.'

'Call it what you like. The subject isn't open for any more discussion,' he stated harshly, and his coldness and then the slamming of the bathroom door hurt her almost as much as the first time Niall had hit her.

CHAPTER TEN

CONAN came out of the villa carrying Sienna's and Daisy's cases. The morning was still and warm, with a mist lying over the distant mountains, but the sun shining on the water beyond the terraced gardens was making it appear piercingly blue.

The boot of the Mercedes was open, where his chauffeur had been loading his own luggage earlier, but at the moment he could only see Sienna tossing her jacket onto the rear seat of the car.

He knew he had hurt her by making his intentions clear, even if she had seemed quite adamant about not making a commitment herself. Whether she was simply bluffing or whether she meant it, he still wasn't sure. He just hadn't wanted her thinking that he was intending to settle down and play happy families when he clearly wasn't. However, that still didn't stop him feeling like a first-rate heel. A feeling only made worse as he remembered how she had refused to take any of the money he had promised her for coming here when he had offered it to her recently, and how she had firmly rebuffed any suggestion of his buying her a new car.

Daisy was still inside, saying her last goodbyes to Claudette and the staff, and so, grabbing this precious last chance to be alone with Sienna for heaven knew how long, Conan quickened his stride past the marble columns above the steps.

She was leaning with her bent arms resting on the roof of his car. The short yellow dress she was wearing with simple black pumps—which was no doubt from a high street store—

did as much, if not more for her in its chic simplicity, he decided, than any of the expensive designs she had obviously worn to please his brother.

She hadn't heard him approaching, giving him time to enjoy the quiet pleasure of admiring her.

With silent masculine appreciation he took in the swanlike elegance of her neck beneath the shining dark cap of her hair, the way the flattering cut of the dress left one arm and shoulder completely bare, that delicate butterfly design on her silken skin.

He'd always disliked tattoos, and yet this one somehow seemed to underline the intrinsic gentleness in her character—as though its subject had actually chosen to settle there and was feeling too safe to fly away.

Impatient with himself for indulging in such sentimental codswallop, he gave himself a mental shake, and from just a few yards away said coolly, without any preamble, 'You've been avoiding me.' And wound up berating himself for catching her off-guard when she swung round, startled, because that was what he had been intending.

'No, I haven't,' she responded cagily, looking up at him with one slender hand shielding her eyes.

But she had been, he assured himself. She had made sure of involving herself with whatever it was Daisy and Avril had been doing all the previous afternoon and evening, before she'd taken herself off to bed early under the pretext, he was sure, of having a headache. And he was certain that she'd only been pretending to be asleep when he'd looked into her room after knocking quietly on her door.

'I'm sorry if what we were discussing yesterday upset you.' He felt uncomfortable bringing it up. But why on earth should he? he wondered, lifting each heavy individual suitcase with remarkable ease into the boot.

Was he sorry? Sienna viewed him guardedly. Sporting that dark executive image—he'd said he had a business meeting to attend as soon as they touched down in London—and with the sunlight striking brilliance from the glittering gold of his eyes, he looked anything but penitent.

'It didn't.' Her smile was forced. How could he still take her breath away when she now knew what he had been open enough to warn her of in his bedroom yesterday? There was absolutely no future for them. Not that she had been expecting that there would be, but it still hadn't stopped it hurting to have him spell it out. 'I'm made of sterner stuff than to fall apart merely by being told the truth,' she told him, brazening it out. Taking a deep breath, she asked far more lightly than she was feeling, 'So what happens now?'

'You tell me. If you wish it, there's no reason why we shouldn't carry on as we are.'

So he'd really meant that yesterday, about not ending what they had. They could still carry on having great sex just so long as she realised that for him it didn't mean anything other than that.

With her heart giving an almost painful lurch, she echoed breathlessly, 'Carry on...?'

'I don't see why not. But it has to be your decision.'

Because he could just walk away from her without turning a hair, seeing her as just another satisfying interlude in his life, while she...

She would just have to grin and bear it when he *did* walk out of her life for good.

Except that it never would be for good, would it? she realised hopelessly. Because there was Daisy. Daisy who bound them both together and with whom he would naturally want to keep in touch, like the father he was determined never to be.

Turning her gaze away from him, to hide all that she was feeling, she uttered, 'And if I decide against it?'

'It would be a pity,' he exhaled, his chest lifting beneath that immaculate white shirt, 'when we seem to gel so well.'

'In bed, you mean.' He didn't answer. How could he? she thought, when in doing so he'd be admitting to reducing what there was between them to little more than an animal coupling?

'As I said, it has to be your decision. But I don't think you're ready to let go, Sienna, any more than I'm prepared to let you. You know I can't get enough of you, and you don't have to say a word for me to know that it's entirely mutual.'

'I might be weak,' she murmured, 'but I'm not a total fool.'

Like hell she wasn't! she thought, despairing of herself. If she'd listened to her head instead of her heart at the beginning she wouldn't be in the mess she was in now.

'Don't think about breaking things off between us, Sienna. Right now I need you in my life like I've never needed anyone.' Where had *that* come from? he asked himself, wondering how he could possibly have allowed any woman to impel him to admit a thing like that—let alone the woman against whom he had harboured a three year long grievance, and a desire to teach her a lesson without any regard for what the cost might be. 'Right now you're good for me—we're good for each other,' he appended, thinking how selfish he was in danger of sounding. But there wasn't a woman anywhere he felt so desperate to keep in his bed. 'Of course if you're asking me to prove it to you...'

'No!' Her hands came up to protect herself from his particular brand of persuasion as his sudden nearness and that roughness in his voice—which could only be inspired by his desire for her—called to an answering need deep down inside. All right, he had been hurt, she thought. And badly. But then so had she. And she didn't intend letting a man use her or hurt her—either physically or emotionally—ever again. Apart from which, she had Daisy to consider now. 'This isn't a very good idea,' she told him tremulously, finding it took every ounce of emotional strength she had to be able to say it. 'We had a fling. We had a good time. Let's leave it like that.' She was amazed at how nonchalant she managed to sound.

'A *fling?*' His face creased up as though he couldn't fully comprehend what she was saying. 'Is that what you want to call it?'

'Wasn't it?' she murmured, the lightness of her tone hiding the real anguish behind her words.

Something hardened his jaw and he started to say something, but was stalled by the sound of childish chatter.

They both looked up as the little girl came skipping out of the house ahead of her grandmother. Carefully negotiating the steps, she ran straight up to Conan and held up her hippo.

'I told him we were going home, but he says he wants to stay with you,' she told him breathlessly, the innocent little gesture striking at Sienna's heart.

'No, Daisy,' she advised firmly, guessing just what Conan would think of that. 'Uncle Conan's coming back to England anyway, so Hippo's only going to be lonely.'

'No, he won't!' Daisy remonstrated, sticking out her bottom lip. 'He says he wants to stay until he comes back.'

'I said no, Daisy...'

The little girl squealed in protest, shrugging off Sienna's hand.

'Let her leave it if she wants to.'

Conan's voice cut impatiently across the altercation between mother and daughter, leaving Sienna wondering, after they had said their goodbyes to Avril and were on the open road, whether his off-handedness sprang from his niece's innocent attempts to squeeze her way into his affections, or from her own refusal to continue an affair that was going nowhere.

She had been back at the gym for a couple of weeks, juggling her courses with Daisy's new schooling schedule and trying to keep her mind off Conan by plunging herself into the daily reward of helping others—particularly her older class members—to reach healthier levels of fitness, when he suddenly turned up out of the blue.

It was a Thursday, which she remembered telling him once

was usually her morning off. What she hadn't reckoned on was that he would remember that.

It was with a surprised leap of her heart therefore, after coming back from dropping Daisy off and taking a shower, that she padded to the front door in her short cotton robe to find him standing there on the step.

'Conan!'

Impeccably groomed as always, power-dressed in his dark executive suit, he made her feel at an immediate disadvantage, with her hair still damp and dishevelled, and far too conscious of being totally naked under her robe.

'Hello, Sienna,' he said, against a backing of excited barks. 'May I come in?'

She pressed herself back against the door, and as he stepped in was reminded of the first time he had come here. Except now he stooped to pet Shadow, who had rushed in from the garden at the first peal of the doorbell, no longer viewing the dog as a cold reminder of that dreadful attack he had suffered in the past. But as he moved past her, with that evocative scent of cologne almost spelling his signature, she was far too aware that—unlike that first time he had come here—he now knew every secret pathway of her body; knew just what to do to make it respond with shameless abandon to his irresistible masculinity. Just as it was doing now—and without any help from him!

'How's Daisy?' he asked, before she had gathered herself enough to say anything.

'She's fine.' Searching for words, so that he wouldn't guess how his dark allure was making her breasts ache and making that familiar heat at the heart of her pool into honeyed moistness in unwitting preparation for his hard invasion, she added croakily, 'So, to what do I owe this unexpected visit?'

An elevated eyebrow acknowledged the tremor that destabilised her voice as he held back for her to precede him into the living room, his manners impeccable as always.

'I wanted to let you know that Avril's well enough to return to London and will be moving into her new apartment within the next couple of weeks,' he informed her smoothly, with no sign apparent of the kind of upheaval going on inside Sienna. It was an apartment that Conan was buying his mother especially to make it easier for her to see Daisy, she remembered Avril telling her before they had left France.

'You could have phoned.' She said it too curtly, and wondered if he could sense the panic that was rising in her.

'I could have.' His eyes were resting on hers—probing, too discerning—before they slid to the betraying movement of her rapidly rising breasts. 'I've missed you, Sienna.'

Through an escalating tension she was aware of Shadow padding back out to the garden.

And I haven't missed you?

With her body turning weak from the velvety caress of his voice, she couldn't tell him how she couldn't keep her mind on anything. That all she could see was his face swimming in front of her eyes every minute of every day. And that she woke up in the night aching for his loving and had to get up and walk about, make herself tea she didn't want to stop herself succumbing to humiliating and unfulfilling self-release.

'Don't!' She made to sweep away from him, put some distance between them, but strong fingers were suddenly clamping around her wrist.

'Sienna…'

'It's over,' she breathed, panic showing in her eyes as electricity crackled through her from the sensuous agony of his touch.

'No, it isn't.'

His determination outstripped any protest she might have made as his other hand reached up and tugged gently on the belt of her robe.

The garment fell open, leaving her exposed and vulnerable.

A tense heat radiated through her and she pressed her eyes tightly closed, feeling his gaze like a hot brand as he groaned in satisfied acknowledgment of her body's shameless betrayal. 'You still want me, Sienna,' he said deeply. 'Every bit as much as I want you.'

Even now, as his hand slid up around one burgeoning breast and her body arched involuntarily towards him, she wanted to deny it. But it was only her head she was trying to fool, because as his mouth came down over hers her physical responses were telling her something else entirely.

Dear heaven! How long had it been?

Her arms went joyously around him, her body glorying in its triumph over her brain, her pulsing flesh exulting in the recognition of its master, its dark, exciting Svengali, whose command it craved to obey.

'You can't give this up any more than I can, can you?' He broke their kiss to speak breathlessly, not needing to hear her answer because her instinctive responses said it all. 'So why did you think you could?'

His voice was rough and ragged, his mouth and hands moving urgently over her body as though not knowing which part of her to savour first. But her need for him was just as desperate, her laboured breathing coming just as rapidly as his, her hungry fingers tugging at his shirt, pulling it out of his waistband so that she could slip her hands beneath it and feel the throbbing heat of his sinewy body before he lifted her up, with her legs entwined around him, and carried her in a few purposeful strides across the room.

They made love on her old wooden table, amongst the debris of unironed washing, pending bills and a box bursting with Daisy's toys. It was a quick, hot, urgent coming together, but neither of them wanted anything else, both driven by the only thing that mattered right then, which was the swift, hard locking of bodies in an immediate climax so intense that Sienna cried out from the blistering pleasure of it, feeling the tremors that ran through Conan from the hard propulsion of his body until he gave a shuddering groan as he found his own release and collapsed heavily down on top of her.

A little later, as their breathing returned to normal, she said—surprisingly shyly in the circumstances, 'You came prepared.' Because even in their uncontrollable need for each other he had taken effortless time to protect her.

'Around you I can't afford to do anything else,' he responded with a wry grimace as he brought himself up on his elbows, then carefully withdrew from her.

Of course he wouldn't want to make her pregnant and risk finding himself in the sort of family situation he despised. Which was slap-bang in the midst of another stepfamily, she realised, if he did what he would probably consider to be his duty and married her. Which she wouldn't agree to anyway, she thought wretchedly—even if she hadn't had that bad experience with Niall—because there was no way that she'd be prepared to marry a man who resented having to take on Daisy, however strong his reasons were for not doing so, any more than she'd be prepared to marry a man whose only reason for marrying her was because she was having his child.

'Conan…' With her forehead creasing from the effort, she tried to tell him that this was all a mistake. That she hadn't intended to make love with him and that the decision she'd made in France had been the right one. But the unintentional brush of his fingers against her inner thigh as he inspected the condom caused her breath to catch—which he capitalised on by turning the back of his hand against the still swollen bud of her femininity until she started to writhe against him, effectively silenced as his long skilled fingers did his bidding and tipped her over the brink for a second time, because he had known instinctively what she had been going to say.

'Better get dressed,' he whispered when it was over, pressing a feather-light kiss on her nose, drawing her attention to the fact that she was as good as naked while he had done very little more than unzip his trousers and loosen his tie. 'You're far too much of a temptation looking like this.'

A temptation to do what? See how many more times he could get her to capitulate? she demanded of herself, noting that dark satisfaction in his voice. To have her bucking at his command, knowing that having sex with him was going against everything she'd made up her mind not to do? Because that was all it was to him, she thought fervently, scrambling up off the table and fastening her robe around her. Just sex.

Hurting and ashamed, berating herself for being too weak to resist him, and annoyed with him for reducing her to such a quivering mass of need, before she knew it she was flinging at him, 'And you're far too much of an arrogant swine to take no for an answer!'

Anger leaped like green fire in his eyes, but was quickly brought under control by his daunting self-command.

'I wasn't aware that what has happened between us here was anything but mutual,' he rasped in a dangerously soft voice, and she could tell that he was only just managing to hold his anger in check. 'You're as hooked as I am, Sienna, so don't blame me if that doesn't tie in with your misplaced delusions of innocence in all this. You made love with me because you wanted to. Because where you and I are concerned you can't help yourself any more than I can! And if you think I'm proud of myself for getting us both into this situation, then I can assure you categorically, darling, I'm *not!*'

Smarting from his words, shamed by her statement which had provoked them, she stood tensely, wishing she could retract it as he brushed past her and moved out to the minute little room off the kitchen that housed her small downstairs bathroom, telling herself that he had every right to be angry.

Because of course what she had been accusing him of was his failure to respect the decision she had made in France about not continuing an affair with him. But because of her frustration with herself for falling into his arms the minute he arrived, it had come out sounding like something far, far worse. With just that one remark she had relegated him to the worst kind of man imaginable. The type who bullied and bulldozed his way into a woman's bed. Like his stepfather had with his mother. Like Niall.

She shivered as the memory of her marriage came back with shuddering force. She'd thought the past was over—done with. And it was, she assured herself rationally. It was just that sometimes things happened to bring it all back…

A familiar clunk from beyond the kitchen had her darting through to investigate.

Conan had just emerged from the bathroom, pulling the door closed behind him. As she'd expected, the loose handle, with its spindle still attached, had come clean off in his hand.

'The one on the bathroom side keeps dropping off,' she uttered by way of apology for her shabby little home, thinking how devastatingly sophisticated he appeared in her modest little kitchen—which certainly wasn't the place for an enterprising self-made billionaire. 'I bought some screws on the way home this morning. I was going to try and fix it when I had a minute.'

'Then give them to me.'

She wanted to tell him that it was all right—that she didn't need anyone to help her. But he was already taking off his jacket, so she went and fetched the packet of screws that was still in her handbag in the living room. When she came back he was repositioning the handle on the bathroom side, and she tried not to notice how his skin showed bronze through the fine white shirt as she handed him the screwdriver from the kitchen drawer.

As he worked he didn't seem to care that he was kneeling in his best designer trousers, or that he was in danger of scuffing his expensive hand-made shoes on her rather worn quarry-tiled floor.

Perhaps he wasn't too sophisticated to be able to fit in anywhere, she decided, admiring him, her heart swelling involuntarily, noticing how the morning sun shining through the kitchen window seemed to strike fire from his gleaming hair. She restrained the strongest urge to run her fingers through it, deciding that that would betray far too much of what she was feeling and might make him think she was getting serious about him. Which was crazy, she thought, after all the intimacies they had shared.

'There.' He was trying the door handle he had just fixed, making sure it was working properly. 'That should do the trick.' His personal masculine scent impinged on her senses as he got to his feet.

'Thanks.' She watched him secure the packet of remaining screws before putting them with the screwdriver back into the drawer. A neat and tidy workman, just like her father, she decided. And, just like her father, a man who would never hurt her. Not physically anyway. Only emotionally, she thought. And only then if she allowed him to. But she wasn't going to, was she? she tried convincing herself. Even so, her throat felt raw with emotion as she uttered tentatively, 'What I said earlier...' He was shrugging back into his jacket, his eyes dark and inscrutable, and she knew that deep down he was still angry with her for saying what she had. 'I didn't mean it like it sounded. I only meant—'

A broad thumb against her lips cut short what she had been trying to tell him. 'I think we've both said enough for one day.'

The next second she was in his arms, with her cheek pressed against his jacket, her hand moving in an involuntary caress over the soft fabric of his sleeve. One steely arm was tightening with torturous possession around her middle, the other a clamping bar that lay diagonally across her back.

They were as one, she thought, enlivened by the power and the strength and the warmth of him. Joined at the chest and the hip and the thigh, her pelvis pressing with equal possession against his, drawn like a magnet to his hard masculinity, while her head swam with his scent and her heart beat out a message that she feared he wouldn't fail to hear.

I love you!

She bit back the phrase that sprang too easily to her lips, knowing the words would be anathema to him after what he had told her that day at the villa. He was quite prepared for them to carry on as lovers, but that there could never be any future for them. He'd never be a stepfather to Daisy, or any other man's child for that matter, because of the violence he'd witnessed by his stepfather towards his mother, and because of the ridicule and brutality directed at him by the man who had shaped his early life.

Aching for him almost as much as she was aching for herself, she wanted to blurt out that she understood all the fear and misery that he must have gone through. That she had experienced the same sort of fear and misery herself. But what good would it do? she thought. The past was gone—as she had reminded herself earlier. So what benefit would it be to Conan to drag it all up? He knew that his mother was weak and his stepfather had been brutal. How could she destroy Niall's image so completely in his eyes by telling him that the brother he'd loved had not only been weak—which he already knew—but that he had been afflicted with the same brutal streak? She couldn't. Any more than he could forget the past and even think about building a happy, normal relationship with someone like her and Daisy.

All she could do, she decided, trying to drum up the strength, was tell him that she was sticking to the decision she had made in France—which was that she had no intention of sleeping with him again.

And she would have done it, too, she assured herself, if his pager hadn't bleeped at the exact moment she decided to.

'I'm sorry about this.' He grimaced, releasing her so that he could take the call.

Which was curt, brief and to the point. He was needed and he had to go.

'I'll be in touch,' he promised, touching her mouth fleetingly with his.

A few moments later she heard the powerful car growling away, leaving her frustrated and despairing with herself for not telling him when she had had the chance.

CHAPTER ELEVEN

SIENNA had been determined to finish with Conan after that last time he had called, when they had wound up making love on her sitting room table. But that was easier said than done, she'd soon discovered, when she was drawn to him physically in a way that defied all rational argument, and when emotionally she was head over heels in love with him, even while her head kept warning her of the hopelessness of the situation.

Because when he'd called the next time—aware that his niece was off on a school trip—and taken her out for a lunch she had been too weak to refuse, and then the time after that, when he'd dropped Daisy off at her grandmother's and whisked Sienna to an exhibition by her favourite artist that she had been longing to attend, on both occasions he'd brought her back to the house and they had inevitably wound up making love.

Now, hearing his car purring away after another abandoned hour of paradise with him on her little single bed, Sienna tugged her duvet straight with intensifying annoyance at herself as common sense reminded her that if she was stupid enough to imagine that he might suddenly have a change of mind-set and want a long-term relationship with her—and consequently Daisy—then she was just living in cloud-cuckoo-land. Apart from which, she reminded herself with increasing self-recrimination, she didn't just have her own feelings to consider, but Daisy's.

The little girl had become extremely attached to him, and

was continually asking Sienna when he was coming round. But she knew for a fact that when he did pick Daisy up to take her to see Avril he was merely acting as a go-between for his mother and his little niece. He seldom stayed to spend that much time with Daisy. And when he did eventually bring her home, having bought her ice cream, a book of animal stories or various other treats he obviously thought a caring uncle should provide, Daisy never wanted to see him leave—something that had started to spark off tantrums the minute he did.

Sienna was glad, therefore, when towards the end of September he went away for three weeks, tied up with the potential take-over of a floundering communications network in Europe. It gave her some space to think, although it wasn't easy being left to question the inadvisability of what she was doing—for her own sake as well as Daisy's—when another part of her—the part that wouldn't listen to reason—was aching for him with a need that was almost unbearable.

Her mother rang a couple of times while he was away, fishing for any whiff of intimacy between Conan Ryder and her daughter. Sienna knew her mother would have loved to be able to tell her friends that her daughter was romantically involved with the illustrious billionaire, but managed to stay firmly non-committal. Jodie's questions, however, weren't so easy to evade when she came round to show off her new baby boy.

'He comes to see Daisy,' Sienna dissembled, when her friend teasingly remarked upon the number of times she had seen the BMW parked outside the house.

'Even when she isn't here?' Jodie responded knowingly.

Which just went to show how dishonestly her relationship with Conan was making her behave, Sienna realised, rebuking herself. Not only with her friend, but with her own daughter! Because she had made sure from the outset that Daisy didn't get to know that she was sleeping with Conan—something that Conan himself had had no problem going along with. After all, he had exercised the same discretion in France, she remembered, although it wasn't until after he had warned her not to fall in love with him that day at the villa that she had realised why. He didn't want his niece seeing him as anything more than the dutiful uncle he was—least of all as a potential father!

Well, that's all right by me! Sienna thought grittily, forcing herself to see what a complete idiot she was being in allowing him to use her in the way he was—although that didn't stop her impulses going into immediate overdrive the following day when he telephoned to let her know he was back.

She was expecting to see him on her own when he came round that Thursday morning, but an unexpected school closure for some emergency repairs had found her having to delegate her afternoon's training sessions at the gym. It also meant that Daisy was there when he called.

'Let me take you both out,' he suggested generously, spectacularly clad in dark jeans and a black leather jacket, and concealing any disappointment he might have felt—if he was harbouring any.

Reluctantly Sienna agreed, and wasn't sure afterwards whether he'd really enjoyed being in the pet and aquatic centre that he took them to, or whether he had just been making the best of it, when what he had really intended that morning was to have her alone, naked and in bed. Something his eyes told her he still wanted every time they met hers over Daisy's oblivious little head, and which produced a throbbing response in Sienna even while she nursed a sort of torturous satisfaction from knowing he'd been denied having his own way.

It was late in the afternoon when Conan drove them back to her place. Daisy had slept most of the way home, but was her usual energetic self by the time Sienna let them all into the house, and immediately flew out into the garden after Shadow.

Shortly afterwards, having finished the coffee that Sienna had made for them both, Conan set his mug down on the draining board and moved back to her where she was standing at the kitchen counter.

Her breath seemed to lodge in her lungs as his arm snaked around her.

'I'm going to have to go,' he whispered from behind, causing her blood to race as his hand slid upwards to cup one soft responsive breast which yielded too eagerly beneath her bra and the smooth fabric of her sweatshirt. His lips inside the wide neckline sent hot and tingling sensations along her spine.

'I don't want you to go!' Daisy's torn little appeal had Sienna pivoting away from him. Too late, she realised, because her daughter had already seen everything. 'I don't want you to go!' the little girl reiterated passionately, already starting to cry, and Sienna could feel another tantrum coming on. 'Why can't you stay with us? *Why* can't you?' Daisy was sobbing bitterly as she clung to one jean-clad leg, looking up with tears streaming down her face at the man she had clearly grown to adore.

'Because I have to be somewhere else, Daisy.' Conan dropped to his haunches to talk to her.

Immediately sturdy little arms went around his neck. 'No, you don't,' her muffled little voice sobbed above the creak of his straining leather.

'Yes, I do, Daisy.' There was an odd inflexion in his voice, Sienna noted, as his arms moved tentatively around the little girl, the sight so painfully heart-wrenching that she had to turn away and busy herself with the tin of dog food she had just opened.

'Then why can't we come and live with you?'

When she turned around there was such an intensity of emotion in the eyes that lifted to hers that she felt it as tangibly as her own. What was it? she wondered achingly. Hopelessness? Desperation? An appeal to her to get him out of this situation he had unintentionally created?

'Go and take this out to Shadow, Daisy,' she advised tremulously, holding out the dog's bowl and looking helplessly at Conan when the little girl didn't even turn around.

'Go and do as your mother wishes and then we'll talk about it, Daisy.' He spoke softly—deeply—with just enough promise in his voice to get her to comply, which after a few moments' hesitation she did.

'What the hell are you trying to do?' Sienna threw at him angrily as soon as Daisy was out of earshot.

'What do you mean, what am I trying to do?' He was upright, dominating her tiny living space again.

'Giving her reason to hope like that! She might only be four years old but she isn't an idiot! She saw us, Conan. And now she thinks we're all going to be one hunky-dory little family!'

'Then you're going to have to somehow explain to her that we're not.'

'*I'm* going to have to explain? And what am I supposed to say to her, exactly?' she demanded, refusing to acknowledge how much his last insensitive statement was affecting her. 'She's had one man in her life snatched away from her. How am I going to tell her not to get to attached to another who's likely to be disappearing at any minute?'

'What's that supposed to mean?' he challenged impatiently.

'It means,' she informed him, punching the swing bin open with unnecessary force and dropping the dog food tin inside, 'I don't want her thinking you're for real!'

'Well, of *course* I'm for real.' His eyes were incredulous as they followed her movements around the limited space. 'I'm her uncle, for goodness' sake!'

'Unfortunately she isn't old enough to compartmentalise!' The spoon she'd been using clanged noisily as she tossed it down on the stainless-steel drainer. Behind her she caught Conan's heavily released breath.

'I've told you. I can't be a father to her, Sienna—or make a lifelong commitment to you, if that's what you're intimating.'

'It isn't!' Heaven keep him from guessing that she might

have ever dared to imagine that. That she had had enough of this pretence and waiting around for precious phone calls from him. Had enough of aching for him night after night. Loving him while knowing that because of his past and all the brutality he had suffered he would never, ever allow himself to love her back.

'I can't give her what my brother would have given her,' he went on, as though he hadn't heard her, 'and I won't even begin to try. You think I'm guilty of a closed mind? Well, just consider the hypothetical situation of us marrying. Daisy's *your* daughter. Yours and Niall's. You must have had plans for the way you were going to bring her up—still have those plans to teach her what's right from wrong, prepare her for adult life. Supposing I had conflicting views and we disagreed over her upbringing, or anything else she did or might want to do? Then we'd find ourselves in the unenviable situation of taking sides, and that would only lead to jealousy and animosity—or worse,' he expressed, grim-mouthed. 'And that sort of hypothetically perfect family I can do without!'

'Like yours, you mean?' Her tortured little reminder hung like a pollutant on the air between them.

'Yes, if you're so determined to press home the point,' he rasped, his nostrils flaring. 'Exactly like mine!'

'And I've told you before…every stepfamily on the planet isn't exactly like yours. Not that it affects *me* one iota…' She had to keep him believing that, and to emphasise that point she added, 'I don't want to be tied down any more than you do…but you're too ready to generalise. Every one of those families isn't always at each other's throats or…' She hesitated, still less than comfortable with describing the cruelty that had not only dogged his childhood but had tainted her short marriage. 'Or turning violent,' she got out at last.

From the way his face hardened she knew she had touched a raw nerve. 'Tell that to someone who's prepared to share your rose-tinted opinion,' he said coldly. 'And if you'll pardon me for saying so, Sienna, you're hardly in any position to judge.'

Oh, aren't I? her heart screamed bitterly, almost driven to reveal exactly what she had had to endure in being married to his brother. But it would have been a useless exercise in retaliation, she realised, which would serve no purpose but to hurt him. And only because she had been careless enough to fall in love with him, she thought miserably. But that was her problem, not his.

His problem was that he'd been shaped by the destructive jealousy and aggression that had sculpted his early life, and there was nothing she could do or say that could chisel away at those prejudices of his—because they were set in stone.

'Perhaps I just happen to have more faith in human relationships than you do, Conan?' she told him painfully. And with all the courage she could muster pressing like a lead weight against her chest, she said, 'I don't think we should see each other like this any more.'

She almost felt the tension that ripped through his body. 'You don't mean that?' he whispered, taken aback.

No, she didn't, she agonised, clamming up, because how could she bring herself to say anything that would end this love affair with him for good?

As he moved towards her, though, her hands shot up to stave off any intention he might have of trying to change her mind. If he touched her, she wouldn't have a chance, she thought, panicking, and he knew it. 'I'm serious, Conan,' she croaked.

He drew up sharply, his mouth moving in a parody of a smile. 'You're tired. We both are,' he remarked, as though that was the answer to all their problems. 'We'll talk about this some other time.'

With his lips lightly brushing her forehead, he was gone before she could utter another word.

When he telephoned the next day she refused to see him, and when he rang again each day for the rest of that week her answer was the same. When she didn't hear from him the following week, she remembered he was away on a business trip. Then, during that week, with the half-term holiday coming up, she received a call from her parents, inviting her to Spain. With time off from the gym for Daisy's school holiday, Sienna was more than happy to accept.

At least she wouldn't be tempted to go back on her word about making a clean break with Conan—which she knew she had to do for Daisy's sake, if not her own. She knew that if it hadn't been for Daisy she wouldn't have been strong enough to do it. And she'd had to. She had to remain strong for the sake of her sanity and her self-respect. She owed herself that much at least.

But all the pep-talks in the world, which she was constantly having with herself, didn't help to lessen the pain she was suffering being without him. As it had stood she had started to despise herself for being his ready mistress whenever he took it upon himself to call her. But even that less than happy state of affairs had been preferable to this empty longing, this burning need for him that kept her awake each night and left her chastising herself as, like an automaton, appearing normal on the outside, she somehow managed to get through each day.

There was also something else worrying her, that she couldn't even bring herself to dwell on while she was in the state she was in. She was glad, therefore, when Saturday came and she could pack Daisy and Shadow into the car.

Her cell phone rang just as they were leaving for the airport. Fortunately she was just passing a retail park, and pulled off the main highway to answer it.

'Sienna?' Conan's voice at the end of the line sent her mind into chaos. 'Sienna, don't hang up on me. I want to see you. We need to talk.'

'There isn't anything to talk about,' she protested, wishing he would leave her to recover from the pain of loving him, even while her body was turning traitor on her, forcing her to remember the insurmountable pleasure of being his. 'I can't talk right now anyway. I'm going away. I need some space.'

'I know what you need—what we both need,' he stated firmly. 'And it isn't space.'

Sienna sucked in her breath as every erogenous cell in her body reacted to the stimulus of his words just at his incredible voice. 'I've got to get going.' Her own voice cracked under the weight of her hopeless feelings for him. 'We're going to be late.'

'Where are you going anyway?' he demanded, controlled and authoritative in comparison.

'If you must know we're going to Spain!'

Behind her an excited Daisy was kicking her legs against her car seat, asking to speak to her uncle. It didn't help either that Shadow, catching the familiar tones of the disembodied voice, was leaning through the gap in the seat and panting into her left ear.

'No, Daisy. Not now!' Regretting her impulse to snap at the little girl, Sienna had to bite her tongue to stop herself telling Conan to leave her alone—to leave them all alone. He had ties with Daisy and always would have, she reminded herself ruefully, knowing she should have given far more thought to this situation before she had gone so eagerly into his bed.

'It sounds like you've got your hands full. Why don't I come and meet you at the airport?'

'For what reason, Conan?'

From the deep breath she heard him draw he was clearly becoming impatient. 'For the simple reason that I'd like to see my niece.'

Of course. What was she expecting him to say? That he loved her? That the past couple of weeks had been torture and that he couldn't live without her? There was a painful little twist to her mouth as she told him, 'Then you'll just have to wait until she gets back. Now, if you don't mind, I've got a plane to catch so I can start to get on with my life!'

'And that's really how you feel?'

No, I want you, and I can never have you! she agonised silently. Bravely, though, with her shoulders drawn back, she murmured into the mouthpiece, 'That's how I feel.'

At the other end of the line, Conan took another deep breath and held it. She wanted to get on with her life, she'd said, and what right did he have to try and stop her? None whatsoever, his conscience told him, even if he couldn't bear the thought of her sleeping with any other man.

There was no future for them and he'd known it from the start. He just hadn't listened to the voice of reason when it had told him how awkward sleeping with his niece's mother would make things for them in the long term. He had wanted Sienna too much for that. He guessed now that he would just have to arrange for his chauffeur to pick up Daisy whenever he or her grandmother planned to see her. That wouldn't be too difficult, and at least it would mean that his and Sienna's paths wouldn't cross, which surely was the most sensible thing all round. It was time to let her go.

That decision made, it was in a tone devoid of any emotion that he breathed into the phone he was gripping with a tension that surprised him, 'Then goodbye, Sienna.' The click as he cut them off signalled the end of an era.

Sienna stared at her phone as though it was something she had never seen before, let alone just used to terminate her affair with the only man she knew now she had ever truly loved.

Harrowed and shocked, she willed him to ring back, so she could tell him that she hadn't meant it. That she didn't want to get on with a life when he wasn't in it. But the plain and simple truth was that she had to. Wasn't that why she'd allowed the argument to take the turn it had? Wasn't it better that they ended the affair now, when they could both walk away with their dignity intact, rather than at some later date when Conan, having tired of her and started seeking new pastures, walked away under his own steam, leaving her dignity in tatters?

Except that right then she didn't care about her dignity or

her self-respect, because the ache that spread outwards from the region of her heart seemed to be suffocating her.

Emotion welled up in her until she could scarcely draw breath and the busy car park in front of her was nothing but a blur.

She had to breathe. Focus on that, she thought. She was wondering how she was going to keep from breaking down in front of Daisy—until a little voice piped up from the back seat, 'Mummy, I want to go to the toilet.'

She was grateful for that mundane demand that made her focus on something else. Her responsibilities. Not this stifling and all-consuming agony that she knew would take her over if she let it.

'All right, darling.'

That duty discharged, she led Daisy back from the public conveniences and told her to stand beside her and not move while she got the orange juice that the little girl had been asking for out of the boot.

Rummaging in her bag, and then in the pocket of her casual jacket, it hit her suddenly that she had been so wound up over Conan when she had got out of the car that not only had she forgotten to lock it, she had even left her keys in the ignition!

Berating herself for her carelessness, she was only half aware of a dog barking somewhere in another vehicle as she opened her door to retrieve them. What she didn't expect was for Shadow to come leaping over her seat, nearly knocking her off-balance as he shot out of the car and went haring off across the tarmac.

The only thought in her mind to strap Daisy safely in the car, so that she could go after the dog, Sienna spun round—to meet every mother's worst nightmare.

The little girl who had been standing beside her less than half a second ago had darted out after Shadow into the busy car park.

'Daisy!' Sienna screamed, her feet flying as she tried to

reach her. But, too late, life suddenly took on the aspect of some horrifying dream.

Almost in slow motion, it seemed, she saw the wheels of the brake-screeching four-by-four skidding on the wet tarmac, and then the little figure in the red anorak and pale leggings went down before her eyes.

CHAPTER TWELVE

CONAN felt as though he had been sitting there in that hospital ward for days, when in fact it must only have been a matter of hours.

When Sienna had rung him, sounding almost hysterical, at first he hadn't been able to grasp what she was saying. When he had, a dread had taken hold of him such as he had never experienced before, immobilising him, rendering him speechless, unable to think.

He who could turn vast corporations around, who had been clear-headed enough to build a commercial empire from next to nothing, had suddenly been thrown into chaos. One minute he had been arguing with Sienna on the phone and the next she was ringing to say that Daisy had had an accident and was being rushed to the hospital. And when she'd managed to tell him what had happened he'd found himself praying as he'd never prayed in his life.

Not Daisy! he had heard himself silently begging. *Please! Not Daisy!* He'd been tortured then by all the chances he had had to show the little girl his affection and hadn't, when she had shown him so much. Like climbing on his knee when he'd reluctantly agreed to read her a story. Like leaving him her precious hippo. Like clinging to him, sobbing, that last time he had seen her because she hadn't wanted him to go. *You've taken Niall!* he'd thundered silently to anyone who might have been listening, battling with anger, guilt and a cold, overriding fear. *Isn't that enough? Or won't you be satisfied until you've taken Daisy too?*

Except that the four-by-four hadn't hit her, as they had at first feared, he reflected now with agonising relief, although no one could believe how it had managed to miss her. It had been tripping over a kerbstone and banging her head on the ground that had left her worryingly concussed. But even that frightening interlude was over now, because she had regained full consciousness not long after he'd arrived at the hospital and, with thorough tests revealing no other serious injuries, she was sleeping quite normally.

'She's going to be fine.' From the other side of the bed, Sienna almost mouthed the words across the little slumbering form, her smile tremulous, her moist eyes tired and dark, her face racked with the same pained relief that he was feeling.

He nodded, but didn't say anything, tension clamping his jaw as he turned away, battling with the welling of emotion.

He had taken off his jacket and tie earlier, and unfastened the top button of his shirt. His hair was dishevelled from where he had been raking his fingers through it, Sienna noticed. His chin was heavily shadowed with a day's growth of stubble, and his rugged features appeared so lined that he seemed to have aged five years since she had seen him last. But then he'd been worrying about Daisy, she thought. After all, she was his brother's child. And in that moment she was immensely grateful that she had never had to tell him the truth about Niall.

'The nurse I spoke to on my way in here thought she was my daughter,' he imparted in an oddly gruff voice.

Because of their shared surname, Sienna realised. It was a natural mistake to make.

Doing her best to hide the anguish of his crushing, final goodbye over the phone, before this awful thing had happened to Daisy, with an ironic little twist to her mouth, she murmured, 'I hope you put them straight.'

Again he didn't answer—but then neither did she expect him to. He was just being considerate in not telling her he had after all she had been through this evening, she thought, closing her eyes against the pain of ultimately losing him.

Sienna had telephoned her parents earlier, to tell them what had happened, and Faith Swann had been almost hysterical, insisting on flying over from Spain immediately. Conan had arranged for them to be flown over in one of his private jets, and they'd arrived in the early hours, her mother crying with relief to know that her granddaughter was going to be all right, her father fishing for his handkerchief before turning away, saying he had something in his eye.

Conan had also arranged for them to be put up in one of the best hotels near the hospital, putting a car and driver at their disposal so that they wouldn't have to worry about getting around while they were in England. Just as effortlessly, Sienna remembered, he'd arranged for someone to pick up her car from that car park, along with Shadow who, having returned, had been lying dutifully beside her when the ambulance arrived, and was now being looked after by a member of Conan's staff in the exclusive penthouse apartment he occupied when he was in town.

'Conan hasn't been able to do enough for us. And all at his own expense!' her mother crooned, enjoying dropping his name for the benefit of a nurse who had just come to check on Daisy. 'Which tells me that he's more than a little bit interested in you, Sienna.'

Sienna pretended to smile, fixing her gaze on the pink patterned curtain that hung beside Daisy's bed so that no one would see the raw emotion slashing her face.

The hospital discharged Daisy that afternoon.

Conan had left earlier, called back to his office by some business only he could sanction, and Sienna couldn't help wondering whether, now that he knew Daisy was going to be all right, he'd felt relieved to get away. After all, he wouldn't want any further complications with his niece's mother.

Faith and Barry Swann had already left the ward with their granddaughter a few minutes ago. Now, checking there was nothing of Daisy's left in the room, Sienna swung the holdall her parents had brought in with fresh clothes for them both over her shoulder and took the lift down to the ground floor, trying not to think about Conan and how empty her life was going to be without him, or even how she was going to cope, although she knew she had to. Had to hang on to that self-sufficiency she prized—especially in the light of what that shockingly revealing test she had done two days ago had confirmed.

Her parents weren't actually waiting for her in Reception, as expected, but *he* was, and Sienna's legs seemed to turn to mush as he looked up and saw her.

Tall and imposing, he had freshened up in the short time he had been gone, and his dark physical presence was utterly mind-blowing.

In black jeans and a grey, white and black multi-striped shirt, with his clean, sleek black hair just brushing his collar, he exuded a lethal blend of ruggedness and sophistication that no woman—herself included, Sienna thought hopelessly—could ever hope to resist.

'Conan!'

Her anguished sapphire gaze locked with the green-gold of his, and there was such dark emotion beneath the black fringes of his lashes that her heart seemed to stop from the intensity of it.

Nothing in his tone, however, revealed what he was thinking as he said, 'I gather the little invalid's been pronounced fit enough to leave?' When she nodded, he asked, 'What about you?'

'I'm fine,' she murmured, although having nearly lost her precious little daughter last night she was feeling anything but. Yet he'd been there too, she remembered, sharing every minute of those worrying hours with her after Daisy had been brought in. And through the night they'd kept up an almost silent vigil beside her bed. Like parents, she thought achingly, united in their worry and their love for a child they had created—longed for—though in reality nothing could have been further from the truth.

'You don't look it,' he said.

'Neither do you.'

He had shaved since she had last seen him, though there were still dark shadows under his eyes. And although he was casually dressed, and looking coolly magnificent, she sensed an air about him that was far from relaxed—like a caged animal wanting to be free.

Which was exactly what he was, she realised, harrowed.

'I can manage,' she protested, as he relieved her of the holdall.

He merely indicated for her to precede him through the sliding doors.

Sienna didn't argue, because that cedarwood scent of him was enervating, and because when his sleeve had brushed her arm just then it had sent a flood of torturous memories coursing through her. Making love with him on his yacht, the boat a white pearl against the blue water. Being worshipped like a goddess on the table in that vast kitchen in the villa. Lying naked on his bed and provoking him with that glass of wine until his control had snapped.

Outside the day was gentle, with the mellow warmth of autumn, and a golden sun was shining through a gap between the buildings on the other side of the busy road, making even the concrete city look kind.

'Where are Mum and Dad?' she asked, looking towards the parking bays for the Mercedes and the chauffeur he had provided them with.

'They've gone ahead with Daisy. I assured them I would see you got home safely,' he said.

Which would have pleased Faith Swann immensely, Sienna

decided, guessing that his popularity couldn't go up any more notches with her mother if he had tried.

'Why?' she demanded, hurting, but he didn't respond as he guided her across the tarmac to where his car was park.

The BMW shut out the world as Conan closed the passenger door and came around the bonnet, a secure and achingly familiar bubble of luxury that was exclusively his.

He didn't say anything to her as he steered the big car through the London traffic. Perhaps he knew she didn't want to converse, she considered. Or maybe he was just thinking that everything had been said.

'Where are we going?' Lost in her thoughts, she didn't notice the slip road for her suburb until they'd cruised past it.

'We have to talk,' Conan said.

She darted him a glance, her forehead puckering. 'What about?' Her stomach started churning queasily.

'We didn't part very amicably over the phone yesterday. And then what happened afterwards…' He cast his eyes across the space between them. 'I can't help feeling that I somehow managed to contribute to it in some way.'

By saying goodbye?

If he meant she'd left her keys in her car, which had set off the train of events that had led to Daisy's accident, because she hadn't had her mind on what she was doing—something she'd been rebuking herself for ever since—then, yes, perhaps he might have contributed just a little.

Instead, though, she said, 'No, you didn't,' desperate to keep him from guessing how cut up she was about breaking up with him. 'It was all through my own stupidity. It had no bearing on anything you said—anything either of us said. It was just one of those unfortunate things.'

He exhaled heavily through his nostrils. 'It isn't my usual policy to end a relationship over the phone like that. I think I just lost patience with you, Sienna.'

So he was going to do it now, like a civilised human being? But how civilised was it tearing someone's heart to shreds!

'Over the phone. By text. Even by carrier pigeon…' She shrugged, uttering a forced little laugh to hide the anguish that was only increasing with every mile they covered, using the very words he'd used when he'd accused her of being difficult to contact that day, endless weeks ago, at the gym. 'What does it matter?' It would still have been like a knife in her heart if he'd dressed it up with roses and champagne! 'Anyway you were right. It was pointless going on as we were.'

'Nevertheless…' That one word, drawn so erratically from him, seemed to emphasise the finality of what he was about to add. 'After all we shared together I had no right treating you like that. Even with a more casual association I would have chosen a much kinder way.'

Was there a kinder way? Some easier option than telling someone who was desperately in love with you that they would never mean a thing to you?

Only kinder to yourself! she thought, biting the inside of her cheek to stop herself from making a complete fool of herself and breaking down in front of him.

He didn't say anything else, and so Sienna sat gazing out of her window at the rows upon rows of houses whizzing by, grateful if only for the silence that delayed their inevitable parting as the houses gave way to offices and shops and the shops became leafy suburbs. Eventually suburbia became open fields bordered by russet and amber hedges, green swathes of pasture grazed by gentle cattle, acres of ploughed earth creating a rich patchwork against harvested gold.

Almost without her realising it Conan pulled off the main highway, bringing the car to a standstill in a leafy lane.

'Shall we get some fresh air?'

She nodded, taking too long to get out, so that he was around her side of the car and offering his hand before she could avoid it. The contact was painfully electric.

Hastily she dragged her fingers out of his and moved towards the riverbank alongside which they were parked. Here a narrow ribbon of water flowed silently beneath shading trees, glistening silver as it twisted and turned, cutting a path across the mellow fields.

They had to talk, he had said. So now he had brought her to this quiet place to make it easier on himself to finish with her. She couldn't bear that. Didn't think she could take the pain of hearing him say it again.

He came to stand beside her, a man who had witnessed such mental and physical brutality by his stepfather that he had closed himself off and was too afraid to love, and yet he had stolen her heart with the depth of tenderness he was capable of.

Taking the initiative, she said quickly, trying to get it out before her voice could crack and betray what she was really feeling, 'There's no need for either of us to add anything to what was said over the phone yesterday. Let's just leave it like that. We can make arrangements for Daisy to see Avril through one of your staff. I'm sure you've got people who can handle these things, or I can always take her there myself. We don't need to stay in touch with each other.'

He dipped his head—rather hesitantly, she felt, but then it was all part of his act of being kind. And suddenly as the reality of what was happening hit her, it felt as though the earth had stopped spinning. Any second now she'd be slipping off the edge and tumbling down and down into some dark and timeless chasm, and all this pain and misery would mercifully end.

But it didn't. With a violent little shudder, too much of a coward to stand there and take any more of his "kindness", she pulled the brown corduroy jacket she'd draped over her shoulders more closely around her, saying, 'I have to get back to Daisy.' She was already moving back to the car. 'She'll be wondering where I am.'

'Sienna…'

There was such a depth of anguish in his voice that she turned round, saw the same emotion reflected in his eyes. But then he'd been worried sick about Daisy, hadn't he? she told herself painfully. That must surely have left him feeling as battered as she was.

She was leaning against the car as though she needed its support, so petite and desirable beneath her creamy light-weight sweater and jeans that he wanted to take her in his arms and kiss away that harrowed look on her face. But he forced himself to hold back, not sure whether it would do more harm than good. She'd always denied wanting a serious in-volvement with him, although because of the way she made love—as if no other man existed for her—he'd been presump-tuous enough to imagine she was just saying it to save face. But now—because of what happened to Daisy—when there was so much that he needed to say to her—he had been dealt a blow that left him wondering whether in fact she had ever been his.

'Indulge me,' he suggested heavily. 'If only for one last time.' Silently he held out his hand.

Sensing something in his manner that brooked no resis-tance, Sienna took it this time, following his lead a little way along the riverbank.

Unusually, he seemed to be having some inner struggle with himself, and needing to say something, no matter how trivial, to ease the anguish his silence was only intensifying, she grasped the first thing that came into her head and said, 'Thank you for helping Mum and Dad.' She'd been meaning to express her gratitude ever since last night.

'It was the least I could do,' he said.

'Mum hasn't been able to stop talking about it. About you,' she emphasised poignantly, and then, with a hopeless little glance up at him that seemed to squeeze the life out of her heart, she murmured, 'Sorry about that.'

His smile was jerky. 'As I said…' He brought her hand up, studying their clasped fingers with an almost pained absorp-tion. 'It was the least I could do—especially as it gave me the opportunity to get to know them a little, and to tell you that I think your mother and father are great. They're warm, easy-

going and hard-working, and on top of that they're honest—
which it seems is more than you've been with them, isn't it,
Sienna?' His breath caught before he tagged on, 'Or with me.'

She looked at him quickly, her expression guarded. She
thought she'd never seen such bleakness in anyone's eyes.
'What's that supposed to mean?'

He stopped on the way-worn path, pulling her gently round
to face him. 'I mean you did a very good job of convincing
me that Tim Leicester was nothing more than a caring big
brother. But that isn't what your mother very innocently led
me to believe.'

The hands that were holding her loosely dropped away as
she took a step back. She couldn't understand what it was he
was trying to say.

'That week my brother went away... She told me this
morning she'd arranged to come over from Spain to see you.
But you told her you were joining Niall in Copenhagen and
that you weren't going to be around. But you didn't go to
Copenhagen, did you, Sienna? And, knowing my brother, he
wasn't exactly the type who would have welcomed his wife
turning up at one of his friends' stag affairs.'

'What are you saying?' She was shaking her head, her eyes
pained, her small features tense. 'And why would she have
told you about that anyway?'

His mouth tugged downwards at one corner. 'Quite innocently, as I said. She happened to mention when I passed her
in the hospital corridor earlier how you were supposed to be
in Spain with her and Barry this week, and that something
dreadful always seems to happen when you made plans to
go away. I knew she was exaggerating, but she told me then
about your trip to Copenhagen, and how it hadn't happened
because of Niall's accident. I couldn't help but put two and
two together. Work out that you could only have put her off
because you were planning to go to this Tim's. Did you love
him so much that you couldn't miss out on the opportunity to
be with him—even if it meant lying to your mother?' He was

looking at her with a painful intensity that seemed to mirror the anguish in her own heart. 'Are you still in love with him, Sienna?'

'No!' Her denial seemed futile now he had the facts. But why did it matter to him, she thought achingly, when he didn't even love her?

'Then why did you lie to her?' he asked, and then more softly—so softly that it was almost a whisper, 'To *me?*'

In an adjoining field a cow lowed—a lonely sound, almost desolate. As desolate as the fathomless emotion that seemed to be scoring his face.

He was disappointed in her; that was all. Because she had just destroyed all his trust in her that it had taken months—no, years, she thought, agonised—to actually gain.

'I'm sorry.' Conan's voice was hoarse. 'I had no right to ask.' That desolate look about her told him all he needed—yet had dreaded—to know. She was still in love with the man she'd been prepared to wreck her marriage for.

The warmth of her almost broke his resolve to let her go as he placed his hand on her shoulder, and it took every ounce of the calibre he possessed to say, 'Let's get back to the car.'

Sienna turned to go with him, but drew away almost immediately, noticing the glance he gave her before continuing on ahead.

There was a weary slump to his broad shoulders, and his hands were stuffed in his pockets. She was the adulteress. The girl he had always believed she was. And he would walk away always believing the worst about her if she didn't do something to stop him. And she *had* to stop him! Even if it meant going back on every resolution she'd made to protect him from knowing.

'I lied because—' She broke off before he turned round, the admission choking her. Or was it the ravaging anguish she could see on his face? 'Because despite what you think there was no way Tim was ever going to see me with my clothes off. But if I'd let Mum come over, as she was planning to, I knew she might.'

He was moving slowly back to her, his strong features contorted. What on earth was she getting at? He shook his head, bewildered, trying to fathom her out.

She was standing on the path, looking sightlessly towards the river. He could only see her profile, but he thought he had never seen her look more beautiful or more defeated, her lovely face blanched by some painful emotion he could almost feel.

She was small, courageous and proud. Above all else she had a fierce pride and independence he had seldom witnessed in anyone. He would even have said loyalty, if it hadn't been for...

And then it hit him with the sudden weight of a demolition ball thudding into his chest. The way he had found her on that fateful morning. The demure black dress—long-sleeved, high necked—and black leggings hiding her lovely legs even though it had been sweltering outside. He'd thought it was an image she had been trying to cultivate—looking prim to hide her promiscuity. But then he remembered his mother, her face bright and unblemished, wearing those stiff concealing clothes, that same haunted look...

'Niall...*hurt* you?' Shock widened his eyes and Sienna watched his mouth contort with something like disgust and horror through a haze of regretful tears. 'Oh, my love...' Suddenly she was in his arms and he was clasping her to him as though he would protect her from anything that might threaten her. 'Why didn't you tell me?' he rasped. 'Before this? Years ago? Why didn't you say something? *Why?*'

'I couldn't.' The words spilled out on a note of aching remorse, and yet contrarily she felt a strange relief, too, now that he knew. 'He never meant to do it—and he was always so sorry afterwards. He begged me not to tell anyone. More than anyone else,' she murmured, sniffing back tears, 'he didn't want you finding out. I think he wanted to hang on to what little respect he felt you had left for him, and I—I didn't want you to have to face knowing something like that about your own brother.'

'So you kept quiet to safeguard *my* feelings?' Incredulity softened the strong angles of his features as he pulled her closer. 'I would have lynched him,' he growled against the dark pelt of her hair, amazing her with the depth of feeling in his voice. She was still trying to come to terms with the fact that she was in his arms, that he hadn't walked away, that he was holding her and speaking to her as though he really cared. 'How long?' he demanded in a muffled voice, the question seemingly wrenched from his lungs. 'How long had it been going on?'

'I'm not sure. From just after Daisy was born. He couldn't bear to share me with anyone. Not Mum and Dad. Not Tim. Not even with his own daughter. That last time it happened it was because he'd started shrieking at Daisy when she wanted my attention, and when I tried to defend her...' She didn't need to say any more.

Like father—like son, Conan thought, fuming, finding it inconceivable that she—and little Daisy—had suffered so much at the hands of someone she'd loved, and so bravely and silently too. He reproached himself now for the part he had played in compounding her misery, for misjudging her all these years.

'The next day he went off on that stag do, and when Mum said she was coming over I just panicked,' she admitted against the warm strength of his shoulder. 'I didn't want her to see me, or for Dad to know either. It would have upset them too much.' And so she had run to Tim's, not knowing where else to go. Too young still to know how to cope. 'Nothing was visible, so I didn't need to tell him anything except that Niall was away and I'd come up to London for a few days. I made him swear not to tell anyone I'd been to see him. He couldn't understand why, but he went along with it. If he hadn't my parents would have asked questions, and Niall would have gone ballistic if he'd found out. But then he had that accident…'

And she could no more have betrayed his character than she could fly.

She didn't need to say it, Conan thought, caressing her hair, and definitely added loyalty to her list of qualities.

'I wanted Daisy to grow up only thinking the best about her father. Can you understand that?' she queried, looking up at him.

His face, though grave, had less of a bleak look about it now as he nodded in response. 'Can you ever forgive me?' he breathed.

'For what?' she asked, as though all his accusations and suspicions about her meant nothing.

'For not realising that I was in love with you,' he admitted, recognising that she had just wiped the slate clean of those accusations and suspicions. 'I think I have been for a long time, but I refused to accept what my feelings were trying to tell me because…well, you know why. Because I'd convinced myself I could never be a stepfather to Daisy and that I was doing the right thing in not allowing myself to get too close to either of you. But you were right in what you said that day at the villa. I *was* afraid. It took nearly losing her yesterday—or thinking I was going to lose her—to make me realise just how much I love her and what a complete idiot I've been. I want to take care of her, Sienna, and with you beside me I know I can be the loving father she needs and the one I want to be. I want to take care of you both. Of you all,' he amended, wryly, making her look at him quickly. 'Even that darn dog of yours,' he clarified, because of course he didn't know. 'I love you, Sienna. Will you marry me?' Desperately his eyes searched hers. 'What is it?' he enquired, frowning.

'It isn't just three of us. It's four of us. I'm pregnant,' she told him anxiously. 'I don't know how it could have happened—' hadn't they always used protection? '—but you're going to be a father—big-time. Do you think you can handle that?'

He looked incredulous, but pleasantly shocked, and then his lips began to curve in a way that made his face look lit from within.

'With you and Daisy beside me I can handle anything,' he vowed, placing a tender hand over the as yet unnoticeable little life that was growing inside her. 'Especially such a precious gift as a little brother or sister for our daughter.'

'Are you sure?' she queried uncertainly, even though her heart was singing. She couldn't believe that something so good could come out of something as awful as Daisy's accident.

'I've never been surer of anything in my life,' he admitted deeply, smiling down at her, and then, understanding her fears, he said gently, 'Don't worry, darling. I know you had it rough. So did I. But you and I together are going to put things right. I love you, Sienna. I'm ashamed to say I think I fell in love with you from the moment I saw you standing beside Niall in that register office—though I would never allow myself to admit it. And then that night I danced with you...' He shook his head sharply, as though to clear it of a burden he had carried for a very long time. 'I've never wanted anyone as much as I wanted you that night.'

'Is that why you scarcely said a word to me?' she challenged breathlessly—almost mischievously. 'And made me feel as though you were almost relieved when the dance was finished?'

'Did I?' He made a self-deprecating sound. 'That couldn't have been further from how I was feeling. And what about you, Sienna? How did *you* feel?'

A chilly wind rustled the turning leaves of a silver birch tree that was overhanging the path, penetrating her thin sweater. Discerningly, Conan placed the jacket he'd caught when it had slipped unnoticed off her shoulders earlier around her.

'Scared. Excited. Confused.' She could say it now. 'But on

top of all that…' She looked down at her hand, resting on the multi-striped fabric covering his chest, thinking of his values, his conduct, his consideration for others, and his tenderness that was as much a part of him as the hard steel of his body. Now, with eyes that were misty with emotion, she looked up at him and said candidly, 'I felt so…*safe* with you.'

'Oh, my love…' he breathed for the second time, his mouth capturing hers in a kiss that fuelled her desire for him as much as she could feel it fuelling his. When he lifted his head, his eyes seemed to reflect the green-gold fields of an autumn sunset. But there was uncertainty in them too, as huskily he asked, 'Do I take it that's a yes?'

'What do you think?' Sienna said smilingly, brushing a strand of hair away from his face from the teasing wind. But seeing the crease furrowing his forehead, and realising that he was still harbouring doubts, she said simply, and from the bottom of her heart, 'I love you, Conan.'

Clasped against his hard warmth, she thought about all those women who might regret the end of his bachelorhood— even one in particular—but she knew she didn't need to worry. His actions said it all. This man was hers. For eternity.

They stood there in each other's arms until the shadows lengthened over the river and the cool breeze struck up more keenly, scattering bronze and golden leaves around them like sudden handfuls of confetti.

'Let's go home,' Conan murmured deeply, and from his lips the word seemed to mean so very much more. A safe haven. A place where love could grow. A peaceful harbour.

'I am home,' Sienna whispered, tightening her arms around him, and knew that home for them both was where the other one was—and always would be.

* * * * *

WE'LL ALWAYS
HAVE PARIS

JESSICA HART

*For Isabel, dear friend and research advisor,
with love on her own Chapter Ten.*

Jessica Hart was born in west Africa, and has
suffered from itchy feet ever since, travelling and
working around the world in a wide variety of
interesting but very lowly jobs—all of which have
provided inspiration on which to draw when it
comes to the settings and plots of her stories. Now
she lives a rather more settled existence in York,
where she has been able to pursue her interest in
history—although she still yearns sometimes for
wider horizons.

If you'd like to know more about Jessica visit her
website: www.jessicahart.co.uk

CHAPTER ONE

Media Buzz

We hear that MediaOchre Productions are celebrating a lucrative commission from Channel 16 to make a documentary on the romance industry. MediaOchre are keeping the details under wraps, but rumours are rife that an intriguing combination of presenters has been lined up. Stella Holt, still enjoying her meteoric rise from WAG to chat show host, says that she is 'thrilled' to have been invited to front the programme, but remains coy about the identity of her co-presenter.

One name being whispered is that of the economist, Simon Valentine, whose hard-hitting documentary on banking systems and their impact on the very poorest both here and in developing countries has led to a boom in micro-financing projects that is reputed to be revolutionising opportunities for millions around the world. Valentine, a reluctant celebrity, shot to fame with his crisp analysis of the global recession on the news, and has since become the unlikely pin-up of thinking women throughout the country. MediaOchre are refusing to confirm or deny the rumour. Roland Richards, its flamboyant executive producer, is un-

characteristically taciturn on the subject and is sticking to 'no comment' for now.

'No,' SAID Simon Valentine. 'No, no, no, no, no. *No.*'

Clara's cheeks were aching with the effort of keeping a
cheery smile in place. Simon couldn't see it on the phone, of
course, but she had read somewhere that people responded
more positively if you smiled when you were talking.

Not that it seemed to be having an effect on Simon
Valentine.

'I know it's hard to make a decision without having all
the facts,' she said, desperately channelling her inner Julie
Andrews. *The Sound of Music* was Clara's favourite film of
all time. Julie had coped with a Captain and seven children,
so surely Clara shouldn't be daunted by one disobliging economist?

'I'd be happy to meet you and answer any questions you
might have about the programme,' she offered brightly.

'I don't have any questions.' Clara could practically hear
him grinding his teeth. 'I have no intention of appearing on
your programme.'

Clara had a nasty feeling that her positive smile was beginning to look more like a manic grin. 'I understand you
might want to take a little time to think about it.'

'Look, Ms…whatever you're called…'

'Sterne, but please call me Clara.'

Simon Valentine ignored the invitation. 'I don't know how
to make myself clearer,' he said, his voice as tightly controlled
as the image that stared out from Clara's computer screen.

She had been Googling him, hoping to find some chink in
his implacable armour, some glimpse of humour or a shared
interest that she could use to build a connection with him, but
details of his private life were frustratingly sparse. He had
a PhD in Development Economics—whatever *they* were—

from Harvard, and was currently a senior financial analyst with Stanhope Harding, but what use was that to her? You couldn't get chatty about interest rates or the strength of the pound—or, at least, you couldn't if you knew as little about economics as Clara did. She had been hoping to discover that he was married, or played the drums in his spare time, or had a daughter who loved ballet or…something. Something she could *relate* to.

As it was, she had established his age to be thirty-six and the story of how he had quietly used his unexpected celebrity to revolutionize the funding of small projects around the world. So great had been the uproar in response to the programme he had written and presented that the big financial institutions had been forced to rethink their lending policies, or so Clara had understood it. She had read lots of stories from small collectives in sub-Saharan Africa, from farmers in South America and struggling businesses in South East Asia, as well as in the more deprived parts of the UK, all of whom had credited Simon Valentine with changing their lives.

It was all very impressive, but Simon himself remained an elusive figure. As far as Clara could see, he had been born a fully fledged, suit-wearing economist who had no interest in celebrity for its own sake.

There were no snaps of him staggering out of a club at four in the morning, no furtive shots of him shopping with a girlfriend. The ideal, of course, would have been some cheesy shots of Simon Valentine showing his 'lovely home' in the gossip mags, but Clara wasn't unreasonable. She had known that was a long shot, but she had thought she might at least find a picture of him at some reception, glass in hand.

But no. All she had was this corporate head and shoulders shot. He had the whole steely-jawed, gimlet-eyed thing going on, which Clara could sort of see the appeal of, although it didn't do much for her. His tie was straight and rigidly knotted, his jacket stiff, his shoulders squared. The guy had some serious control issues, in Clara's opinion.

Come to think of it, he had a definite Captain von Trapp quality to him, although he wasn't nearly as attractive as Christopher Plummer. *Obviously.* Still, Clara could imagine him summoning his children with a whistle.

Hmm. The thought gave her a definite frisson. Perhaps a rousing rendition of *Edelweiss* would do the trick?

'Are you listening to me?' Simon Valentine demanded.

Hastily, Clara jerked her mind back from Salzburg. 'Of course.'

'Good, then I say this for one last time. I have no intention of appearing on your programme.' Simon spoke very distinctly and with exaggerated patience, as if addressing a naughty child. 'I don't need time to think about it now, just as I didn't need time when you emailed me the first time, or when you rang me for the fourth. My answer was no then, just as it's no now, and as it is always going to be. N. O. *No.* It's a very simple word. Do you understand what it means?'

Of course she understood. She might not be an academic like the rest of her family, but she had mastered the English language. It was Simon Valentine who didn't understand how important this was.

'If I could just expl—' she began desperately, but Simon, it appeared, had had enough explanations.

'Please do not try and call me again, or I will get very angry.'

And he cut the connection without waiting for her reply.

Clara slumped, making a face at the phone as she switched it off and tossed it onto the desk in defeat. *Now* what?

'Well? What did he say?'

She spun her chair round to see the director of *Romance: Fact or Fiction?* hovering in the doorway. 'I'm sorry, Ted,' she said. 'He's just not going to do it.'

'He's got to say yes!' Ted wrung his hands, the way he had been wringing them ever since Clara had first come up against a flat refusal from Simon Valentine. 'Roland's already promised Stella that Simon Valentine is on board!'

'Ted, I *know*. Why else do you think I've been harassing him?' But Clara was careful not to snap. Ted was one of her closest friends, and she knew how anxious he was about the new flat he and his partner had just bought.

More wringing of hands. 'What are we going to do?'

'I don't know.' With a sigh, Clara swung back to contemplate her computer screen. Simon Valentine gazed austerely back at her, the inflexible set of his lips taunting her with the impossibility of ever getting him to change his mind.

Puffing out a frustrated breath, Clara stuck her tongue out at him. Maturity was everything.

'Why can't Stella front the programme with someone else? Someone more approachable and more likely to take part? The Prime Minister, for instance, or—I know!—the Secretary General of the United Nations. Now there's someone who'd make a great presenter. I could give the UN a ring now...I'm sure it would be easier than getting Simon Valentine to agree.'

Her mouth turned down despondently. 'Honestly, Ted, I've tried and tried to talk to him, but he just isn't interested. You'd think he'd at least consider it after doing that programme on micro-financing, but he won't even let me explain.'

'Did you tell him Stella was super-keen to work with him?'

'I tried, but he doesn't know who she is.'

'You're kidding?' Ted gaped at her. 'I don't see how he could have missed her!'

'I don't get the impression Simon Valentine watches much daytime television,' said Clara, 'and I'm guessing the *Financial Times* doesn't devote much space to footballers' wives and girlfriends. This isn't a guy who's going to have a clue about celebrities.'

Ted grimaced. 'Better not tell Stella he's never heard of her or the fat really will be in the fire!'

'I can't think why she's so obsessed with Simon Valentine anyway,' grumbled Clara. 'He's so not her type. She should be going out with someone who's happy to be photographed all loved-up in *Hello!*, not a repressed economist. It's mad!'

Ted perched on the edge of her desk. 'Roland reckons she wants a relationship with Simon to give her gravitas,' he confided. 'Apparently she's desperate to shake off her WAG image and be taken seriously. Or maybe she just fancies him.'

'I just don't get it.' Clara studied Simon's photo critically. Even allowing for the vague Christopher Plummer resemblance, it was hard to see what all the fuss was about. Talk about buttoned-up!

'Did you hear that audience figures for the news have rocketed since he's been doing those analyses of the economic situation?' she said, mystified. 'Women all over the country have been switching on specially in the hope of seeing him, and now they're all tweeting each other about how sexy they think he is.' She shook her head at the photograph.

'They're calling him the Dow-Jones Darling now,' said Ted, and Clara snorted.

'More like the Nikkei Nightmare!'

'You ought to watch the news. You can't understand Simon Valentine's appeal until you've seen him in action.'

'I do watch the news,' Clara protested. She wasn't entirely superficial! She caught Ted's eye. 'Sometimes, anyway,' she amended.

'I made a point of watching the other night before I called him the first time so that I could tell him how brilliant he was—not that I ever got the chance to suck up,' she remembered glumly. 'I can see that he knows what he's talking about, but the whole he's-so-gorgeous thing has passed me by. He didn't smile once!'

'He's talking about the global recession,' Ted pointed out. 'Not exactly laugh-a-minute stuff. You can hardly expect him to be cracking jokes. What do you want him to say? Have you heard the one about the rising unemployment figures?'

'I'm just saying he doesn't look as if he'd be much fun.'

'Simon Valentine appeals to women's intellect,' said Ted authoritatively, and Clara rolled her eyes.

'Like you'd know!'

Ted ignored that. 'He's obviously fiercely intelligent, but he explains what's happening in the financial markets so clearly that you can actually understand it, and that makes you feel clever too. He only got invited to comment that first time because someone else wasn't available but he's a natural on camera.'

'I know. It's odd, isn't it? It's not as if he's incredibly good-looking or anything.'

'It's not about that,' said Ted with all the authority of a film director. 'It's about a complete lack of vanity. He clearly doesn't care what he looks like, and he's talking about a subject he's utterly comfortable with, so he's relaxed, and the camera loves that. I can see exactly why the BBC snapped up that documentary. There's a passion about the way he talks about economics…it *is* kind of sexy.'

'If you say so,' said Clara, unconvinced.

'It was Simon who sold the proposal when Roland pitched it to Channel 16. The suits loved the idea of putting him with Stella.'

Clara could just about get that. Stella Holt was a popular daytime television chat show host, famous for her giggle and revealing dresses. Who better to contrast with her than Simon Valentine, the coolly intelligent financial analyst who had somehow managed to make the global recession a sexy subject? The commissioning editors at Channel 16 had lapped it up, just as Roland Richards had said they would.

You didn't need to be Simon Valentine to know that the economic outlook was bleak for small television production companies like MediaOchre. They were incredibly lucky to have a programme commissioned at all, as Roland kept reminding them. If it wasn't for that, the whole company would be folding.

As it was, they had the money—an extraordinarily generous budget under the circumstances. They had Ted as an award-winning producer, and a camera and sound crew lined up. They had the locations chosen and deals set up with airlines and hotels. They had Stella Holt to add the celebrity glamour that would pull in the viewers.

All they needed was Simon Valentine.

As Roland also kept reminding Clara.

'You're the production assistant,' he told her. 'I don't care what you do, but get him on board or this whole thing is going to fall apart, and it won't just be you that's out of a job. We'll all be out on the streets!'

So no pressure then.

Remembering, Clara put her head in her hands. 'There must be some way of persuading Simon to take part. He won't talk on the phone or respond to emails… I need to talk to him face to face. But how?'

'Can't you get contrive to bump into him at a party?' Ted suggested.

Clara lifted her head to jab a finger at the screen. 'Does he look like a party animal to you? He doesn't do anything but work, as far as I can see. They even do those interviews in his office, so I can't even throw myself at him in the lift at the BBC.'

'He must go home some time. Hang around outside his office and then follow him.'

'Excellent idea. I could get myself arrested as a stalker.

Although it might come to that. Anyway, he drives to work. It's very un-ecological of him,' said Clara disapprovingly.

They brooded on the problem for a while. Ted took the other chair and spun thoughtfully round and round, while Clara Googled in a desultory fashion.

'We could send a surprise cake to the office,' Ted suggested at last.

'And I could deliver it.' Clara paused with her fingers on the keyboard and considered the idea, her head on one side. 'I'd be lucky to get past reception, though.'

'I was thinking more of you jumping out of it,' said Ted, and she flattened her eyes at him.

'Oh, yes, he's bound to take me seriously if I jump out of a cake! Why don't I turn myself into a call girl and be done with it? And don't even *think* about mentioning that idea to Roland!' she warned, spotting the speculative gleam in Ted's eyes. 'He'll just make me do it.'

She turned back to the computer. 'Shame he doesn't appear to have any children. I could inveigle my way in as a governess and charm him into agreeing with my heart-warming song and dance routines.'

'You'd be better off pretending that you're setting up a weaving cooperative somewhere in the Third World,' said Ted, who was used to Clara drifting into *Sound of Music* fantasies. 'He's very hot on credit systems for small organisations that are struggling.'

'*We're* a small organisation that's struggling,' Clara pointed out. 'Or we will be if he doesn't agree to take part!' She scrolled down the screen, looking for something, *anything*, that might help her. 'Pity he isn't hotter on self-promotion, but it's always the same story. It's about the projects, not about him—oh…'

Ted sat up straighter as she broke off. 'What?'

'It says here that Simon Valentine is giving a lecture at the

International Institute for Trade and Developing Economies tomorrow night.' Clara's eyes skimmed over the announcement. 'There's bound to be drinks or something afterwards. If I can blag my way in, I might be able to corner him for a while. I'd have to miss my Zumba class, mind.'

'Better than losing your job.' Ted sprang up, newly invigorated. 'It's a brilliant idea, Clara. Wear your shortest skirt and show off your legs. Times are too desperate to be PC.'

Clara sniffed. 'I thought I'd dazzle him with my intellect,' she said, and Ted grinned as he patted her on the shoulder.

'I'd stick to my legs if I were you. I think they're more likely to impress Simon Valentine.'

Clara tugged surreptitiously at her skirt. She wished now that she had worn something a little more demure. Surrounded by a sea of suits in varying shades of black and grey, she felt like a streetlamp left on during the day in a fuchsia-pink mini-dress and purple suede killer heels. The other members of the audience had eyed her askance as she edged along the row and collapsed into a spare seat at the back of the room. On one side of her a brisk-looking woman in a daringly beige trouser suit bristled with disapproval. On the other, a corpulent executive leered at her legs until Simon Valentine began to speak.

There had been no problem about talking her way in without a ticket—Clara suspected the mini-dress had helped there, at least—but once inside it was clear that she was totally out of place. She fixed her attention on Simon, who was standing behind a lectern and explaining some complicated-looking PowerPoint presentation in a crisp, erudite way that appeared to have the audience absorbed.

It was all way over Clara's head. She recognised the odd word, but that was about it. Every now and then a ripple of laughter passed over the room, although Clara had no idea what had been so funny. She picked up the occasional word:

percentages and forecasts, public sector debt and private equity. Something called quantitative easing.

Hilarious.

Abandoning her attempt to follow the lecture, Clara planned her strategy for afterwards instead. Somehow she would have to manoeuvre him into a quiet corner and dazzle him with her wit and charm before casually slipping the programme into the conversation.

Or she could go with Ted's suggestion and flash her legs at him.

Clara wasn't mad about that idea. On the other hand, it might be more effective than relying on wit and charm, and it would be worth it if she could stroll into the office the next day. *Oh, yeah,* she would say casually to Roland. *Simon's on board.*

Roland would be over the moon. He would offer her an assistant producer role straight away, and then, after a few thought-provoking documentaries, she could make the move into drama. Clara hugged the thought to herself. She would spend the rest of her career making spell-binding programmes and everyone would take her seriously at last.

A storm of applause woke Clara out of her dream.

OK, maybe an entire high-flying career was a lot to get out of one conversation, but she was an optimist. Climb every mountain, and all that. It could happen and, at the very least, convincing Simon Valentine to take part would save her job and mean that Ted could stay in his flat.

There was the usual scrum to get out of the room to the drinks reception afterwards. The International Institute for Trade and Developing Economies was as stuffy as its name suggested. It was an imposing enough building, if you liked that kind of thing, with elaborately carved plaster ceilings, portraits of stern Edwardian economists lining the walls, and a grand staircase that Clara longed to dance down. It was just

begging for a sparkly dress and a Ginger Rogers imperson-
ation.

The reception was held in the library and by the time Clara
got in there the glittering chandeliers were ringing with the
rising babble of conversation. Grabbing a glass of white wine,
she skulked around the edges of the crowd, trying to look as
if she understood what everyone was talking about. She recognized several famous journalists and politicians, and the
air was thick with talk of monetary policy frameworks, asset
bubbles and exchange rate policies.

Oh, dear, if only she was a bit more knowledgeable. She
would never be able to dazzle Simon Valentine at this rate.
Clara was careful to avoid eye contact with anyone in case
they asked her what she thought about the credit crisis or interest rate cuts. She didn't want to be exposed as the impos-
ter that she was.

The atmosphere was so intimidating that Clara was
tempted to turn tail and go home before she was outed as
utterly ignorant, but this might be her only chance to talk to
Simon Valentine face to face. She *couldn't* go until she had at
least tried. It would be too shaming to go into work the next
day and admit that she'd lost her nerve.

Humming under her breath to bolster her confidence, Clara
scanned the crowds for her quarry and spotted him at last,
looking so austere in a grey suit that everyone else seemed
positively jolly in comparison. Several women in monochrome suits of various shades were clustered around him,
nodding fervently at everything he said. Those must be his
groupies, thought Clara disparagingly, unable to see what it
was about Simon Valentine that made obviously intelligent
women fawn over him.

Not that he seemed to be enjoying the experience, she had
to concede. He had a definite air of being at bay, and she saw
him steal surreptitious glances at his watch.

Seriously, the guy needed to relax a bit, Clara decided. He was holding a glass but not drinking from it and, as she watched, he put it back on a passing tray, offered a smile so brief it was barely more than a grimace to his disappointed fans and started to make his way out of the crush.

Terrified that he was leaving already, Clara drained her second glass for courage and headed after him. She couldn't let him get away without at least trying to buttonhole him.

Pushing her way through the crowds, she followed him out into the cavernous entrance hall in time to see him striding purposefully towards the cloakrooms. He was going to get his coat and leave, and her chance would be gone. She would have sat through a lecture on economics for nothing!

It was now or never.

Her heels clicked on the marble floor as she hurried after him. 'Dr Valentine?' she called breathlessly.

Simon bit down on an expletive. His lecture had gone very well, but he would much prefer to have left immediately afterwards. Instead, he'd had to stand around and make small talk. He'd barely stepped into the library when a whole gaggle of women had descended on him. Ever since he had appeared on the news explaining the blindingly obvious about the financial situation, he had become a reluctant celebrity.

At first it had seemed an excellent idea. His firm was all for it, and Simon himself believed it was important for people to understand the economic realities of life. He had no problem with that, and the opportunity to bring new thinking about micro financing to global attention was too good to miss. He was delighted that the ensuing documentary had had such an impact, but had been totally unprepared for the effect of his television appearances on female viewers.

It was all very embarrassing, in fact, and the intent way some women had taken to hanging on his every word made him deeply uncomfortable. If they were that interested in economics, why didn't they go away and read his articles instead?

And now, just when he'd managed to escape for a few minutes' quiet, here was another one.

For a moment Simon considered pretending that he hadn't heard her, but some of his so-called fans could be annoyingly persistent, and he wouldn't put it past some of them to pursue him right into the Gents. So he paused, clenched his jaw, and fixed on his least welcoming expression.

But when he turned, the young woman coming after him didn't look at all like one of his normal fans, most of whom tended to hide their silliness at being fans in the first place beneath a veneer of seriousness. There was nothing serious about this girl.

His first impression was of vivid colour, his second of a spectacular pair of legs. In spite of himself, Simon blinked. He doubted very much that the Institute had ever seen a skirt that short before, or shoes that frivolous.

He allowed himself a moment to appreciate the legs before he made himself look away from them. Just because Astrid had left, he didn't have to start leering at the first pair of decent legs to come his way.

'Yes?' he said uninvitingly.

She offered him a friendly smile. 'I just wanted to say that I enjoyed your talk very much,' she said, still breathless from the effort of hurrying after him in those absurd shoes. 'I thought you made some excellent points.'

Simon eyed her suspiciously. 'Oh? Which particular points?' he said. Maybe it was unfair to put her on the spot, but he didn't feel like being helpful.

'All of them,' she said firmly, only to falter as her gaze met his. She had an extraordinarily transparent expression, and Simon could see her realising that as an answer it was less than impressive and dredging up something she remembered from the lecture.

Which turned out to be not very much.

'What you said about qualitative easing was particularly interesting,' she offered with an ingenuous smile.

'Really? That's strange, as I was talking about *quant*itative easing.'

'That too,' she said.

He had to give her points for trying. Most of his 'fans' did their homework in an attempt to impress him when they met. This one clearly hadn't bothered.

'You're interested in the banks' asset policies?'

'Fascinated,' she said, clearly lying, but meeting his eyes with such limpid innocence that Simon felt an unfamiliar tugging sensation at the corner of his mouth. It took a moment before he recognized it as amusement, and he pressed his lips together before he actually smiled.

Now that he looked at her properly, he could see that she wasn't particularly pretty. Once you got past the animated expression, her features were really very ordinary, with ordinary brown hair falling in a very ordinary style to her shoulders. And yet she seemed to shimmer with a kind of suppressed energy, as if she were about to break into a run or fling her arms around, that made her not ordinary at all.

She made Simon feel vaguely unsettled, and that wasn't a feeling he liked.

'Were you even *at* my lecture?' he demanded.

'I sat through every riveting minute of it,' she assured him.

'And how much did you understand?'

He saw a brief struggle with her conscience cross her face before she opted, wisely, for honesty. 'Well, not everything… that is, not a lot…in fact, none of it, but I do admire you a lot, obviously.' She cleared her throat. 'The truth is, I don't know anything about economics. I'm here because I really need to talk to you.'

'I'm afraid I only talk about economics, so if you don't know anything about the subject it's likely to be a very short conversation,' said Simon curtly and made to turn away but she clutched at his arm.

'I won't keep you a minute, I *promise*,' she said and plunged into a prepared speech before he could shake his arm from her grasp. 'My name's Clara Sterne, and I—'

But she had already said enough. Simon's eyes narrowed. 'As in the Clara Sterne who has been ringing and emailing me and apparently doesn't understand the meaning of the word *no*?'

'Oh, you recognize my name? Good,' said Clara brightly.

Simon's mouth tightened. 'Spare your breath!' he said, flinging up a hand as she opened her mouth to go on. 'No, I will not participate in your ridiculous television programme. Once and for all… *No*!'

'But you haven't even given me a chance to explain about the programme,' she protested. 'It's not ridiculous at all. We want it to be a serious examination of the romance industry.'

'Clara, in case you haven't noticed, there's a global recession going on. I think there are more serious issues to examine than romance, even if such a thing existed.'

Clara pounced on that. 'So you don't think romance exists?'

She might as well have asked him whether he believed in the Jolly Green Giant. 'Of course I don't,' he said. 'It's clearly an artificial construct dreamed up by marketing teams.'

'Then that's all we want you to say on the programme! That's the whole point, in fact. It'll be a serious discussion, with you and your co-presenter putting different sides of the argument.'

'A serious discussion? I seem to recall you told me the

other presenter was a footballer's wife who hosts a daytime chat show!'

'*Ex*-wife,' Clara corrected him. 'We think the contrast between the two of you will be very effective.'

She had an extraordinarily mobile face. Her eyes as she leant eagerly towards him were an undistinguished brown, but her expression was so bright that Simon was momentarily snared, like the proverbial rabbit in the headlights. Irritated by the image, he still had to make a physical effort to jerk himself free.

'I don't care how "effective" the contrast would be,' he said sharply. 'It's not going to happen.'

Clara regarded him in dismay. How could she persuade him if he wouldn't even listen to her? 'I'd have thought you would be pleased at the chance to convince people about your point of view,' she said. 'Your last documentary was really important, and we want this one to be the same.'

'My last documentary was about the alleviation of poverty! I hope you're not going to try and convince me the importance of that can be compared to *romance*?'

Uh-oh. Wrong track. Clara did some swift back-pedalling. 'No, of course not,' she said quickly. 'But we could offer the opportunity to do a follow-up programme on the projects you mentioned in your film,' she offered, seized by inspiration, and mentally crossing her fingers that Roland would agree. 'It would be great publicity for you.'

But that was the wrong thing to say too. 'I'm not interested in publicity,' said Simon quellingly. 'I'm interested in making systems work so that the people who need help get it. It's nothing—'

He broke off, obviously catching sight of someone over Clara's shoulder, and stiffened.

Curious, she turned to see a couple coming towards them.

The woman was coolly elegant, her companion dark and Mediterranean-looking and seriously hot.

There was an awkward pause, then the woman said, 'Hello, Simon.'

'Astrid.' Simon inclined his head in curt acknowledgement, his voice clipped.

Clara looked from one to the other with interest. There was something going on here. Astrid was rather lovely, Clara thought enviously, with perfect skin, perfect bone structure and a perfect shining curtain of silvery-blonde hair.

And no prizes for guessing Simon thought so too. He was looking wooden but Clara prided herself on reading body language and, unless she was much mistaken, Astrid was an ex of some kind.

'You haven't met Paolo before.' Astrid sounded composed enough, but there was a telltale flush along her cheekbones as she introduced the two men, who eyed each other with undisguised hostility. 'Paolo Sparchetti, Simon Valentine.'

'Ciao,' drawled Paolo, and put a possessive arm around Astrid's waist.

Lucky Astrid, was all Clara could think. Paolo was sulkily handsome, with a wide sensuous mouth and just the right degree of stubble to make him look sexily dishevelled. Now if *he* was commenting on the stock markets, she might take an interest in the economy. It was bizarre to think that Simon was the one with all the fans.

Simon was definitely jealous. He barely managed a jerk of his head to acknowledge the introduction.

Ver-rr-ry interesting, thought Clara.

It was hard to imagine two men more different. Simon was all buttoned up and conventional, while Paolo was smouldering passion in an open-necked shirt and a designer jacket, with a man purse slung over his shoulder. Clara was prepared to bet her life on the fact that Simon would die rather than carry a handbag.

There was another taut silence.

Clara looked from one to the other, intrigued by the fact that Astrid seemed torn. Her body seemed to be attuned to Paolo's—and, frankly, Clara didn't blame it—but her mind was apparently focused on Simon's reaction.

Hmm. Clara scented an opportunity. Somehow she needed to get Simon and Astrid back together, which would make Simon so grateful that he would offer her, Clara, anything she wanted in return for restoring his lost love to him. At which point she would mention MediaOchre's pressing need for him to appear in the programme.

Of course I'll do it, he would say. *Anything for you, Clara.*

Well, it was worth a shot.

CHAPTER TWO

CLARA considered her options. She could try and draw Paolo's attention away from Astrid, but that was frankly unlikely. Clara could scrub up well enough when she tried, but she had none of Astrid's cool beauty.

The alternative was to make Astrid jealous of Simon.

It shouldn't be too hard, Clara decided. A look, a hint, a suggestion that Simon had found someone else ought to be enough.

All she had to do was pretend to be in love with Simon.

And how hard could that be?

Years earlier, when she had still been dreaming of making it to Broadway, Clara had done a drama course. Her acting career had been humiliatingly short, but she could still pull out the stops when she tried.

Putting on a bright smile, she stepped just a little closer to Simon and stuck out her hand to Astrid. 'Hello, I'm Clara.'

It was pretty clear that Astrid hadn't registered Clara's presence up to that point. Clara wasn't offended. If she had Paolo on her arm, she wouldn't notice anyone else either, and it wasn't as if Clara was a likely rival for his interest, more was the pity.

Still, Astrid's perfect brows drew together as she took in Clara's appearance, and when her perfect green eyes reached the hem of Clara's mini-dress, the perfect mouth definitely tightened.

'Hello,' she said with marked coolness.

Clara pretended not to notice. 'Simon was *brilliant*, wasn't he?' She threw Simon an adoring look.

The feedback at the end of her drama course had been succinct: stick to dancing. If only her tutors could see her now! They might change their minds about her acting abilities. She deserved a gleaming statuette at least for convincing Astrid that she was starstruck by Simon Valentine, Clara decided.

'I've just felt so *inspired* about the economy since meeting Simon,' she cooed. 'I've learnt so much, haven't you?'

Simon unfolded his lips. 'Astrid is a hedge fund manager.'

Clara didn't have a clue what a hedge fund manager was, but she gathered from Simon's tone and Astrid's expression that there was little the other woman had to learn about economics.

'How exciting,' she said, bestowing a kind smile on Astrid. 'Did you enjoy Simon's lecture anyway?'

'Of course,' said Astrid. She glanced from Clara to Simon. 'I've heard him talk before, obviously.'

Obviously.

'It's still a thrill for me every time.' Clara thought that was a clever touch, hinting that she had sat through hours of economic lectures just for the pleasure of listening to Simon's voice. Talk about devoted!

Astrid hesitated. 'I just thought it would be a good idea for you and Paolo to meet, Simon,' she said, effectively cutting Clara out of the conversation.

It was Clara's cue to make an excuse and leave, but instead she put a hand on Simon's arm and beamed at the other two, not budging. 'It's lovely to meet *you*,' she assured them, very aware of Simon, who had gone rigid at her touch.

Baulked of the tête-à-tête she so plainly desired, Astrid had to concede defeat. 'Well, I'll see you in the office tomorrow,' she said to Simon, pointedly ignoring Clara. 'Paolo, we'd better go.'

'Whenever you want, *cara*.' The smirk Paolo sent Simon was a classic, and Simon glowered after the Italian as he sauntered off with Astrid.

'Did you see that?' he demanded. 'She's actually with a man who carries a handbag!'

She had got that right, anyway. 'I think you'll find they're called carry-alls,' said Clara.

'It looked like a handbag to me,' snarled Simon. Then he remembered who he was talking to, and rounded on her.

'And what did you think you were doing barging in on a private conversation, anyway?'

The brown eyes looked guilelessly back at him. 'I thought you'd be glad of my help.'

'Help?' He glowered at her. 'What for?'

'You want Astrid back, don't you?'

'What?' Simon was completely thrown. 'How did you know that?' he asked involuntarily and then glowered some more, furious with himself for such a revealing remark.

'Well, you *could* have hung a sign saying "jealous loser" round your neck,' said Clara, evidently quite undaunted by his thunderous expression, 'but otherwise it's hard to see how you could have made it more obvious!'

Feeling his mouth fall open in a gape, Simon snapped it shut. Who *was* this girl? She had some nerve, he had to give her that! Nobody else he knew—apart from his mother, perhaps—would think of talking to him that way.

'Astrid didn't like me being with you, you know,' she went on knowledgeably.

'You're not with me!'

'But she doesn't know that, does she?'

Simon was beginning to wonder if he was having a particularly vivid and unsettling dream. His life was black and white and firmly under control. He didn't talk about relationships. He didn't let himself get trapped into bizarre conversations with young women who wore vibrant colours and inappropriately short skirts and who appeared to have no compunction about barging in on other people's conversations or offering unsolicited advice.

'Any fool can see why Astrid is with Paolo—I mean, he's seriously hot—but she's clearly still got a thing about you.' Clara couldn't quite manage to keep the bafflement from her voice, Simon noted. 'Instead of you glaring at Paolo, you need to make *her* jealous.'

'Jealous?' echoed Simon, even as he wondered why he was even having this conversation.

Clara nodded encouragingly. 'Make her wonder what she's missing,' she said.

'And this is any of your business because…?'

'Like I say, I can help you. I don't mind hanging around and simpering at you whenever you're likely to meet Astrid. She won't like the idea that you're with me at all, and if you can't make the most of the situation when she tells you how jealous she is, I wash my hands of you.'

Unbelievable. What kind of world was Clara Sterne living in? Simon regarded her with his most sardonic expression.

'And in return for this sacrifice on your part? Or can I guess?'

'Well, you're not stupid,' said Clara, 'so yes, you probably can. All you'd have to do in return is present a one-hour film.' She looked at him hopefully. 'Well? Do we have a deal?'

She didn't seriously expect him to agree to that nonsense, did she? Ruin his reputation as a serious economist by taking part in some sentimental twaddle?

'Not exactly,' said Simon, 'but I do have a deal to offer *you*.' He crooked a finger in conspiratorial fashion and her face lit up. 'Really?' she said, leaning closer. Simon got a whiff of a fresh citrusy scent.

'Really,' he said.

'What's the deal?'

'It's a very simple one. *You* go away and leave me alone, and *I* won't call Security to throw you out. How's that for an offer?'

Clara recoiled in disappointment. 'Oh, but *please…*'

Unmoved by the pleading brown eyes, Simon looked at his watch. 'I'll count to ten, then I'm calling Security.'

'All right, I'm going!' she said hastily. Digging in her purse, she produced a business card and pushed it into his hand. 'But here are my contact details, just in case you change your mind.'

Shaking his head with a mixture of exasperation and reluctant admiration at her persistence, Simon permitted himself a last look at her legs as she left, clearly disappointed but still with plenty of verve to the swing of her hips. As the click of those precipitous heels faded and she disappeared around the corner, he found that he was turning her card round and round between his fingers, and he stopped himself irritably.

Clara Sterne, Production Assistant, MediaOchre Productions, the card read. Who in God's name would want to have anything to do with a company that called itself MediaOchre? The name was either prescient or indicated an ominous taste for puns. Simon had no intention of getting involved either way.

Unable to spot a bin, he shoved the card in his jacket pocket. He would dispose of it later, as he certainly wouldn't be needing it. That was the last he would see of Clara Sterne.

Simon drummed his fingers on his desk. When they were going out, it had been very convenient that Astrid worked in the same office, but now it felt…well, awkward.

Simon didn't *like* feeling awkward. He had always liked the fact that it had been so *comfortable* being with Astrid. She didn't make scenes or get all emotional, and she never got personal in the office.

So why she wanted to spoil it all by throwing everything up for a pretty Italian, Simon couldn't begin to fathom. He thought she had been happy with him. She had *said* she had been happy. And then one day it had been all about being swept off her feet and wanting 'passion' and 'romance'.

Madness.

Astrid had put her head round his door earlier and asked if she could have a word. He'd been glad to see her. If they could have sat down together and chatted about financial sustainability for NGOs or risk analysis, he was sure she would have remembered how much better off she was with him. It wasn't as if she could have a meaningful conversation with a man who carried a handbag, after all. Surely she would get bored with Paolo soon?

Not that he was jealous, whatever Clara Sterne had had to say about it. That was nonsense. He didn't get jealous. That wasn't how he and Astrid had operated, and he wasn't about to start now.

Simon had every faith that Astrid would come to her senses but, apparently, it wasn't yet. She had no time for economic policy nowadays, and was determined to talk about bloody Paolo instead. How he made her feel. How guilty she then felt about Simon. Feelings, feelings, feelings… Simon couldn't understand it. It was so unlike her.

Now Astrid was pacing. That was another thing she had never used to do.

'Who was that you were with last night?' she asked abruptly.

'Last night?'

'That girl. Clara. I got the impression she was with you.'

Simon opened his mouth to deny any acquaintance with Clara Sterne, but the words died on his tongue as her words came back to him.

She's clearly still got a thing about you. Instead of glaring at Paolo, you need to make her jealous.

Was it possible that Clara was right?

Simon was unsettled by how clearly he could remember her. Clara wasn't a beautiful woman like Astrid, of course, but there had been a sort of quirky appeal to her undistinguished features, he had to admit. Something to do with the warm brown eyes, perhaps, or that mouth that seemed permanently tilted at the corners.

Or maybe those spectacular legs.

Simon was prepared to admit to a sneaking admiration for her daring, too, if he were honest, although he had no intention of changing his mind.

In his jacket pocket he'd found her card, which he'd forgotten to put in the bin. Now he turned it on the desk, frowning slightly.

'How long have you known her?'

To his relief, Astrid stopped pacing and sat down on the other side of his desk. A tiny crease had appeared between her immaculately groomed brows.

'Not long.' Simon shifted, uncomfortably aware that he wasn't being entirely truthful.

'It's just that I worry about you,' Astrid said unexpectedly. 'I know we're not together any more, but that doesn't mean I don't care about you, and I'd hate it if you were to do anything foolish.'

Simon paused in the middle of turning the card on its side. 'Foolish?' Pretty rich coming from someone who had thrown over a perfectly satisfactory relationship for a handbag-carrying Italian!

'Clara's very...' Astrid paused delicately '...*colourful*, but she's hardly your type, Simon. And that dress! Totally inappropriate, I thought.'

It had been, but Simon couldn't help remembering how good Clara's legs had looked in it.

'I know you're too intelligent to be taken in by a girl in a miniskirt,' Astrid went on, 'but I hope you'll be careful.'

'I'm always careful,' said Simon.

It was true. He liked his life firmly under control. Risk analysis was his speciality. He didn't do reckless or spontaneous. And he certainly didn't do foolish. He'd seen just how disastrous recklessness and foolishness could be, and neither were mistakes he would be making.

'I know.' Astrid's expression softened. 'Look, it's hard to talk about these things in the office. Why don't we meet for a drink later?' Then, just when he was congratulating himself on being right about her returning to her senses, she spoiled things by adding, 'I'd really like you to get to know Paolo.'

So much for a quiet drink sorting things out. Simon wanted to be with Astrid, but he had no desire to get to know any more about Paolo. As far as he was concerned, he already knew more than enough.

'I'm sorry, Astrid,' he said, 'but my mother is coming to town this evening, and I promised to take her out to dinner. I'm expecting her any minute, in fact. Another time, perhaps.'

Preferably when Paolo was unavailable.

As if on cue, his PA buzzed him from her office. Not sorry for the distraction, Simon flipped the switch. 'Yes, Molly?'

'I've just had a call from Reception,' said Molly. 'Your mother's there. She's fine, but there's been some kind of incident. Could you go down?'

When the lift doors opened, Simon spotted his mother straight away. She was at the centre of a cluster of people on the far side of the atrium, but when she saw him she hurried over to meet him. 'Thank goodness you're here!'

Simon's brows snapped together at the sight of her flustered appearance. Frances Valentine was still an attractive woman, but now her highlighted blonde hair was dishevelled, and there were spots of colour in her cheeks. 'What on earth has happened?'

'I've been mugged!' she announced with her usual flair for the dramatic.

'Are you all right?' he asked in quick concern.

'I'm fine. It's Clara I'm worried about.'

'Clara?'

'She saw what happened, and tackled the mugger,' Frances said admiringly, tugging him over to a bedraggled figure sitting on one of the low leather sofas, nursing one arm. 'Wasn't it brave of her?'

With a sinking sense of inevitability, Simon recognized the long legs first. His gaze travelled up over the torn tights, mud-splattered skirt and top to a face that was already unsettlingly familiar. Above the colourfully striped scarf that was wound several times around her neck, Clara Sterne's face was paler than the night before but, even shaken, she managed to look more vivid than the other women clucking over her and, as her brown eyes widened at the sight of him, he felt an odd little zing pass through him.

'*You're* Frances's son?' she exclaimed.

'You know each other?' his mother said in delight.

'No,' said Simon.

Just as Clara said, 'Yes.'

How did a woman as warm and friendly as Frances have a son as stiff as Simon Valentine? Clara wondered. She hadn't been expecting to see him just then, and surprise had sent her heart jumping into her throat at the sight of him.

At least she hoped it was surprise.

He looked as disapproving as ever, as if she had thrown herself into that puddle and torn her tights and hurt her wrist just to annoy him. She had wanted to see him, of course, but not like this.

'What happened?' he asked his mother.

Frances launched into her story. 'I was just crossing the road when I felt this thump on my shoulder and this awful oik grabbed my bag.' She shuddered. 'I got such a fright! It's my favourite bag too. Do you remember I bought it in Venice last year?'

Judging by Simon's expression, he knew nothing about his mother's handbags and cared less. Clara saw him keeping a visible rein on his impatience.

'How did Clara get involved?'

'She saw what was happening.' Frances sat down next to Clara and patted her knee. 'Lots of other people must have seen too, but no one else moved. Clara took off after him straight away, and she got hold of my bag, but they had a bit of a tussle and he pushed her to the ground before he ran off.'

Drawing breath, she looked up at her son. 'I'm very much afraid she may have broken her wrist, but she says there's no need to call an ambulance. You try and talk some sense into her, Simon.'

'There's no need, really.' Clara managed to get a word in at last. 'I'm perfectly all right. I can walk.'

'You're not all right! Look at you. You've ruined your tights, and I can tell your wrist is hurting.'

It was. When the mugger had shoved her, Clara had lost her balance and her wrist had taken the whole weight of her body as she fell. But her legs were all right, thank goodness, and she hardly counted as an emergency.

'I'll get a taxi,' she compromised.

'You'll do no such thing!' said Frances roundly. 'Simon has a car. You'll take her to hospital, won't you, darling?'

Clara had never seen anyone look less like a darling than Simon Valentine right then. It was almost worth a sore wrist and scraped knees to see the expression on his face, where impatience, frustration and reluctance warred with the mixture of exasperation and affection he obviously felt for his mother.

'Of course,' he said after a moment.

'Really, it's not necessary…'

'Nonsense!' said Frances. 'You're a heroine, and so I shall tell the police.'

'All right.' Rather to Clara's relief, Simon interrupted his mother's account of her heroics and took charge. Her wrist was getting more painful by the minute, and she was glad to be able to sit numbly while he despatched the cluster of receptionists who had been clucking ineffectually and arranged for his mother to be taken to his home in a taxi.

Only then did he turn his attention to Clara.

'There's no need to look at me like that,' she said as she got stiffly to her feet.

'Like what?'

'Like you think I arranged the mugging on purpose.'

'It crossed my mind.' Simon pushed the button for the lift to take them down to the basement car park. 'If you were desperate enough to sit through a lecture on monetary policy, who knows what you'd be prepared to do.'

'I was desperate to talk to you, but not quite desperate enough to tackle a mugger,' said Clara. She didn't add that Roland would certainly have pushed her into it if he thought it would get results.

As it appeared to have done. She mustn't waste this opportunity, she told herself, but her knees were stinging where she had grazed them and the pain in her wrist made it hard to concentrate.

Simon looked at her sideways as the lift doors slid open and they stepped inside.

'And yet you did it anyway. It was a dangerous thing to do. What if the mugger had been armed?'

'I didn't think,' Clara confessed, cradling her forearm. 'I saw your mum stagger, and then this young guy snatched her bag. It just made me mad. She looked so shocked that I ran after him and grabbed the bag back.'

She was very aware of him in the close confines of the lift. He seemed bigger than he had the night before. Stronger and more solid. More male. More overwhelming, and she found herself babbling.

'It would have been fine if he'd just let me take the bag back,' she rattled on. 'I suppose that was too much to hope after he'd gone to all the trouble of stealing it. Anyway, he turned round and shoved me, and the next thing I was crashing into a puddle.'

She grimaced down at herself. Her favourite skirt was ruined. 'I kept hold of the bag, though, and everyone was looking by then, so I think he just cut his losses and ran off. Your mother had caught up with us by then, so I was able to give her the bag back. She insisted that we come in here, but I honestly didn't know that you were her son!'

'I believe you,' said Simon with a dry glance. The lift doors opened, and they stepped out into the garage. 'But I hope you're not going to ask me to believe that it was coincidence that you were outside the building?' he asked, leading the way to a sleek silver car.

'No.' Clara didn't see any point in denying it. 'I was hoping to catch you when you left work. I thought you might be in a better mood today.'

Simon jabbed the key in the direction of the car to unlock it. 'I was in a perfectly good mood yesterday!' he said as the lights flashed obediently. 'Just as I'm in a perfectly good mood today,' he added through clenched teeth, opening the passenger door for her with pointed courtesy.

'Gosh, I hope I never meet you in a bad mood,' said Clara.

There was a dangerous pause, and then Simon shut the door on her with a careful lack of emphasis.

'I'm grateful to you for going to my mother's rescue,' he said stiffly when he got behind the wheel and started the engine, 'but if you're thinking of using this situation to press your case about this wretched programme of yours, please don't bother. I'm not changing my mind.'

Clara heaved a martyred sigh. 'All right. My wrist is too sore to grovel right now, anyway.' She slid him a glance under her lashes. 'I guess I'll just have to resign myself to pain and the prospect of losing my job.'

'You know, there is such a thing as employment law,' said Simon, unimpressed. 'They can't sack you because you had an accident and hurt your wrist.'

'No, but they can for failing to do your job, which in my case was to get you to agree to present the programme.'

'Emotional blackmail.' Simon put the car into gear and drove up the ramp and out into the dark January evening. 'The perfect end to a perfect day.'

'You're right.' Emotional blackmail was all she had left. 'It's not your problem if my career is over, or if I can't pay my rent and have to go back to live with my parents and admit I'm a total failure.'

Simon spared her a brief glance. 'Save it,' he advised. 'If you've done your research, you'll know that I'm completely heartless.'

'I have, and you're not,' said Clara. 'I know how many times you've volunteered for emergency relief projects after disasters. A heartless person doesn't do that.'

'Don't make me into a hero,' he said curtly. 'I'm not getting my hands dirty. I just make sure the money gets to those who need it.'

Quite a big 'just', Clara would have thought. Simon might not be pulling people out of the rubble or a doctor saving lives, but he regularly left his comfortable life in London to spend several weeks in extremely difficult conditions. Nothing happened without money, and relief efforts depended on financial managers like him to channel the funds where they were most needed and stop them being siphoned off by fraud and corruption.

Simon was clearly anxious to change the subject. 'Besides,' he said, cutting across her thoughts, 'it's totally unreasonable for anyone's job to depend on one person.'

'Tell that to my boss,' said Clara glumly.

'They must be able to find someone else. It's not even as if I'm a professional broadcaster.'

'It has to be you.' Faced with his intransigence, she had nothing to lose, Clara decided. She might as well be straight. 'The budget is based on your participation, and Stella Holt won't take part unless you do. The whole thing falls apart without you,' she told him. 'And so does MediaOchre. There are only three of us as it is. That's why I've been so persistent.'

'Basing the entire future of a company on one individual is an extremely risky economic strategy,' said Simon severely.

'I suppose so, but you have to take a risk every now and then, don't you?'

She knew immediately she had said the wrong thing. Simon's expression didn't change, but she felt him withdraw, like a snail shrinking back into its shell, and his voice was distant. 'Not in my experience,' he said.

There was a pause. 'Well, you can't say I haven't tried,' she said after a moment.

'No,' said Simon, 'I can't say that.'

A dreary drizzle misted the windscreen, and the streetlamps cast a fuzzy orange glow over the commuters hurrying for the tube, collars turned up against the cold and the damp.

How was she going to break it to Ted and Roland? Clara's heart sank. She had failed them both. Now she could wave goodbye to her shiny new career and her hopes of becoming a producer. Just when she had filled the aching gap in her life left by Matt and found something she really wanted to do too.

Where was Julie Andrews when she needed her? As so often, Clara opted for frivolity when things looked like getting desperate. It was better than the alternative, which was crying hopelessly and which never really helped anyway. That was a lesson she had learnt the hard way in the weeks and months after Matt had left.

Well, she would just have to cheer herself up. Clara hummed a few bars of *My Favourite Things* under her breath while Simon negotiated an awkward junction.

'What are you doing?'

'Singing to myself.'

'What on earth for?'

'To make myself feel better.' It seemed obvious to Clara.

'I thought that's why I was taking you to hospital.'

'Music is the best medicine,' she said. 'Musicals taught me that.'

She might as well have claimed to have learned it from aliens. 'Musicals?' asked Simon as if he had never heard the word.

'Shows where the actors sing and dance around,' said Clara helpfully. 'And some of the greatest movies ever made. Take *The Sound of Music*. You must have seen that?'

'I've heard of it.' He eased into a gap between a bus and a taxi.

'I'll bet you know most of the songs.' She hummed the tune again. 'Is it ringing any bells?'

Simon glanced at her, shook his head slightly, and turned his attention back to the traffic. 'I have no idea what you're talking about, Clara.'

She gaped at him, astounded by his ignorance. This was probably how he felt about anyone who didn't know all about quantitative easing and interest rate policies.

'It's a classic song,' she told him. 'And, what's more, it really does work. When things go wrong—like you refusing to take part in the programme and ruining my career, for instance—all I have to do is sing a bit and I instantly feel better.'

It had worked when she missed Matt. Most of the time.

'Who needs a doctor when you've got *The Sound of Music*?' she said cheerfully, and Simon shook his head in disbelief.

'I think I'd still take my chances at the hospital if I were you.'

At least three of the nurses in the A and E department recognized Simon, and there was a rather unseemly tussle as to who would help him. Initially triumphant at securing the task of dealing with Clara, the staff nurse was positively sulky when she realised that Simon planned to wait outside, and that the other two were left to fuss around him.

Not that Simon even seemed to realise that he was getting special treatment. 'I'll be here when you're ready,' he said to Clara. Taking a seat on one of the hard plastic chairs, he unfolded the *Financial Times* and proceeded to ignore everyone else.

By the time she emerged with a plaster cast up to her elbow and her arm in a sling, Clara was tired and sore and feeling faintly sick. She wanted Matt. Usually she was very good at persuading herself that she was fine, but at times like this, when her defences were down and she just needed him to put his arms round her and tell her that everything would be all right, his absence sharpened from a dull ache to a spearing pain.

Matt wasn't there for her any more. There was no one there for her.

Except Simon Valentine, who was sitting exactly where she had left him, and the rush of relief she felt at the sight of him made her screw up her face in case she burst into tears or did something equally humiliating.

'The sister said your wrist is broken,' he said, folding his newspaper and getting to his feet as she appeared. 'I'm sorry, it must be very painful.'

Clara put on a bright smile. She wasn't going to be a cry-baby in front of Simon Valentine.

'It's not too bad.' She moved her arm in its sling gingerly. 'I have to come back to the fracture clinic in a week, and they'll put a lightweight cast on it then.'

'My mother rang while you were being X-rayed,' he told her. 'It seems she picked up your bag when you dropped it to go after that mugger.'

Clara clapped her good hand to her head. 'Thank goodness for that! I forgot all about it in all the kerfuffle.'

'We'll go and pick it up, and then I'll take you home.'

'Honestly, I'm fine,' she said quickly. 'I can get a cab.'

'You might as well resign yourself,' he said. 'My life wouldn't be worth living if my mother got wind of the fact that I let you go home in a taxi!'

His suit was still immaculate, and she was horribly aware all at once of her scuffed knees and mud-splattered clothes where she had fallen. His hand was strong and steadying through her jacket as he took her good arm and steered her out through the doors to the car park, and she was guiltily grateful to his mother for insisting that he go with her to the hospital.

Being driven was a luxury too, she thought, sinking into the comfortable leather seat. It certainly beat the tube, or squeezing onto a bus with everyone else, coats steaming and breath misting the windows.

'You don't strike me as a man who's scared of his mother,' she said, turning slightly to look at him as he got in beside her.

'She has her own ways of getting what she wants,' said Simon in a dry voice. 'I've learnt it's easier just to do what she says.'

Throwing his arm over the back of her seat, he reversed out of the narrow parking slot. Clara sat very still, afraid to move her head in case she brushed against him. All at once it felt as if there wasn't quite enough oxygen in the car.

'I thought she was charming,' she said breathlessly.

'Oh, yes, she's charming,' he said with a sigh and, to Clara's relief, he brought his arm back to put the car into forward gear once more. 'Great fun, wonderful company and completely irresponsible, but she gets away with it. She can be utterly infuriating, but if you try and reason with her, she just smiles and pats your cheek and, before you know where you are, you're doing exactly what she wants.'

Now why hadn't she thought of patting his cheek? Clara wondered. Somehow she felt it wouldn't have worked for her.

She liked the sound of Frances, though. She seemed a most unlikely mother for Simon.

'You must take after your father,' she said.

It was a throwaway comment, but Simon's face closed and his mouth set in a compressed line.

'No, I don't,' he said harshly. 'I don't resemble him at all.'

CHAPTER THREE

'Wow.' A-glitter with lights, London lay spread out below Simon's apartment. Across the Thames, the bridges were illuminated as if strung with fairy lights, and Clara could see right down to the Houses of Parliament and the huge circle of the London Eye. In the darkness, the streets seemed to be shimmering with energy.

'Wow,' she said again. 'What a fabulous view! It feels like you're on top of the world, doesn't it?'

She turned back to admire the rest of the apartment, which was stark and stylish, and somehow not at all what she had expected of someone as conventional as Simon Valentine. 'What an amazing place.'

Simon shrugged as he pocketed his car keys. 'It's a convenient location for the City, and these properties make sound investments.'

'Right,' said Clara, who had never invested in property in her life.

'I think it's *ghastly*!' said Frances. She had changed and was looking remarkably relaxed and elegant for someone who had been mugged hours earlier. 'I keep telling him that he should at least put up some curtains.'

She looked around her disparagingly. 'Soulless is the only word for it. What this place needs is a woman's touch,' she said as Simon blew out an exasperated breath, having clearly heard it all before. 'Don't you agree, Clara?'

Clara thought of the cluttered flat she shared with Allegra. It was cosier than Simon's apartment, that was for sure, but she couldn't see Simon wanting cushions and throws and magazines scattered on the sofa. He wouldn't like cold mugs of tea left lying around, shoes discarded on the floor or bras and tights drying over the radiators. That coffee table would never be buried under nail polishes and phone chargers and old newspapers and empty crisp packets and menus from the Indian takeaway round the corner.

In fact, the woman's touch was probably the last thing Simon needed.

'It's very spacious,' she said diplomatically.

Frances sniffed. 'I don't know why he doesn't buy a nice house in Chelsea or somewhere. It would be so much nicer for me to visit.' She heaved an exaggerated sigh but, when Simon remained unmoved, turned back to Clara.

'Anyway, come and sit down.' Without giving Clara an opportunity to protest, she drew her over towards one of the cream sofas and spoke over her shoulder to her son.

'Darling, do get Clara a drink. You must be gasping for a G&T,' she told Clara. 'I know I am! Or I suppose Simon could make tea,' she added doubtfully.

'Mother—' Simon's teeth were audibly gritted '—Clara's anxious to get home. She might not want a drink.'

'Nonsense, of course she does. Don't you, Clara?'

Clara was torn. Simon was clearly desperate to get rid of her, but it had been a long day and now that Frances had mentioned gin…

'I'd love a gin and tonic,' she confessed.

'There you are!' Frances turned triumphantly to her son. 'And I'll have one too, darling, to keep her company.'

Simon sucked in a breath. 'Of course,' he said tightly and disappeared to what Clara presumed was a kitchen.

'Don't mind him,' Frances said with a sunny smile. 'He likes to disapprove, but it's good for him to relax a bit. He works so hard, poor darling, and now he's on his own again…' She leant towards Clara confidentially. 'Well, I always thought Astrid was a bit of a cold fish, but at least she would make him go out.'

Clara was dying to gossip, but didn't think she ought to. She asked Frances how long she was visiting instead, and Frances chatted happily about herself until Simon reappeared with drinks.

'Now you must tell us all about you,' she insisted, and proceeded to grill Clara about her family, background and job.

'Oh, you work in television? How exciting! Simon's on television sometimes.'

Clara's eyes met Simon's fleetingly over the rim of her glass. 'Yes, I know.' She had to give him points for being able to pour a mean gin and tonic. It was long and fizzy, with just the right amount of lime and ice. She was feeling better already and she settled back into the sofa, prepared to enjoy herself before she had to face the reality of failure again.

'You must be very proud,' she said to Frances.

'Oh, I am, *terribly*. Of course, the idea of him being a pin-up is a bit of a hoot. Not that he wasn't a *gorgeous* baby.'

'*Mother*…'

Clara smothered a smile at Simon's expression as Frances rattled on. 'I see him on the news, and he sounds so clever and *sensible*. You'd never guess what a reckless little boy he was, would you?'

'Mother—' said Simon again, warning in his voice '—Clara's had a long day. She doesn't want to listen to a lot of boring family stories.'

Frances ignored him and spoke to a fascinated Clara. 'He

was full of mischief when he was little. Your hair would stand
on end if I told you half the things he got up to! But then
his father died...' She trailed off sadly. 'That was a horrible
shock. I don't know what I would have done without Simon
then. He sorted everything out, and he's been looking after
us ever since.'

Simon's jaw was set. 'That's not true—'

'It *is* true,' insisted Frances. 'I always wonder how different you'd have been if your father hadn't left things in such
a mess.'

What mess? Clara wondered. It sounded as if there was an
interesting story there, but when Simon caught her eye his
expression was so tense that she couldn't help responding to
his unspoken appeal.

'I really should be going,' she interrupted Frances, who
was clearly ready to tell the whole story. Draining her glass,
she put it down and, one-armed, manoeuvred herself awkwardly to her feet from the deep sofa.

'Must you go?' Frances looked disappointed. 'It's been
such fun meeting you, and I'm so, *so* grateful to you.'

'It was nothing, really.'

'It wasn't nothing. You were an absolute *heroine*, and
you've broken your wrist rescuing my wretched bag. I can't
possibly thank you enough. You must *promise* to tell us if
there's ever anything we can ever do for you. Mustn't she,
Simon?'

A nerve jerked in Simon's cheek. 'Of course,' he said after
the tiniest of hesitations.

'That's settled then.'

Frances fussed around, trying to remember where she'd
put Clara's bag, while Clara and Simon waited in awkward
silence. Eventually it was found, and Frances handed it over,
kissed Clara on the cheek and made her promise to keep in
touch.

At last she let them go, waving them off from the door of Simon's apartment.

He waited until the lift doors were closed before he spoke.

'Thank you,' he said gruffly.

Clara didn't pretend not to know what he was talking about. 'My mother can be really embarrassing, too.'

'Does she regale perfect strangers with stories of what you did as a little girl?' he asked, but his expression lightened a little.

'Not exactly. She and Dad are both academics, and my brothers are really clever too. They all listen to classical music and read highbrow novels and if they go to the theatre, it's to watch some avant-garde play, while I flick through magazines and love show tunes.' Clara sighed. 'My family are lovely, but sometimes I can feel them thinking that there must have been some mix-up at the hospital when I was born.'

'They don't sound too embarrassing,' said Simon.

'That's because you've got a PhD,' she pointed out. 'Try taking a boyfriend home.'

She had a momentary pang when she thought about Matt, who had done better than most at coping with her family. But then, of course, he would have done. Matt got on with everybody. Clara pushed the memory aside.

'He gets grilled on what he thinks about existentialist literature or Saint Augustine's theology, and if the poor guy is brave enough to ask a question of his own about what they do, he gets a whole lecture on the spatial politics of post Reformation churches.'

'The what?'

'I think it's something to do with kneeling,' said Clara. 'I ought to know. My mother's been writing a book about it since I was five. I used to envy my friends who had proper mothers who read *Glitz* and watched television and talked about make-up and celebrities. The only famous people Mum knows about have been dead four hundred years!'

'At least she doesn't keep running off and marrying unsuitable men,' said Simon as they headed back to the car.

'How many times has your mother been married?'

'Three, and every time she manages to pick someone who'll leave her high and dry.' Clara could hear the bitter undercurrent in his voice as he unlocked the car and helped her in so that she didn't jar her wrist. His hand, she noticed, was firm and his grip surprisingly strong.

'You'd think she would learn from experience, but no!' Simon said, unaware of the tiny and disturbing frisson shimmying its way down Clara's spine. 'She'll throw everything up for "love" and, before we know where we are, she's having to extricate herself from another mess.'

Or was he the one who had to extricate his mother every time? Clara wondered, glad to feel that the frisson had reached the coccyx and appeared to have vanished. Perhaps she had imagined it?

'I think it's nice that she hasn't lost her faith in love,' she said neutrally when Simon settled himself behind the steering wheel.

'She thinks she needs a husband, but that's not true. Mother likes to tell everyone that I looked after her when my father died, but that's not true. *She* was the one who kept us going, and it was hard for her. Whenever she's at her most exasperating—which is often—I remember that.'

'Is that why you won't do a programme about romance? Because it never worked out for your mother?'

'No,' said Simon with a withering look. 'I won't do it because (a), I'm extremely busy with more important things and (b), frankly the last thing I want at the moment is more media exposure. I didn't mind when I could draw attention to the micro-financing crisis, but nobody ever mentions that now, and instead I get sackloads of fan mail from silly women who have obviously got nothing better to do with their time. I wouldn't keep doing the news interviews at all if the CEO of Stanhope Harding hadn't insisted it was good PR.'

Clearly remembering that particular conversation, he shoved the car into gear with unnecessary force. 'He didn't quite tell me that my job depended on continuing to comment, but I got the message.'

'Mmm,' said Clara, unable to resist. 'It's hard, isn't it, when your job depends on your boss, who insists that you do something you don't particularly want to do.'

Simon said nothing, but the distinctly abrasive quality to the silence told her that he had got the point.

You must promise to tell us if there's ever anything we can ever do for you, Frances had said.

And then Simon had been forced to say, *Of course.*

He must know that there was indeed something he could do for her.

Apart from directions to the flat she shared in a shabby street in south-west London, the journey passed in silence. Clara folded her lips together and heroically refrained from reminding Simon of his mother's promise, but she knew that he was thinking about it. Whenever she sneaked a glance at him from under her lashes, she could see a muscle jerking in his jaw.

Miraculously, Simon managed to find a parking space only a little way down the street from Clara's flat. He switched off the engine, but neither of them moved.

The silence lengthened. His jaw was still working, Clara noted. It would be a mistake to say anything, but he could do with just a *tiny* push.

Lifting her arm in its sling, she winced. Not too much. Just enough to suggest great pain, bravely borne, but not so bravely that he didn't notice. It was a delicate balance.

'Oh, all *right*!' Simon ground out as if she had been nagging him for the entire journey.

Clara opened her eyes at him, all innocence. 'What?'

'I'll do your bloody programme, all right?' he snarled. 'There's no need to keep going *on* about it!'

'I didn't say a word,' protested Clara, careful to conceal her jubilation.

'You didn't need to. I know perfectly well you registered what my mother said. *You must promise to let us know if there's ever anything we can do for you*,' he mimicked Frances savagely. 'One of these days I'm going to wring her neck!'

'Oh, don't do that! She's so lovely.'

Far from agreeing, Simon blew out a breath and glowered through the windscreen. 'You'd better tell me what she's let me in for,' he said heavily.

'It won't be that bad, honestly.' Now that he was on the point of agreeing, Clara perversely began to feel a little sorry for him. 'We're not asking you to take part in any stunts or cheap tricks. Ted is a brilliant director. MediaOchre has won several awards for documentaries we've made, and we're expecting this one to be just as successful.'

She could hardly believe she was getting to do the speech she had practised so carefully at last. This was worth a broken wrist!

'*Romance: Fact or Fiction?* will be a serious examination of romance,' she assured him. 'We're going to look at what it is and how it works and why it's so popular around the world, but we want to get beyond the clichés.'

'Right.' Simon's voice dripped disbelief.

'Your presence will give the programme real gravitas,' Clara went on, ignoring his scepticism. 'Stella Holt is incredibly popular at the moment, so she'll represent the "romantic" idea while you would be in the "anti-romance" camp, if you like. I know Stella is very keen to work with you on this,' she added. 'We think the contrast between the two of you will make for intriguing television.'

'Intriguing television…ye gods.' Simon rubbed a hand over his face. 'I can't believe I'm even listening to this!'

Clearly she wasn't converting him to the idea. Clara ploughed on. 'The plan is to shoot the film in three classic "romantic" locations. One will be Paris, obviously.'

'I thought you were going to avoid clichés?'

'We're *testing* the clichés,' she said firmly. 'After Paris, we'll film on a tropical island and, for the last segment, Ted wants me to find somewhere wild and stormy—a cottage in the Highlands, for instance.' She looked at him hopefully. 'What do you think?'

'I think it's the most ridiculous idea I've ever heard,' said Simon, not mincing his words. 'What's it supposed to prove?'

'Well, for a start, we'll consider whether those places are romantic or not—will you feel more romantic when you're there, and do they make you behave differently?'

'I can tell you now that I won't,' he said, his mouth set in an implacable line. 'I don't do romance.'

'Then that's what you'll say.' Clara kept her voice calm. It was like dealing with a skittish horse. Having got this close, she didn't want to spook him now, before she'd slipped that bridle over his head and got him to finally agree. She was *almost* there. Already her fingers were itching to pull out her phone and call Ted with the news.

Simon sighed and rubbed his hand over his face again. Reluctance incarnate.

'So it would just be those three trips?'

'Three short trips, which we would accommodate to your schedule, of course. For you it'll mean free trips to Paris, the Indian Ocean and Scotland,' Clara added, still in economist whisperer mode. 'That can't be bad, can it?'

Oops, wrong thing to say. 'If there's one thing people need

to understand about the economy, it's that there's no such thing as "free",' said Simon quellingly. 'Everything has to be paid for somewhere along the line.'

'I can assure you we wouldn't be asking you to pay anything.'

'I'd be paying with my professional reputation. And my time.'

Personally, Clara would have thought the chance to go to the tropical island of St Bonaventure alone was worth the trade, but she bit her lip on the comment.

'We'd make all the arrangements,' she said, trying another tack. 'You wouldn't have to do anything but turn up and do your piece to the camera.'

'And if I agree, will you shut up and leave me alone?'

'Absolutely.'

'No more phone calls, no more emails, no more throwing yourself at muggers?'

'Well, I'd need to get in touch with you about travel arrangements, but other than that, you won't even know I exist,' promised Clara.

Simon thought that was deeply unlikely. Once you knew Clara Sterne existed, it would be very hard to forget her. There weren't that many people who would tackle a mugger to save a stranger's bag. She sat there, shimmering with energy, brimming with colour even in the dim light, her eyes fixed expectantly on his face.

God only knew what he had got himself into! But now that she had explained the deal, perhaps it wouldn't be *quite* as bad as he'd imagined. It might even be possible to salvage something from the whole mess.

'You mentioned a follow-up programme on the micro-financed projects,' he reminded Clara.

'Er…yes, I did, didn't I?'

Simon was fairly sure Clara didn't have the authority to

agree which programmes the company would make, but if MediaOchre wanted him badly enough, he might have some leverage to get the follow-ups made. It would be good for the projects and keep the issue alive in the fickle media.

'Can you guarantee that will be your next project?' he pressed her.

'I can say we'll do our very best to get it commissioned,' she said and he could practically see her crossing her fingers.

'All right,' he said, resigned, 'in that case, you can tell your boss I'll do it and you get to keep your job.'

Her face lit up with a smile, and for the strangest moment Simon had the dazzling sensation that the car had filled with sunshine. 'Oh, *thank* you!' she said. 'Thank you, thank you, thank you! You won't regret it, I promise you. It's going to be fantastic!'

Simon doubted that too, but he got out to open her door, take her bag and help her out. It wasn't that easy one-armed, and he saw her wince as she knocked the plaster on the door frame. A real wince, not that fake remember-what-your-mother-promised wince she had done earlier.

A slight frown touched his eyes. 'Are you going to be all right?'

'Oh, I'll be fine,' she said buoyantly, glancing along at the house, where lamps were lit in the window of what was obviously an upstairs flat. 'It looks like Allegra is home, so she can let me in.'

She hoisted her bag onto her good shoulder and beamed at him. 'Thank you again, Simon. I'll be in touch.'

One hand on the open door of the car, Simon watched her literally dancing down the pavement. She had her phone to her ear already. 'Ted!' he heard her say joyfully. 'He's agreed! It's going to be all right! Everything's perfect.'

* * *

The concourse at St Pancras was crowded. Simon checked his watch, and then the name of the coffee bar behind him again. He had agreed to meet Clara there ten minutes ago.

He was in no mood for a so-called romantic trip to Paris. His last hope, that the CEO of Stanhope Harding would refuse permission for him to take the time off had been quashed when the board had decided that in the current economic climate it would be politic to show the 'friendly face' of financial services.

One more disaster to chalk up to the banking crisis, in fact.

And as if it wasn't bad enough being roped into this charade—a programme about romance, for God's sake!—a signal failure on the Circle line had meant that he was five minutes late, and Simon hated unpunctuality. It smacked too much of a lack of control.

He hadn't been looking forward to apologising to Clara, but there had been no sign of her when he'd arrived, and that made him even crosser.

Surely she could have made an effort to be there on time after all the fuss she had made about getting him to agree to take part in her ridiculous programme? Simon was bitterly regretting having succumbed to that martyred little wince.

This was all his mother's fault! If she hadn't carried a ridiculous handbag just begging to be snatched by a mugger, Clara would never have broken her wrist and he would have felt under no obligation whatsoever.

Simon eyed the passing crowd morosely. It was coming up for Valentine's Day. February was never a good time to be burdened with his surname. Why couldn't his ancestors have chosen a decent Anglo-Saxon name like Smith or Brown? The shop windows were plastered with red hearts, and the concourse was full of loved-up couples wandering hand in hand. They were probably all going to Paris for a romantic weekend too, as if this trip wasn't going to be excruciating enough.

Where was Clara? Frowning, he looked at his watch again. True to her word, she had restricted herself to contacting him about practical arrangements, and had proved surprisingly efficient. Until now, anyway. Offered the choice between flying and taking the train, Simon had opted for Eurostar, which was quicker and more convenient than hanging around airports. He had his laptop with him and could work more effectively on the train.

If Clara ever turned up with the tickets.

A few yards away a crowd had gathered. They were all watching something, and laughing and cheering. Simon took a few steps closer to see what they were all so damned happy about.

Craning his neck, he was able to see round two women talking volubly in French, and his astonished gaze fell on Clara. Dressed in a denim jacket, a red jumper and a short skirt, with the same vividly striped scarf wound carelessly several times around her throat, she was performing a tap dance routine to much encouragement and applause from her audience. From the elbow downwards, her arm was encased in a lime-green cast, but it didn't seem to be bothering her at all. Her cheeks were pink and her hair swung wildly around her face, while her skirt swished, revealing long legs clad in diamond-patterned tights.

She was laughing, responding to the crowd, but when her gaze met his with an almost audible clash, her feet faltered and she stopped in dismay.

'Omigod!' she said, clapping a hand to her forehead. 'What time is it?'

As one, the crowd turned to stare at Simon, making him feel like a monster for interrupting their entertainment.

'Twenty past,' he said.

'I am *so* sorry.' Clara grabbed her bag, waved a general farewell with her lime-green cast, and pushed through her admirers towards him. 'I was here on time, honestly I was, but there was this little girl who was so miserable,' she explained breathlessly. 'Her mother said she had a bad ear and they were going home without seeing *Cats*, which they'd come specially to London to see, so I just did a little routine from the show to entertain her, and suddenly there were all these people watching, and I forgot the time, I'm afraid. I always wanted to be Ginger Rogers...'

She trailed off at the unresponsive look on Simon's face. 'Sorry, I get a bit carried away when I dance, and it's not often I get an audience.' She was digging around in her bag for the tickets with her good hand. 'I don't suppose *you* dance?'

'Do I look like Fred Astaire to you?'

Clara stopped, her hand still buried in her bag, and studied him. Simon Valentine had dressed for a romantic weekend in Paris in a suit, with a pale blue shirt and a darker blue tie with some kind of crest on it. He had a laptop case in one hand and an overnight bag in the other, both black and nononsense, and his expression was distant.

No, not a man about to burst into song or twirl her around the concourse.

'Not really,' she said. 'But I'm always ready to be surprised.'

'I'm afraid what you see is what you get,' said Simon, and she sighed.

'I thought that might be the case.'

Clara had arranged a Business Premier ticket for Simon, and Roland had grudgingly agreed that she could travel in the same class. Which was big of him, given that she had spent the past three weeks setting up deals with airlines and hotels and saving him thousands of pounds on the budget.

It had been a frantic time to get it all organised, and Clara was looking forward to travelling in comfort. She accepted the glass of champagne that was offered as soon as they boarded with the aplomb of one born to travel first class, as opposed to one who spent most of her time on buses or battling the rush hour on the underground. This was the life! Settling into her seat, she looked around appreciatively.

'This is exciting, isn't it?'

She beamed at Simon, who had taken a glass of water instead of champagne and was opening his computer.

'Thrilling.'

Clara tutted at his deadpan tone. 'Can you really say you don't feel even a tiny frisson at the idea of going to Paris for a weekend?' she asked as she attempted to unwind her scarf one-handed.

'I don't even know what a frisson is,' said Simon as his laptop whirred and bleeped into life.

'And then you wonder that your girlfriend dumped you for an Italian hottie!' Clara grimaced as her scarf got caught behind her, and she tugged at it fruitlessly until Simon sucked in an exasperated breath and got up to help her.

'Stand up,' he ordered, and Clara wriggled obediently out of her seat. She stood very still as he disentangled her briskly. Her eyes were fixed above his collar where his throat met his jaw, and for some reason her heart started to thud against her ribs. All at once he seemed very solid and very male.

He smelled nice too, and she wondered what it would be like to lean forward and press her lips to his skin.

The thought veered out of nowhere and caught Clara unawares, so much like a blow to the stomach driving all the air from her lungs that she actually flinched.

'What?' said Simon.

'Nothing.' Clara bundled the scarf up in her hands. 'Thanks,' she said, avoiding his eyes and slipping back into her seat. Her heart was still pattering ridiculously, and she found that she was breathing very carefully.

At least Simon didn't appear to have noticed anything. He sat down, produced a pair of horn-rimmed spectacles and put them on before turning his attention to the computer screen.

Clara studied him covertly. It wasn't that he was *un*attractive, but he was so stern, so conventional. Nothing there to make her heart hammer in her throat, or the breath leak out of her lungs.

'Did you ever take Astrid to Paris for a romantic weekend?' she asked the moment her breathing had settled, just to prove that it had been a momentary aberration.

Simon didn't even look up from the screen. 'We didn't have that kind of relationship,' he said stiffly.

'What kind of relationship *did* you have?'

'A good one,' he said, but this time he did meet her gaze over the laptop. 'It worked very well. We both had our own space. We *agreed*.' A faint defensive edge had crept into his voice. 'It was what we both wanted. No complicated emotions.'

Clara considered that. 'It doesn't sound like much fun.'

'It wasn't about fun. It was about companionship…mutual satisfaction.'

Sex, presumably. Clara chose not to examine why the idea of that should leave her feeling nettled.

'So what happened if it was so satisfying for both of you?'

At first she thought Simon wasn't going to answer. He pressed a key and watched something appear on the screen. 'Paolo was at some reception we both went to. God knows how he got in! He doesn't have a clue about finance. He's something to do with fashion.' Simon said it as if it were a dirty word. 'Apparently he sent Astrid roses the next day, and begged to meet her again. She said she'd been swept off her feet.'

He looked so baffled by the idea that Clara felt quite sorry for him.

'It sounds like she wanted some romance, and she wasn't getting any from you.'

'She said she didn't want any of that nonsense!'

'She might have said that, but when she found out what it could be like, she obviously changed her mind.'

Clara put down her champagne and leant forward. She was feeling herself again, thank goodness. 'You know, I think making this programme will be good for you, Simon. You should be able to pick up all sorts of little hints this weekend, and then put them into action when you get home.'

Simon had been running his finger over the mouse pad, but he glanced up at that, his brows drawn together. 'Hints?'

'If you want Astrid back, that is. Paolo might have swept her off her feet, but you could always sweep her back now that you know that she likes some romance. You could organise a lovely weekend for her in Paris. I'm sure she'd love the hotel where we're staying, for instance,' said Clara, warming to her theme. 'You could arrange for champagne and flowers in the room and then take her out to dinner. I've researched the perfect romantic restaurant, and the best place for dancing…'

Picking up her glass once more, she sighed a little wistfully and sipped her champagne. 'I'd love it if someone did that for me!'

'So why isn't your boyfriend taking *you* to Paris this weekend?' said Simon nastily.

There was a tiny pause. 'Mainly because he married his childhood sweetheart and they're expecting their first baby any day now.'

Clara smiled hard to show Simon that she was perfectly fine about it.

'Ah,' said Simon.

CHAPTER FOUR

AWARE that the tables had turned, and that it wasn't that comfortable to be quizzed about your failed relationship, Clara fiddled with the cast on her hand as she looked out of the window. Simon had told her about Astrid, so it was only fair that she told him her own story.

'Matt was very romantic. He took me to Seville for my birthday two years ago. It was perfect. He was everything I'd ever wanted,' she remembered. 'I was sure he was The One, and that we'd be together for ever. I was *so* happy.'

Simon didn't say anything but, when she glanced back, she saw that he was watching her rather than his computer screen, so she went on.

'I thought he was going to ask me to marry him while we were in Seville, but he didn't. So I thought maybe he would do it when we got home, and when he sat me down and said he wanted to talk to me, I was so excited I couldn't really take in what he was saying at first.'

Her mouth twisted a little at the memory. 'And when I *did* take it in, I couldn't believe it. He told me that he'd met Sophie again a couple of weeks before, and that they'd realised that they were meant to be together. It turned out that I was just a rebound relationship.'

Simon would never have made an agony aunt. Clara could tell that she was making him uneasy. Now, if only she could talk to him about the derivatives market or public sector debt, he might be some use. Still, he was listening, even if it clearly terrified him that she was about to cry or do something equally alarming and emotional.

Which she wasn't. Clara put a bright smile back in place just to prove it.

She didn't do crying. She did singing, dancing, joking. She did anything that would stop her thinking about how much it had hurt when Matt had left, about the rawness of her heart and the loneliness she tucked away deep inside her.

'Why did he bother taking you to Seville if he was going to end things as soon as you got home?' Simon asked after a moment.

'He didn't want to spoil my birthday,' she said. Even now, the memory of that awful evening made her wince. 'He was being kind. He did really like me, he said. If it hadn't been for Sophie, we could have been happy together, he said. It was just that as soon as he'd seen her again, he'd known that he loved her still. Sophie was the love of his life, he said, but he wanted us to stay friends.'

'And are you friends?'

'Oh, well, you know how it is,' said Clara, super-casual. 'Life's just one hectic social whirl. There's television to be watched and analysed in depth, nails to be painted, magazines to be read… Allegra and I have to keep up to date with all the latest fashion disasters and celebrity news. It's a wonder we have time for work at all!'

'I take it that's a no,' said Simon sardonically.

'We're not *not* friends,' she said. 'It's just that our lives have gone in different directions.'

Matt had married Sophie and was blissfully happy, and she had been left on her own.

'We keep in touch,' she added, very slightly on the defensive. 'I know about the baby. And I'm glad for him.'

She *was*.

'There would have been no point in us staying together if he was in love with someone else,' Clara said, just as she'd said to herself so many times. 'We'd have both been miserable.'

'You seem happy now,' said Simon after a moment.

'I've got a lot to be happy about.' Clara drained her champagne with a sort of defiance and set the glass back down on the table between them with a click. 'I've got my family, I've got friends. I've somewhere to live and a job I love.

'Actually, it was the job that made the most difference to me,' she told Simon. 'I'd never had a career before. I used to dream about starring in a musical, maybe going to Broadway, but I wasn't dedicated enough, and the truth is that I wasn't good enough either. I did a couple of tours with a third-rate company, and got the occasional job doing ads, but it wasn't exactly starry stuff, and even that dried up and I had to keep myself going by waitressing and temping. So when Matt left me I fell apart, and it felt as if I had nothing. It was Ted who saved me.'

'Ted?'

'You'll meet him in Paris. He's the director, and brilliant at it too. He also happens to be one of my best friends. I was an absolute mess, but Ted mopped me up, and when MediaOchre Productions had a vacancy for a research assistant he bullied me into applying for it. He said it was time I tried a proper job, and the fact is I've loved working there. I'm much better at making arrangements and pulling together all the loose ends on a project than I am at dancing.'

'I'm glad to hear it,' said Simon dryly, clearly thinking about her performance at St Pancras.

Clara ignored that. 'I'm a production assistant now, and I want to be a producer, and eventually work in drama. That's my dream, anyway,' she confessed.

It was a dream that kept her going, and filled the awful gap Matt had left in her life.

'Roland Richards—he's executive producer and owns MediaOchre—promised me a shot at producing a programme if we could get *Romance: Fact or Fiction?* made.'

'Oh, so that's why you kept hassling me?'

'Well, yes.' Clara looked contrite. 'But I do really think it'll be a great programme,' she added hastily. 'It's just that I love this job, and I've never made a success of anything before now. I can't imagine feeling for anybody else what I felt for Matt, so I'm determined to focus on my career now, and this programme is part of that and a step towards what I really want to do.'

'It's unwise to invest emotion in a job,' said Simon disapprovingly. 'It's not logical.'

'Not everything can be decided by logic,' Clara protested.

'It would be a lot better if everything was,' said Simon. 'As soon as people start substituting emotion for clear thinking, that's when things go wrong. It all gets muddled and messy. If everyone understood that all relationships are at heart economic ones, there would be a lot less agonising.'

'That's rubbish!' said Clara. 'You can't reduce love to economics.'

'You can dress it up all you like in hearts and flowers, but the reality is that economic imperatives drive the way we think, the way we behave, and the way we feel.'

Simon leant back and regarded Clara over the rim of his glasses. 'Take you and this job that you "love". You wouldn't do it if it didn't give you an income that means you can pay for the basic necessities of food and shelter, would you?'

'I have to earn my living, sure, but that doesn't mean I don't love what I do,' she objected.

'What exactly do you "love" about it?'

'Well, there's the opportunity to meet charmers like you,' said Clara sarcastically before she could help herself.

'But you only want me because you need my cooperation to get the programme made and, if I've understood the situation correctly, if you don't get the programme made, the future of MediaOchre Productions is at risk. No MediaOchre Productions means no job for you, no matter how much you love it, which means no income, which means you'll be struggling for your essentials again. So we're back to economics.'

'So what are you saying? I'm not allowed to enjoy my job?'

'Not at all. I'm saying when you talk about having a dream, you should ground it in economic reality, not in waffly concepts like "loving" what you do.'

'Well.' Clara felt quite huffy. 'So what's your dream? Or is dreaming too illogical for you?'

'Dream is a very emotive word. I've got goals and ambitions, certainly.'

'Like what?'

Simon eyed Clara across the table. She had shrugged off her jacket and, above the red jumper, her eyes looked bright and brown, like a robin's. All at once he found himself remembering the softness of her scarf as he unwound it, the downward sweep of her lashes, the fresh fragrance that drifted up from her hair.

Things he didn't usually notice at all.

It was odd. Taken feature by feature, she wasn't particularly pretty, but there was a quirkiness about her that was quite appealing, he supposed. She was nowhere near as lovely as Astrid, of course. Astrid was coolly elegant, even serene— except when she was being swept off her feet by passionate Italians—while Clara was all colour and movement. Astrid would never have made an exhibition of herself in the middle of the station concourse, that was for sure.

Clara reminded Simon uneasily of his mother, who had

the same impulsiveness, who gave exactly the same impression of being on the verge of doing something crazily illogical. Even Clara's face was full of movement. The edges of her mouth, her cheekbones, her lashes, even the corners of her eyes seemed to be tilting very slightly upwards, as if she were on the point of breaking into a smile. It annoyed Simon that he kept watching her, waiting for it to happen.

Not that there was much sign of her smiling right then. She was leaning forward, her expression combative, as she waited for him to answer her question.

'What *are* your goals?' she insisted.

That was easy. 'I want people to understand the economic forces that shape their lives. I want them to have access to financial systems that help them to help themselves,' he said. 'That's what the micro-finance projects are all about.'

'But that's general,' Clara objected. 'I was thinking about personal goals. What do you want for *yourself*?'

Simon adjusted his glasses, annoyed to find that he had to think about it.

'Financial security,' he said.

'That's it?' She stared at him. 'Not love? Not happiness?'

'Security is the basis of everything else,' said Simon. 'That's enough for me.'

Pointedly, Simon turned his attention back to his computer, and to his relief she fell silent. He allowed himself to hope that she'd lost interest, and made a show of looking up the markets, but the truth was that he was unsettlingly aware of her still. There was a warmth and vibrancy to Clara that made the very air around her shimmer.

He frowned at the thought. It wasn't like him to be so fanciful. He ought to be able to ignore her easily. If only she didn't ask such awkward questions! Now, instead of focusing on his laptop, he was thinking about what he really wanted, and what was the point of that?

Simon had never doubted it before. Ever since his father's death, he had preferred figures to people. Figures made sense. They stayed still so that you could grasp them. They didn't veer off course illogically, or plunge from one ridiculous situation to the next the way his mother did. They weren't reckless or disturbing. They were *safe*.

Astrid had made him feel like that. She wasn't alarming or demanding. She never insisted on talking about their relationship or knowing what he was feeling. She never wittered on about goals or looked at him as if he were somehow deficient for not wanting to take risks.

Perhaps it wasn't a very exciting goal to stay as you were, Simon thought, vaguely defensive, but once you had what you wanted, once you had everything under control and no one could throw your world upside down, why keep on striving for more?

It was pouring when they arrived in Paris. Ted was there already, with Steve the cameraman and Peter on sound. 'They're doing establishing shots,' Clara told Simon in the taxi to the hotel.

'What the hell is an establishing shot?' Simon was still in a bad mood. He had made it clear that he wanted to work but, instead of sitting and reading quietly, or working herself as Astrid would have done, Clara had left him to it, and gone wandering off. Before he knew what had happened, she was sharing another glass of champagne with an American couple and a businessman from Lyons, and they were all getting on like a proverbial fire in a match factory.

They were too far away for Simon to hear their conversation, so he couldn't even complain that they were disturbing him, but he was aware of them laughing all the same. It was obvious that Clara was having a great time, and was clearly not the slightest bit bothered that he was too busy to talk.

All in all, he hadn't managed any work at all, and now it was raining!

The entire trip was turning out to be a disaster, he thought grouchily.

Clara was explaining about establishing shots, as if he really cared. 'They're location shots,' she said. 'You know, the Eiffel Tower, to signal to the viewer that we're in Paris and general views to give a sense of place. I had a message from Ted, who said the weather wasn't too bad this morning, so they'll be glad they came early.'

She looked eagerly through the taxi window, apparently unfazed by his unresponsive mood. 'It's great to be here at last! Now we just need Stella. She said she wanted to fly, so Roland's accompanying her. They should be arriving later and you'll have a chance to meet her before we start shooting tomorrow.'

'So why are we here so early?' Simon asked grumpily.

'You said you wanted to work on the train,' she reminded him. 'There's plenty to do. I've got to check the equipment, and block out some scenes with you and Ted.'

'What scenes?' he asked in alarm.

'Nothing is rehearsed, but obviously we need an idea of what you and Stella are going to say,' Clara said patiently. 'I'll just list some bullet points for you to cover when you're talking. We'll need to recce some special locations. I've done quite a lot of research, but you never really know how good a place is going to look on camera until you actually get there. I can't wait to see the hotel,' she added, craning her head as if she could get the taxi to move faster through the heavy traffic on the *périphérique*. 'It sounds fab.'

Fab wasn't a word Simon would ever have used, but even he had to admit that it was a very attractive hotel, tucked into a quiet street near the Luxembourg Gardens. The taxi dropped them by a heavy Parisian door, and they stepped through into a hidden cobbled courtyard and another world.

Inside, the hotel was chic and charming, and it reeked of expense down to the last light switch. A hush of wealth hung over the reception, where Clara managed to look utterly out of place and yet completely at ease.

'I thought MediaOchre were tottering on the brink of bankruptcy,' Simon muttered out of the corner of his mouth as he waited with Clara for the lift. 'How on earth did you afford a place like this?'

'I negotiated a deal,' Clara whispered back. 'There will just happen to be a couple of shots of the hotel in the final edit. You'd be surprised what we can get in return for a bit of free publicity.'

To Simon's critical eyes, the room was over-decorated, with a flounce too many around the bed, but Clara was thrilled with it. 'Oh, isn't it *gorgeous*?' she said, opening the bathroom and oohing and aahing at the polished taps, fluffy towels and free toiletries.

Careless of the rain, she threw open the French windows and stepped out onto the tiny balcony. 'Look, you can see the Eiffel Tower from here!'

Her face was alight as she turned back to Simon, wiping the raindrops from her cheeks, and he was alarmed to feel an odd little clutch in the area of his heart.

'Oh, this is perfect!' she said, waving the lime-green cast around. 'I'm so excited! You can't get more romantic than this, can you?'

It was just a room to Simon, but he was reluctant to burst her bubble. 'I'm glad you like it,' he said gruffly. 'Well, if you tell me where my room is, I'll go and get settled.'

Clara laughed. 'This *is* your room! You don't think they put the crew in rooms like this, do you? I negotiated three lovely rooms for you, Stella and Roland, but the rest of us are in rooms at the back.'

'That's not very fair,' said Simon, frowning, but Clara shrugged.

'It's how it is. We're lucky we're in the same hotel. Often the talent get a smart hotel, while the rest of us are in some grotty place round the corner.'

'The talent?'

'That's you, in this case,' she said with a grin. 'You and Stella.'

He made a face. 'Look, why don't we swap rooms?' he heard himself suggesting.

'Swap?' Clara stared at him, and Simon gestured around the room.

'It's just somewhere to sleep to me. I don't care what the décor is like or how fluffy my pillows are. It sounded to me as if you would really enjoy sleeping here.'

'Of course I would, but—'

'I don't care where I sleep,' he added irritably.

She looked at him closely, as if to check that he wasn't joking. 'That's really generous of you,' she said, still uncertain, 'but I've hired a whole lot of equipment, and anything Ted isn't using at the moment will be in my room so that I can check it tonight.'

'Get it moved here.'

'Simon, I can't…' Clara protested, half laughing. 'You're one of the presenters. I can't put you in a poky room at the back!'

'You're not putting me anywhere. I've made the decision.'

Unsure quite why he was making such an issue of it, Simon scowled and stomped over to the door. 'A room like this is wasted on me. I saw the rates downstairs and, no matter how good a deal you got, you're still paying a lot of money for somewhere to sleep. That's only worth it if the room is used by someone who will appreciate it, and I won't. It's exactly the kind of bad economic practice that I find offensive,' he added austerely. 'Squandering money for the sake of it... I refuse to be part of it,' he said, ending the discussion.

'Roland would have a fit,' said Clara, but he could tell she was tempted.

'Tell him I insisted.'

Brushing her attempts to protest aside, he dragged her back to Reception and made her switch their rooms. A bell-boy was despatched with a trolley to transfer all the camera and sound equipment to the room at the front, while Clara and Simon went back to retrieve his case.

'I don't know what to say.' Clara looked around her a little helplessly. 'I can't believe I'll really get to sleep in a room like this! Thank you,' she said, smiling at him. 'It's beautiful.'

When Simon saw the room that Clara had been expected to share with a great pile of kit, he was quite cross. Barely more than a cupboard, it was adequate for his own needs, of course, but she would have been really uncomfortable.

He tossed his bag on the bed, and opened his laptop on the desk. They had agreed to meet a couple of hours later, but for now he was alone and could get on with some work. At last!

Rolling up his sleeves, Simon settled down at his computer, but the figures on the screen kept wavering as Clara's smile shimmered before his eyes instead. It was exasperating. There he was, trying to work, and all he could see was Clara, turning around, all bright red sweater and lime-green cast and long legs, smiling at him. *Thank you. It's beautiful.*

There was absolutely no reason for her smile to make him feel that good.

No reason for his chest to tighten.

No reason for him not to focus on work.

None at all.

* * *

In the end, Simon gave up and went down early to the chic lobby, where he sat on possibly the most uncomfortable chair he had ever tried and tried to focus on the *Financial Times*. Clara breezed in a few minutes later, brandishing an old-fashioned umbrella.

'Look what they gave me in Reception!' she said. 'It's going to be perfect!'

'Perfect?' Simon got to his feet and looked out through the doors, to where the rain was falling like stair rods into the courtyard. 'Clara, have you seen the weather? It's hard to imagine anything *less* perfect!'

But Clara refused to be daunted. 'What could be more romantic than sharing an umbrella as you wander around Paris? Maybe we'll get you and Stella to have a discussion under an umbrella,' she said excitedly.

'It won't be much of a discussion if no one can hear anything except the rain crashing onto the umbrella,' Simon pointed out and she waved her plaster cast to dismiss the problem.

'Details, details. The sound guy can work all that out.'

Swinging the umbrella in her good hand, she offered him a sunny smile quite at odds with the weather. 'Now, let's go and find us some romantic locations!'

She sounded so jaunty that Simon eyed the swinging umbrella with foreboding. 'Please tell me you're not going to start singing in the rain!'

Even he had heard of that song.

'It's funny you should mention that.' Clara sent him a wicked smile. 'It's one of my favourite routines.' And before Simon could stop her she was tap dancing around the umbrella and humming loudly while assorted well-dressed guests turned to stare.

'For God's sake, everybody's looking!' Simon scowled and snatched the umbrella back. 'I'm keeping this!'

Taking her by the arm, he propelled her towards the entrance. A doorman leapt to open the doors for them, and Simon let Clara go so that he could put up the umbrella with a snap.

'I forgot for a moment there what an exhibitionist you are!'

Clara wasn't in the least chastened. 'I just love to dance when I'm happy.'

'What is there to be happy about?' he grumbled as they picked their way through the puddles.

'Oh, it's not so bad, is it?'

'Clara, it's tipping it down! My shoes are soaked already. If you're trying to convince me that this is romantic, you're going the wrong way about it.'

'Wait till we're in Montmartre,' said Clara. 'Even you will have to admit it's romantic then!'

She made him climb all the way up the hill to the great white basilica of Sacré-Coeur. Simon was prepared to admit that the narrow streets would have been picturesque if they had been able to see much beyond the confines of the umbrella, and the view from the top probably was impressive if only it hadn't been obscured by sheets of rain.

He had been to Paris before, of course, but only to meetings in the financial district. Even if he had had the time, Montmartre's bohemian charm and street painters wouldn't have appealed. Perhaps because of the rain, it wasn't quite as touristy as he had feared. It felt as if they had the *quartier* to themselves. Everyone else was sensibly inside.

Only Clara would think of going out in this weather, he thought, exasperated. She was relentlessly upbeat about it, too, her face animated as she wittered on about mood and atmosphere and what she persisted in calling 'the romance of it all', while the neon-green cast swept through the gloomy light.

'Remind me again why this is romantic,' sighed Simon.

They were standing under the umbrella in front of Sacré-Coeur, peering out over the terraced gardens to where Paris was lost in the murk. The rain drummed on the plastic over their heads, and splashed into the puddles. The bottom of Simon's trousers were soaked to the knees, and as for his shoes…!

Worst of all was being so aware of Clara beside him, exuding a warmth and vitality that banished the cold and the wet and the greyness beyond the shelter of the umbrella. They had to stand close together to keep out of the rain, and the shininess of her hair kept catching at the edge of his eye. Simon could smell it, a fresh, flowery fragrance that made him think of hot summer nights, which was odd when it was hard to imagine a more miserable February day.

It irritated Simon that he was finding it so hard to concentrate, especially when Clara herself didn't seem at all bothered by how close they were standing.

'I fail to see what's romantic about wet feet,' he added crossly.

'All right, it might not be romantic for us, but if we were lovers, you wouldn't be thinking about your feet,' said Clara, who hadn't been thinking about hers since they left the hotel. She had been too busy thinking about how much bigger Simon was when you were standing right next to him, how much more solid and steadying. How safe it felt to be with him.

It was weird now to remember how boring she had thought him at first. There was something about him that grew on you, Clara had decided. Simon was never going to be gorgeous, of course, but once you had started noticing the cool line of his mouth, or the firm angle of his jaw, you kept *on* noticing.

In fact, Clara wished that she could stop finding little details that made him, if not exactly hot, at least more attractive than expected: the squareness of his hands, the set of his shoulders, the creases at the edges of his eyes. There was a bit beneath his ear where his jaw met his throat, and every time Clara looked at it she felt a slow, disturbing thump that started low in her belly and muddled up her breathing.

The way it was doing then.

Simon was still grouchy. 'It would take a lot to make me forget about my feet right now,' he said.

'That's because you don't get romance.' Clara forced herself to sound bright and breezy, and not as if the blood was thudding along her veins and booming in her ears. 'If you were a romantic, it would be enough for you to be alone with your lover.'

She dragged her eyes from his throat and gestured at the umbrella above them. 'I mean, what could be more intimate? Just two of you under an umbrella, cut off from the rest of the world by the rain. You wouldn't care about how wet your feet were then. You'd just care that you were alone.'

Her expression grew misty. 'And when you kissed, the rain would disappear and you'd forget about your feet...'

'Then let's try it,' said Simon.

'Try what?' said Clara, who was still caught up in her imagined scene. She could picture it perfectly. The two lovers, the rain, the passion... She should be producing romantic films, not documentaries.

'A kiss.'

Clara snapped back to attention. *'What?'*

'I'm prepared to try anything to forget about my wet feet,' he said, straight-faced, and she smiled uncertainly.

'You're not serious?'

'Why not? You keep telling me this is all romantic. I thought you could demonstrate.'

'But you don't want to kiss me!' Clara objected, still unable to decide whether he was joking or not.

'I thought *you* could kiss *me*,' said Simon. 'I'm prepared to be persuaded that there's something romantic about this situation,' he added, looking down at his sodden shoes, 'although I've got to say I'm not convinced so far!'

His gaze came back to Clara's doubtful face and he raised his brows. 'No? Fair enough. I suppose it's not *that* romantic, but if nothing else I thought it would take my mind off my feet.'

'Oh, I expect I could do that,' said Clara with an assumption of nonchalance that covered a pounding pulse and a mouth that was suddenly dry.

And the alarming knowledge that there was nothing she would like more than to kiss him.

'You're the talent, after all,' she said, 'and Roland would expect me to do whatever it took to keep you happy, even if it's just distracting you from your wet feet!'

That was it, she congratulated herself. Make a joke of it. She was good at that. And really, what was the problem? It would only be a kiss. She had been an actor, hadn't she? Kissing was just part of the job at times.

Besides, she might not get a better chance to convince Simon that there *was* such a thing as romance. He was so determinedly pragmatic about everything. Surely even *he* couldn't kiss pragmatically?

She would show him what a kiss could do, thought Clara, on her mettle. Simon might not want to admit that romance existed, but she would show him. She would pretend that he was Matt and give him a kiss he would never forget!

Lifting her chin, she turned to face him and stepped a little closer. It didn't take much to rest her palms flat against his chest. His body was broad and solid beneath the black coat.

Clara studied the raindrops spangled on the wool before she raised her eyes to Simon's. He was watching her steadily, his expression indecipherable.

'We have to imagine that we're in love,' she said as she slid her hands up to his shoulders.

Simon's expression didn't change, but Clara could see a muscle jumping in his cheek. It made her think that he might not be *quite* as cool as he seemed, and her confidence grew.

'Whatever *that* means,' he said.

'It means that when we're together, we don't need anybody else,' said Clara, letting herself remember how she had felt when she was with Matt. 'It means that all we want is to be together, and to be able to touch each other.' Her palms smoothed thoughtfully around the collar of his coat. 'We can't keep our hands off each other, in fact. We don't care who might be watching.'

'Nobody is going to be watching in this rain,' Simon pointed out, but that telltale muscle in his cheek was still twitching.

'We don't even notice the rain when we're together,' Clara told him firmly.

'Why are we bothering with an umbrella in that case?'

'Don't be difficult,' she said, folding her lips together to stop herself laughing. She wasn't supposed to be laughing! But perversely it was easier now that she had remembered what she was doing. She had forgotten to be sad about Matt, and could tell herself that she was just trying to convince Simon of the power of romance.

Lowering her voice until it was suitably husky, she murmured, 'We're so in love that we don't care about anything but how right it feels when I kiss your throat like this...'

She touched her mouth to that tantalising place beneath his ear, and tried not to notice how good it *did* feel. His skin smelt wonderful: clean, crisp, male.

'If we were in love, you'd like it when I did that,' she told him.

'Maybe I like it anyway.' Simon's voice had deepened too. Clara could feel it reverberating through her, and she smiled.

'And this?' she asked, pressing little kisses along his jaw to the corner of his mouth.

'That too.'

'Then maybe you're getting the idea,' she said.

CHAPTER FIVE

THE rain beat down around them but beneath the umbrella it felt as if they were in a cocoon. Angling her mouth more comfortably, Clara pressed her lips against the firm warmth of his, and she felt him smile a little.

Simon Valentine, smiling. Who would have thought it? Heat fluttered through her, snaring the breath in her throat.

'How are those feet?' she asked, her voice not as steady as she would have liked.

'What feet?'

She laughed breathlessly, and Simon's arm came round her to pull her closer, while the hand holding the umbrella lowered until it was almost touching their heads.

Then *he* kissed *her*.

Well.

Well. Who would have thought that a stuffed shirt like Simon Valentine could kiss like *that*?

Clara was gripped by a strange giddy feeling. She forgot that she was supposed to be proving a point. She forgot the programme. She forgot everything but the warmth of Simon's skin and the comforting solidity of his body as she leant against it.

Kissing him felt wonderful. His lips were so sure, and his arm around her so solid. It felt so good, in fact, that Clara was aware of a momentary disquiet. It was enough to make her consider drawing back before the kiss went any further, but the bit of her brain that thought that was a good idea didn't stand a chance against the whoosh of response that ignited deep inside her, that pressed her tighter against him and sent her arms winding round his neck as if of their own accord.

Perhaps it would have been sensible to stop then, but Clara had never been one to choose the sensible option when there was a reckless, exciting one on offer. She gave herself up to the kiss, to the sheer pleasure of it, as it grew deeper and hungrier and more urgent.

Clara never knew how long they would have stood there, kissing, or how they would have ended it—although she had a nasty feeling that it wouldn't have been her who called a halt. As it turned out, the decision was taken out of their hands, or their lips, or whatever other organs were driving the kiss.

One moment they were deep in the kiss, oblivious to anything but the heat surging between them. The next a gust of wind blew up the hill, turned the umbrella inside out and hurled a sky's worth of rain into their faces. It was like being pitched into a river without warning.

Gasping in shock, Simon and Clara jerked apart.

'Yeurgh…!' Pointlessly, Clara tried to rub the rain from her eyes while Simon cursed as he wrestled the umbrella back into shape.

Eventually he managed to get it the right way out and held it above their heads, but by then they were both drenched and Clara was shivering. 'So much for romance,' he said, his voice the only dry thing about them. 'Still, I think I needed that!'

Take it lightly, Clara told herself. She wrung out her hair and wiped her cheeks with the back of her hand, not that it made much difference. 'Well, it took your mind off your feet, didn't it?'

'It certainly did that.'

'It works better when you're in love,' she added, just in case he misinterpreted the eagerness of her response to him.

'I'll take your word for it,' said Simon. 'Look, I've had enough rain, if you don't mind. Can we go somewhere dry and unromantic?'

The romance of rain was rather lost on Clara too by that point. Her teeth were chattering, and water from her wet hair was running down her neck. She was more than happy to follow Simon into the first café they came across. It turned out to be a cosy bistro, and they sat together on a banquette near the fire where they could hang up their sodden coats and steam gently in the warmth.

Simon took charge, ordering a bottle of red wine and *steak-frites* in excruciating but effective French, while Clara plucked at her damp clothes and grimaced.

The wine made her feel much better, though, and as she began to dry out she looked around her, because that was easier than looking at Simon and remembering that kiss.

It had ended so suddenly. One minute locked together, the next running for shelter. Clara could almost believe that it had never happened at all.

Except for the fact that her lips were still tingling, and her heart was still thudding and every last cell in her body was sulking at the interruption.

And except for the fact her senses jumped with awareness when Simon had finished hanging up their coats and sat down beside her.

It was just as well that gust had blown the umbrella inside out when it did, Clara told herself. She had got a bit carried away there, and she didn't want to give Simon the impression that she was unprofessional. She was supposed to be focusing on her career, after all.

And it wasn't as if the kiss had meant anything to either of them. Simon clearly wasn't that bothered. He certainly didn't look as if he was twitching with awareness or wondering how she would react if he laced his fingers with hers and tugged her towards him.

Clara cleared her throat. Not that she was wondering that either.

Not at all.

So, back to business.

She rummaged in her bag for her phone. 'I should ring Ted and find out where they are. I think they'd be interested to see this place.'

'Why?' said Simon, looking around him. 'It's all right, but it's pretty tatty, isn't it?' He fingered a jagged tear in the plastic banquette seat. 'Look at this. And the menus are grubby. As for the wine…' he took a sip from his glass '…a fruity little paint-stripper.'

He broke off as he caught Clara's eye, and flung up a hand. 'Don't tell me! This is romantic too?'

'Well, it *is*. OK, the banquettes have seen better days, but they're so private and so Parisian,' she said. 'I like the fact that there are no white tablecloths or fancy menus. No tourists, either,' she noted, inspecting the few fellow guests. 'It's authentic.'

Simon sighed. 'Is there *any*where that isn't romantic to you?'

'This is exactly the kind of tucked-away place we want you and Stella to have your discussion,' said Clara, searching for Ted's number on her contact list. 'Intimate, private. Waiters in long white aprons, the smell of garlic, *Madame* at the till…it's perfect!'

Ted and the rest of the crew were also in Montmartre, it seemed. They appeared a few minutes later and when they saw what Clara and Simon were eating, ordered lunch too. Even Simon had to admit that the food was excellent, Clara thought. She was very glad that Ted agreed with her about shooting a scene between Simon and Stella over dinner.

By the time she had talked to *Madame*, made all the necessary arrangements and called a couple of taxis to take them back to the hotel, Clara was feeling much more in control. She was back in production assistant mode. Calm, efficient, resourceful…not at all the kind of girl who would kiss the talent or make a fool of herself by wanting to kiss him again.

Really, there was no need to make a fuss about it. It wasn't as if she or Simon would want to repeat it, and no one else would ever guess they had kissed at all.

'What's going on between you and Simon Valentine?' Ted asked under his breath as they made their way out to the taxis.

'What do you mean?' asked Clara, miffed that he had apparently picked up on something. After she had been so careful to behave normally too!

'You're being too polite to him.'

'I'm being *professional*.'

'And he keeps looking at you, whenever you're not looking at him.'

'Really, Ted, I don't know what you're talking about.'

He looked at her closely. Sometimes it was a curse to have a friend who knew you too well. 'You've fallen for the Dow-Jones Darling, too, haven't you?'

'Don't be ridiculous.' Ted would never let her forget it if he knew about the kiss. 'I'm still getting over Matt, remember? I'm here to do my job and nothing else.'

And that meant not kissing Simon again.

By the time they all got back to the hotel, Roland and Stella had arrived and were having a drink in the bar. Stella was instantly recognizable. Clara had never watched her show, but she had seen Stella plenty of times, smiling out from magazine covers at supermarket checkouts everywhere.

'There you are!' Roland beckoned Clara and Simon over, while Ted and the crew took the opportunity to slip away.

Lucky things, thought Clara. Roland was looking displeased, and she guessed that Stella hadn't been happy to discover that Simon wasn't waiting for her. Stella's ratings might have been dropping recently, but there was plenty of the star about her still. Stella was used to having whatever she wanted and, if Ted was to be believed, she wanted Simon.

Eyes narrowed, Clara watched as Stella greeted him effusively and offered perfumed cheeks for a mwah-mwah kiss. She was petite and very pretty, with a gloss of celebrity that made her look faintly unreal. Her hair was just a little too blonde, her teeth too white, her make-up too perfect.

Nothing that anyone could ever accuse Clara of. 'What on earth have you been doing?' Roland demanded, scowling at her. 'You look a bloody mess,' he said bluntly.

Clara looked down at herself. Until that moment, she had forgotten how bedraggled she must look after her drenching. Her boots were still damp, her jacket stained and wrinkled, and she hadn't given a thought to her hair after squeezing out the worst of the rain.

'We were looking for locations,' she said. 'We got a bit wet.'

Roland turned to Simon. 'Please tell me Clara didn't drag you out to look at locations in this rain?'

'She was explaining the romance of Paris in the rain,' Simon said. His eyes met Clara's fleetingly. 'It was very instructive.'

Stella, Clara noticed, had kept a possessive hand on Simon's arm. Now she shuddered lightly. 'We won't be filming in the rain, will we?'

'Of course not,' said Roland quickly.

Simon looked thoughtful. 'You don't think there's some-

thing romantic about lovers under an umbrella?' he said, un-
obtrusively moving away from Stella's clutch.

'Well, now you come to mention it...' Stella fluttered her
lashes at him. 'Perhaps it *might* be fun if we did a piece together in the rain.'

It looked as if Ted was right, thought Clara, conscious of
a sinking feeling that she chose not to analyse. Stella clearly
wasn't planning to play hard to get, although Clara wished
her luck in trying to flirt with someone quite as unflirtable
as Simon. If Stella wanted Simon to improve her image, she
would have to work hard for him.

But perhaps Ted was wrong, and she wasn't interested in
Simon's image. Perhaps she was more interested in his mouth
and his hands and his lean, solid body.

Something stirred queerly in the pit of Clara's stomach.
Only that morning she would have pooh-poohed such an idea,
but that was before she had kissed him. Now she could understand it far too easily.

She turned away. 'I'd better go and check the equipment,'
she said to Roland.

'I'll go with you,' said Simon quickly. 'I want to change
out of these wet things.'

Stella's perfect lips tightened slightly. Clara imagined she
was thinking that she was worth a bit of discomfort, but there
was only the tiniest of hesitations before she offered a dazzling smile.

'Of course. We'll have a chance to talk properly tonight,
anyway. Roland is taking us to the Tour d'Argent.'

'That would have been nice, but I'm afraid I've already
agreed to have dinner with Clara here and the rest of the crew,'
said Simon pleasantly.

Stella registered Clara's presence for the first time. Her
blue gaze took in the hair hanging in rats' tails around Clara's

face, the neon-green cast on her wrist and the scruffy wardrobe. She was not impressed, and Clara didn't blame her.

'I'm sure they'll manage without you,' she said to Simon, dimpling charmingly and peeping a glance at him under her lashes that would have had a lesser man crumbling at her feet. 'I think it's so important that we get to know each other before we start filming.'

'That's true,' said Simon. 'Why don't you and Roland join us, in that case? Clara, you can change the booking, can't you? I'm sure the restaurant can squeeze in another two.' He turned back to Stella before Clara could reply. 'You'd love this place, Stella—but perhaps you and Roland would rather go to the Tour d'Argent?'

Clara felt almost sorry for Stella as conflicting emotions crossed the flawless face. Obviously Stella didn't enjoy having her will crossed, but just as obviously she wasn't ready to give up a chance of seducing Simon, and had no intention of being stuck with Roland all night.

'No, it sounds like fun to eat with the crew, don't you think, Roland?' To give her credit, Stella managed a smile, even if it was on the tight side.

Clara avoided Roland's accusing glare. 'I'll give the restaurant a ring,' she said, backing away towards the lift. 'I'll go and do that now.'

Simon was halfway to the lift too. 'You're not to leave me alone with that woman,' he muttered to Clara under his breath.

'I'm sure you're more than a match for Stella.' Clara was ashamed of the lift of her heart.

'That's what you think. Women like that terrify me. They're all breathy voices and fluttery hands, but pure tungsten under the fluff. It's been like this ever since Astrid left,' he grumbled. 'They latch on to you, and before you know it you're taking them out to dinner, and then they invite you in for a coffee and next thing you're expected to ring them every five minutes.'

Shoving his hands in his pockets, he eyed the lift doors morosely.

'Most men would be grateful,' Clara pointed out.

Simon's mention of Astrid had come just in time. Like a fool, she had just allowed herself to believe that he really liked her. Why else would he make it so clear that he preferred her company to Stella's? A little glow had settled around her heart, but it was fading fast at the reminder of Astrid.

How could she have forgotten the woman Simon really wanted?

The way Matt had really wanted Sophie.

'Stella is gorgeous. Men all over the country fantasise about her wanting to spend the evening with them!'

'I don't like being pursued.' The lift doors slid open and they stepped in. 'Why can't women accept a man can be perfectly happy on his own?' he asked grouchily.

'You're not, though. You want Astrid back.'

'Well, I don't want anyone else,' said Simon. 'I certainly don't want to get involved with Stella Holt!'

What was the point of feeling disappointed? Clara asked herself as she checked every connecting cable and tested the batteries in the mikes. What had she expected? That one kiss in the rain would make Simon forget about Astrid and fall in love with her?

It hadn't even been a real kiss. She had just been a distraction from his wet feet.

Besides, she didn't want Simon either. He was *so* not her type, Clara reminded herself. OK, maybe he was more attractive than she had thought at first, and yes, he was a great kisser, but she was only just getting over Matt. There was no way she was putting herself through the agony of falling for a man who really wanted someone else again!

Astrid was perfect for Simon. Cool, clever Astrid. *I don't want anyone else,* he had said. If he was prepared to make just a little effort, Clara was sure he could get Astrid back, and then he would be happy again.

And she would be pleased for him. Really, she would.

Meanwhile, she needed to focus on her career. She had something to prove to her over-achieving family.

And to herself.

Clara ticked the tripod off her list. Roland had promised her a chance at producing if this programme was a success. She should be thinking about that, and not about the dizzying warmth of Simon's mouth on hers. About how good it would feel to tell her parents that she was a producer now, not about how good it had felt with Simon's arm solid around her.

That kiss had been a mistake. She wouldn't think about it again, Clara vowed. It had been a momentary indulgence, that was all, and it was time to pull herself together. Ted had promised to take her dancing after dinner. That would make her feel better.

She could forget everything when she was dancing.

Even that kiss.

She hoped.

Where was Clara? Backed against the bar, Simon kept a grim eye on the lifts. Turning up at the time agreed had clearly been a mistake. The MediaOchre crew obviously weren't bothered about punctuality, and he had been alone when Stella floated into the bar, looking glamorous and sultry and utterly terrifying.

Now she had him pinned into the bar, and was rabbiting on about how much she loved watching him on the news. She was standing too close, and her perfume was giving him a headache. There was something suffocating about her. She was one of those women who liked to touch you all the time. Simon had to grit his teeth to stop himself brushing her hand away.

He was feeling very twitchy. For all her fluffy femininity, he sensed a steely purpose in Stella. She had set her sights on him—God only knew why!—and intended to have him. Simon didn't care for feeling like a gazelle to her lion. He had *told* Clara not to leave him alone with Stella, but had she listened? No! She was probably still upstairs, singing in the shower she had spent so much time oohing and aahing over.

His mind stumbled at the thought of Clara, wet and naked, and as his eyes focused on Stella's lovely face, he felt oddly winded.

'Don't you agree?' said Stella with a winsome look.

'What?'

Stella's laugh was silvery and notably lacking in humour. 'Simon, I do believe you haven't been listening to a word I said!'

It was true. Simon made an effort to pull himself together. It wasn't like him to be thrown off his stride, but he had been aghast at how clearly he had been able to imagine Clara under the shower, all long legs and soft breasts, her face tilted up to the spray, her hair streaming down her back. Her eyes would be squeezed shut against the water, and she might be holding her cast out of the shower, but she would be singing, he was sure of that.

And she would be swaying from side to side, shimmying her hips, not caring what she looked like.

She wouldn't care if he was watching her. She would just smile that tilting smile of hers and invite him in with her eyes, and she would keep dancing until he slid open the shower door to join her, until he kissed her against the tiles and let his hands roam over her wet, supple body.

Simon's mouth dried. God, what was he *thinking*? This was all the fault of that stupid kiss in the rain. It had been madness, and he should never have provoked her into it, but she had been so close and so warm and that easy way she moved had gone to his head.

It had just been a joke, of course. He knew that, Clara knew that. But then suddenly it hadn't been. Suddenly the light-heartedness had intensified into something deeper, sweeter, more urgent. Something that made his blood pound and his mind reel.

And here she came at last.

Simon's heart jerked alarmingly as he caught sight of Clara crossing the lobby with Ted. She was talking, waving that absurd green cast around, her face animated and her hips swaying. Even if he hadn't been able to see her, he would have known that she was there. Her vibrant presence stirred the air, like an eddy of wind lifting autumn leaves.

Catching sight of him, she smiled and waved, just as if she hadn't left him alone here with Stella.

Simon scowled.

'Aren't you going to be cold?' he asked austerely as she came up.

Clara looked down at herself. On that filthy February night, she had chosen a skirt that swirled and floated around her knees as she walked, a top with thin straps and, in what he supposed was a concession to the weather, a teeny-tiny silky cardigan, all in colours that reminded Simon of nothing so much as a tropical fruit salad. On her feet she wore a pair of bright green shoes with precipitous heels that clashed horribly with the cast on her arm. Next to Stella, in designer black, she looked ridiculous.

Ridiculous, but gorgeous.

'Ted promised we could go dancing after dinner,' said Clara as if that explained everything. 'He's heard of a brilliant salsa club. Do you want to come?'

She included Stella in the question with a friendly smile.

Simon could see Stella's lip curling in a sneer. She had already forgone an expensive restaurant in favour of a meal with the crew, and she clearly had no intention of being any more familiar.

'I don't think so, darling,' she said. 'Salsa's not my kind of thing.'

It wasn't Simon's kind of thing either, but he wasn't risking another tête à tête with Stella. 'I'll give it a go.'

'Are you sure, Simon?' Stella's perfectly groomed brows drew together. 'We're shooting tomorrow,' she reminded him. 'You don't want a late night.'

'I'm sure Clara and Ted don't want a late night either. They'll be working too.'

'They're not the ones in front of the camera,' said Stella. 'Tiredness shows up so horribly on film.' She moved a little closer and lowered her voice flirtatiously. 'I was thinking we could come back after dinner and have a quiet session together,' she said. 'We could get to know each other properly and plan what we're going to say.'

'Clara's got that all blocked out, haven't you, Clara?'

Without waiting for Clara's reply, Stella snatched her hand from his arm and flounced off to find Roland. Simon turned to Clara with satisfaction, only to find that she was glaring at him.

'What?'

'Couldn't you be a bit nicer to her?'

Simon was affronted. 'What do you mean?'

'She's not happy. She only agreed to come on the programme because it meant working with you, and if you keep avoiding her she's going to be really miffed,' said Clara worriedly. 'We can't afford to lose her. Stella's got a reputation as a prima donna, and she hates not getting her own way. We don't want her taking her bat and ball and going home because you won't play with her!'

'It's not my fault she can't get the hint that I'm not interested in her,' grumbled Simon.

'It'll be your fault if we can't make the programme. We
really need the two of you, Simon. It's only until tomorrow.'
Clara looked at him pleadingly. 'Couldn't you pretend to be
interested in her, or at least not give her the brush-off just yet?
You know how much the programme means to MediaOchre.
It's make or break for us.'

She must have seen the stubbornness in Simon's expression because she held out her cast and winced.

Simon rolled his eyes. 'Isn't that old cast trick getting old?'

'It's jolly sore.' She rapped the knuckles of her good hand
on the cast. 'Ouch.'

Simon sighed.

'You know, I didn't think you were the kind of man who
would stand by and let the woman who saved your mother's
bag suffer the agony of uncertainty,' Clara went on, shaking
her head in disappointment. 'I do believe the word "heroine"
was bandied around,' she remembered artlessly, 'but that obviously doesn't mean anything to you. If it did, you'd never
let me face the collapse of the company and the loss of my
job, just because you couldn't be bothered to be nice to your
co-presenter.

'But I can see that's too much to ask,' she went on, clearly
enjoying herself. 'I suppose I'll just have to find another job.
Oh, and somewhere else to live, because I certainly won't be
able to pay the rent any more. I won't be able to go and stay
with Ted, because he'll lose his flat too, so we'll be wandering the streets together. But we'll be fine,' she said bravely.
'Don't worry about us.'

'Oh, very well,' said Simon, goaded. 'I'll be nice to Stella.'

'Promise?'

'Promise. But I'm not sleeping with her,' he warned. 'My
mother's bag wasn't worth that much!'

So he had to sit next to Stella at dinner, and let her monopolise his attention, while Clara, all smiles, had a great time at the other end of the table with the cameraman, Steve, and Peter, the sound guy.

Restored to good humour by his attention, Stella was fluttering her lashes at him over the rim of her glass. 'My accountant says I should be investing my money, but what do you think? I'm just so confused by finance.'

Suppressing a sigh, Simon set his jaw and explained how the markets operated while at the other end of the table Clara threw back her head and laughed at some joke Steve had told, and Ted and Roland were immersed in a long discussion which Simon strongly suspected was intended to leave him at the mercy of Stella.

Evidently taking his gritty conversation as encouragement, Stella inched her chair closer. She found excuses to touch his thigh, his arm, his knee, and only the memory of Clara's smile at his promise stopped Simon from edging back into Roland's lap. Stella was monumentally self-absorbed, he decided. She ignored everyone except Roland, snapped at waiters, and pushed her food away barely touched.

When at last the meal was over, Stella started dropping hints that the two of them should head back to the hotel alone, but Simon felt he had endured enough by then.

'I said I'd go dancing,' he said, trying to sound regretful.

Stella flicked a dismissive glance down the table to where Clara was telling some uproarious story. 'They'll just be going to some ghastly club and getting drunk,' she said. 'You know what crews are like. They're halfway there already, I'd say,' she added contemptuously.

'Someone ought to tell that girl Clara that she can't carry off those colours,' she went on, when Simon didn't respond. 'Still, I suppose she has to get attention some way. She's not exactly a stunner, is she?' Complacent in her own beauty,

Stella smoothed her fingers along her clavicle. 'It's a shame she ends up looking so vulgar.'

'I think she's attractive,' said Simon stiffly, and Stella's celestial blue eyes sharpened.

'Be careful, darling. You're quite an innocent in the world of television, I can tell. These production companies are full of girls like Clara who just sleep their way to the top. I've seen her eyeing you up.'

'That's ridiculous. I've got no influence in television.'

'You'd be surprised,' said Stella. 'I'm quite sure Clara knows just how useful you could be to her. Anyway, she's having a good time with the crew. They won't mind if you and I go back to the hotel and get cosy with a little *digestif*. Wouldn't you rather do that than go to some noisy club?'

Simon wasn't over-enamoured of the club idea, but he would rather cosy up to a crocodile with PMT than be alone with Stella. Mindful of Clara's instructions, though, he bit back the comment and forced an approximation of a smile. 'I won't be long.'

Stella put her lips close to his ear. 'Knock on my door when you get back.'

It was a huge relief when she made Roland take her back to the hotel. As soon as they had gone, the rest of the party relaxed and headed off for the club. 'Thank you. ' Clara smiled at Simon. 'Stella looked much happier when she left.'

'I don't want to hear any more about being nice to her,' said Simon. 'She got a free financial consultation out of me!'

'And I appreciate it,' Clara promised him. 'Now you can relax and enjoy yourself.'

They were pushing their way into a crowded bar, and they had to raise their voices over the sound of the catchy salsa beat. Clara's feet were tapping. 'Come on, let's dance,' she said, grabbing his hand unselfconsciously, but Simon dug in his heels at that.

'I don't dance.'

Clara stopped and stared at him. 'Why on earth did you come then?'

'It was a choice between this and a nightcap with Stella, and I've been nice enough to her tonight.'

'Well, since you're here, you ought to try it. Dancing's good for you.'

Simon grunted. 'I fail to see how making a fool of myself on the dance floor could possibly be good for me.'

'It's about letting go.'

Exactly the reason he didn't dance.

'I don't do letting go either,' said Simon.

'Well, *I'm* dancing.'

Clara disappeared into the crowd, and Simon found a spot to lean against the wall with a lager. It was dark and very hot, and the smell of beer and sweat fought with the throb of music in the darkness. Every surface was sticky as far as Simon could make out. He could feel the clagginess of the floor every time he moved his feet.

Astrid liked the theatre, or classical music. Simon had gone with her occasionally but usually they went to receptions, to drinks parties or expensive restaurants where it was all very quiet and tasteful, and there were no grinding, gyrating bodies, no pounding music reverberating up through the floor.

Simon felt as if he had been transported to a different world. Once his eyes had adjusted to the dim light, he kept getting glimpses of Clara through the crush on the dance floor. She was impossible to miss with that neon-green cast.

Not that it seemed to be cramping her style. Her skirt swirled up round her thighs and her arms waved and her body swayed and spun. Simon couldn't take his eyes off her. She was like a flame, dancing and flickering mesmerizingly in the darkness.

Sometimes she danced with Ted, sometimes on her own,

but sometimes with other men, strangers presumably. Simon watched, scowling, as they put their hands on Clara's waist, or swung her round them, their hips thrusting suggestively. Why didn't they just get a room? Simon wondered savagely.

God, there was another one! His fingers tightened around his glass. Dressed like a gigolo in a vest and obscenely tight jeans, he was undulating around Clara, and she was *laughing*! Dammit, couldn't she see the guy was a slime ball, and probably a pervert to boot? She shouldn't be allowed out on her own.

The music was just coming to an end, thank God, but Simon saw the slime ball shout something in Clara's ear, obviously suggesting another dance.

Simon couldn't bear it any longer. Smacking down the glass he had been nursing on a nearby table, he stalked onto the floor.

CHAPTER SIX

'MY TURN, I think,' Simon said, taking her by the arm and giving her admirer such a glare that the man threw up his hands, shrugged and retreated.

'I thought you didn't dance?' said Clara, but the music had started again and she had to lean close and shout in his ear.

'I don't,' he shouted back. 'I can hold you, though. Will that do?'

Without giving her a chance to reply, he put one hand at the small of her back and drew her close, holding her good hand against his chest with his other. Clara stared at him for a moment, then rested the hand with its absurd cast on his shoulder and relaxed into him.

Simon could feel the warmth of her body through her flimsy top. She was soft and supple, and she swayed in an attempt to dance while he shuffled around a bit, which was the best he could do. *He* wasn't going to gyrate in tight trousers and a vest.

Luckily, the music had slowed, but it was still impossible to talk, and Simon was glad of it. Succumbing to temptation, he rested his cheek against her hair. It felt silky against his skin, and he breathed in the same fresh scent he had noticed earlier that day. There on the crowded floor, with the other dancers jostling around them and the music making the floor vibrate, for the first time in as long as he could remember, Simon felt himself relax.

Which was odd because there was nothing restful about Clara. She was all warmth and movement and challenge, and he liked coolness and calmness and control. That was what had always attracted him to Astrid.

Simon frowned slightly against Clara's hair. It worried him that he had been in Paris less than twenty-four hours and already he was having trouble picturing Astrid clearly. All he remembered was an impression of serenity and contentment. It was always easy to be with Astrid. She never made him walk in the rain or dance in dark, noisy clubs.

So he should be thinking about getting Astrid back, not about how warm and soft Clara was. It was Astrid he really wanted.

Wasn't it?

Clara shut the hotel room door and leant back against it, letting out a long breath as she closed her eyes. Her heart was still thudding from that last dance with Simon.

By unspoken agreement, they had left when it had ended. Ted, Steve and Peter were ready to move on to another bar, but Clara and Simon had come back to the hotel. There had been silence in the taxi but Clara's body was thrumming with awareness, and her pulse was roaring in her ears so loudly that she was sure Simon must be able to hear it.

He must know that her senses were still jerking, that her back felt as if the imprint of his palm were seared onto it, that her fingers tingled where he had held her. It had been so, so tempting to lean closer, to let her hand slide a little higher up onto his shoulder. She tried not to, but how could she help remembering how easily they had kissed before? If they had turned their faces just a little way, they could have kissed again, but Simon kept his cheek against her hair, and she kept staring at his collar.

Which was just as well.

Because what a mistake that would have been. Simon didn't need another groupie, fantasising about that lean, angular body and that cool, cool mouth. Clara couldn't understand how she had missed the appeal of it before. Now she couldn't think about anything else.

But that was pointless. For a start, it was deeply unprofessional to lust after the talent, quite apart from the fact that she would be treading on Stella's toes and possibly putting the whole programme at risk.

Hadn't she vowed to focus on her career? It wasn't long since she had been desperate about Matt, Clara reminded herself. She had had enough of longing for someone who was hopelessly out of reach. She was tired of being liked, but not quite enough to be more than second best.

Simon had been very clear. He needed Astrid, just as Matt had needed Sophie. *I don't want anyone else,* Simon had said.

He might have held her close on the dance floor, but he didn't want any more than that. Why else would he have simply wished her a cool goodnight in the lift?

Deliberately, Clara made herself remember those terrible weeks after Matt had left. The jagged pain in her heart, the aching loneliness. The bitter realisation that all she could do was put one foot in front of another and trudge on without him.

She had survived. More than survived. Brick by brick, joke by joke, she had built up a defensive barrier of gaiety around her heart and it had served her well. She wasn't going to let it crumble now, not for a man who was clearly interested in another woman, no matter how good it felt when he held her.

No matter how well he kissed.

Sighing, Clara pushed herself away from the door. She

was very tired, almost too tired to enjoy this lovely room. The bed was wide, inviting, with crisp white linen. It was a shame not to have someone to share it with, and her mind flickered treacherously to Simon, who was making do in the basic room that had been hers, Simon, on whom the romance of this room would have been quite wasted.

Clara stepped out onto the balcony. It had stopped raining while they were in the club, but the roads were still wet. She could hear tyres swishing on the tarmac, and the occasional horn. Laughter and music spilled out of a bar down the street, and the air shimmered with the pulse of the city.

Hugging her arms together, Clara looked down onto the courtyard, where the cobbles gleamed in the yellow light that spilled out of the lobby windows. It was perfect, just like the room behind her was perfect, and she sighed again, depressed and lonely and aware that, for the first time in years, it wasn't Matt she most wished for.

But there was no point in wishing for Simon. He wouldn't appreciate this anyway. He had no idea about romance. Matt would have done, if he'd been here, but Simon would tell her she would catch her death, and for God's sake come in and close the window.

He wouldn't draw her down onto those white sheets and make love to her all night. He would remind her that they had to get up early next morning and make sure that she had set the alarm.

Clara crawled into the bed. She was exhausted, but she couldn't sleep. She lay luxuriating in the soft sheets and trying not to feel lonely. Trying not to think about that kiss or how it had felt dancing with Simon—if you could call it dancing! The man had no sense of rhythm.

It had been like trying to dance with a block of wood, Clara thought, encouraging the train of thought. So what if he had strong hands and a solid body and a mouth that made the air leak out of her lungs? She could never fall for a man who couldn't dance.

Never.

She had just drifted off to sleep when there was a tap at the door. She rolled over with a groan and pulled the pillow over her head, but the tap came again. If Ted had lost his room key again, she was officially going to demote him from best friend to most annoying colleague imaginable.

Blearily, Clara rolled out of bed and grabbed the throw to cover her nakedness. Ted was a good friend, but not that good. She was still wrapping it round her when she opened the door in mid yawn.

'This had better—'

She broke off. Stella stood there, dressed in a sheer negligee that left little to the imagination, her hand raised to knock once more.

There was a moment of appalled silence as they stared at each other.

'I see,' said Stella, blue eyes blazing. 'So that's how it is! I warned Simon about you, but did he listen?'

'What? No!' Clara came abruptly awake. 'Wait!' she said, realising too late what Stella had assumed. 'Wait, Simon's not here!'

But Stella was already stalking back to her room next door and, by the time Clara had tripped over the cover and disentangled herself, the door had slammed.

That was the end of Clara's sleep that night.

Stella woke Roland and screamed at him down the phone. Roland rang Clara and screamed at her.

'What the hell are you doing sleeping with Simon Valentine?'

In vain did Clara try and explain that she and Simon had just swapped rooms. At two in the morning Stella insisted on being found another equally luxurious hotel. 'I'm not staying here to be humiliated another moment, and if you think I'm taking part in your pathetic programme, you can forget it!'

Ted, on his way back to bed, returned to the hotel in time to see Stella flouncing out, and the realisation that his programme had just lost one of its stars.

'I'm going to call Simon,' he said, when he'd heard the story from a desperate Clara. 'Perhaps he can talk some sense into Stella.'

Only Simon could be woken at two in the morning and look as crisp and capable as ever. Clara had an absurd desire to burst into tears when he walked into Roland's room, where they had gathered.

Still buttoning his cuffs, his gaze swept around the room. Incandescent with fury, Roland was pacing in a magnificent dressing gown, while Ted hunched on a chair, his head in his hands. Clara was still wrapped in the coverlet, and her expression must have been desperate for Simon's brows snapped together.

'What in God's name is going on?'

In the end, it was Ted who explained the situation, with unhelpful interruptions from Roland, who blamed Clara for everything.

'What were you thinking, changing rooms, anyway?' he bellowed. 'Simon was supposed to be in that room! Of course Stella was going to think you were sleeping with him!'

'It was my idea,' said Simon levelly. 'It's not Clara's fault. And it's not as if it's the end of the world, anyway.'

With an effort, Roland clamped down on the obvious retort, which was that it was Simon's fault for not letting himself be seduced by Stella.

'Easy for you to say! You haven't spent half your budget on a programme that's not going to happen!'

'You can make the programme without Stella, can't you?'

'Not really,' said Ted. 'We sold it on the basis of the two

of you.' He hesitated. 'I don't suppose you'd consider going after Stella, maybe tomorrow when she's calmed down a bit?' he asked hopefully.

'You suppose right,' said Simon. 'If you ask me, you're better off without her. It's unprofessional to have a tantrum over something so silly. I didn't think she had anything of interest to say in any case.'

'The whole point of the programme was the contrast between two points of view,' Roland said tightly. 'It's not going to work with one presenter, and we can't afford to get anyone else out here, even if we could arrange it at short notice.'

The three of them started worrying away at the problem, putting forward increasingly wild suggestions that the other two would shoot down as impractical.

Simon listened in increasing exasperation. The solution seemed obvious to him.

'Why can't Clara do it?'

They all stopped and stared at him. 'What?'

'Clara could take Stella's place.'

'Clara?' echoed Roland with unflattering incredulity. 'Are you mad?' He had evidently forgotten that he was talking to his only remaining presenter. 'Clara couldn't do it!'

'Why not?'

'For a start, she doesn't have any experience.'

Simon turned to Clara. 'You told me you'd done some acting.'

'Well, yes, a little, but—'

'We're not looking for a song and dance routine,' Roland interrupted. 'What we need is glamour and, not to put too fine a point on it, Clara doesn't have the looks.'

'At least she's here, and hasn't stormed off in a huff,' said Simon, who was feeling guilty, and then cross with himself for feeling that way. No one had told him he was expected to take Stella to bed to keep her sweet! He'd done his best at dinner, hadn't he?

But Clara looked so devastated, and he remembered how important this wretched programme was to her. It wasn't her fault that Stella couldn't take a hint.

'You know, it might work,' said Ted.

'How?' Roland was too angry to be tactful. 'Look at her! Does she look like a presenter to you?'

Clara shifted under the gaze of the three men, and tucked the coverlet more tightly round her. 'I dare say she can put some decent clothes on,' said Simon, distracted by the creaminess of her bare shoulders.

'Oh, I don't know.' Clara lifted her chin and made a brave attempt at a recovery. 'Coverlets are bang on trend this year.'

Roland ignored that. 'And what about that stupid cast on her arm?'

'We could shoot round her,' said Ted eagerly. 'It'll be much easier for Simon if he's got someone to talk to on camera. Clara can put the pro-romance point of view so they're having a conversation. We've got two cameras, so we can shoot both of them, but we can always edit Clara out if necessary later.'

'Great,' said Clara. 'I've always wanted to be edited out!'

But Roland seemed to be considering the matter at least. He rubbed his nose. 'But what am I going to say to Channel 16? They're expecting Stella, or someone with a similar profile at least.'

'Tough,' said Simon in a flat voice. 'It's Clara or no one if you want me involved. You can have me, or you can grovel to Stella, in which case I'll be the one flouncing off. I'm not working with that woman again!'

'This is the best option, Roland,' said Ted.

'Don't you think you'd better ask Clara if she's prepared to do it?' Simon interrupted.

'Of course I'll do it,' said Clara as they turned to look expectantly at her. 'I'll do whatever it takes to save the programme. You can cut me out later.'

'You're looking tense.'

'Of course I'm tense,' snapped Clara. 'I've put the entire programme in jeopardy! I'll be lucky if Roland lets me keep my job, and if I make a mess of today, I'll be lucky if there's a job to keep.'

On top of which, her eyes felt as if they were bulging with lack of sleep, her wrist was aching, and Roland's remarks about her unimpressive appearance had stung more than Clara wanted to admit. She had done her best to brush up that morning but, short of a fairy godmother to wave a wand, there wasn't that much she could do to transform herself into a glamorous Stella lookalike.

All in all, her confidence was down in her unglamorous boots. Now she was expected to sparkle in front of the camera—and Simon wondered why she was tense!

They were standing in one of the semi-circular embrasures on the Pont Neuf, looking down onto the Seine, while Peter manoeuvred a boom over their heads and Ted and Steve discussed camera angles. Having thrown off the rain overnight, Paris had confounded them with a beautiful day. It was still cold, but the sky was a bright, brilliant blue and the city seemed to be preening itself in the winter sunshine.

Clara was in no mood to appreciate it, though. Roland never got involved in the practicalities of filming and, anyway, he was still too angry to speak to her. Even if MediaOchre Productions survived this debacle, he would sack her as soon as they got back to London, Clara was miserably sure.

'He can hardly sack you because I didn't want to sleep with Stella,' said Simon when she told him that, but Clara wouldn't be comforted.

'I shouldn't have upset her by being in your room.' She hugged her arms together fretfully. 'I just feel so guilty about spoiling everything...'

'Don't you think you're overreacting?' said Simon, crisp as ever. 'I don't see why you're beating yourself up. None of this is your fault.'

But Clara wasn't convinced. 'The whole future of MediaOchre hangs on this programme, and it's not going to work without Stella. You heard what Roland said. I'm too ordinary to be in front of the camera.'

'That's ridiculous,' said Simon shortly. 'I've never met anyone *less* ordinary.'

He studied her. She was wearing jeans today. Since there was no way she was going to rival Stella's sophisticated look, Ted had decided as director that Clara should look casual, but not scruffy. Her red jumper made her look too bulky, he said, so she only had a long-sleeved T-shirt on under her jacket. Ted wouldn't let her have her scarf either.

'What does it matter what I wear?' she had grumbled. 'I thought you were going to edit me out.'

'We'll see,' was all Ted would commit himself to. 'We can't do much about the cast, but it would be good to get in some shots of you as well so Simon doesn't look as if he's talking to himself the whole time.'

So Clara was shivering on the bridge. The sun might be shining, but it was still February. 'I'm freezing,' she said.

'Here.' Simon took off his jacket. 'Put this on until the cameras are rolling.'

'But now you'll be cold,' Clara objected, even as she hugged his jacket gratefully around her shoulders.

'I don't feel the cold.'

The heaviness of the jacket felt very intimate somehow. 'Like you don't dance, and you don't let go?'

Simon glanced at her, and then away. 'Yes, like that.'

There was a tiny silence. Peter was shouting something to Ted about the boom, and a party of tourists eyed them curiously, momentarily distracted from their admiration of Paris's oldest bridge, but for a moment it felt to Clara as if she and Simon were quite alone.

'Look, there's no point in fretting about Stella,' said Simon, watching a pleasure boat slide beneath them, the guide's commentary echoing out over the water. 'You can't do anything about it now. You just have to deal with the situation as it is, and there's no reason why you shouldn't do just as good a job as Stella would have done.'

Clara hunched her shoulders. 'I hate it when people are reasonable.'

'That's a very unreasonable thing to say,' he said, but she thought she saw a smile hovering around his mouth.

'Well, there you are, all ready to enjoy a good old moan, and then someone like you comes along and spoils it by pointing out that things aren't that bad...' Clara sniffed, and that suspicion of a smile became almost a certainty.

'They're not. You'll do fine as a presenter.'

'If I don't freeze to death first—and don't tell me I'm highly unlikely to freeze in the middle of a city in this temperature!'

'You were very eloquent about romance yesterday. Now you just have to do that again, but on camera. Just pretend you're under that umbrella and it's pouring with rain.'

Clara wished he hadn't mentioned the umbrella. Suddenly the memory of the kiss they had shared was throbbing right there between them on the Pont Neuf. Simon could feel it too, she knew he could. Their gazes glanced, jarred, skidded away from each other, and the silence tightened. Her heart was banging against her ribs as she tried to think of a way to break it but, in the end, it was Simon who spoke first.

'Anyway,' he said. Was it her imagination, or did he sound

huskier than usual? He stopped and cleared his throat. 'You told me you wanted to be a star,' he reminded her. 'Now's your chance.'

'Getting ready to be edited out of a documentary wasn't quite what I had in mind,' said Clara, gloomy again. She leant back against the old stones, almost able to convince herself now that the sticky moment when the kiss had shimmered between them hadn't really happened. 'I was thinking more a spangled costume and lots of singing and dancing.'

'If you can even *think* of dancing in a spangled costume, you can do this,' said Simon. 'Come on, there must be some inspiring song in your repertoire of musicals!'

'I suppose so.' Clara liked the idea. She mulled over it for a while. 'I could be like Julie Andrews. Remember when she set off to be a governess in *The Sound of Music*?'

'You have to remember that I don't have your encyclopaedic knowledge of musicals,' he said with asperity.

She straightened, clutching the jacket around her, her face vivid with new enthusiasm. 'You must remember! She was nervous about taking on a Captain and seven children.'

'I imagine she would be.'

'And she sings herself into feeling confident.'

Simon was just congratulating himself on having restored the brightness to her face when she launched into the song— some nonsense about having confidence in sunshine and rain—and, being Clara, she didn't hum it under her breath the way anyone else would have done. No, she belted it out as if the Pont Neuf were her stage, and the passers-by her audience. One or two smiled, but most averted their eyes and hurried past.

Simon was tempted to do the same. '*Clara*…I didn't want a demonstration. I just wanted you to feel more confident.'

'It worked!' said Clara, arms outstretched, feet tapping.

He pinched the bridge of his nose. 'Ted, can we get on before she makes even more of an exhibition of herself?'

But Ted already had the camera pointing their way. 'Sure,' he said. 'Shut up, Clara. Let's start.'

Clara gave Simon back his jacket. 'Did you know that the Pont Neuf is one of the top ten places to make a marriage proposal? It's what makes Paris one of the most romantic cities in the world.'

'A romantic city is just a myth manufactured by marketing teams,' Simon said. 'It's got nothing to do with relationships, and everything to do with what tourism contributes to the economy. In the case of Paris, that's a lot.'

And they were off, arguing backwards and forwards about whether or not romance was real or not. Clara was so absorbed in their discussion that she forgot about Peter dangling the mike from an eight-foot pole over their heads. She forgot about the cameras, and her nervousness and even the whole fiasco with Stella. There was just Simon, stubbornly refusing to accept that love could change everything, and that there was magic in the most ordinary things if you cared to look for it.

From the Pont Neuf, they wandered around the Ile de la Cité. They paused to admire Notre Dame, climbed the Eiffel Tower, and strolled down the Champs-Élysées. Clara was still acting as production assistant, so ran backwards and forwards, checking permissions and equipment and making notes for Ted, then rushing back to Simon, waiting imperturbably in front of the camera, and picking up the argument where they had left off. Every now and then, Ted would make them back up and start the discussion again, and Clara soon lost track of whether the cameras were filming them or not.

They broke at lunch, and Clara was glad to go back to the hotel and crash for a few hours. She felt better after a nap and a shower and, by the time they were back at the restaurant in Montmartre, she was much more herself again.

Simon had raised his brows when she turned up in exactly the same outfit as the night before, but as she pointed out, she didn't have an extensive wardrobe to choose from. 'I wasn't expecting to be in front of the camera,' she told him. 'This is as smart as I can get.'

Madame welcomed them back to the restaurant and had kept them a secluded table as arranged. Clara handed out clearance forms to all the other diners, making sure they wouldn't object if their image was glimpsed on screen, and with Ted ordered a meal that would be easy to eat on camera.

'No spaghetti,' she told Simon as she slid into the banquette opposite him. 'We vetoed snails, mussels and crayfish as well. Too messy.'

'I'm glad to see Ted's allowed us some wine,' he said, pouring her a glass from the bottle that had arrived compliments of the house. 'Are we allowed to start?'

'I think so. They'll be ages yet.'

Simon glanced across the restaurant to where Ted and Steve had their heads together. 'What are they doing?'

'They're setting up a two shot. It's better with two cameras. If they get them in the right place, they can film us both at the same time from a distance instead of swinging the camera from face to face, or having to do those awful noddy shots, where you ask the questions again and nod encouragingly when the interview is over.'

'They do that sometimes after I've done a piece for the news.'

'Of course. I forget that you know all about television.'

'I've got to admit that this is more interesting,' said Simon. 'I'm usually just sitting in my office—and there's never any wine included!'

Clara eyed him over the rim of her glass. 'So you're not regretting I persuaded you into taking part?'

'I think I'd use the word blackmail rather than persuasion,' he said, and she laughed.

'It hasn't been that bad, has it?'

'What, apart from being made to stand around in the pouring rain, dodging the seduction attempts of a monstrously self-absorbed chat show hostess, being woken at two in the morning and standing around half the day waiting for Ted to decide on the light he wants?'

'See, I knew you'd have a good time!'

Simon took a sip of his wine. The truth was that he *had* been enjoying himself, much to his own surprise.

'It makes a change from my usual routine,' was all he would concede, though.

'So what would you be doing if you were at home now?' asked Clara, settling back into the banquette.

He glanced at the clock on the wall. It was nearly half past eight. 'Working, probably.'

'It doesn't sound to me like you have enough fun.'

'Fun is overrated,' said Simon flatly.

Clara was dismayed. 'That's sad.'

'No, what's sad is when people throw away perfectly good lives just for momentary fun.' He couldn't keep the bitterness from his voice. 'My father was a great believer in fun. He liked to do things on the spur of the moment, the more extravagant and exciting the better. He'd come and take me out of school without warning, and we'd go hang-gliding or sailing, or we'd be on a plane for a weekend's skiing. "Let's have some fun", he'd say.'

'It sounds like a great childhood,' said Clara with a touch of envy. 'My parents were the opposite. I mean, they weren't cruel or anything, but their minds were always on their research. I spent my childhood either being dragged round medieval churches or being told to be quiet so they could read. I was forever being banished to the bottom of the garden to practice my song and dance routines because I was giving them a headache.'

She tried to imagine her own father, vague about anything that didn't relate to ecclesiastical architecture, whisking her out of school to go skiing for the weekend.

'My family's idea of fun is to discover a medieval pyx they haven't seen before, and they can get really animated about double hammer-beam roofs or wardmote court records,' she said, reassured to see that Simon was looking baffled. 'They spent all of last Christmas dinner arguing about later Franciscan thought instead of discussing the TV Christmas specials like a normal family.'

She sighed. 'I wouldn't have minded a bit of fun.'

'At least your parents take their work seriously,' said Simon. 'My father never took anything seriously. He inherited his money, and never thought about where it came from. In theory, he was on the board of a few companies, but it was just an excuse for some good lunches and it never interfered with the real business of life, which was amusing himself.

'I sometimes wonder,' he said, contemplating his wine, 'whether things would have been different if my father had been forced to work for what he wanted, but it was always easy come, easy go with him.'

'You must have some good memories of him, though, don't you?' said Clara. 'It must have been exciting to be taken out of school, wasn't it? And at least he was thinking of you and wanted to be with you.'

Simon's face closed. 'He wasn't thinking of us when he drove too fast down that mountain road. He wasn't think-ing of us when he gambled away most of his inheritance and invested what was left in a scam that a two-year-old should have been able to see through. He was having fun, not thinking about what it would be like for my mother to be left on her own.'

Or what it would be like for his son to lose his father, Clara thought.

'She lost everything,' Simon said. 'Her husband, her house, her car, her money and a lot of her so-called friends. But she did have one good friend, who gave her a job in her dress shop. It was the first job she'd ever had, and she hated it, but she stuck at it until I could earn enough to support us both. Whenever she's at her most exasperating, I remember that.'

Frances had struck Clara as utterly charming, but flighty and frivolous. It was hard to imagine her gritting her teeth and knuckling down to an unfamiliar job. Now Clara could understand why Simon gritted *his* teeth and put up with his mother's extravagances.

'How old were you when your father died?' she asked him.

'Nearly fifteen.'

It must have been hard for him, too, thought Clara, rolling her glass slowly between her hands. It was bad enough losing a father without losing everything else you'd always taken for granted at the same time.

'What happened to you?'

'Well, there was no question of school fees any more, so I switched to the local school.'

'What was that like?' A private schoolboy pitched without warning into the local comprehensive. Clara couldn't imagine that had been easy for him, but he brushed her concern aside.

'It was fine,' he said briefly. Too briefly, Clara couldn't help thinking. 'As soon as I could, I got a part-time job so that I could help my mother and put myself through university. Once I started earning, I made sure that I was never going to be in the position of not having any security again. And I never will be.'

CHAPTER SEVEN

CLARA picked at the dribble of wax that had trickled down the side of the candle, thinking about Simon and how his father's death had turned him from the mischievous little boy Frances Valentine remembered into the self-contained man sitting across the table from her.

Easy now to understand why control was so important to him. No wonder he was so resistant to letting go, to rocking the boat the way Astrid had done and plunging into the tempestuous waters of passion.

'Your mother seemed like a person who still has plenty of fun,' she said cautiously.

'Oh, yes, she's big on fun too,' said Simon with a sigh. 'She'd just got back on her feet and had some security when she threw it all up for someone she met at a party.'

'Gosh, really?'

'She said she was "madly in love".' He hooked his fingers in the air to emphasis the strangeness of the concept. Clara had the sense that the phrase might as well have been in Hungarian for all it meant to him.

'She and Tim had only been together a month when she announced that they were going to get married and live happily ever after,' Simon went on with remembered weariness. 'I suggested that she wait a few months until she knew Tim a bit better but no! I didn't understand, it was *love*.'

He made a face as if the word tasted bad in his mouth. 'Well, it might have been, but it certainly didn't last. They were divorced barely a year after they married, and I had to pick up the pieces again.

'My mother,' he said with evident restraint, 'is not a moderate person. When she's having fun, she's having more fun than anyone else, but when she's down, there's a very, very big mess!'

He sipped his wine, remembering. 'A couple of years later, it was Rob. At least she didn't go as far as getting married that time, but the effect was just as devastating. After Rob, there was Geoffrey, and that ended in tears too...'

Setting down his glass, Simon looked at Clara across the table. 'I don't understand why she keeps putting herself through it,' he said, baffled. 'Is it really worth it?'

'If you'd ever been in love, you'd know that it is,' said Clara. 'Loving means making yourself vulnerable to being hurt, and yes, it is a risk, but if you try and protect yourself against that, you'll never know the wonder of falling in love.'

She twisted the stem of her glass between her fingers, looking at the wine and remembering Matt. Bitter as the ending had been, she wouldn't have missed loving him for anything. 'When you love someone, it just feels so...exhilarating. The whole world seems better, brighter. It's like you feel *connected* in a way you can never be if you're not prepared to open your heart to loving.'

'Is that from a musical?' Simon raised derisive brows, and she flushed a little.

'You can mock, but the reason so many songs from musicals are popular is because they're *true*. People recognize them from their own experience.'

'You can't live your life by a philosophy according to musicals, Clara,' he said astringently.

Ruffled, Clara stuck her chin in the air. 'There are worse philosophies to live by.'

'Dear God.' He shook his head.

'Look, all I'm saying is that you have to be brave to love. It's not just a passive thing that happens to you. You can stay safe and never be hurt, but if you do, you'll never be truly happy either. Your mother knows that. That's why she's prepared to have a go. I admire her for it.'

'Yes, well, you're not the one who has to pick her up when it all goes wrong,' said Simon with a touch of defensiveness. 'It's not even as if your approach has brought you much of this famous happiness. You're still pining for your ex.'

Good point. Clara took a slug of her wine, unwilling to concede. 'I'm not *pining* for him.'

Much.

'When you love someone, you want them to be happy, even if it isn't what you want. I've accepted that Matt is happier with Sophie. Yes, I was unhappy for a time, but I don't regret loving him. Being with Matt was one of the best experiences of my life. I know what it's like to love someone utterly, and how good that feels. If I haven't met anyone else, it's because I won't settle for anything less than that feeling again. That's not pining.'

Simon was unconvinced. 'Maybe not, but it is unrealistic. You're pinning your hopes for the future on some vague, indefinable feeling. You might as well read the stars or consult tea leaves for all the good a "feeling" is going to do you when it comes to thinking about your long-term happiness.

'Isn't it better to get to know someone first?' he went on, leaning over to top up her wine. 'To make sure that you share the same interests, and that you're able to build a relationship on a sound economic footing? Those things are much more likely to give you long-lasting happiness with someone than what is no more than a fleeting sexual attraction.'

Clara's mouth was set in a mulish line. 'Love is about more than sex.'

'Do you really believe that?' he asked sceptically.

'Of course I do! Love is about needing someone, about feeling as if the day isn't quite right if they're not there.' The way she had felt about Matt. 'It's about knowing that, no matter how bad a day you've had, the moment you see them again or hear their voice, the world is back in its place.'

'Uh-oh.' He made a show of looking frantically around for an escape route. 'I can feel a song coming on!'

Clara ignored him. 'It's about looking at the one you love and feeling your heart swelling and swelling as if it would burst,' she said, pressing her fist against her chest, remembering the power and pain of it. 'It's about feeling a bigger and better and braver person for loving them, about feeling as if you've come home when you can rest against them...'

Feeling the way she never would again.

To her horror, Clara heard her voice crack at the memory, and she took another gulp of wine.

'And you want someone to feel all this for you?' Simon didn't even bother to hide his derision. 'Isn't that a bit of a tall order?'

'Maybe, but it's how I felt about Matt.' The wine had steadied her, thank goodness, and she sounded normal again. 'I know that it's possible. Matt was everything I've ever wanted. He's funny and charming and kind and when I was with him I was in heaven. I want to feel like that again, and I want someone to feel that way about me.

'Go ahead,' she said, her eyes meeting Simon's, 'sneer all you want, but one of these days you'll fall in love, and then you'll know what I mean!'

'That's not going to happen,' said Simon, matter-of-fact as ever. 'Always supposing I believed such a thing were possible, if I were going to fall in love, it would have been with

Astrid. We were equals—socially, economically, intellectually—and that's a far better foundation for a lasting relationship than any amount of swelling hearts.'

Well, that was her put in her place, thought Clara. There was no way *she* was ever going to be Simon's economic or intellectual equal.

Not that she cared, she reassured herself hastily. She couldn't imagine anything worse than being stuck with someone who didn't believe in love and insisted on being rational about everything. It would be like being with her family, and always feeling as if she belonged in a parallel universe.

Only it hadn't felt like that when they had kissed.

When Simon kissed her it had felt alarmingly like coming home.

Clara wriggled her shoulders to shake off *that* idea. True, Simon grew more attractive every time she looked at him, but there was no way she was going to fall in love with him. No, no, no. That would never do.

It was just a passing sexual attraction, the way Simon thought all relationships were. It was important, but it wasn't enough on its own. It wasn't *love*.

'Being equals wasn't enough for Astrid, though, was it?' she said a little pettishly. 'Maybe she wants passion now. Maybe she wants to feel loved and desired. Paolo will make her feel that.'

Simon snorted at the mention of Paolo. 'Astrid will soon get tired of him. What has she got in common with him? Nothing! We've talked about it plenty of times. We're perfectly suited. Astrid agreed that! We have the same interests, and we want the same things out of life. We were comfortable together.'

'Comfortable isn't romantic!'

'What could be better than finding someone you feel at ease with? Someone you don't need to try with?'

'Because not needing to try is only a short step from not

bothering,' said Clara. 'Romance requires a bit of effort, it's true. A little edge, a little frisson of danger. If you want Astrid back, you'll need to step out of your comfort zone and risk showing her how you really feel about her. And I'll give you a little tip for free: telling her that you feel comfortable with her isn't going to win her back!'

She stopped as Ted came weaving his way between the tables. 'Can you do that last bit again?' he said. 'Someone clinked a glass at just the wrong moment.'

'You've been *recording* us?' They looked at him with identical expressions of horror.

'That's generally the idea of filming,' said Ted. 'When we put that little mike on you and gave you the radio mike to put in your pocket, it was so that we could hear you talking,' he explained kindly, as if to two not very bright children. 'See Steve with the camera over there? It's pointed at you because we're filming you. You do understand that means we're taking pictures of you?'

'We didn't think you were ready,' Clara protested.

'I know,' he said, pleased. 'It worked really well. You both looked super natural.'

Simon didn't look natural now. He had pokered up and was regarding Ted with disapproval.

'We were discussing personal matters,' he said severely.

'Oh, don't worry, we can edit out anything personal.' Ted waved away their concerns. 'Visually, it's wonderful. The restaurant, the two of you absorbed in each other…great stuff.'

He beamed at them both. 'So, can you go back to when you were talking about what love is, Clara?'

They did their best to have a neutral discussion, but it felt stilted now. They had managed fine that morning, but there was too much in the air now. Clara kept thinking about Simon as a boy, discovering that his father was flawed. He hadn't said it, but she was certain that he had adored his father and that he had been bereft when he had died.

Ever since then he had been building a wall around his emotions. It would take a lot to bring it down. A very special woman might do it.

But it wouldn't be her.

Clara fiddled with her cutlery, unaccountably dispirited. It was stupid to feel so low. What had she expected? That one kiss would change Simon's view of love?

And, even if it had, what then? They were different in almost every way. Simon might be wrong about love and romance, but he was probably right about the kind of woman he needed. Clara was too noisy, too muddled, too much of a failure. She wouldn't fit into his ruthlessly ordered life any more than he would fit into her somewhat less ordered one. He was no easy-going Matt.

Simon needed Astrid, who was calm and controlled except when she was being swept off her feet by Paolo. Clara suspected Simon was right when he thought Astrid would get tired of the pretty Italian. A toyboy might be fun for a while, but Paolo could never compare to Simon.

No, Astrid would go back to Simon sooner or later. Clara just hoped she recognized just how much love and reassurance Simon needed. Did Astrid understand the desolate boy who was buried deep inside the austere economist?

Clara pulled herself up. What was she thinking? That *she* understood Simon? She had known him for barely twenty-four hours and kissed him once, as a joke. What made her such an expert all of a sudden?

Perhaps she had moved on from Matt after all? That she could even be thinking about Simon this way was a good sign, Clara told herself, but she wasn't going to get carried away. She wanted what she had told Simon: someone special who would love her as she loved him. Someone who would need her and want her, not a substitute or second best, but *her*, Clara.

And that someone wasn't going to be Simon any more than it had been Matt.

So she should stop thinking about his mouth and his hands, and start remembering everything she had said to herself about concentrating on her job.

While she still had one.

'Welcome to Paradise!'

Clara was waiting for Simon when he arrived at St Bonaventure's tiny airport. He walked off the plane looking as crisp and cool as if he was heading into the office instead of stepping into the soupy heat of the tropics.

No board shorts or Hawaiian shirts for Simon Valentine. Instead he wore pale chinos and, in a concession to the heat, a short-sleeved shirt, although he looked as if he would much rather be in a suit.

Clara, who had given herself a stern talking to while she waited for the plane to land, was annoyed to find that her heart gave a great bounce the moment she saw him, momentarily depriving her of breath.

He threw up a hand before she could speak. 'Please, no singalongs from *South Pacific*!'

She was ridiculously glad to see him, grouchy as he was. Forcing her heart back into place, she asked him about his flight. 'I asked them to give you a good seat,' she said, dismayed to find that her voice came out thin and reedy as if there wasn't enough air in her lungs.

Fortunately Simon didn't appear to notice. 'Extremely comfortable,' he said. 'It was very extravagant to send me out first class, though.'

'Don't worry, we didn't pay for first class. Our budget won't stretch *that* far!'

Disturbingly aware of a dangerous fluttery feeling inside her, Clara shifted her sunglasses to her bad hand and pulled the straps of her brightly striped basket back onto her shoulder with her good one. She wasn't supposed to be feeling fluttery. She was supposed to be cool and professional.

'I managed to get you a free upgrade,' she told Simon, horribly afraid that she was babbling. 'We'll just make sure the airline's logo is in the final programme. Ted's outside getting some shots of planes landing now, in fact.'

She stopped, inhaled, made herself slow down. 'Is that all you've brought with you?' she asked, nodding at the neat cabin bag which was all he carried.

'I'm only here for three nights,' Simon pointed out. 'You do realise that it's economic madness for four of us to come all this way just to talk about romance? We could have done that in London!'

'The whole point is that this is another super-romantic place,' said Clara as they headed for the exit. 'You may have resisted the appeal of Paris, but that's a big city, and I'll admit the rain didn't help. But not even you will be able to say that St Bonaventure isn't romantic,' she said. 'Wait till you see where we're staying! It's perfect.'

If only her heart would settle down and her lungs start working properly! It had been two weeks since that trip to Paris, and since then Clara had hardly thought about him at all. Not more than five or six times a day, anyway.

Perhaps she had caught the news once or twice—or maybe a bit more than that, if she was truthful—on the off-chance that Simon would be on, giving one of his concise assessments of the current economic situation, but that was purely for research purposes, Clara reassured herself.

It wasn't because her stomach jerked itself into a knot every time she remembered that kiss they had shared under the umbrella in Paris, or how it had felt to be held firmly against him in the club while everyone else danced around them.

Not at all.

And if she had been absurdly jittery when she emailed him with details of the trip to St Bonaventure, that was just because it was her job, and she was anxious about getting everything right. She'd never had to organise shooting in so many different locations. Naturally she was nervous!

Simon's reply to her email had been uninformative. *Fine*, was all he had said.

Fine! What was she supposed to make of that?

Well, that was fine by her too. Clara arranged to fly out with Ted and Peter. There was no need to accompany Simon, who was more than capable of getting on a plane by himself and, anyway, they only had one upgrade, so she would have had to sit on her own in cattle class. So it made perfect sense. It was the *professional* thing to do.

Clara had it all worked out. The moment she laid eyes on Simon again, she would wonder what on earth all the jittering had been about. Why, she would think, had she wasted even a minute thinking about him? Her stomach would promptly disentangle itself, that odd fluttery feeling would fade, and she would see the man she had seen at first: uptight, cold, dull.

But it hadn't worked like that. Clara glanced at Simon as he walked easily through the airport terminal with her and saw a self-contained man with a tautly muscled body and a lean, intelligent face. A man with a stern mouth and eyes that seemed to reach right inside her to snare the breath in her lungs. A man with warm hands and a caustic turn of phrase.

He was restrained, not uptight. Guarded, not cold. And when she looked at the hard, exciting angles of his face and remembered the touch of his mouth, dull was the very last word that came to mind.

And he was a man who didn't believe in love and who was looking for an equal. Remember that, Clara?

Outside the air-conditioned terminal, the heat hit them like a blast and they had to screw up their eyes against the glare. Clara put on her sunglasses, glad of the excuse to shield her expression.

She had loved the island as soon as she had arrived the previous day but now, with Simon beside her, all her senses had intensified and she was acutely aware of the warm breeze lifting her hair and making the palms sway. It carried the scent of the ocean and dried coconut husks from the beach, battling with the airport smell of kerosene and taxi fumes. The sun was warm on her back and the bougainvillaea scrambling over a fence was so intensely pink it hurt the eyes.

And then there was Simon himself, pulling a pair of sunglasses from his shirt pocket but otherwise apparently impervious to the heat. He had nice arms, Clara couldn't help noticing. They were strong with broad wrists and flat, dark hairs on his forearms, and when she found her gaze lingering on his hands, she had to jerk her eyes away.

Ted was waiting for them at the taxi rank. They climbed into a rattling old cab with cracked plastic seats that burnt the back of Clara's legs. She wished she hadn't worn shorts now. She'd picked them because she thought they would be cool.

And flattering, an uncomfortable little voice at the back of her mind reminded her. Her legs were her best feature, and she had wanted to look nice when she met Simon again, admit it.

But if Simon had noticed her legs, he was giving no sign of it.

And that was fine, Clara told herself fiercely. She was here as a professional, not to flaunt her legs in front of the talent.

She cleared her throat. 'It's not far,' she told Simon. 'Once we get to the port, we'll get a sea plane out to the island... Given that we don't have much time, we thought we'd get there as quickly as possible.'

'It would have been even quicker if you'd booked somewhere on the mainland.' Simon was clearly in an astringent mood. 'The sea is the sea, after all.' He was holding onto the roof through the taxi's open window and he looked out at the coconut palms lining the road, making the sunlight flicker as they sped past. Every now and then they got a glimpse of the ocean, a harsh glitter in the midday sun. 'You can't tell me there aren't beautiful beaches here.'

Ted turned round from the passenger seat by the driver. 'Not like Paradise Island,' he promised Simon.

'It's the ultimate romantic hideaway,' said Clara. 'It's gorgeous, isn't it, Ted?'

'I'm sure it's very nice. I'm just questioning the economic justification for travelling quite so far to make a short segment of the programme.'

Clara rolled her eyes, but she was glad he was being crabby. It made it easier to pretend she wasn't noticing the line of his throat where his open collar lifted in the breeze through the window, that she wasn't burningly conscious of his hand on the seat between them.

The hand she absolutely mustn't lift to see if it felt as warm and firm as she remembered. Clara could feel her fingers twitching with the need to curl around his, and she looped the straps of her basket firmly around them to keep them in place.

'Wait and see,' she promised.

Paradise Island lay in the outskirts of the archipelago that was flung like carelessly discarded jewels in the Indian Ocean west of St Bonaventure itself. Never had an island been better named, in Clara's opinion. It was tiny, set in the middle of a pale, pale green lagoon, with the dark blue ocean surging against the reef beyond. The water was so clear they could see the reflection of the sea plane on the sandy bottom as they flew over the lagoon.

There was a central area with a bar and restaurant, but the guests stayed in individual wooden huts, simply but luxuriously decorated, each opening out onto the beach. Simon and the MediaOchre crew all had a hut to themselves in the same part of the beach.

'We're all the same,' Clara told him. 'There's no need to swap rooms this time.'

By the time Simon had washed and changed into shorts and a loose shirt, the glare had gone from the sky, and he went out to find Clara.

She was sitting at the end of a long wooden dock that speared out into the lagoon, etched against the horizon in blocks of vibrant colour. Green shorts, a turquoise-blue sleeveless top. The neon-green cast on her arm that clashed horribly with both. It was so much part of Clara now that Simon had almost stopped noticing it. Her hair hung loose to her shoulders, pulled back by the sunglasses perched on top of her head, and her legs dangled in the water.

At the sound of his footsteps, she looked over her shoulder and smiled.

'Go on,' she said as he sat down next to her and let his own feet hang in the translucent water. It was very quiet, with just the gentle slap of the lagoon against the dock and the faint boom of the ocean beyond the reef. 'Admit it,' she said. 'This is paradise.'

'It's very attractive,' he conceded.

'Attractive?' Clara threw up her hands in disbelief. 'It's more than just attractive. It's incredibly, amazingly, stunningly beautiful!'

Simon had been watching the way the sunlight threw wavering reflections over their legs, but he turned his head to look at her then.

He liked the fact that Clara was tall. Their eyes were almost at the same level. Hers were brown and indignant, with the tilting lashes he had remembered, and her skin had already picked up a glow from the sun.

His gaze dropped to the warm, curving mouth that he had been unable to banish from his mind. If he were a more fanciful man, Simon would have said that mouth had haunted him since their return from Paris, but how could it do that? It was just a mouth after all, and that was just a throat, just a chin, just a cheek with a sweet curve to it. Taken one by one, there was nothing special about any of them.

But, put together, they made Clara. Warm, humorous Clara, forever on the point of breaking into a song or a smile.

Simon examined her face. It reminded him of a picture his mother had showed him when he was a small boy. If you looked at it one way, you saw a profile of an old woman, but when you looked again, you could see an elegant young one instead. Clara was like that. Sometimes she was a perfectly ordinary young woman, but if you blinked and looked again, suddenly she was gorgeous.

His gaze came back to hers. 'All right,' he said, without looking at the view. 'It's beautiful.'

Too late, he realised that he had made a mistake. Why was he looking into her eyes? Now he was pinioned, trapped, unable to look away, while the silence stretched around them and time seemed to stop and there was nothing but that moment. Nothing but the hard wooden dock beneath his thighs, nothing but the silky warmth of the water against his skin.

And Clara's gaze tangled with his, the indignation fading to an expression Simon couldn't identify but that made his throat tighten painfully all the same.

Deep inside him, Simon felt something inside him unlock,

so clearly that he could almost hear it click, and the sensation was so vivid it jerked him back to reality.

Because unlocking was a bad idea. A bad, bad idea. Unlocking was the first step to opening up, to letting go, and letting go meant losing control. Simon's heart was actually thumping in alarm at the prospect, and he dragged his eyes away from Clara's with an effort.

He found himself staring at her legs instead, but that wasn't any better. She had great legs, long and bare and smooth. Simon calculated that he would only have to shift an inch or so for his left thigh to be touching her right one, for their shoulders to touch. And, if that happened, it would be so easy to slide a hand under her hair and pull her towards him…

The impulse was so strong that it seemed to Simon that Clara was a powerful magnet, tugging him towards her. The effort of resistance had his heart going like a steam engine, and it was only by sheer force of will that he managed to wrench his gaze away from her legs. He stared out to where a cat's paw of wind ruffled the surface of the lagoon, sending shivers across the pure green water, until he felt his pulse settle and whatever it was that had unlocked had clicked firmly back in place.

They sat on the end of the dock, carefully watching the horizon, carefully not touching, while the silence yawned around them.

Simon cleared his throat. 'How's the wrist?' he managed to ask at last, but his tongue felt thick and unwieldy in his mouth, and he was excruciatingly aware of how close Clara was. An inch, two, that was all it would take. He swallowed hard. 'I thought you'd be out of the cast by now.'

'Another couple of weeks.' The words came out oddly squeezed as she lifted the cast to show him. 'It's fine, though. I hardly notice I've got it on most of the time.

'It's a pain here, though,' she said, sounding more like herself, as if she had shifted her voice down a gear. 'I can't swim or snorkel, and I have to wear a plastic bag on the beach to stop sand getting down my cast. I tried sitting in the water with my arm in the air, but I look a complete idiot,' she said glumly.

'It's the mark of a heroine, remember?' said Simon and her mouth pulled down at the corners.

'Frankly, I'd rather be a coward and be able to swim.'

'But then you wouldn't have been able to blackmail me into being here.'

'True.' Clara sat up a bit straighter and swung her legs in the water, making the reflections rock wildly. 'So, tell me, what have you been doing since Paris?'

'Working.'

'Have you seen Astrid?'

'Yes,' he said reluctantly.

'And?'

'And what?'

'And did you sweep her off her feet? Were you romantic? Did you win her back from Paolo?'

Simon presumed she was joking. 'We went out for a drink,' he said. 'Astrid seemed…concerned.'

'Concerned? What about?'

'About you.'

Clara's feet stopped swinging and she turned to stare at him. *'Me?'*

Simon didn't want to spoil the mood, but she probably ought to know. 'Apparently Stella spread a few nasty rumours after she got back from Paris,' he said, picking his way carefully.

'What kind of rumours?'

'I thought you might have heard.'

'No.' Clara fixed him with those bright brown eyes. 'What did she say?'

'Stupid things.' Simon shifted uneasily. 'How you had thrown yourself at me and we'd spent the entire time in bed and refused to turn up for filming or do any work at all.'

Her eyes widened. *'What?'*

'It's all rubbish, of course,' he said, 'but I gather Stella was quite persuasive, and I've always been so straight-laced it was a story everyone enjoyed, so it's been doing the rounds.'

'You mean people really think that…*you*…and *me*…?' She pointed at him and then at herself. 'How ridiculous!' she said unevenly when he nodded.

'Quite.'

Her gaze slid away from his.

'But Astrid can't have been concerned about *that*?' she said after a moment. 'She must know you better than that!'

'I think she was afraid I'd gone off the rails,' said Simon.

There was a pause. Clara glanced at him, clearly thinking that it was impossible to imagine anyone more firmly *on* the rails and under control, and when she looked away he saw her bite her cheeks to hide a smile.

'Go ahead,' he said, resigned. 'Laugh.'

CHAPTER EIGHT

CLARA's peal of laughter rang out across the lagoon, and Simon felt an answering smile twitch at the corners of his mouth.

For some reason, that broke the intensity of the mood and lessened the constraint between them. Clara pulled one foot out of the water so that she could hug her knee and half turn towards him, amusement still dancing in her eyes.

'I hope you were able to reassure her!'

'I think so.' Simon squinted out at the reef, remembering the conversation. 'She was in a strange mood, though. She kept going on about you and how "vulnerable" I was.'

'That's because she's jealous!' Clara gave him a *duh* look. 'I told you she would be. It's a good sign.' She flicked her hair back over her shoulder with her good hand. 'What did you say?'

'Nothing. She's still with Paolo.' Simon had wondered whether Astrid might be jealous himself. She had been very conciliating, almost as if she were waiting for him to ask her to come back.

It would have been easy, and he *had* thought about it, but somehow the words hadn't come. Simon still didn't really know why he had held back. He had spent a lot of time since Paris reminding himself how perfectly he and Astrid were suited, but when she was right in front of him, he felt… nothing.

But after she had gone he had been exasperated with himself. That was Clara's fault, he had decided. It would never have occurred to him to worry about feelings until he had met her.

'You don't want to play it too cool,' Clara warned. 'You could send her some flowers when you get home. Ask her to dinner and tell her you missed her. Or say you'd like to take her to Paris. If she really is jealous, she'll want to come back, but you have to show her that you've changed and that you really want her.'

'I'd forgotten that you were the great romance expert,' said Simon, a faint edge to his voice. She seemed absolutely determined to get him back with Astrid, and the thought left him vaguely disgruntled.

Clara was leaning forward, her eyes intent. 'If Astrid gets a glimpse of passion from you, she'll drop Paolo like a shot,' she told him. 'You can have your nice comfortable life back. Surely that's worth a romantic gesture or two?'

'I suppose so.' Simon could hear the doubt in his own voice.

'That is what you want, isn't it?'

'Of course,' he said, but Clara had noticed that tiny hesitation, he could tell.

It *was* what he wanted, Simon insisted to himself. He'd had much the same conversation with his mother only the week before, and he'd been absolutely sure then.

Frances had wanted to know all about Paris, and how he had got on with Clara. Simon had told her everything—oh, not about the kiss, but everything else. She knew about the way Clara danced, about her exasperating habit of humming under her breath, and the leaps of logic that left Simon wanting to tear his hair out.

'She sounds perfect for you,' Frances had said and Simon had stared at her, convinced that she had finally taken leave of her senses.

'*Astrid* is perfect for me,' he'd corrected her, but his mother only looked at him pityingly.

'For such a clever man, darling, you can be very stupid,' she had said. Simon was still puzzling over that one.

Now he sat on the dock beside Clara and made himself remember everything he liked about Astrid. Her clear mind. Her poise and elegance. The way she had never pushed him. She understood his work, understood how he thought.

No, they were perfect for each other.

'Of course that's what I want,' he said more firmly.

They were a smaller crew this time. Ted was acting as cameraman as well as director to save money, and Peter was doing sound again. Later that evening, Clara and Simon walked over to join them in the restaurant.

'I'm surprised Roland isn't here,' said Simon, distracted by the way she looked, with her shoulders bare and a frangipani flower in her hair. A sarong patterned with hibiscus flowers was wrapped around her hips, and the night was so warm all she wore with it was a strappy top and spangled flip-flops.

'He's wheeling and dealing,' said Clara. 'That's what he really likes doing. He calls himself executive producer, but he's not really interested in the practicalities. He only came to Paris to make sure you and Stella were happy—and we know how well *that* turned out,' she added ruefully.

'Has he forgiven you yet?'

'Just about.' Clara made a face. 'Ted seems to have convinced him that it's going to work fine without Stella, but I've been keeping a low profile. I can't afford to alienate Roland again. He promised me a chance at producing if this programme was a success, but I suspect I can wave goodbye to that for now. It's a shame, as I'm not likely to get a better chance.'

Catching herself up on a sigh, she smiled at Simon. 'Never mind. I'm not going to think about that now. I'm lucky I've still got a job at all, frankly.'

'It's not unreasonable to want financial security,' said Simon, who was having some trouble keeping his attention on economic realities when those hibiscus-clad hips were swaying.

'Simon, we're on Paradise Island,' said Clara as they climbed the steps to the restaurant. Candlelit tables were set out over a large covered deck area, decorated with plants and huge pots and open on all sides.

'This is not the place to think about practicalities,' she said. 'This is the place to think about how warm the night is, how starry it is. Look at how many honeymooning couples there are here. This is a place made for romance, not reality.'

'We're not here for romance, though, are we?' Simon heard himself say, and then regretted it when a guarded look flickered across her face before she pinned on a smile.

'No, of course not,' she said brightly, 'but that doesn't mean we can't enjoy the rest of it.' She waved her good arm in an all-encompassing gesture. 'The tropical night, the quiet…oh, and the food, of course.' Catching sight of Ted and Peter on the far side of the restaurant, she waved and set off through the tables. 'I can recommend the prawns,' she said over her shoulder. 'They were to die for last night.'

An uneasy feeling in her stomach woke Clara in the early hours. For a while she lay hoping it would go away, until unease became urgency, and then panic. She only just made it to the luxury bathroom in time.

When Simon knocked on her door that morning, she could barely lift her head off the pillow to croak, 'Come in.'

'Clara?' He was barely through the door before she had to make another humiliating dash to the bathroom.

It was Simon who produced a bucket, Simon who broke the news to Ted and Peter that there was no way Clara could stand in front of a camera, Simon who made sure that she had fresh water to drink and then held her head as she threw it all up again.

Having disposed of the contents, he came back with a wet flannel so that she could wipe her face.

'Is this when I start singing about your favourite things? Or what about a spoonful of sugar?'

Clara dragged the flannel over her face. Even that was an effort. Her hair was tangled and she strongly suspected that she was an unattractive shade somewhere between grey and green. That was how she felt, anyway.

'I can't believe you're making fun of me when I'm dying.'

Simon smiled. 'I don't think it's quite as bad as that. You've obviously had a nasty little bout of food poisoning. One of those prawns you were raving about last night, probably.'

'Uuurrrgghhh…' Clara clapped one hand to her mouth, the other to her stomach at the very thought of prawns.

'You'll be fine,' said Simon soothingly. 'It just needs to work its way through your system. Twenty-four hours and you'll be right as rain.'

Twenty-four hours! She struggled up on her pillows. 'I have to get up. We've only got today and tomorrow morning.'

The words were barely out of her mouth before the cramps hit her again. Obligingly, Simon passed the bucket.

'Oh, God, Ted's going to kill me,' she moaned when she could.

'He's fine. I'm going to do a few pieces to camera about the economic exploitation of these islands and what happens to indigenous populations when tourism takes over.'

'That sounds like fun,' Clara managed, still hanging over the bucket.

'We'll fit you in later when you're on your feet.'

Clara just groaned. 'Go away and let me die in peace.'

Simon smiled and smoothed some stray strands of hair from her clammy forehead. 'I'll come back and check on you later.'

So Clara lay and, between vile episodes in the bathroom and hanging over the bucket, alternated between wanting to die and squirming with humiliation whenever she remembered how kind Simon had been. Ted, never the most stoical of friends, had only managed to blow a kiss from the doorway before blenching and departing hastily, but Simon had been infinitely reassuring. Clara was torn, partly longing for his visits, and partly horrified that he had seen her at her absolute worst.

'I must look terrible,' she said on his last visit. She hadn't been sick for an hour and was hoping the worst was over.

'You're feeling better if you care what you look like,' he pointed out. 'Do you think you could manage a shower?'

Clara sat up cautiously. 'Does Ted want me now?'

'Don't fret. It's all decided. There's time to do your bits tomorrow before the flight back.'

'I can't believe I've wasted half my time here throwing up!' she said, slumping back against her pillows.

'It's all been terribly romantic, I know,' said Simon, then ducked as she threw a pillow at him.

'You're definitely on the mend,' he said. 'You'll feel even better if you have a shower.'

Clara did. She had a shower, washed her hair and brushed her teeth vigorously, but she was so weak she had to keep sitting down. Eventually, she managed to drag on a T-shirt and another sarong, and made her way on wobbly legs to the hut's little verandah.

Simon was coming along the sandy path from the beach, silhouetted against the setting sun. He stopped at the bottom of her steps and looked up at her, the stern features relaxing into a smile.

'You're up.'

The hollow feeling in her stomach was entirely due to food poisoning, Clara told herself. That was the only reason her knees were so weak that she had to hold onto the door frame for support.

'I couldn't stay inside any longer.'

'How are you feeling?'

She patted her stomach cautiously. 'Empty. Thinner.'

'Can you manage a little walk?'

In the end, she could only make it as far as the beach, which wasn't very far at all, but it was worth it when she was sitting on the soft sand, still warm after a day under the tropical sun.

Clara dug her bare toes into it and sighed contentedly. 'It's beautiful.'

Simon sat beside her and together they watched the sun set in a spectacular flush of orange and red. Further down the beach, a honeymoon couple wandered hand in hand along the edge of the lagoon. Clara remembered doing that with Matt on a beach in Greece. Funny how the memory didn't hurt any more.

Her eyes followed the couple as she absently picked up handfuls of the fine sand and let it trickle through her fingers, enjoying its fineness. Beside her Simon was lying back on his elbows, his ankles crossed. He looked cool and contained, and her mouth dried with wanting him.

What would it be like if they were on their honeymoon, like the couple further down the beach? If they loved each other and were starting their life together? If she could reach out and touch him whenever she wanted, and know that he would smile and pull her down to him? If Simon had lowered his guard and let himself love?

A lot of ifs there, Clara realised with a sigh, and face it, none of them was going to happen.

And, anyway, some honeymoon it would have been with her chucking up all day.

She was getting as bad as Simon, she thought wryly, puncturing a lovely dream with reality.

The sky was crimson, fading to purple and then dark, and out of nowhere came the thought that romance was like the sunset, a flush of something amazing and wonderful that faded to mundane reality.

A tiny crease between her brows, Clara lay back beside Simon, who had stretched out flat and was looking up at the fringed palm leaves that stirred and rustled in the warm breeze.

'What's the matter?' asked Simon.

'Nothing.'

'You keep sighing.'

Clara was ruffled. 'I sighed *once*!'

'Twice. You sighed just now when you lay down.' He turned his head to look at her. 'I'd have thought you'd have been in heaven.'

'I am,' she said with a shade of defiance. 'This is about as romantic as it gets.'

The tropical night had fallen with dizzying suddenness. Clara was agonisingly aware of Simon's dark, solid bulk next to her on the sand. It was as if the night had closed around them, sealing them in a tiny bubble that was slowly leaking oxygen. She found that she was breathing very carefully so as not to use it up too quickly.

Desperately, she made herself focus on the night, on the soft sigh of the lagoon and the whirr of the cicadas, on the silkiness of the sand under her toes and the scent of the frangipani drifting in the warm air. Closing her eyes, she began to hum softly.

'What's that?' asked Simon lazily. 'Another gem from *The Sound of Music*?'

Clara opened her eyes and stared at him in disbelief. 'It's from *South Pacific*. Even you must know *Some Enchanted Evening*!'

He made a non-committal sound, and she shook her head at the depths of his ignorance as she sang the first few lines.

'It *is* an enchanted evening,' she said, heaving a sigh. 'Can't you feel it? A deserted beach, a starry night, the only sound the hot wind soughing through the palm trees…'

'I can hear a generator, too,' Simon pointed out.

Clara clicked her tongue, provoked. 'You're just being difficult. I don't believe you can't understand how fabulously romantic this all is. It's a perfect tropical night, and Paradise Island is exactly what I imagined a coral island to be like. I don't see how you could possibly improve it.'

'Oh, surely it can get better than this,' he said.

'I don't see how.'

Simon propped himself up on one elbow so that he could look down at her. 'We could kiss.'

He made the suggestion so casually that Clara wasn't sure that she had heard properly.

The little breath that was left in her lungs leaked away. 'Do you think that's a good idea?'

'Well, according to your theory it would make it even more romantic, wouldn't it?'

'It might,' she agreed unevenly, and Simon's teeth gleamed in the darkness as he smiled.

'It worked in Paris in the rain.'

'Hmm…that's true.'

This was probably a big mistake. Hadn't she spent the last

two weeks talking herself out of being attracted to Simon? Didn't she *know* that it could never work with him?

But wouldn't it feel good? And shouldn't it be her mission to convince him that romance was possible, even if it was just a kiss on a tropical beach in the dark?

Just one kiss. What harm could it do? Neither of them was committed to anyone else.

And it would feel so good…

'If this evening is as enchanted as you say, it seems a waste not to make the most of it, don't you think?' Simon lifted her hair and smoothed it behind her ear, letting his fingers linger against her cheek, making her tremble with need.

'Rude not to,' she agreed raggedly.

'We could think of it as a useful comparative exercise,' he said, leaning over her. 'Which is more romantic? To kiss in Paris when you're soaked to the skin or on a tropical beach when one of you has spent the day groaning over a bucket?'

'Ugh, don't mention food poisoning,' said Clara, but she was fingering the bottom of his shirt and made no effort to move away as Simon lowered his head.

'The thing is, I'm a rational man,' he said. 'I can't make a decision based on feelings. I need to test the empirical evidence before I make up my mind as to which is the more romantic place.'

Clara's toes were curling in the sand and, without quite meaning to, she lifted her hands to his shoulders. 'Good point,' she said.

Very slowly, Simon lowered his head until his mouth was almost—*almost* touching hers. 'So shall we test the hypothesis?'

'I suppose so,' she managed unsteadily. 'Just in the interests of scientific research.'

'Naturally,' said Simon. She felt his mouth curve in a smile.

It fitted hers perfectly, and she realised that she was smiling too.

At the back of her mind, a small, sensible part of Clara
had retained just enough grip on reality to think *uh-oh, perhaps this isn't such a good idea after all,* and was frantically
waving a warning flag, but she frowned it down.

How could it not be a good idea when Simon was pressing
her into the sand and his body was warm and wonderfully
solid? When his competent hands were unwinding her sarong
and his kisses swamped her with pleasure? When there was
only the distant boom of surf against the reef and the lap of
the lagoon on the shore and the warm darkness that wrapped
itself around them like a caress?

When it really *was* an enchanted evening?

So Clara turned her mental back on that warning flag and
kissed Simon back. She moved her hands down his flanks to
slide them under his shirt, hissing in a breath at the feel of his
bare skin. His back was broad and smooth and powerfully
muscled beneath her palms, and she arched into the sand with
a gasp as his lips travelled down the side of her neck to the
curve of her shoulder in a trail of wicked pleasure.

How could this possibly be a bad idea? Clara abandoned
herself without regret to the honeyed delight of feeling him,
touching him, *tasting* him.

To the bone-melting pleasure that dissolved in its turn to
a dizzying rush of heat.

To the insistent pulse of excitement as his hungry hands
unlocked her, as his mouth drove her to the pitch of need and
she clutched at him, loving his hard weight on her, fingering
the bumps in his spine, smiling as he flexed in response.

'This is madness,' Simon mumbled against her throat.

'I know.' Her arms slid around his neck, pulled him closer.
'Madness, I know.'

And then they sank back down into the glorious, giddy heat once more.

Mouths, hands. Touch, feel. Gasp, sigh.

Kiss. Kiss, kiss, kiss.

Time slowed and swirled. 'We should stop,' Simon muttered, not stopping.

The warning flag struggled to the top of Clara's consciousness once more, waving exhaustedly. 'Probably,' she agreed reluctantly.

Simon drew a long steadying breath. Levering himself off her, he rolled back onto the sand beside her. For a while they lay there, letting their breathing quieten.

Having caught her attention at last, the sensible part of Clara's mind was firmly back in charge. It had been a wonderful kiss, but she mustn't read too much into it. Simon Valentine might kiss better than any other man she had ever kissed, but he was still a man who didn't believe in love.

He might desire her now, on the beach, in the dark, skimpily dressed—he was a guy, after all—but she wasn't the one he really wanted.

Clara made herself remember everything he'd told her about Astrid in Paris. *I don't want anyone else*, he had said. Astrid was perfect for Simon, he had said so and, no matter how much he might resist the idea, Clara thought he probably did love Astrid. As much as he dared to, anyway.

And Clara wasn't playing second best again. She wasn't going to be a substitute, a temporary replacement, until the one he really wanted became available. She had been there with Matt, and she wasn't going there again. It had hurt too much.

So she would treat it lightly, the way she had learnt to do. It was easier that way.

'So what did you decide?' she asked Simon.

'Decide?' He sounded distracted.

'Is the beach more romantic than Paris?'

A tiny, tiny pause. 'It's definitely more convenient. It's dark and dry and we're lying down for a start, so yes, I vote for the tropical paradise.'

His voice was back to its normal astringency by then, but his hand found Clara's in the darkness, and her throat tightened at the intimacy of their entangled fingers.

'It's easy to get carried away in the dark,' she agreed after a moment. 'I knew you wouldn't be able to resist the romance of it all.'

'Is it romance or is it physical attraction?'

'It's probably a bit of both,' said Clara, hearing the wariness in his voice. 'But you don't need to panic. I'm not talking about love. I'm talking about the way a place like this helps you let down your barriers.'

It was true, thought Simon. He had lowered his guard, but was that because of the darkness and heat and the scents of the tropical night, or was it because of Clara herself?

I'm a rational man, he had told her, but reason had evaporated the moment his mouth had touched hers and he had succumbed to the wild sweetness. The world had swung round them, but there at its centre, holding everything steady, had been Clara.

Now he lay, his fingers entwined with hers, and felt the earth turning beneath them, and he felt exposed and vulnerable and yet as if everything was in its right place.

'I know you don't do love,' said Clara.

That was true, too.

Simon wondered what he was feeling now. Desire, certainly, but beyond that, something new, something disturbing, was coiling around his heart. Something that made him shift uneasily on the sand.

'I don't like feeling out of control.'

'I know you don't. And you don't need to worry,' she told

him, sounding remarkably cheerful, Simon couldn't help noticing.

How could she kiss like that, and then bounce straight back to normal? It wasn't natural. Wasn't her blood still pounding? Wasn't her body still clenched with desire?

'I'm not falling in love with someone who can't love me back completely,' she said. 'So we both know where we are.'

He ought to be glad she was so businesslike about it. He *was* glad. It was just… Well, Simon didn't *know* what it was. He just knew he felt edgy and faintly aggrieved, and how irrational was *that*?

I'm a rational man. Hah!

Disentangling her fingers, Clara sat up and tried to wrap her sarong around her once more. The sarong he had unwound so efficiently so that he could smooth his hand down her thigh and stroke the inside of her knee.

Simon wrenched his mind back on track and sat up as well, resting his wrists on his bent knees.

The sarong was hopelessly twisted, and Clara had given up. She was brushing sand off herself instead.

'Anyway,' she said, 'I know it's Astrid you want, so there's no danger of either of us misinterpreting what just happened.' She glanced at him, trying to gauge his reaction. 'That doesn't mean I didn't enjoy it.'

If Clara the great romantic could be casual about a kiss that had shaken him to his core, *he* certainly could!

'I enjoyed it too,' he said.

'Perhaps we should test the hypothesis again in Scotland,' Clara suggested tentatively.

'Scotland?'

'That's going to be the last segment of the programme. We'll have done Paris, and a tropical paradise. An isolated cottage in the Highlands is another kind of romantic place, and it'll be the perfect contrast to the other two.'

'Aren't the Highlands cold and wet and plagued with midges? What's romantic about that?'

'There won't be any midges when we go,' said Clara firmly, omitting the cold and wet issue. 'It'll be wonderful.'

'When have you been to the Highlands?'

'Never, as it happens, but I know I'm going to love it. It'll be *elemental*.' She hugged herself at the thought. 'Wild hills, the mist on the heather, the rain lashing at the windows…'

Simon sighed, but actually he was feeling better. More himself. This was Clara in normal, exasperatingly illogical mode, and he could deal with that much better than he could with the Clara whose softness and warmth made his mind reel.

'What is it with you and rain? Didn't we have enough rain in Paris?'

'It'll be different in Scotland. You expect it there.'

Above their heads, the palms rustled in the breeze and somewhere in the darkness there was a thud as a coconut dropped into the sand.

Bizarre to be having a conversation about hills and cold and rain on this tropical beach. Scotland was another world— a world where things would be back to normal, Simon hoped. Where he would be back in control. Where there would be no warmth and languid nights to seduce him into lowering his guard once more.

'When are we going up there?' he asked.

'The end of March, if that works for you,' said Clara, head bent over her knees as she combed the sand from her hair with her fingers.

'And you think we should have another kiss there?'

She peered up at him through her hair. 'Just for comparative purposes, of course.'

'Of course.'

'And if you're not back with Astrid,' she added.

'Of course,' he said again, distracted by the sweet curve of the nape of her neck. He made himself look away. If it was anything like the kiss they'd just shared, it would be worth all that lashing rain. 'I'll look forward to it.'

'When you said it was isolated, you really meant it.'

Simon rested his arms on the steering wheel and peered through the windscreen at the whitewashed cottage lit by the beam of his headlights.

They had been driving along a bumpy track in the pitch-dark for what seemed like hours. The last sign of human habitation was miles behind them, and it was a long time since either of them had been able to get a signal on their mobile phones.

And it was starting to snow.

Excellent.

When Simon turned off the engine, all that could be heard was the keen of the wind screaming down from the mountains that were shrouded in the snowy darkness. It buffeted the car, making it rock slightly. The prospect of getting out into it and fighting their way to the dark cottage was uninviting, to say the least.

Clara eyed the cottage doubtfully. 'It looked nicer on the Internet.'

'The snow is a nice touch.' Simon allowed sarcasm to lace his voice. It had been a very long drive. 'You've certainly covered a range of weather in this programme of yours.'

'Well, getting snowed in is always romantic.' Clara slid a glance at Simon, wondering if it would be pushing things too far to sing *Always Look on the Bright Side of Life*, and deciding against it after one look at the set of his jaw.

'It's a pity it's not Christmas,' she said instead. 'That really *would* have been romantic.'

Simon was looking sceptical. 'We just need the others to

arrive,' she said, trying to cheer him up. Ted, Peter and Steve were driving up in a van loaded with equipment and the food Clara had bought the day before. 'I did a big shop so there'll be lots of nice things to eat. We'll make a fire. It'll be cosy.'

'You're doing Julie Andrews again,' he said sourly. 'Stop it.'

Simon had elected to drive his own car north, obviously not trusting Clara's driving, in spite of the fact that her wrist was out of its cast at last. She had to admit that it was more comfortable than a hired car, and certainly than the van would have been.

He was a good driver, fast and competent, his hands very steady on the steering wheel, but it had still been a very long drive. Clara had entertained herself—and Simon, she had thought—with a repertoire of all the songs from the musicals she knew until he had told her that he would put her in the boot if he had to hear one more.

'That damn tune about the lonely goatherd is in my head now,' he growled.

'You should sing along,' said Clara. 'That'll let it out of your head.'

One look from Simon was enough to tell her what he thought of *that* suggestion.

Fine. She wouldn't sing then. After a while, without really being aware of it, she began humming under her breath.

'Stop buzzing!' said Simon, exasperated. 'Why can't you just sit quietly and look at the scenery?'

'I don't like silence.' Clara hunched a sullen shoulder.

It had been nearly a month since that kiss on St Bonaventure, and she had done her best to put it out of her mind, but she couldn't help remembering that they had agreed to kiss again in Scotland.

Just as a light-hearted test.

I'll look forward to it, Simon had said. Every time Clara

thought of it, which was more often than she wanted, anticipation shivered down her spine and clenched her entrails.

It was madness, they had agreed on that beach, and it still was. This was the last time she and Simon would meet. Once the filming was over, their lives would go their separate ways for good. Ted would edit her out of the film, so they wouldn't even stay together digitally. How symbolic was that?

She and Simon had nothing whatsoever in common, Clara knew that, but still she couldn't stop the excitement buzzing under her skin when she thought about him, and the moment she had seen him again it was as if a light had been switched on inside her.

CHAPTER NINE

IT DIDN'T make sense. Yes, he was a fantastic kisser, but he was also cross, critical and infuriatingly unromantic. He didn't sing, couldn't dance. He was her very own Captain von Trapp, in fact.

Which made Astrid the Baroness.

Who, let's face it, had much nicer frocks and in reality would have made him a much more suitable wife than a guitar-strumming nun.

Clara suppressed a sigh. 'I suppose Astrid behaves perfectly in the car?'

'At least she can sit still for more than a minute at a time, and doesn't subject me to the complete works of Andrew Lloyd Webber and Rodgers and Hammerstein!'

Clara didn't normally like long car journeys, which did indeed involve too much sitting still for her liking, but she hadn't been bored. How could she be bored when being with Simon made her feel so alive? Every one of her senses was on high alert, and she was intensely aware of the beating of her own heart.

Of the smell of the leather seats and the smoothness of the glossy wood trim, of the length of Simon's thigh, and the dashboard lights which threw a muted glow over his features, catching the line of his nose and the set of his mouth in a way that dried the breath in Clara's throat whenever she looked at it.

When not providing Simon with a free cabaret—which he hadn't appreciated at all—Clara had spent the journey curled up in her seat, half-turned towards him, and they had talked and argued their way all the way up the motorway.

Simon was one of those drivers who hated breaking the momentum of their journey and, in spite of constant lobbying for a proper meal, Clara had barely been allowed the occasional brief loo stop. She had a sandwich and a packet of crisps that earned her a ticking off for dropping crumbs all over his car, but now they were there and she was starving.

'Well, let's see what it's like inside,' she said, digging in her bag for the key they had picked up a lifetime earlier. 'I'm sure it'll be fine once we've got the kettle on and a fire going.'

She had to push hard to open the car door. The wind snatched at her hair and spat snow into her eyes as soon as she got out, and she made a bolt for the cottage. She was shivering so much she couldn't get the key in the lock.

'What are you doing?' Simon had to raise his voice above the howling wind and, even fumbling around in the dark with the snow swirling around them, she was acutely aware of his body behind her.

'My hands are cold,' she yelled back.

'Let me do it.' His fingers were warm and sure as he reached out and took the key from her, and for an instant Clara was transported back to Paradise Island and his hand on her thigh, on the back of her knee.

The rush of heat warmed her as Simon opened the door without any difficulty and groped around for a light switch.

'Ah,' he said as he encountered one and clicked it on.

Nothing.

He switched it off and then on again. Still nothing.

'What's the matter?' said Clara, who was shivering again after that brief, welcome spurt of warmth.

'No power.'

'Ohmigod...' Clara's dream of a cosy cottage was rapidly fading.

'Perhaps it's just the bulb.'

But when Simon located another switch, that didn't work either.

'Now what?' Clara said as he cursed.

'See if you can find the fuse box.'

Muttering under his breath, Simon fought his way back through the wind and snow to the car and stomped back with a torch.

Clara was very glad of his competence. She certainly wouldn't have known what to do. Tasked with holding the torch, she huddled behind him, pulling her sleeves down over her hands, while he examined the fuse box.

'I can't see if you wave the torch around like that,' Simon said irritably.

'It's cold,' she grumbled, but she eased her fingers out of her jumper to hold the torch steadier.

Simon straightened, and they were suddenly standing very close. Clara took an instinctive step back, which seemed a better idea than throwing herself at his chest, which was what she really wanted to do.

'The fuses are OK,' he said, taking the torch from her briskly and playing it around the room. 'That means the power is out further down the line. There's nothing we can do about that.'

Clara hugged her arms together in dismay. 'What are we going to do? This is a nightmare.'

'You were the one who thought an isolated cottage would be romantic,' he reminded her.

True, she had.

'It'll be cosy, you said,' Simon added maliciously. 'It'll be wonderful, you said. It'll be *elemental*.'

'We'll make it cosy,' said Clara, pulling herself together. 'There must be a fire. Let's have that torch. Look, there,' she said in relief, spotting a mantelpiece.

'That's something,' grunted Simon. 'You get it going and I'll bring our stuff in from the car.'

Fortunately the fire had been laid, and Clara found some matches. They were the first tenants of the year, the agent had told them, and the matches were rather damp, but she eventually managed to get one to light. She was shivering so hard by then that the match nearly went out as she held it to the paper with a shaking hand, but at last a tiny flame caught the edge of the paper.

Clara watched it anxiously as it wavered, then steadied. Puffing out a sigh of relief, she sat back on her heels, holding out her hands to the fire as it crackled into life. Now she knew how cavemen must have felt. There was something infinitely comforting about the leaping flames in the darkness.

Simon pushed the door shut with his foot and dumped their things by the door while he brushed the snow from his jacket. They didn't have much with them. It had seemed silly to load up the car when the van could bring everything more easily.

Which might have been a mistake.

'I'm starving,' said Clara, switching off the torch to save the battery. 'I hope Ted and the others arrive soon. They've got all the food.'

'We won't be able to cook it,' Simon pointed out as he dropped wearily into a chair on one side of the fire and stretched out his legs to the flames. 'The oven's electric.'

Clara's shoulders slumped. She had been fantasising about the piece of lamb she'd bought to roast.

'There's bread and cheese.' She perked up a little as she

remembered what else they could eat. 'Crisps, olives…oh, and wine, of course.'

She sighed. 'I must stop thinking about it. I'm drooling! I can't even find out how far away they are.' Just in case a signal had miraculously winkled its way through the mountains, she dug her phone out of her bag. It was still blank, but she did find the end of a packet of mints that she had forgotten was there.

'Want a mint?' she offered Simon.

'Why not save them until we're desperate?'

'I'm desperate now!' But she put the mints back, and got to her feet and picked up the torch.

'I'm going to see if there's anything in the kitchen.'

'Don't waste the battery,' Simon warned.

'I'll be quick.'

It was too cold to be away from the fire for too long anyway. Clara hunted through the kitchen cupboards but could only find some old instant coffee and two cans of kidney beans.

'No can opener either,' she reported glumly when she was huddled back in front of the fire. 'We'd better eke out those mints or we'll be reduced to gnawing our own limbs.'

Simon added a log to the fire and poked it into place. 'That's right,' he said. 'A quick step from a twinge of hunger to cannibalism. Why am I even surprised?' He threw himself back into the chair. 'Do you ever react moderately to anything?'

'I don't need to be moderate when you're sitting there being moderate enough for ten of us!' said Clara pettishly.

'There's no point in me doing drama when you're sitting there being dramatic enough for twenty!'

There was an unpleasant silence, and then Clara sighed. 'I'm sorry,' she said. 'I'm just cross because this is turning into a nightmare.'

Dispirited, she looked around the cottage. It was difficult to make out much in the firelight, but she didn't hold out much hope of the charming, cosy décor she had imagined. There were some bulky pieces of furniture, most of it dating from the Seventies to judge by the knobbly material on the three-piece suite in front of the fireplace, and a musty smell pervaded everything.

'You're right,' she told Simon miserably. 'It's not romantic at all. It's awful. Maybe I've got it all wrong.'

Simon sat up in mock alarm. 'That's not like you! Isn't there some song you can sing to make you feel better?'

'I don't feel like singing,' said Clara, settling herself with her back against the sofa.

'Now you've really got me worried,' he said, only half-joking.

She tucked her hair behind her ears and forced herself to face up to the truth.

'All these romantic situations have turned out to be disasters,' she said in a hollow voice. 'Pouring in Paris, food poisoning on Paradise Island, and now freezing and starving in the middle of nowhere! Of *course* it's not romantic. What am I going to say tomorrow when we're filming? I'll have to admit that I've changed my mind and that I don't believe in romance any more.'

Simon looked at her in concern. He ought to have been pleased that she had seen sense and come round to his way of thinking, but it felt all wrong. Clara's shining belief in romance was part of her. He didn't like it when she was sensible and rational.

'You're just tired and hungry,' he said. 'You'll feel better when Ted gets here and you've had something to eat.'

But three hours crawled by and there was still no sign of the van. Clara gnawed the inside of her cheek. 'Do you think they've been in some terrible accident?'

'No,' said Simon. 'I think they're sensibly holed up in a comfortable hotel somewhere rather than drive through the snow in the dark.'

'I wish we knew what had happened to them!'

'They'll be here in the morning. In the meantime, there's nothing we can do about it except resign ourselves to no supper.'

The torch beam was already weak, but he used it to explore upstairs, where he found ample bedding, which was something, and then he went around the living room opening and closing cupboard doors.

'What are you looking for?' asked Clara, following his progress.

'Survival rations…ah!' Simon came back to the fire with a bottle of whisky and two glasses. 'I thought a Scottish cottage had to have an emergency supply somewhere.' He held up the bottle and inspected it in the firelight. 'Half empty— I suppose you'd say half full—but it'll keep us going.'

He sloshed whisky into the glasses, and handed one to Clara. 'This will cheer you up.'

They both sat on the floor, backs against the sofa, not quite touching. Their legs were stretched out towards the fire, and the flames sent flickering shadows leaping over their faces.

Clara wasn't used to drinking whisky, she told him. She choked and spluttered at first, but she soon got the hang of it, and they drank in companionable silence for a while, their hands brushing occasionally when they set their glass on the floor between them.

Simon looked down into his glass contemplatively. He had driven for twelve hours that day and he was very hungry. Astrid would never have got him into a situation like this. On the few occasions they'd been away together, Astrid would book them into five-star hotels, and always made sure that she got a good deal by booking in advance. Simon couldn't imagine her here.

But he was oddly comfortable sitting in front of the fire in this musty old cottage. Outside, the wind worried at the windows, and the rest of the rooms were dank and bitterly cold, but within the circle of firelight it was quite cosy. They had long ago finished the mints, but the whisky was warm in his stomach and Clara was beside him, long legs sprawled in front of her, humming as she watched the fire, one of those wretched show tunes he was going to have running round his head for the rest of the week.

His eyes rested on her profile, on the tilt of her lashes, the line of her cheek, the sweet curve of her mouth, and his heart turned over. Had there really been a time when he had thought of her as ordinary? Now, every time he looked at Clara she seemed more beautiful to him. Not perfect in a cool, classic way, but with a warmth and an allure that made his senses swirl.

There was a tight feeling around his chest, and he found himself remembering what she had said in Paris. *It's about looking at the one you love and feeling your heart swelling and swelling as if it would burst.*

The way his heart felt right then.

Sensing his gaze, she glanced at him and smiled.

And that was it. The world tipped and the tight band around Simon's chest that had been keeping his emotions in check for so long snapped open, and his head reeled before the rush of feeling, as terrifying as he had feared and as exhilarating as Clara had promised.

One of these days you'll fall in love, she had said. *Then you'll know what I mean.*

Simon was glad that he was sitting down. Very carefully, he put his glass on the floor beside him. He had been afraid letting go would be like this, that the feelings would surge and slosh around out of control and that he'd be left grappling for something to hold onto. In the maelstrom, there was only one certainty.

Clara, and the fact that he loved her.

The panicky feeling subsided and the world righted itself once more, the same but with everything in a subtly different alignment. Clara was beside him and nothing else mattered. He might be tired and hungry and uncomfortable, but she was there and he was happy.

When had she become so necessary to him? Simon couldn't take his eyes off her now. Unaware of the effect of her smile, she had turned back to watch the fire, absorbed in the wavering flames.

Why her? Why Clara, with her absurdly romantic view of life, with her chaotic outfits and her infuriating singing and her exuberance? She was completely wrong for him.

And yet completely right.

He wanted to slide his hand under her hair, to see her turn towards him, her eyes widening and that smile tugging at her mouth. He wanted to draw her close, to lay her down in the firelight and make love to her until she promised that she would never leave him.

But why would she promise that? Simon picked up his glass and took a steadying sip of whisky. He had locked away his feelings after his father's death and turned inward. Clara was braver than that. She had been hurt too, but she had hidden it beneath a gaiety and a zest for life.

She had loved Matt so much. Simon's jaw tightened as he faced the truth. He could never match up to the love of Clara's life. Matt had been everything she had ever wanted. She had told him that outright. Kind, romantic, Mr Nice Guy...everything Simon wasn't, in fact.

When you love someone, you want them to be happy. That was another thing Clara had said. She wanted a man who was passionate and funny and wildly romantic, and he could never be that, Simon knew. But now the truth was out there, slapping him with his stupidity—how could he not have known how much he loved her?—he had to find a way to tell her how he felt.

He cleared his throat. 'Astrid wants us to try again.'

Clara broke off in mid hum and straightened to look at him. 'Well…that's good news,' she said a little awkwardly before she turned back to study the flames. 'I knew that was what she wanted really. What happened to Paolo?'

'She said that he was too demanding, and jealous of the time she spent at work. At first she found it flattering, she said, but after a while she wanted someone she could talk to about work. Me, in fact.'

'So what did you say?' asked Clara.

'I said no.'

'*No?*' The whisky slopped in her glass as she jerked in surprise. '*Why?* I thought Astrid was perfect for you?'

'I thought she was too.' Simon turned his glass between his hands, remembering the scene. 'I can't explain it. She was so practical about it. She seemed to take it for granted that we would just pick up from where we left off and go back to the way we were before, that we'd pretend that she had never said that she wanted passion and excitement and romance.'

He put the glass back on the floor beside him. 'It was only then that I realised we couldn't do that. I told her I thought we had both changed too much to pretend everything was the same.'

'Do you think you *have* changed?' Clara asked softly, and he nodded.

'The truth is that I would never have kissed you in Paris if Astrid had been really important to me. I wouldn't have wanted to kiss you on Paradise Island.' His voice deepened and his eyes rested on her face. 'I wouldn't want to kiss you now.'

Clara's eyes met his almost unwillingly, and the air between them thrummed with the memory of what that last kiss had been like.

'We did say we would try a third kiss,' she said with difficulty.

Simon's heart was pumping as he laid his hand to her cheek, twisted a strand of her silky hair around his finger. 'What if I want more than three kisses? What if I want to kiss you in London, say?'

Clara stilled. 'I don't think that would work,' she said slowly.

'Why not? Why does it matter where we are?'

'Because this isn't real,' she said, gesturing at the fire. 'The way Paradise Island wasn't real, or Paris.'

'It felt pretty real to me when I went upstairs,' said Simon. 'It's freezing up there.'

'It's real, but it's not real life,' Clara struggled to explain. 'The whole point about the places we've been is that they're special. They're places where we can step outside our normal existences for a while and do things differently, *be* different. That's what makes them so romantic.'

'Can't London be romantic?'

'For some people maybe, but not for us. London is where we both work. It's real for us. There's no way I could ever fit into your life there,' she said. 'I'd drive you crazy in five minutes.'

'You're driving me crazy now,' said Simon with a rueful smile.

'You know what I mean,' Clara said. 'We're too different. You want calmness and order, and I want music and dancing.'

Simon's heart sank. He let her hair fall and dropped his hand. She sounded so clear. *We're too different.*

What if she was right? He might have fallen in love, but he hadn't lost his mind. He still believed that shared interests were a far better basis for a successful relationship in the long run. He *did* like order. Clara probably *would* drive him crazy, just as he would drive her crazy by not singing along or sweeping her off her feet with wildly romantic gestures.

Perhaps, in the end, it was better to be sensible?

'I'm waiting for someone who isn't afraid to love me completely,' said Clara, as if she could read his mind. Pulling up her legs, she hugged her knees as she looked dreamily into the fire.

'I want someone who will take a risk for me,' she said. 'Someone who'll dance for me, sing for me… Oh, I know it's just a fantasy, I know I've probably watched too many musicals, but that's what I want. To be the star of someone's show, not an understudy or a walk-on part.'

Simon watched her profile. 'Do you really think it's possible to find someone like that?'

'Maybe not.' Her eyes were dark and huge and she turned to look at him again. 'I don't know, but I'm not prepared to settle for less than that now. I don't want to be second best again.'

Reaching out once more, Simon's hand slid beneath her hair to caress the nape of her neck and ignored the crack in his heart. 'So…it looks like we're incompatible.'

'I'm afraid so,' said Clara, but he felt her shiver of response and she leant into his hand. 'In real life, anyway.'

'What about now? Didn't you say this isn't real life?'

A smile tugged at the corners of that lush mouth. 'No, it isn't real. For now we're both here, and we don't have to be sensible. We don't have to think about the future. We can just think about this place and this moment and the fact that there's just the two of us.'

'And that it's very cold,' Simon agreed, slowly drawing her

closer. 'It's a well-established fact that the best way to keep warm is to share body heat.'

'I've heard that.' Clara smiled. 'But I know you like to test the evidence,' she said as she pulled free of his hand and clambered over him until she straddled him on the floor.

'We should do a little experiment,' she said, leaning forward to press little kisses along his jaw, and Simon's senses reeled at the feel of her, at the tickle of her hair against his cheek, the scent of her, the way she fitted so perfectly against him.

When she reached his mouth, she angled her face to kiss his lips. He tasted whisky and something that was instantly, unmistakably Clara and the tightness inside him unravelled as he sank into the heat and the piercing sweetness and the world came right at last.

'You can tell me to stop any time you're warm enough,' she murmured against his mouth and he smiled as his arms came up to pull her tight where she belonged.

'Don't stop yet,' he said. 'Don't stop at all.'

Ted, Steve and Peter arrived just before ten the next morning. 'I'm so sorry, my dears,' said Ted, hugging Clara. 'The wretched van broke down.'

'You poor things! You must have been frozen,' she said in concern. At least she and Simon had had a fire to keep them warm.

And each other.

Inside the cottage, there was no evidence of the night before. Clara had taken the bedding back upstairs, while Simon relit the fire that had died in the early hours.

Making love with him had been beyond anything Clara had ever experienced before. She told herself that it was because of the whisky and the firelight and the fact that they were marooned on a Scottish hillside, but deep down she knew that it was more than that.

She loved him. No matter how hard she tried to persuade herself that it was just a fleeting, inexplicable physical thing, the way she told Simon it was, it made no difference. Lying in his arms in the firelight, her head on his chest, Clara had listened to the slow, steady beat of his heart and her own had turned inside out. She had felt her heart expanding, while a glorious, irrevocable sense of rightness had settled in the pit of her belly.

It hadn't been like that with Matt. She had adored him, but had always sensed that she was never really the one he wanted. The more she had clutched at him, the more Matt had held back, and Clara had been permanently tense. She'd been afraid to be herself in case he realised that he didn't really love her, but in the end he had realised that anyway.

Clara knew Simon couldn't love her. She hadn't wanted him to love her, and she hadn't tried to be anything other than what she was. Perhaps that was why it felt so utterly right being with him, why she felt more herself than she had ever been before. When they had made love, the differences between them hadn't mattered. They were just two people who fitted together perfectly.

Now I understand, Clara had thought in the middle of the night. All those love songs she sang with such gusto weren't just lovely tunes. They were true.

But loving Simon didn't change anything. They wanted different things. *Needed* different things. She would irritate Simon, and he would disappoint her. His father's irresponsibility had scarred him, Clara understood that. It wasn't that he was too stubborn to let go. He *couldn't*. Letting go was too much of a risk for him, and she couldn't spend her life being careful.

So Clara told herself that this short time with him would

be enough. That morning when they woke up tangled in the covers in front of the ashes in the fireplace, they had made love once more, but when they got up, they both knew that it was over.

The power had come on in the middle of the night, startling them both with the glare of light bulbs. Clara had a hot shower, and mentally braced herself to hide the love that wanted to spill out of her. But it wouldn't be fair to tell Simon. It would just make everything awkward. Already, she could see that he had withdrawn behind his defences. That was fine, Clara told herself. It would be easier to say goodbye that way.

Now Ted and the crew were here, and she had a job to do.

'Did you get any sleep?' she asked Ted as Steve and Peter started unloading the van.

'Oh, yes,' said Ted. 'The mechanic fixed it, but by then it was so late, and it was snowing, so we stopped at the next pub and set off first thing this morning. It was surprisingly comfortable.'

'I told you so,' Simon said to Clara, who put her hands on her hips and glared at Ted.

'I was imagining you'd skidded off the road and were freezing to death on some isolated hillside, and all the while you were tucked up in a warm pub!'

'I did try to ring you, but I couldn't get through.' Ted tucked his arm through hers. 'How did you two get on?'

'We were starving,' said Clara lightly, 'but otherwise we survived, didn't we, Simon?'

She thought they both looked perfectly normal, but Ted's eyes sharpened as he looked from one to the other. 'So, are you ready to shoot?' was all he said though.

'Not until we've had breakfast.'

It was a strange day. The snow had cleared overnight, leaving a dusting of white on the heather. Having arrived in the dark, Clara was unprepared for the sight of the massive hills looming around the cottage, and she had actually gasped when she'd stepped out of the cottage that morning. The photos on the Internet hadn't done the scenery justice, and it made a spectacular backdrop for the outside shots Ted wanted.

Clara and Simon sat on a great granite boulder with the hills behind them, while Peter struggled to keep the boom in place above their heads in the bitter wind. They stuck to the arguments that they had played out in Paris and on Paradise Island, but all the time Clara was remembering the feel of Simon's body, the wicked pleasure of his hands, the darkness and the heat that had burned between them.

She knew Simon was remembering too. Sometimes she would catch his eye and a crackle of awareness passed between them. The stern line of his mouth would soften then, and he would cough and raise his hand to hide the hint of a smile, until Ted yelled at him that he was spoiling the shot and they would have to do that bit again.

'Sorry, Ted.'

It was so cold that they were all glad when Ted decreed some fireside shots, but it was even harder then to maintain a professional distance. They were sitting in exactly the same spot where they had made love the night before, and it was impossible not to remember how it had been, impossible not to wish that it could be just the two of them again.

Clara was afraid that Ted would make some comment about them not concentrating—he could be very cutting when he wanted—but when he said nothing, she presumed that she and Simon had brushed through it without giving themselves away.

At last it was over. 'And…it's a wrap!' Ted spread his arms in his best Hollywood movie mogul mode. 'Well done, my dears. Let's all have an enormous drink!'

Now that filming was over, they could relax. The power

stayed on, so they cooked all the food and drank all the wine Clara had packed for two nights.

Clara refused to think about the fact that there would be no reason to see Simon again. Roland had been lukewarm, to say the least, about the idea of follow-up documentaries on Simon's micro-finance projects. 'Not exactly a sexy subject, is it?' he had said.

When Clara had steeled herself to tell Simon, he had been phlegmatic. 'It was worth a try,' he said.

If only Roland had leapt on the idea! He could make things happen when he wanted them to, and they could have had a commission lined up already. Then this wouldn't have been the end. She could have driven back to London with Simon and, instead of saying goodbye, she would have had the perfect excuse to call him. *I'll be in touch*, she could have said, and then they would have been working together again and then—

And then what? Clara interrupted herself. Nothing would really have changed. Everything she had said the night before was true. She and Simon were too different to make it work. Astrid might not be the right one for him, but there would be someone else, someone more sensible and suitable than Clara.

Better to accept it now. Simon would drive her back to London the next day and that would be it. Oh, perhaps they would have a polite chat over a screening of the preview, or a stilted phone call to inform him of the release date, but there would be no more trips, no more times alone.

No more making love.

But she had known all along that it would end, Clara reminded herself. There was only ever the moment, and she would live for it now. So she tucked her feelings away, the way she had always done, and smiled brightly and probably drank more than she should.

OK, she *definitely* drank more than she should. All she really remembered the next day was standing on the table and using a wooden spoon as a microphone as she belted out show tunes, cheered on by Steve and Peter. Simon hadn't encouraged her, but she knew that his eyes were on her and, although he shook his head in mock despair, he was smiling.

CHAPTER TEN

SIMON was unsympathetic about her hangover the next morning. 'It serves you right,' he said. 'Does this mean no singing down the motorway?'

Clara held her aching head. 'No anything,' she croaked.

It was a very quiet journey. They listened to Radio 4 the whole way, just as Simon had wanted to do when they drove up. Except he couldn't appreciate it as much as he should have done.

This time there was no incessant singing and humming, no tapping of the feet or dancing of the hands. No chomping of crisps. No low, wicked laugh, no teasing smile. It wasn't the same when she was quiet. He even began to wish that she would sing again, and who would ever have thought that?

Simon glanced across to where she was huddled in the seat, her face wan and her eyes closed, and he had to suppress a grin at the thought of her the night before, up on that table, singing into the wooden spoon and kicking her legs.

God, he was going to miss her.

Simon held grimly onto the wheel and tried not to think about how empty his life was going to be from now on. He couldn't regret their night together but how long was it going to be before he stopped aching for what he was missing? How long before he forgot the heat and the wildness of losing control? The moment he had that sweet, luscious body under his hands, he had been lost, all sensible thought obliterated as his mind went blank and black with desire, and his heart shifted at the memory.

One night, that was what they had agreed. It was sensible. It was practical. It was better for both of them.

Clara was a very special person, and she deserved to be happy, thought Simon. She had made it clear that one night was all that she had wanted. He couldn't give her the fantasy she craved, and she didn't want to settle for less.

So she would go her way, and he would get back to his nice, ordered life and that would be that. There was no point in telling her how he felt. It would just make things more difficult.

Simon told himself that it was all for the best. He liked it quiet, didn't he? There would be no more singing, none of those smiles that made his heart lurch alarmingly. No illogical arguments, no rolling of the eyes, no fear that any moment she would break into a dance routine.

No Clara.

There was a space right outside her flat. Simon parked and switched off the engine. On that busy London street, the silence was suffocating.

'Well,' said Clara.

'Well,' said Simon.

The air was clogged with tension. He undid his seat belt for want of anything else to do. 'I suppose this is it,' he said after a moment.

'Yes.' Her voice was strained. 'At least, there's no more filming. Ted will edit it now, and we'll record the voice-over. Obviously we'll let you know when it's done, and let you have a preview copy.'

'Fine.'

'But you've done your bit.' Clara cleared her throat. 'I know you didn't want to do it, but I'm really grateful to you, Simon.

We would never have been able to make the programme without you.'

Simon shifted round in his seat so that he could look at her. 'It wasn't so bad,' he said slowly.

The truth was that it had been the most fun he could remember having since before his father died.

And look how that had turned out.

The heat and sweetness and the need that had engulfed him at the cottage had blotted out all else, but now the reminder of where too much fun could lead jerked Simon back to reality just as he was on the point of begging to see her again.

Better to call an end to this—whatever *this* was—now. It would just get complicated and end in Clara being disappointed, and he couldn't bear to do that to her.

Clara would always have a good time. She had a zest for life that Simon both yearned for and feared. She needed someone who could enjoy the good times with her and not spoil things by pointing out the practicalities or considering the consequences.

Someone who wasn't him.

'I enjoyed it,' he said.

'I'm glad.' Clara's smile was uneven as she unclipped her seat belt and reached for the door. 'I'd better go.'

He didn't want to let her go. 'Clara…'

She turned back, still holding the door handle.

'I did enjoy it,' he said as if she had said she didn't believe him. 'And that night—'

'You don't need to say anything,' she interrupted him. 'That night was fantastic, but we both know it wouldn't be like that again.'

'Wouldn't it?'

'I mean, look at us,' she said, gesturing from Simon's neat navy Guernsey to her layers of mismatched colours and patterns, topped off with the vividly striped scarf she always wore. 'We couldn't be more different.'

'It didn't matter at the cottage.'

Clara bit her lip. 'And it might not matter tomorrow, or next week, or the week after that, but sooner or later, it would. You taught me that,' she said. 'You have to find someone who shares your goals and your interests and fits into your life. We've had some romantic moments, but moments are all they are.'

She was right. It was what he had said all along, Simon knew, but it sounded all wrong coming out of her mouth.

'Well, I enjoyed them,' he said.

Clara's brave smile evaporated from her face. 'Me too,' she whispered.

'Goodbye, Clara.' Simon leant across and gently kissed her mouth, and she laid her palm against his cheek and kissed him back. It was short and achingly sweet. A farewell kiss.

'Goodbye, Simon.' Her eyes were shimmering with tears as she dropped her hand, and his heart shook with wanting her.

Before he could jerk her back into his arms, she was out of the car, grabbing her bag from the back seat, running up the steps to the front door. He watched her put the key in the door, push it open. At the last minute she turned and lifted a hand to him. Simon lifted a hand in return.

Then she went inside and closed the door.

She was gone.

'You can't show this!' Clara looked from Ted to Roland in horror. They had just shown her the preview copy of *Romance: Fact or Fiction?*, now titled *How to Fall in Love (When You Really Don't Want To)*.

'Lovey, it's a great programme,' said Ted gently.

'It's not! It's nothing like we planned. This is a completely different film! It's...*private*.'

Clara was near to tears. She hadn't been looking forward to watching the preview, knowing it would bring back bittersweet memories of Simon, but she had never dreamed that it would be this bad.

She knew that she had made the right decision. Going their separate ways was the sensible thing to do. Sometimes she saw Simon on the news, and he looked cool and contained and like the grown-up that he was, while she was still muddling along, not knowing anything except the fact that she missed him.

Nothing was right without him. She couldn't dance any more because there was a leaden weight inside her that threw her off balance, and her heart was too bleak for her to be able to sing. Always before she had been able to bury her feelings beneath a light-hearted veneer, but not this time.

This time it was too hard.

Getting through every day was a chore. Clara had thrown herself into work, and put in long hours while Ted and Roland were closeted in the editing suite. Her job had been her only consolation.

Until now.

Clara turned an accusing glare on Ted. 'Why didn't you warn me?'

'I didn't think you'd like it.' Ted had the grace to blush. 'I thought that if you saw the finished result, you might realise what a great story it is now.'

Oh, she could see that. It was a clever piece of film-making. All the locations were lovingly shot. Ted had taken everything she and Simon had said for the camera and edited it so that the arguments came across as an interesting, engaging debate. He had made the programme that they had planned.

But he hadn't stopped there. Their set pieces were intercut

with shots of Simon and Clara when they thought they were off camera.

There they were in Paris. Simon putting his jacket around her shoulders on the Pont Neuf, rolling his eyes as she sang herself into a confident mood. Absorbed in each other in the Montmartre bistro. Dancing close together in the club. Ted took his camera wherever he went. Why hadn't she remembered that?

There they were sitting on that granite boulder, the wind whipping Clara's hair around her face. She held it back with one hand and looked at Simon with her heart in her eyes. And Simon, watching her as she danced on the table. How could she possibly have thought their body language wasn't revealing? They might as well have hung out a sign that they had slept together.

There they were on Paradise Island, on the end of the dock. Clara supposed she should be grateful Ted hadn't filmed her throwing up, but he had been there later because there they were on the beach, watching the sunset together.

Kissing.

It was dark, and not that clear, but there was no doubt about what they were doing.

Clara's face was hot. 'What were you doing spying on us on the beach?' she said furiously to Ted. 'That was just pervy!'

'I just happened to be getting some establishing shots of the sunset,' he said, but his eyes slid away from hers.

'Hah!'

'Clara, I know how it seems, but it was just so clear what the real story was,' Ted tried to explain. 'Simon was saying one thing and it was obvious that he really believed it, but at the same time he was feeling something else entirely. I could tell right from the start that he was falling in love with you.'

Ted didn't bother to say that it had been just as obvious that she had been falling in love with Simon at the same time.

'It wasn't like that,' said Clara dully.

'You only need to watch the programme to see that he is.'

'You don't understand!' Clara took a breath and fought to stay calm. 'Yes, we had a fling, but that's all it was. That's not how Simon is. You know what his reputation is. If you show this, he'll be a laughing stock! It's wrong!'

She turned imploringly to Roland, who was leaning back in his chair, picking his nails. 'You can't do this!'

'I think you'll find I can,' he said. 'This is all very sweet, but Simon Valentine signed a release and there's nothing in there about having to approve what goes out.'

'He didn't know you were going to put this...this *travesty* together!'

'Tough,' said Roland. 'They're going to lap this up at Channel 16. I've got to admit that I had my doubts when Ted suggested you as a stand-in for Stella in Paris,' he admitted frankly, 'but it's turned out brilliantly. I said to him when he first showed me the edits, "I think you've got something here, mate." Didn't I, Ted?'

Ted nodded. The traitor. He looked uncomfortable. As well he might, thought Clara, clenching her fists in frustration. She knew Ted would hate upsetting her, but he was a passionate film maker and if he believed in this programme, she wouldn't shift him.

'Look, this is going to turn out fine,' Roland said. 'I think we'll get more commissions on the back of this one, and you can produce them if you want. Get your own production assistant. How about that?'

Clara stared at him. She felt sick. Her dream job, in return for letting them expose Simon to the media wolves. Simon, who was so famously controlled, so self-contained, his guard down for everyone to jeer over. The press would have a field day. It had been bad enough for him when Stella had spread those silly rumours, but this would be on television for everyone to see and laugh about.

'No,' she said.

'No what?'

'No, I won't let you do it,' she said clearly. 'Simon may have signed a release, but I didn't. I won't give you permission to show this.'

Roland's face darkened. He turned to Ted. 'She didn't sign a release?'

'It's Clara's job to make sure they get signed,' said Ted nervously.

'Oh, that's just great!' snarled Roland. 'Then it's a straight choice, Clara. Sign the release and keep your job, or take a walk.'

'Roland—' Ted started to protest, but Clara didn't wait to hear or stop to think. Pushing back her chair, she snatched up her bag and jacket.

'I'll take the walk.'

Clara sat at the table in her parents' comfortably shabby Oxford kitchen. Outside, it was a soft spring day, but the blue sky and the tubs of cheerful daffodils weren't enough to stop the world looking grey. Dispiritedly, she scrolled through the 'jobs vacant' on her laptop. She had to find a job somehow.

Television was out. Roland had plenty of contacts in the media, and she knew he had put the word out that she was unreliable. Competition was cut-throat as it was. She'd lucky if she ever got another job in production, Clara thought miserably.

If she didn't get a job soon, she would have to tell Allegra couldn't afford to pay rent any more. Staying in London had been too painful, and she had come home to Oxford for a few days to regroup. Her parents had welcomed her back with their usual vaguely baffled kindness.

'Of course you can stay,' her mother had said, deep in an article about ecclesiastical reform in the sixteenth century. 'What about your job, though?'

'I told you,' said Clara. 'I had to leave.'

'Oh, dear. I thought you liked working in television too.'

Clara supposed it was something that her mother remembered what it was she'd been doing.

'I did,' she said.

She missed her job. She missed working with Ted. She missed Allegra and the flat and the in-depth discussions about Saturday night TV.

But, most of all, she missed Simon. Ted's film had been a shock. She hadn't realised their feelings were quite so obvious. A little bit of Clara had rejoiced to see Simon falling for her, of course—the bit that had urged her to pick up the phone, to call him and tell him how she felt. But a saner, more sensible part held her back.

Simon might be attracted to her, but he hadn't changed. Neither of them had changed. He was still logical, practical, a man who needed order and control, and she was still a girl who needed to be loved completely. Simon would never be able to do that. Clara understood just how carefully he guarded his emotions. She needed more than he was able to give, and it was better to accept that now than hope and hope the way she had done with Matt.

Anyway, it wasn't really love, whatever Ted's film made it look like. It was an attraction, Clara decided. A physical thing. That wasn't the same. But there was still a tight band around chest, making it hard to breathe properly. Her back was still stiff, her limbs still rigid, her heart locked down.

Ted had been in touch, miserably torn and desperate to make amends. He was worried about her. When Matt had left her for Sophie, it was Ted who had dragged her along to a *Sound of Music* singalong, and her spirits had been instantly boosted, but this time Clara didn't even have the heart for that.

Her father had disappeared to answer the doorbell. He was expecting a PhD student, and had forgotten that he still had a piece of toast in his hand. Her mother was sitting at the other end of the table, drinking coffee and marking essays.

'What are you doing today, Clara?' she asked absently.

'Looking for a job,' said Clara. London had too many painful memories. Perhaps she should try and find something in Oxford? It would be humiliating to have to move back in with her parents, but what did a bit of humiliation matter now?

'Why don't you think about doing a degree?'

'What in? The collected works of Rodgers and Hammerstein?'

'There must be something you want to do.'

See Simon. Touch Simon. Be with Simon. Did they offer a degree in that?

'I don't think I'm university material, Mum.' Clara sighed and slumped back in her chair. 'I don't seem to be very good at anything.'

Her mother lifted her head at that and inspected her daughter over the top of her glasses. 'Oh, I don't think that's the case at all,' she said but before Clara could ask her what she meant, her father wandered back in, eating his toast.

'What have you done with your student?'

'It wasn't her. It's some man for you, Clara,' he said vaguely.

'Me? But nobody knows I'm here.' Ted might have guessed, but her parents knew him well and not even her father was vague enough to not recognize him. 'Are you sure it was me he wanted?'

'I may be a little absent-minded sometimes, but I'm not senile,' her father said, pouring himself some more coffee. 'Of course it was you.'

Puzzled, Clara pushed back her chair and went to the door. And there was Simon.

Her heart leapt with joy and the world, which had been dully monochrome and all askew, abruptly righted itself and sprang back into colour.

'Simon!'

She drank in the sight of him on the doorstep. He was looking positively casual in an open-necked shirt and jacket, but otherwise he was wonderfully *Simon*. She loved the austere angles of his face, the stern mouth that made her knees go weak, the quiet solidity of him.

She wanted to throw herself into his arms, but the strained look in his eyes, the tautness around his mouth, made her pause.

'Is everything OK?'

'Fine.' Simon cleared his throat. 'That is…fine. I just came by because…well, I wondered if you had a summer house here,' he finished in a rush.

Clara's jaw dropped. She didn't know what she had been expecting, but it wasn't that. 'A *summer house*?'

'Do you?'

Was this a peculiarly vivid dream? 'There's a shed in the back garden,' she said cautiously.

'The back garden. That'll do fine.'

'Whatever for?'

'Could we go there now?' he asked tensely. 'If you're not too busy?'

Clara stared at him. 'Simon, are you sure you're all right? You're behaving very strangely.'

'I know,' he said. 'It's just there's something I need to do before I lose my nerve.'

'*In the shed?*' But she stood back and Simon stepped past her into the house.

Still half convinced that this was a dream, Clara led him

down the narrow Victorian tiled hall to the back door. They passed the open door of the kitchen, where her parents were having an erudite discussion about Derrida interspersed with requests to pass the marmalade.

There was a flash of the old Simon as he raised his brows at Clara. 'They mixed up the babies at the hospital,' she whispered. 'My real parents are out there somewhere slumped in front of the television and watching soaps.'

Neither of her parents was much of a gardener, and the long walled garden was rather neglected. The borders were straggly and overgrown, and dandelions were starting to sprout in the grass and between the worn stones of the patio.

'That's the shed,' said Clara, pointing. It was faded and listing slightly to one side, and she couldn't imagine what Simon wanted with it.

'It's all right. This will do.' Simon was looking around the patio, moving a pot out of the way and pulling out a rickety garden chair. 'Sit down,' he said as he steered Clara towards it.

'Simon, what's going on?'

'Just a minute.' He took a deep breath, and opened his mouth. And then closed it again.

'What?' Clara was getting really worried.

Simon cleared his throat savagely. 'Sorry,' he said. 'I'll start again.'

Another breath and then, to Clara's astonishment, he launched into a cracked and uncertain rendition from *The Sound of Music*.

A dazzling hope blurred Clara's eyes with tears. It was unmistakably *Climb Every Mountain*, even if he forgot the words halfway through and had to improvise.

And he was dancing! True, Simon was no Nureyev, but he was definitely shuffling from side to side and every now and then he even tried a twirl. His expression was intent, and he was frowning as he tried to remember the words and coordinate with the movements. Several times he found himself facing the wrong way, and had to turn round hastily and pick up his routine again.

Clara covered her mouth with her hand. She didn't know whether to laugh or cry. Simon was there, it was really him, and he was dancing for her.

And then he was holding out his hand, inviting her to dance with him, drawing her up from her chair. Smiling through her tears, she let him swing her round until he came to a halt with a flourish.

'...your dree-eam,' he finished tunelessly and looked into Clara's eyes at last with a mixture of relief, trepidation and excruciating embarrassment.

'Simon,' she said, starry-eyed. 'You were singing. You were *dancing*.'

'I'm not very good, I know.'

'That was the best version of *Climb Every Mountain* I've ever heard.' Her voice cracked a little as she put her arms around his neck. 'The *best*,' she whispered in his ear as he pulled her close but, before he could kiss her there was a burst of applause from the kitchen window.

Clara's parents, evidently distracted from Derrida by Simon's singing, were beaming broadly and clapping.

'Excellent! Very well done!'

'Clara's always needed someone who will dance with her,' said her father when Clara introduced Simon to them.

'I'm not really much of a dancer,' he confessed.

'You looked like you were doing fine to us.' Which just went to show how much her parents knew about dancing.

Her mother, it appeared, had noticed more than Clara had thought. 'Are you the reason Clara has been so unhappy lately?' she demanded, regarding Simon with the severity she reserved for students who hadn't prepared for a seminar.

'We don't like Clara being unhappy,' her father added. 'She was born for laughter. The rest of us have our research, but Clara has an ability to enjoy life that we've always envied.'

Clara was astounded. All those years when she had felt inadequate and excluded in the family, and all the time *they* had been envying *her*? Could it be true? 'But I thought…' She broke off as the doorbell rang.

Her mother clicked her tongue. 'That'll be your student, Michael. You'd better go and let her in.' She turned back to Clara and Simon with a twinkle. 'If there are to be any more song and dance routines, you'll have to keep the noise down, I'm afraid.'

'I think once was enough,' said Simon ruefully.

He took Clara's hands as her parents disappeared. '*Was* once enough, Clara?'

'Yes,' she said, her fingers tightening around his. She knew just how much that dance must have cost him. 'Oh, Simon, I can't believe you did that for me!'

'It was the only way I could think of to tell you how much I love you,' he said. 'I remembered what you said at that cottage about wanting to be the star of someone's show, and I wanted to tell you that you'll always be the star of mine.'

Clara's throat was so tight, she could hardly talk. 'Simon…' was all she managed to choke out.

'I love you, Clara,' he said, his eyes locked on hers. 'If you want me to sing and dance for you every day, I will.'

'You don't need to do that,' said Clara, finding her voice at last. Drawing her hands free, she put them on his shoulders, feeling his strength and his solidity. Letting herself believe that that was really happening.

'You don't need to dance for me, or sing for me, Simon. You just need to be you. You just need to be there. You just need to love me.'

'I can do that,' said Simon, so obviously relieved that she

laughed, giddy with happiness, and he laughed too and kissed her. Wild joy surged along her veins, and she wrapped her arms around his neck and kissed him back.

'I missed you,' she mumbled at last between kisses.

'I missed you too.'

He held her tightly, and she leant against him with a great sigh of contentment. 'I imagined you getting on with your quiet, comfortable life,' she confessed.

'I tried to,' said Simon, 'but it wasn't comfortable without you. It was too quiet. There was no one to distract me or to sing or to make me laugh.'

'Why didn't you say anything?'

'Because I was imagining *you* having a great time without me. I thought you'd be out dancing or singing on tables, and I couldn't imagine why you would possibly want to spend time with someone conventional like me.'

Clara's body shook with laughter. 'You're never that, Simon. No one truly conventional would have come and demanded to dance in my parents' garden shed!' She pulled slightly away from him. 'What was the shed about anyway?'

'I wanted a summer house, like in *The Sound of Music*.'

She looked at him in amazement. 'How on earth did you know about that? I didn't think you'd even seen the film?'

'I have now. I missed all those stupid songs you sing so much that I was actually reduced to buying the DVD!'

'*No?*' Clara was delighted. 'So that's where you learnt the words! And how did you work out the dance routine?'

'That was my mother,' Simon admitted, pulling her back against him. 'I was desperate and I couldn't think of anyone else to ask. I don't know anyone else who dances. She enjoyed herself enormously, and said that if you were prepared to talk to me after seeing the way I danced, you must love me.'

'She's right,' said Clara, kissing him. 'I do.'

'Now you know why I was so nervous when I arrived. I was terrified I would lose my nerve.'

'I'm glad you didn't. I'll never forget that dance on the patio!' Her smile faded. 'Seriously, I know how hard that was for you, Simon.'

'I've learnt that letting go doesn't have to mean losing everything,' said Simon. 'You've taught me that. Sometimes, taking a risk and letting go means you can win everything you've ever wanted.' His pale eyes were warmer than Clara had ever seen them. How could she ever have thought of them as cold? 'Sometimes you have to leave your safe home and climb that mountain, in fact.'

Clara laughed and pressed closer, breathing in the wonderful, familiar scent of him. 'Who would have thought you'd ever be quoting from *The Sound of Music*?'

'I'm not the only one who's taken a risk, Clara.' Simon's expression grew serious. 'Ted came to see me. He told me that you'd refused the producer job Roland offered you and walked out of MediaOchre.'

Her eyes slid from his. 'Yes, well, we had a…difference of opinion.'

'Clara, you really wanted to be a producer.'

'Oh, well, you know I'm not very good at sticking with things.'

Simon drew her down onto the patio wall and turned her face to his. 'You gave up that job for me,' he said. 'Ted showed me the film.'

She flushed at the memory. 'It was *awful*, wasn't it? But don't worry, they won't be able to show it. I refused to sign a release so, unless they make the film the way they originally planned it, they're stuck.'

'I know. Ted told me.' Simon smiled crookedly. 'I said I was happy for the film to go out as it was if you agreed. I promised him I'd try and persuade you to change your mind.'

'*What?*' Clara jerked upright to stare at him.

'Ted's right. It's a great film.'

'But it's so...*intimate.*'

'It's *true*, Clara. There I am, fighting it all the way, and it's clear as houses that I'm falling in love with you. I'm standing there saying one thing, and the viewer can see that I'm doing the opposite.'

'I can't understand why you're being so reasonable about this,' said Clara. 'It's embarrassing.'

'I'm not embarrassed to love you,' said Simon. 'Yes, I look a fool, but that's true too! And let's face it, you won the argument. Romance won out over logic, fair and square.'

'I don't think I did win,' she said thoughtfully, settling back into the curve of his arm. 'I didn't fall in love with you because we were in Paris, or on that beautiful beach. I fell in love because even when things went wrong, you were there for me, to hold the umbrella, or fetch a bucket, to give me your jacket or stop me worrying.'

She tilted her face up to his. 'And what did I ever do for you except drag you out into the rain and strand you halfway up a mountain with no food and throw up all over you?'

'They're all precious memories to me,' he said, straight-faced.

'Those places weren't romantic in the end,' said Clara. 'But a truly terrible dance routine...*that* was romantic. I don't need a dance partner, Simon. I need someone who's prepared to take a risk for me, someone who'll grit his teeth and make a fool of himself to show me that he loves me.'

'And I need someone who'll make me laugh and push me out of my comfort zone and make me *feel*,' said Simon, gathering her into him for a long, sweet kiss.

'I think we should let them show that programme, Clara,' he said much later when he lifted his head. 'Tell Roland he can do it if he makes you a producer.'

'It would be good,' said Clara, tempted. 'I've missed my job.'

'I didn't think much of the ending, though, did you? Why don't we suggest a better one?'

'Hmm, there's a thought. We could sing in a music festival and then escape over some mountains. That would give it the drama it's rather lacking at the moment.'

'It's an interesting idea,' Simon agreed, 'but I was thinking that it might be a nice touch to end with something a bit more tame. Like a wedding, for instance.'

Clara primmed her lips, pretending to consider the idea, but her eyes danced. 'A wedding?'

'Yes. I thought it would tie up a few loose ends. Of course, it would mean us getting married,' he said. 'Do you think that would work?'

'Do you know, I think it might,' she said, kissing him. 'I think it would make a perfect ending.'

'Or a perfect beginning,' said Simon, kissing her back.

In the garden, a blackbird started to sing, a pure trill of joy. Clara felt the sunshine on her shoulders and Simon's warm arm around her, and when she pressed her face into his throat and breathed in the scent of his skin, she thought she would shatter with happiness.

Now she knew what Julie Andrews had been singing about when she wondered what she had done to deserve being loved by the Captain.

Clara thought about Simon, about the serious, formidably intelligent, heart-shakingly attractive man he was, and it seemed so incredible that he could actually love her that she wondered if she really were dreaming. They were so different. It was hardly any time since he had categorically refused to have anything to do with her. No, no, no, no, no, *no*, he had said.

'Simon, are you *sure* you want to marry me?' she asked, and she felt him smile against her temple.

'Yes,' said Simon.

Tonight on Channel 16

8.00 p.m. How to Fall in Love (When You Really Don't Want To) *****

Surprisingly absorbing examination of romance and whether it really exists, with Simon Valentine, whose incisive analysis of the financial situation has won him a legion of female fans—all of whom are likely to be disappointed by the chemistry that fairly sizzles between him and his co-presenter. Worth watching just for the ending. Have a hankie handy!

* * * * *

The World of
MILLS & BOON®

HISTORICAL

Awaken the romance of the past
6 new stories every month

MEDICAL ROMANCE™

The ultimate in romantic medical drama
6 new stories every month

MODERN™

Power, passion and irresistible temptation
8 new stories every month

By Request

Relive the romance with the best of the best
12 stories every month

MY GREEK
ISLAND FLING

NINA HARRINGTON

Nina Harrington grew up in rural Northumberland, England, and decided at the age of eleven that she was going to be a librarian—because then she could read all of the books in the public library whenever she wanted! Since then she has been a shop assistant, community pharmacist, technical writer, university lecturer, volcano walker and industrial scientist, before taking a career break to realise her dream of being a fiction writer. When she is not creating stories which make her readers smile, her hobbies are cooking, eating, enjoying good wine—and talking, for which she has had specialist training.

PROLOGUE

'Mum—I'm here,' Lexi Collazo Sloane whispered as her mother breezed into her room, instantly bringing a splash of purple, bravado and energy to the calm cream and gold colour scheme in the exclusive London hospital.

'I am *so* sorry I'm late, darling,' her mother gushed, shaking the rain from her coat and then planting a firm kiss on Lexi's cheek. 'But our director suddenly decided to bring the rehearsal of the ballroom scene forward.' She shook her head and laughed out loud. 'Pirate swords and silk skirts. If those dresses survive intact it will be a miracle. And don't talk to me about the shoes and wigs!'

'You can do it, Mum.' Lexi chuckled, folding her pyjamas into her overnight bag. 'You're the best wardrobe mistress in the theatre business. No worries. The dress rehearsal tomorrow will be a triumph.'

'Alexis Sloane, you are the most outrageous fibber. But, thanks. Now. Down to more important things.' She took a breath, then gently put a hand on Lexi's shoulder and looked into her eyes. 'How did it go this morning? And don't spare me. What did the specialist say? Am I going to be a grandmother one of these fine days?'

Lexi sat back down on the bed and her heart wanted to weep. Time to get this over and done with.

'Well, there's some good news, and some less-than-good news. Apparently medical science has advanced a little over the past eighteen years, but I don't want you to get your hopes up.' She reached out and drew her mother to sit next to her on the bed. 'There is a small chance that I might be able to have children, but…' she caught her breath as her mother gasped '…it would be a long, tough process—and there's no guarantee that the treatment would be a success in the end. According to the specialist, I'd only be setting myself up for disappointment.'

She braved a half smile and squeezed her mother's hand. 'Sorry, Mum. It looks like you might have to wait a lot longer before I can give you those grandchildren after all.'

Her mother exhaled loudly before hugging her. 'Now, don't you worry about that for one more minute. We've talked about this before. There are lots of children out there looking for a loving home, and Adam is happy to adopt. You *will* have your own family one day—I just know it. Okay?'

'I know, but you had such high hopes that it would be good news.'

'As far as I am concerned it *is* good news. In fact, I think we should splash out on a nice restaurant this evening, don't you? Your dad will insist,' she added, waggling her eyebrows. 'It seems the photography business is paying well these days.'

Lexi touched her arm and swallowed down the huge lump of anxiety and apprehension that had made an already miserable day even more stressful. 'Is he here yet, Mum? I've been nodding off all afternoon and now I'm terrified that I might have missed him.'

But her mother looked into her face with a huge grin. 'Yes,' she replied, clasping hold of both of Lexi's hands. 'Yes, he *is* here. I left your dad back in the car park. And he is so different. He really does want to make up for lost time. Why else would he pay for this lovely private hospital at the first mention that you needed treatment? He knew how scared you must be after the last time. Everything's going to be just fine. You wait and see.'

Lexi's heart started to race. 'What if he doesn't even recognise me? I mean, I was only ten the last time he saw me. That was eighteen years ago. He might not even know who I am.'

Her mother patted her cheek, shaking her head. 'Now, don't be so silly. Of course he'll recognise you. He must have albums filled with all of the photos I've sent him over the years. Besides, you're so lovely he'll spot you in an instant.'

She pressed her cheek against Lexi's as she wrapped her in a warm hug. 'Your dad has already told me how very proud he is of everything you've achieved in your life. And you can tell him all about your brilliant writing over dinner tonight.'

Then she patted her hair, snatched up her bag and headed into the bathroom. 'Which means I need to get ready. Back in a moment.'

Lexi smiled and shrugged her shoulders. As if her mother could ever be anything other than gorgeous! She'd aways been so irrepressible, no matter what life had thrown at them. And all she'd ever wanted was a large family around her whom she could shower with love.

Lexi wiped away a stray tear from her cheek. It broke her heart that she wouldn't be able to give her mother grandchildren and make her happy. Just broke her heart.

Mark Belmont stabbed at the elevator buttons, willing them to respond, then cursed under his breath and took off towards the stairs.

The logical part of his brain knew that it had only been

seconds since he'd thanked his mother's friend for keeping vigil in that terrible hospital room until he arrived. The steady weeping hadn't helped him to keep calm or controlled, but he was on his own now, and it was his turn to make some sense of the last few hours.

The urgent call from the hospital. The terrible flight from Mumbai, which had felt never-ending, then the taxi ride from the airport, which had seemed to hit every red light in London on the way in.

The truth was still hard to take in. His mother, his beautiful, talented and self-confident mother, had taken herself to a London plastic surgeon without telling her family. According to her actress friend she had made some feeble joke about not alerting the media to the fact that Crystal Leighton was having a tummy tuck. And she was right. The press were only too ready to track down any dirty secrets about the famously wholesome English movie star. But to him? That was his mother the tabloids were stalking.

Mark took the stairs two at a time as his sense of failure threatened to overwhelm him.

He couldn't believe it. They'd been together for the whole of the Christmas and New Year holiday and she'd seemed more excited and positive than she'd been in years. Her autobiography was coming together, her charity work was showing results and his clever sister had provided her with a second grandchild.

Why? Why had she done this without telling anyone? Why had she come here alone to have an operation that had gone so horribly wrong? She'd known the risks, and she'd always laughed off any suggestion of plastic surgery in the past. And yet she'd gone ahead and done it anyway.

His steps slowed and he sniffed and took a long breath, steadying himself before going back into that hospital room where his lovely, precious mother was lying comatose, hooked up to monitors which beeped out every second just how much damage the embolism had done.

A stroke. Doing what they could. Specialists called in. Still no clear prognosis.

Mark pulled open the door. At least she'd had the good sense to choose a discreet hospital, well-known for protecting its patients from prying eyes. There would be no paparazzi taking pictures of his bruised and battered mother for the world to ogle at.

No. He would have to endure that image on his own.

Lexi had just turned back to her packing when a young nurse popped her head around the door. 'More visitors, Miss Sloane.' She smiled. 'Your dad and your cousin have just arrived to take you home. They'll be right with you.' And with a quick wave she was gone.

'Thank you,' Lexi replied in the direction of the door, and swallowed down a deep feeling of uncertainty and nervousness. Why did her father want to see her now, after all these long years? She pushed herself off the bed and slowly walked towards the door.

Then Lexi paused and frowned. Her cousin? She didn't have a cousin—as far as she knew. Perhaps that was another one of the surprises her dad had lined up for her? She'd promised her mother that she would give him a chance today, and that was what she was going to do, no matter how painful it might be.

Taking a deep breath, she straightened her back and strolled out into the corridor to greet the father who had abandoned her and her mother just when they'd needed him most. If he expected her to leap into his arms then he was sorely mistaken, but she could be polite and thank him for her mother's sake, at least.

If only her heart would stop thumping so hard that she

could hardly think. She'd loved him so much when she was little—her wonderful father had been the centre of her world.

She braced herself and looked around. But all was calm, restful and quiet. Of course it would take a few moments for him to get through the elaborate security checks at the main desk—designed to protect the rich and famous—and then take the elevator to the first floor.

She was just about to turn back when she caught a movement out of the corner of her eye through the half-open door of one of the patient's rooms identical to the one she had just left, but tucked away at the end of the long corridor.

And then she saw him.

Unmistakable. Unforgettable. Her father. Mario Collazo. Slim and handsome, greying around the temples, but still gorgeous. He was crouched down just inside the room, under the window, and he had a small but powerful digital camera in his hand.

Something was horribly wrong here. Without thinking, she crept towards the door to get a better look.

In an instant she took in the scene. A woman lay on the hospital bed, her long dark hair spread out against the bleached white sheets which matched the colour of her face. Her eyes were closed and she was connected to tubes and monitors all around the bed.

The horrific truth of what she was looking at struck Lexi hard and left her reeling with shock, so that she had to lean against the wall to stay upright.

The nurses wouldn't have been able to see her father from the main reception area, where a younger man she had never seen before was showing them some paperwork, diverting their attention away from what was happening in this exclusive clinic under their very noses.